Osceola the Seminole
The Red Fawn of the Flower Land

Captain Mayne Reid

Preface.

The Historical Novel has ever maintained a high rank—perhaps the highest—among works of fiction, for the reason that while it enchants the senses, it improves the mind, conveying, under a most pleasing form, much information which, perhaps, the reader would never have sought for amid the dry records of the purely historic narrative.

This fact being conceded, it needs but little argument to prove that those works are most interesting which treat of the facts and incidents pertaining to our own history, and of a date which is yet fresh in the memory of the reader.

To this class of books pre-eminently belongs the volume which is here submitted to the American reader, from the pen of a writer who has proved himself unsurpassed in the field which he has, by his various works, made peculiarly his own.

The brief but heroic struggle of the celebrated Chief, Osceola, forms the groundwork of a narrative which is equal, if not superior, to any of Mr Reid's former productions; and while the reader's patriotism cannot fail to be gratified at the result, his sympathy is, at the same time, awakened for the manly struggles and untimely fate of the gallant spirit, who fought so nobly for the freedom of his red brethren and the preservation of their cherished hunting-grounds.

Chapter One.

The Flowery Land.

Linda Florida! fair land of flowers!

Thus hailed thee the bold Spanish adventurer, as standing upon the prow of his caravel, he first caught sight of thy shores.

It was upon the Sunday of Palms—the festival of the flowers—and the devout Castilian beheld in thee a fit emblem of the day. Under the influence of a pious thought, he gave thee its name, and well deservedst thou the proud appellation.

That was three hundred years ago. Three full cycles have rolled past, since the hour of thy baptismal ceremony; but the title becomes thee as ever. Thy floral bloom is as bright at this hour as when Leon landed upon thy shores—ay, bright as when the breath of God first called thee into being.

Thy forests are still virgin and inviolate; verdant thy savannas; thy groves as fragrant as ever—those perfumed groves of aniseed and orange, of myrtle and magnolia. Still sparkles upon thy plains the cerulean ixia; still gleam in thy waters the golden nymphae; above thy swamps yet tower the colossal cypress, the gigantic cedar, the gum, and the bay-tree; still over thy gentle slopes of silvery sand wave long-leaved pines, mingling their acetalous foliage with the frondage of the palm. Strange anomaly of vegetation; the tree of the north, and the tree of the south—the types of the frigid and torrid—in this thy mild mid region, standing side by side, and blending their branches together!

Linda Florida! who can behold thee without peculiar emotion? without conviction that thou art a favoured land? Gazing upon thee, one ceases to wonder at the faith—the wild faith of the early adventurers—that from thy bosom gushed forth the fountain of youth, the waters of eternal life!

No wonder the sweet fancy found favour and credence; no wonder so delightful an idea had its crowds of devotees. Thousands came from afar, to find rejuvenescence by bathing in thy crystal streams—thousands sought it, with far more eagerness than the white metal of Mexico, or the yellow gold of Peru; in the search thousands grew older instead of younger, or perished in pursuit of the vain illusion; but who could wonder?

Even at this hour, one can scarcely think it an illusion; and in that age of romance, it was still easier of belief. A new world had been discovered, why not a new theory of life? Men looked upon a land where the leaves never fell, and the flowers never faded. The bloom was eternal—eternal the music of the birds. There was no winter—no signs of death or decay. Natural, then, the fancy, and easy the faith, that in such fair land man too might be immortal.

The delusion has long since died away, but not the beauty that gave birth to it. Thou, Florida, art still the same—still art thou emphatically the land of flowers. Thy groves are as green, thy skies as bright, thy waters as diaphanous as ever. There is no change in the loveliness of thy aspect.

And yet I observe a change. The scene is the same, but not the characters! Where are they of that red race who were born of thee, and nurtured on thy bosom? I see them not. In thy fields, I behold white and black, but not red—European and African, but not Indian—not one of that ancient people who were once thine own. Where are they?

Gone! all gone! No longer tread they thy flowery paths—no longer are thy crystal streams cleft by the keels of their canoes—no more upon thy spicy gale is borne the sound of their voices—the twang of their bowstrings is heard no more amid the trees of thy forest: they have parted from thee far and for ever.

But not willing went they away—for who could leave thee with a willing heart? No, fair Florida; thy red children were true to thee, and parted only in sore unwillingness. Long did they cling to the loved scenes of their youth; long continued they the conflict of despair, that has made them famous for ever. Whole armies, and many a hard straggle, it cost the pale-face to dispossess them; and then they went not willingly—they were torn from thy bosom like wolf-cubs from their dam, and forced to a far western land. Sad their hearts, and slow their steps, as they faced toward the setting sun. Silent or weeping, they moved onward. In all that band, there was not one voluntary exile.

No wonder they disliked to leave thee. I can well comprehend the poignancy of their grief. I too have enjoyed the sweets of thy flowery land, and parted from thee with like reluctance. I have walked under the shadows of thy majestic forests, and bathed my body in thy limpid streams—not with the hope of rejuvenescence, but the certainty of health and joy. Oft have I made my couch under the canopy of thy spreading palms and magnolias, or stretched myself along the greensward of thy savannas; and, with eyes bent upon the blue ether of thy heavens, have listened to my heart repeating the words of the eastern poet:

"Oh! if there can be an Elysium on earth,
It is this - it is this!"

Chapter Two.

The Indigo Plantation.

My father was an indigo planter; his name was Randolph. I bear his name in full—George Randolph.

There is Indian blood in my veins. My father was of the Randolphs of Roanoke—hence descended from the Princess Pocahontas. He was proud of his Indian ancestry—almost vain of it.

It may sound paradoxical, especially to European ears; but it is true, that white men in America, who have Indian blood in them, are proud of the taint. Even to be a "half-breed" is no badge of shame—particularly where the *sang mêlé* has been gifted with fortune. Not all the volumes that have been written bear such strong testimony to the grandeur of the Indian character as this one fact—we are not ashamed to acknowledge them as ancestry!

Hundreds of white families lay claim to descent from the Virginian princess. If their claims be just, then must the fair Pocahontas have been a blessing to her lord.

I think my father *was* of the true lineage; at all events, he belonged to a proud family in the "Old Dominion;" and during his early life had been surrounded by sable slaves in hundreds. But his rich patrimonial lands became at length worn-out; profuse hospitality well-nigh ruined him; and not brooking an inferior station, he gathered up the fragments of his fortune, and "moved" southward—there to begin the world anew.

I was born before this removal, and am therefore a native of Virginia; but my earliest impressions of a home were formed upon the banks of the beautiful Suwanee in Florida. That was the scene of my boyhood's life—the spot consecrated to me by the joys of youth and the charms of early love.

2

I would paint the picture of my boyhood's home. Well do I remember it: so fair a scene is not easily effaced from the memory.

A handsome "frame"-house, coloured white, with green Venetians over the windows, and a wide verandah extending all round. Carved wooden porticoes support the roof of this verandah, and a low balustrade with light railing separates it from the adjoining grounds—from the flower parterre in front, the orangery on the right flank and a large garden on the left. From the outer edge of the parterre, a smooth lawn slopes gently to the bank of the river—here expanding to the dimensions of a noble lake, with distant wooded shores, islets that seem suspended in the air, wild-fowl upon the wing, and wild-fowl in the water.

Upon the lawn, behold tall tapering palms, with pinnatifid leaves—a species of *oreodoxia*—others with broad fan-shaped fronds—the *palmettoes* of the south; behold magnolias, clumps of the fragrant illicium, and radiating crowns of the *yucca gloriosa*—all indigenous to the soil. Another native presents itself to the eye—a huge live-oak extending its long horizontal boughs, covered thickly with evergreen coriaceous leaves, and broadly shadowing the grass beneath. Under its shade behold a beautiful girl, in light summer robes—her hair loosely coifed with a white kerchief, from the folds of which have escaped long tresses glittering with the hues of gold. That is my sister Virginia, my only sister, still younger than myself. Her golden hair bespeaks not her Indian descent, but in that she takes after our mother. She is playing with her pets, the doe of the fallow deer, and its pretty spotted fawn. She is feeding them with the pulp of the sweet orange, of which they are immoderately fond. Another favourite is by her side, led by its tiny chain. It is the black fox-squirrel, with glossy coat and quivering tail. Its eccentric gambols frighten the fawn, causing the timid creature to start over the ground, and press closer to its mother, and sometimes to my sister, for protection.

The scene has its accompaniment of music. The golden oriole, whose nest is among the orange-trees, gives out its liquid song; the mock-bird, caged in the verandah, repeats the strain with variations. The gay mimic echoes the red cardinal and the blue jay, both fluttering among the flowers of the magnolia; it mocks the chatter of the green paroquets, that are busy with the berries of the tall cypresses down by the water's edge; at intervals it repeats the wild scream of the Spanish curlews that wave their silver wings overhead, or the cry of the tantalus heard from the far islets of the lake. The bark of the dog, the mewing of the cat, the hinny of mules, the neighing of horses, even the tones of the human voice, are all imitated by this versatile and incomparable songster.

The rear of the dwelling presents a different aspect—perhaps not so bright, though not less cheerful. Here is exhibited a scene of active life—a picture of the industry of an indigo plantation.

A spacious enclosure, with its "post-and-rail" fence, adjoins the house. Near the centre of this stands the *pièce de résistance*—a grand shed that covers half an acre of ground, supported upon strong pillars of wood. Underneath are seen huge oblong vats, hewn from the great trunks of the cypress. They are ranged in threes, one above the other, and communicate by means of spigots placed in their ends. In these the precious plant is macerated, and its cerulean colour extracted.

Beyond are rows of pretty little cottages, uniform in size and shape, each embowered in its grove of orange-trees, whose ripening fruit and white wax-like flowers fill the air with perfume. These are the negro-cabins. Here and there, towering above their roofs in upright attitude, or bending gently over, is the same noble palm-tree that ornaments the lawn in front. Other houses appear within the enclosure, rude structures of hewn logs, with "clap-board" roofs: they are the stable, the corn-crib, the kitchen—this last communicating with the main dwelling by a long open gallery, with shingle roof, supported upon posts of the fragrant red cedar.

Beyond the enclosure stretch wild fields, backed by a dark belt of cypress forest that shuts out the view of the horizon. These fields exhibit the staple of cultivation, the precious dye-plant, though other vegetation appears upon them. There are maize-plants and sweet potatoes (*Convolvulus batatas*) some rice, and sugar-cane. These are not intended for commerce, but to provision the establishment.

3

The indigo is sown in straight rows, with intervals between. The plants are of different ages, some just bursting through the glebe with leaves like young trefoil; others full-grown, above two feet in height, resemble ferns, and exhibit the light-green pinnated leaves which distinguish most of the *leguminosæ*—for the indigo belongs to this tribe. Some shew their papilionaceous flowers just on the eve of bursting; but rarely are they permitted to exhibit their full bloom. Another destiny awaits them; and the hand of the reaper rudely checks their purple inflorescence.

In the inclosure, and over the indigo-fields, a hundred human forms are moving; with one or two exceptions, they are all of the African race—all slaves. They are not all of black skin—scarcely the majority of them are negroes. There are mulattoes, samboes, and quadroons. Even some who are of pure African blood are not black, only bronze-coloured; but with the exception of the "overseer" and the owner of the plantation, all are slaves. Some are hideously ugly, with thick lips, low retreating foreheads, flat noses, and ill-formed bodies! others are well proportioned; and among them are some that might be accounted good-looking. There are women nearly white—quadroons. Of the latter are several that are more than good-looking—some even beautiful.

The men are in their work-dresses: loose cotton trousers, with coarse coloured shirts, and hats of palmetto-leaf. A few display dandyism in their attire. Some are naked from the waist upwards, their black skins glistening under the sun like ebony. The women are more gaily arrayed in striped prints, and heads "toqued" with Madras kerchiefs of brilliant check. The dresses of some are tasteful and pretty. The turban-like coiffure renders them picturesque.

Both men and women are alike employed in the business of the plantation—the manufacture of the indigo. Some cut down the plants with reaping-hooks, and tie them in bundles; others carry the bundles in from the fields to the great shed; a few are employed in throwing them into the upper trough, the "steeper;" while another few are drawing off and "beating." Some shovel the sediment into the draining-bags, while others superintend the drying and cutting out. All have their respective tasks, and all seem alike cheerful in the performance of them. They laugh, and chatter, and sing; they give back jest for jest; and scarcely a moment passes that merry voices are not ringing upon the ear.

And yet these are all slaves—the slaves of my father. He treats them well; seldom is the lash uplifted: hence the happy mood and cheerful aspect.

Such pleasant pictures are graven on my memory, sweetly and deeply impressed. They formed the *mise-en-scène* of my early life.

Chapter Three.

The Two Jakes.

Every plantation has its "bad fellow"—often more than one, but always one who holds pre-eminence in evil. "Yellow Jake" was the fiend of ours.

He was a young mulatto, in person not ill-looking, but of sullen habit and morose disposition. On occasions he had shewn himself capable of fierce resentment and cruelty.

Instances of such character are more common among mulattoes than negroes. Pride of colour on the part of the yellow man—confidence in a higher organism, both intellectual and physical, and consequently a keener sense of the injustice of his degraded position, explain this psychological difference.

As for the pure negro, he rarely enacts the unfeeling savage. In the drama of human life, he is the victim, not the villain. No matter where lies the scene—in his own land, or elsewhere—he has been used to play the *rôle* of the sufferer; yet his soul is still free from resentment or ferocity. In all the world, there is no kinder heart than that which beats within the bosom of the African black.

Yellow Jake was wicked without provocation. Cruelty was innate in his disposition—no doubt inherited. He was a Spanish mulatto; that is, paternally of Spanish blood—maternally, negro. His father had sold him to mine!

4

A slave-mother, a slave-son. The father's freedom affects not the offspring. Among the black and red races of America, the child fellows the fortunes of the mother. Only she of Caucasian race can be the mother of white men.

There was another "Jacob" upon the plantation—hence the distinctive sobriquet of "Yellow Jake." This other was "Black Jake;" and only in age and size was there any similarity between the two. In disposition they differed even more than in complexion. If Yellow Jake had the brighter skin, Black Jake had the lighter heart. Their countenances exhibited a complete contrast—the contrast between a sullen frown and a cheerful smile. The white teeth of the latter were ever set in smiles: the former smiled only when under the influence of some malicious prompting.

Black Jake was a Virginian. He was one of those belonging to the old plantation—had "moved" along with his master; and felt those ties of attachment which in many cases exist strongly between master and slave. He regarded himself as one of our family, and gloried in bearing our name. Like all negroes born in the "Old Dominion," he was proud of his nativity. In caste, a "Vaginny nigger" takes precedence of all others.

Apart from his complexion, Black Jake was not ill-looking. His features were as good as those of the mulatto. He had neither the thick lips, flat nose, nor retreating forehead of his race—for these characteristics are not universal. I have known negroes of pure African blood with features perfectly regular, and such a one was Black Jake. In form, he might have passed for the Ethiopian Apollo.

There was one who thought him handsome—handsomer than his yellow namesake. This was the quadroon Viola, the belle of the plantation. For Viola's hand, the two Jakes had long time been rival suitors. Both had assiduously courted her smiles—somewhat capricious they were, for Viola was not without coquetry—but she had at length exhibited a marked preference for the black. I need not add that there was jealousy between the negro and mulatto—on the part of the latter, rank hatred of his rival—which Viola's preference had kindled into fierce resentment.

More than once had the two measured their strength, and on each occasion had the black been victorious. Perhaps to this cause, more than to his personal appearance, was he indebted for the smiles of Viola. Throughout all the world, throughout all time, beauty has bowed down before courage and strength.

Yellow Jake was our woodman; Black Jake, the curator of the horses, the driver of "white massa's" barouche.

The story of the two Jakes—their loves and their jealousies—is but a common affair in the *petite politique* of plantation-life. I have singled it out, not from any separate interest it may possess, but as leading to a series of events that exercised an important influence on my own subsequent history.

The first of these events was as follows; Yellow Jake, burning with jealousy at the success of his rival, had grown spiteful with Viola. Meeting her by some chance in the woods, and far from the house, he had offered her a dire insult. Resentment had rendered him reckless. The opportune arrival of my sister had prevented him from using violence, but the intent could not be overlooked; and chiefly through my sister's influence, the mulatto was brought to punishment.

It was the first time that Yellow Jake had received chastisement, though not the first time he had deserved it. My father had been indulgent with him; too indulgent, all said. He had often pardoned him when guilty of faults—of crimes. My father was of an easy temper, and had an exceeding dislike to proceed to the extremity of the lash; but in this case my sister had urged, with some spirit, the necessity of the punishment. Viola was her maid; and the wicked conduct of the mulatto could not be overlooked.

The castigation did not cure him of his propensity to evil. An event occurred shortly after, that proved he was vindictive. My sister's pretty fawn was found dead by the shore of the lake. It could not have died from any natural cause—for it was seen alive, and skipping over the lawn but the hour before. No alligator could have done it, nor yet a wolf. There was neither scratch nor tear upon it; no signs of blood! It must have been strangled.

5

It *was* strangled, as proved in the sequel. Yellow Jake had done it, and Black Jake had seen him. From the orange grove, where the latter chanced to be at work, he had been witness of the tragic scene; and his testimony procured a second flogging for the mulatto.

A third event followed close upon the heels of this—a quarrel between negro and mulatto, that came to blows. It had been sought by the latter to revenge himself, at once upon his rival in love, and the witness of his late crime.

The conflict did not end in mere blows. Yellow Jake, with an instinct derived from his Spanish paternity, drew his knife, and inflicted a severe wound upon his unarmed antagonist.

This time his punishment was more severe. I was myself enraged, for Black Jake was my "body guard" and favourite. Though his skin was black, and his intellect but little cultivated, his cheerful disposition rendered him a pleasant companion; he was, in fact, the chosen associate of my boyish days—my comrade upon the water, and in the woods.

Justice required satisfaction, and Yellow Jake caught it in earnest.

The punishment proved of no avail. He was incorrigible. The demon spirit was too strong within him: it was part of his nature.

Chapter Four.

The Hommock.

Just outside the orangery was one of those singular formations—peculiar, I believe, to Florida.

A circular basin, like a vast sugar-pan, opens into the earth, to the depth of many feet, and having a diameter of forty yards or more. In the bottom of this, several cavities are seen, about the size and of the appearance of dug wells, regularly cylindrical—except where their sides have fallen in, or the rocky partition between them has given way, in which case they resemble a vast honeycomb with broken cells.

The wells are sometimes found dry; but more commonly there is water in the bottom, and often filling the great tank itself.

Such natural reservoirs, although occurring in the midst of level plains, are always partially surrounded by eminences—knolls, and detached masses of testaceous rocks; all of which are covered by an evergreen thicket of native trees, as *magnolia grandiflora*, red bay, *zanthoxylon*, live-oak, mulberry, and several species of fan-palms (palmettoes). Sometimes these shadowy coverts are found among the trees of the pine-forests, and sometimes they appear in the midst of green savannas, like islets in the ocean.

They constitute the "hommocks" of Florida—famed in the story of its Indian wars.

One of these, then, was situated just outside the orangery; with groups of testaceous rocks forming a half-circle around its edge; and draped with the dark foliage of evergreen trees, of the species already mentioned. The water contained in the basin was sweet and limpid; and far down in its crystal depths might be seen gold and red fish, with yellow bream, spotted bass, and many other beautiful varieties of the finny tribe, disporting themselves all day long. The tank was in reality a natural fishpond; and, moreover, it was used as the family bathing-place—for, under the hot sun of Florida, the bath is a necessity as well as a luxury.

From the house, it was approached by a sanded walk that led across the orangery, and some large stone-flags enabled the bather to descend conveniently into the water. Of course, only the white members of the family were allowed the freedom of this charming sanctuary.

Outside the hommock extended the fields under cultivation, until bounded in the distance by tall forests of cypress and white cedar—a sort of impenetrable morass that covered the country for miles beyond.

On one side of the plantation-fields was a wide plain, covered with grassy turf, and without enclosure of any kind. This was the *savanna*, a natural meadow where the horses and cattle of the plantation were freely pastured. Deer often appeared upon this plain, and flocks of the wild turkey.

I was just of that age to be enamoured of the chase. Like most youth of the southern states who have little else to do, hunting was my chief occupation; and I was passionately fond of it. My father had procured for me a brace of splendid greyhounds; and it was a favourite pastime with me to conceal myself in the hommock, wait for the deer and turkeys as they approached, and then course them across the savanna. In this manner I made many a capture of both species of game; for the wild turkey can easily be run down with fleet dogs.

The hour at which I was accustomed to enjoy this amusement was early in the morning, before any of the family were astir. That was the best time to find the game upon the savanna.

One morning, as usual, I repaired to my stand in the covert. I climbed upon a rock, whose flat top afforded footing both to myself and my dogs. From this elevated position I had the whole plain under view, and could observe any object that might be moving upon it, while I was myself secure from observation. The broad leaves of the magnolia formed a bower around me, leaving a break in the foliage, through which I could make my reconnoissance.

On this particular morning I had arrived before sunrise. The horses were still in their stables, and the cattle in the enclosure. Even by the deer, the savanna was untenanted, as I could perceive at the first glance. Over all its wide extent not an antler was to be seen.

I was somewhat disappointed on observing this. My mother expected a party upon that day. She had expressed a wish to have venison at dinner: I had promised her she should have it; and on seeing the savanna empty, I felt disappointment.

I was a little surprised, too; the sight was unusual. Almost every morning, there were deer upon this wide pasture, at one point or another.

Had some early stalker been before me? Probable enough. Perhaps young Ringgold from the next plantation; or maybe one of the Indian hunters, who seemed never to sleep? Certainly, some one had been over the ground, and frightened off the game?

The savanna was a free range, and all who chose might hunt or pasture upon it. It was a tract of common ground, belonging to no one of the plantations—government land not yet purchased.

Certainly Ringgold had been there? or old Hickman, the alligator-hunter, who lived upon the skirt of our plantation? or it might be an Indian from the other side of the swamp?

With such conjectures did I account for the absence of the game.

I felt chagrin. I should not be able to keep my promise; there would be no venison for dinner. A turkey I might obtain; the hour for chasing them had not yet arrived. I could hear them calling from the tall tree-tops—their loud "gobbling" borne far and clear upon the still air of the morning. I did not care for these—the larder was already stocked with them; I had killed a brace on the preceding day. I did not want more—I wanted venison.

To procure it, I must needs try some other mode than coursing. I had my rifle with me; I could try a "still-hunt" in the woods. Better still, I would go in the direction of old Hickman's cabin; he might help me in my dilemma. Perhaps he had been out already? if so, he would be sure to bring home venison. I could procure a supply from him, and keep my promise.—The sun was just shewing his disc above the horizon; his rays were tingeing the tops of the distant cypresses, whose light-green leaves shone with the lines of gold.

I gave one more glance over the savanna, before descending from my elevated position; in that glance I saw what caused me to change my resolution, and remain upon the rock.

A herd of deer was trooping out from the edge of the cypress woods—at that corner where the rail-fence separated the savanna from the cultivated fields.

"Ha!" thought I, "they have been poaching upon the young maize-plants."

I bent my eyes towards the point whence, as I supposed, they had issued from the fields. I knew there was a gap near the corner, with movable bars. I could see it from where I stood, but I now perceived that the bars were in their places! The deer could not have been in the fields then? It was not likely they had leaped either the bars or the fence. It was a high rail-fence, with "stakes and riders." The bars were as high as the fence. The deer must have come out of the woods?

This observation was instantly followed by another. The animals were running rapidly, as if alarmed by the presence of some enemy.

A hunter is behind them? Old Hickman? Ringgold? Who?

7

I gazed eagerly, sweeping my eyes along the edge of the timber, but for a while saw no one.

"A lynx or a bear may have startled them? If so, they will not go far; I shall have a chance with my greyhounds yet. Perhaps—"

My reflections were brought to a sudden termination, on perceiving what had caused the stampede of the deer. It was neither bear nor lynx, but a human being.

A man was just emerging from out the dark shadow of the cypresses. The sun as yet only touched the tops of the trees; but there was light enough below to enable me to make out the figure of a man—still more, to recognise the individual. It was neither Ringgold nor Hickman, nor yet an Indian. The dress I knew well—the blue cottonade trousers, the striped shirt, and palmetto hat. The dress was that worn by our woodman. The man was Yellow Jake.

Chapter Five.

Yellow Jake.

Not without some surprise did I make this discovery. What was the mulatto doing in the woods at such an hour? It was not his habit to be so thrifty; on the contrary, it was difficult to rouse him to his daily work. He was not a hunter—had no taste for it. I never saw him go after game—though, from being always in the woods, he was well acquainted with the haunts and habits of every animal that dwelt there. What was he doing abroad on this particular morning?

I remained on my perch to watch him, at the same time keeping an eye upon the deer.

It soon became evident that the mulatto was not after these; for, on coming out of the timber, he turned along its edge, in a direction opposite to that in which the deer had gone. He went straight towards the gap that fed into the maize-field.

I noticed that he moved slowly and in a crouching attitude. I thought there was some object near his feet: it appeared to be a dog, but a very small one. Perhaps an opossum, thought I. It was of whitish colour, as these creatures are; but in the distance I could not distinguish between an opossum and a puppy. I fancied, however, that it was the pouched animal; that he had caught it in the woods, and was leading it along in a string.

There was nothing remarkable or improbable in all this behaviour. The mulatto may have discovered an opossum-cave the day before, and set a trap for the animal. It may have been caught in the night, and he was now on his way home with it. The only point that surprised me was, that the fellow had turned hunter; but I explained this upon another hypothesis. I remembered how fond the negroes are of the flesh of the opossum, and Yellow Jake was no exception to the rule. Perhaps he had seen, the day before, that this one could be easily obtained, and had resolved upon having a roast?

But why was he not carrying it in a proper manner? He appeared to be leading, or dragging it rather—for I knew the creature would not be led—and every now and then I observed him stoop towards it, as if caressing it.

I was puzzled; it could not be an opossum.

I watched the man narrowly till he arrived opposite the gap in the fence. I expected to see him step over the bars—since through the maize-field was the nearest way to the house. Certainly he entered the field; but, to my astonishment, instead of climbing over in the usual manner, I saw him take out bar after bar, down to the very lowest. I observed, moreover, that he flung the bars to one side, leaving the gap quite open!

He then passed through, and entering among the corn, in the same crouching attitude, disappeared behind the broad blades of the young maize-plants—

For a while I saw no more of him, or the white object that he "toated" along with him in such a singular fashion.

I turned my attention to the deer: they had got over their alarm, and had halted near the middle of the savanna, where they were now quietly browsing.

But I could not help pondering upon the eccentric manoeuvres I had just been witness of; and once more I bent my eyes toward the place, where I had last seen the mulatto.

He was still among the maize-plants. I could see nothing of him; but at that moment my eyes rested upon an object that filled me with fresh surprise.

Just at the point where Yellow Jake had emerged from the woods, something else appeared in motion—also coming out into the open savanna. It was a dark object, and from its prostrate attitude, resembled a man crawling forward upon his hands, and dragging his limbs after him.

For a moment or two, I believed it to be a man—not a white man—but a negro or an Indian. The tactics were Indian, but we were at peace with these people, and why should one of them be thus trailing the mulatto? I say "trailing" for the attitude and motions, of whatever creature I saw, plainly indicated that it was following upon the track which Yellow Jake had just passed over.

Was it Black Jake who was after him?

This idea came suddenly into my mind: I remembered the *vendetta* that existed between them; I remembered the conflict in which Yellow Jake had used his knife. True, he had been punished, but not by Black Jake himself. Was the latter now seeking to revenge himself in person?

This might have appeared the easiest explanation of the scene that was mystifying me; had it not been for the improbability of the black acting in such a manner. I could not think that the noble fellow would seek any mean mode of retaliation, however revengeful he might feel against one who had so basely attacked him. It was not in keeping with his character. No. It could not be he who was crawling out of the bushes.

Nor he, nor any one.

At that moment, the golden sun flashed over the savanna. His beams glanced along the greensward, lighting the trees to their bases. The dark form emerged from out of the shadow, and turned head towards the maize-field. The long prostrate body glittered under the sun with a sheen like scaled armour. It was easily recognised. It was not negro—not Indian—not human: it was the hideous form of an alligator!

Chapter Six.

The Alligator.

To one brought up—born, I might almost say—upon the banks of a Floridian river, there is nothing remarkable in the sight of an alligator. Nothing very terrible either; for ugly as is the great saurian—certainly the most repulsive form in the animal kingdom—it is least dreaded by those who know it best. For all that, it is seldom approached without some feeling of fear. The stranger to its haunts and habits, abhors and flees from it; and even the native—be he red, white, or black—whose home borders the swamp and the lagoon, approaches this gigantic lizard with caution.

Some closet naturalists have asserted that the alligator will not attack man, and yet they admit that it will destroy horses and horned cattle. A like allegation is made of the jaguar and vampire bat. Strange assertions, in the teeth of a thousand testimonies to the contrary.

It is true the alligator does not always attack man when an opportunity offers—nor does the lion, nor yet the tiger—but even the false Buffon would scarcely be bold enough to declare that the alligator is innocuous. If a list could be furnished of human beings who have fallen victims to the voracity of this creature, since the days of Columbus, it would be found to be something enormous—quite equal to the havoc made in the same period of time by the Indian tiger or the African lion. Humboldt, during his short stay in South America, was well informed of many instances; and for my part, I know of more than one case of actual death, and many of lacerated limbs, received at the jaws of the American alligator.

There are many species, both of the caïman or alligator, and of the true crocodile, in the waters of tropical America. They are more or less fierce, and hence the difference of "travellers' tales" in relation to them. Even the same species in two different rivers is not always of like disposition. The individuals are affected by outward circumstances, as other animals are. Size, climate, colonisation, all produce their effect; and, what may appear still more singular, their disposition is influenced by the character of the race of men that chances to dwell near them!

On some of the South-American rivers—whose banks are the home of the ill-armed apathetic Indian—the caimans are exceedingly bold, and dangerous to approach. Just so were their congeners, the alligators of the north, till the stalwart backwoodsman, with his axe in one hand, and his rifle in the other, taught them to fear the upright form—a proof that these crawling creatures possess the powers of reason. Even to this hour, in many of the swamps and streams of Florida, full-grown alligators cannot be approached without peril; this is especially the case daring the season of the sexes, and still more where these reptiles are encountered remote from the habitations of man. In Florida are rivers and lagoons where a swimmer would have no more chance of life, than if he had plunged into a sea of sharks.

Notwithstanding all this, use brings one to look lightly even upon real danger— particularly when that danger is almost continuous; and the denizen of the *cyprière* and the *white cedar* swamp is accustomed to regard without much emotion the menace of the ugly alligator. To the native of Florida, its presence is no novelty, and its going or coming excites but little interest—except perhaps in the bosom of the black man who feeds upon its tail; or the alligator-hunter, who makes a living out of its leather.

The appearance of one on the edge of the savanna would not have caused me a second thought, had it not been for its peculiar movements, as well as those I had just observed on the part of the mulatto. I could not help fancying that there was *some connexion between them*; at all events it appeared certain, that the reptile was following the man!

Whether it had him in view, or whether trailing him by the scent, I could not tell. The latter I fancied to be the case; for the mulatto had entered under cover of the maize-plants, before the other appeared outside the timber; and it could hardly have seen him as it turned towards the gap. It might, but I fancied not. More like, it was trailing him by the scent; but whether the creature was capable of doing so, I did not stay to inquire.

On it crawled over the sward—crossing the corner of the meadow, and directly upon the track which the man had taken. At intervals, it paused, flattened its breast against the earth, and remained for some seconds in this attitude, as if resting itself. Then it would raise its body to nearly a yard in height, and move forward with apparent eagerness—as if in obedience to some attractive power in advance of it? The alligator progresses but slowly upon dry ground—not faster than a duck or goose. The water is its true element, where it makes way almost with the rapidity of a fish.

At length it approached the gap; and, after another pause, it drew its long dark body within the enclosure. I saw it enter among the maize-plants, at the exact point where the mulatto had disappeared! Of course, it was now also hidden from my view.

I no longer doubted that the monster was following the man; and equally certain was I that the latter *knew* that he was followed! How could I doubt either of these facts? To the former, I was an eye-witness; of the latter, I had circumstantial proofs. The singular attitudes and actions of the mulatto; his taking out the bars and leaving the gap free; his occasional glances backward—which I had observed as he was crossing the open ground—these were my proofs that he knew what was coming behind him—undoubtedly he knew.

But my conviction upon these two points in nowise helped to elucidate the mystery— for a mystery it had become. Beyond a doubt, the reptile was drawn after by some attraction, which it appeared unable to resist—its eagerness in advancing was evidence of this, and proved that the man was exercising some influence over it that lured it forward.

What influence? Was he beguiling it by some charm of Obeah?

A superstitious shudder came over me, as I asked myself the question. I really had such fancies at the moment. Brought up, as I had been, among Africans, dandled in the arms—perhaps nourished from the bosom—of many a sable nurse, it is not to be wondered at that my young mind was tainted with the superstitions of Bonny and Benin. I knew there were alligators in the cypress swamp—in its more remote recesses, some of enormous size—

but how Yellow Jake had contrived to lure one out, and cause it to follow him over the dry cultivated ground, was a puzzle I could not explain to myself. I could think of no natural cause; I was therefore forced into the regions of the weird and supernatural.

I stood for a long while watching and wondering. The deer had passed out of my mind. They fed unnoticed: I was too much absorbed in the mysterious movements of the half-breed and his amphibious follower.

Chapter Seven.

The Turtle-Crawl.

So long as they remained in the maize-field, I saw nothing of either. The direction of my view was slightly oblique to the rows of the plants. The corn was at full growth, and its tall culms and broad lanceolate leaves would have overtopped the head of a man on horseback. A thicket of evergreen trees would not have been more impenetrable to the eye.

By going a little to the right, I should have become aligned with the rows, and could have seen far down the avenues between them; but this would have carried me out of the cover, and the mulatto might then have seen *me*. For certain reasons, I did not desire he should; and I remained where I had hitherto been standing.

I was satisfied that the man was still making his way up the field, and would in due time discover himself in the open ground.

An indigo flat lay between the hommock and the maize. To approach the house, it would be necessary for him to pass through the indigo; and, as the plants were but a little over two feet in height, I could not fail to observe him as he came through. I waited, therefore, with a feeling of curious anticipation—my thoughts still wearing a tinge of the weird!

He came on slowly—very slowly; but I knew that he was advancing. I could trace his progress by an occasional movement which I observed among the leaves and tassels of the maize. The morning was still—not a breath of air stirred; and consequently the motion must have been caused by some one passing among the plants—of course by the mulatto himself. The oscillation observed farther off, told that the alligator was still following.

Again and again I observed this movement among the maize-blades. It was evident the man was not following the direction of the rows, but crossing diagonally through them! For what purpose? I could not guess. Any one of the intervals would have conducted him in a direct line towards the house—whither I supposed him to be moving. Why, then, should he adopt a more difficult course, by crossing them? It was not till afterwards that I discovered his object in this zigzag movement.

He had now advanced almost to the nether edge of the cornfield. The indigo flat was of no great breadth, and he was already so near, that I could hear the rustling of the cornstalks as they switched against each other.

Another sound I could now hear; it resembled the howling of a dog. I heard it again, and, after an interval, again. It was not the voice of a full-grown dog, but rather the weak whimper of a puppy.

At first, I fancied that the sounds came from the alligator: for these reptiles make exactly such a noise—but only when young. The one following the mulatto was full-grown; the cries could not proceed from it. Moreover, the sounds came from a point nearer me—from the place where the man himself was moving.

I now remembered the white object I had observed as the man was crossing the corner of the savanna. It was not an opossum, then, but a young dog.

Yes. I heard the cry again: it was the whining of a whelp—nothing else.

If I could have doubted the evidence of my ears, my eyes would soon have convinced me; for, just then, I saw the man emerge from out the maize with a dog by his side—a small white cur, and apparently a young one. He was leading the creature upon a string, half-dragging it after him. I had now a full view of the individual, and saw to a certainty that he was our woodman, Yellow Jake.

Before coming out from the cover of the corn, he halted for a moment—as if to reconnoitre the ground before him. He was upon his feet, and in an erect attitude. Whatever motive he had for concealment, he needed not to crouch amid the tall plants of maize; but the indigo did not promise so good a shelter, and he was evidently considering how to advance through it without being perceived. Plainly, he had a motive for concealing himself—his every movement proved this—but with what object I could not divine.

The indigo was of the kind known as the "false Guatemala." There were several species cultivated upon the plantation; but this grew tallest; and some of the plants, now in their full purple bloom, stood nearly three feet from the surface of the soil. A man passing through them in an erect attitude, could, of coarse, have been seen from any part of the field; but it was possible for one to crouch down, and move, between the rows unobserved. This possibility seemed to occur to the woodman; for, after a short pause, he dropped to his hands and knees, and commenced crawling forward among the indigo.

There was no fence for him to cross—the cultivated ground was all under one enclosure—and an open ridge alone formed the dividing-line between the two kinds of crop.

Had I been upon the same level with the field, the skulker would have been now hidden from my sight; but my elevated position enabled me to command a view of the intervals between the rows, and I could note every movement he was making.

Every now and then he paused, caught up the cur, and held it for a few seconds in his hands—during which the animal continued to howl as if in pain!

As he drew nearer, and repeated this operation, I saw that he was *pinching its ears!*

Fifty paces in his rear, the great lizard appeared coming out of the corn. It scarcely made pause in the open ground, but still following the track, entered among the indigo.

At this moment, a light broke upon me; I no longer speculated on the power of Obeah. The mystery was dissolved: the alligator was lured forward by the cries of the dog!

I might have thought of the thing before, for I had heard of it before. I had heard from good authority—the alligator-hunter himself, who had often captured them by such a decoy—that these reptiles will follow a howling dog for miles through the forest, and that the old males especially are addicted to this habit. Hickman's belief was that they mistake the voice of the dog for that of their own offspring, which these unnatural parents eagerly devour.

But, independently of this monstrous propensity, it is well-known that dogs are the favourite prey of the alligator; and the unfortunate beagle that, in the heat of the chase, ventures across creek or lagoon, is certain to be attacked by these ugly amphibia.

The huge reptile, then, was being lured forward by the voice of the puppy; and this accounted for the grand overland journey he was making.

There was no longer a mystery—at least, about the mode in which the alligator was attracted onward; the only thing that remained for explanation was, what motive had the mulatto in carrying out this singular manoeuvre?

When I saw him take to his hands and knees, I had been under the impression that he did so to approach the house, without being observed. But as I continued to watch him, I changed my mind. I noticed that he looked oftener, and with more anxiety *behind* him, as if he was only desirous of being concealed from the eyes of the alligator. I observed, too, that he changed frequently from place to place, as if he aimed at keeping a screen of the plants between himself and his follower. This would also account for his having crossed the rows of the maize-plants, as already noticed.

After all, it was only some freak that had entered the fellow's brain. He had learned this curious mode of coaxing the alligator from its haunts—perhaps old Hickman had shown him how—or he may have gathered it from his own observation, while wood-chopping in the swamps. He was taking the reptile to the house from some eccentric motive?—to make exhibition of it among his fellows?—to have a "lark" with it? or a combat between it and the house-dogs? or for some like purpose?

I could not divine his intention, and would have thought no more of it, had it not been that one or two little circumstances had made an impression upon me. I was struck by the peculiar pains which the fellow was taking to accomplish his purpose with success. He was sparing neither trouble nor time. True, it was not to be a work-day upon the plantation;

it was a holiday, and the time was his own; but it was not the habit of Yellow Jake to be abroad at so early an hour, and the trouble he was taking was not in consonance with his character of habitual *insouciance* and idleness. Some strong motive, then, must have been urging him to the act. What motive?

I pondered upon it, but could not make it out.

And yet I felt uneasiness, as I watched him. It was an undefined feeling, and I could assign no reason for it—beyond the fact that the mulatto was a bad fellow, and I knew him to be capable of almost any wickedness. But if his design was a wicked one, what evil could he effect with the alligator? No one would fear the reptile upon dry ground?—it could hurt no one?

Thus I reflected, and still did I feel some indefinite apprehensions.

But for this feeling I should have given over observing his movements, and turned my attention to the herd of deer—which I now perceived approaching up the savanna, and coming close to my place of concealment.

I resisted the temptation, and continued to watch the mulatto a little longer.

I was not kept much longer in suspense. He had now arrived upon the outer edge of the hommock, which he did not enter. I saw him turn round the thicket, and keep on towards the orangery. There was a wicket at this corner which he passed through, leaving the gate open behind him. At short intervals, he still caused the dog to utter its involuntary howlings.

It no longer needed to cry loudly, for the alligator was now close in the rear.

I obtained a full view of the monster as it passed under my position. It was not one of the largest, though it was several yards in length. There are some that measure more than a statute pole. This one was full twelve feet, from its snout to the extremity of its tail. It clutched the ground with its broad webbed feet as it crawled forward. Its corrugated skin of bluish brown colour was coated with slippery mucus, that glittered under the sun as it moved; and large masses of the swamp-slime rested in the concavities between its rhomboid scales. It seemed greatly excited; and whenever it heard the voice of the dog, exhibited fresh symptoms of rage. It would erect itself upon its muscular arms, raise its head aloft—as if to get a view of the prey—lash its plaited tail into the air, and swell its body almost to double its natural dimensions. At the same time, it emitted loud noises from its throat and nostrils, that resembled the rumbling of distant thunder, and its musky smell filled the air with a sickening effluvium. A more monstrous creature it would be impossible to conceive. Even the fabled dragon could not have been more horrible to behold.

Without stopping, it dragged its long body through the gate, still following the direction of the noise. The leaves of the evergreens intervened, and hid the hideous reptile from my sight.

I turned my face in the opposite direction—towards the house—to watch the further movements of the mulatto. From my position, I commanded a view of the tank, and could see nearly all around it. The inner side was especially under my view, as it lay opposite, and could only be approached through the orangery.

Between the grove and the edge of the great basin, was an open space. Here there was an artificial pond only a few yards in width, and with a little water at the bottom, which was supplied by means of a pump, from the main reservoir. This pond, or rather enclosure, was the "turtle-crawl," a place in which turtle were fed and kept, to be ready at all times for the table. My father still continued his habits of Virginian hospitality; and in Florida these aldermanic delicacies are easily obtained.

The embankment of this turtle-crawl formed the direct path to the water-basin; and as I turned, I saw Yellow Jake upon it, and just approaching the pond. He still carried the cur in his arms; I saw that he was causing it to utter a continuous howling.

On reaching the steps, that led down, he paused a moment, and looked back. I noticed that he looked back in both ways—first towards the house, and then, with a satisfied air, in the direction whence he had come. No doubt he saw the alligator close at hand; for, without further hesitation, he flung the puppy far out into the water; and then, retreating along the embankment of the turtle-crawl, he entered among the orange-trees, and was out of sight.

The whelp, thus suddenly plunged into the cool tank, kept up a constant howling, at the same time beating the water violently with its feet, in the endeavour to keep itself afloat.

Its struggles were of short duration. The alligator, now guided by the well-known noise of moving water, as well as the cries of the dog, advanced rapidly to the edge; and without hesitating a moment, sprang forward into the pond. With the rapidity of an arrow, it darted out to the centre; and, seizing the victim between its bony jaws, dived instantaneously under the surface.

I could for some time trace its monstrous form far down in the diaphanous water; but guided by instinct, it soon entered one of the deep wells, amidst the darkness of which it sank out of sight.

Chapter Eight.

The King Vultures.

"So, then, my yellow friend, that is the intention!—a bit of revenge after all. I'll make you pay for it, you spiteful ruffian! You little thought you were observed. Ha! you shall rue this cunning deviltry before night."

Some such soliloquy escaped my lips, as soon as I comprehended the design of the mulatto's manoeuvre—for I now understood it—at least I thought so. The tank was full of beautiful fish. There were gold fish and silver fish, hyodons, and red trout. They were my sister's especial pets. She was very fond of them. It was her custom to visit them daily, give them food, and watch their gambols. Many an aquatic *cotillon* had she superintended. They knew her person, would follow her around the tank, and take food out of her fingers. She delighted in thus serving them.

The revenge lay in this. The mulatto well knew that the alligator lives upon fish—they are his natural food; and that those in the tank, pent up as they were, would soon become his prey. So strong a tyrant would soon ravage the preserve, killing the helpless creatures by scores—of course to the chagrin and grief of their fond mistress, and the joy of Yellow Jake.

I knew that the fellow disliked my little sister. The spirited part she had played, in having him punished for the affair with Viola, had kindled his resentment against her; but since then, there had been other little incidents to increase it. She had favoured the suit of his rival with the quadroon, and had forbidden the woodman to approach Viola in her presence. These circumstances had certainly rendered the fellow hostile to her; and although there was no outward show of this feeling—there dared not be—I was nevertheless aware of the fact. His killing the fawn had proved it, and the present was a fresh instance of the implacable spirit of the man.

He calculated upon the alligator soon making havoc among the fish. Of course he knew it would in time be discovered and killed; but likely not before many of the finest should be destroyed.

No one would ever dream that the creature had been *brought* there—for on more than one occasion, alligators had found their way into the tank—having strayed from the river, or the neighbouring lagoons—or rather having been guided thither by an unexplained instinct, which enables these creatures to travel straight in the direction of water.

Such, thought I, were the designs and conjectures of Yellow Jake.

It proved afterwards that I had fathomed but half his plan. I was too young, too innocent of wickedness, even to guess at the intense malice of which the human heart is capable.

My first impulse was to follow the mulatto to the house—make known what he had done—have him punished; and then return with a party to destroy the alligator, before he could do any damage among the fish.

At this crisis, the deer claimed my attention. The herd—an antlered buck with several does—had browsed close up to the hommock. They were within two hundred yards of where I stood. The sight was too tempting. I remembered the promise to my mother; it must be kept; venison must be obtained at all hazards!

But there was no hazard. The alligator had already eaten his breakfast. With a whole dog in his maw, it was not likely he would disturb the finny denizens of the tank for some hours to come; and as for Yellow Jake, I saw he had proceeded on to the house; he could be found at any moment; his chastisement could stand over till my return.

With these reflections passing through my mind, I abandoned my first design, and turned my attention exclusively to the game.

They were too distant for the range of my rifle; and I waited a while in the hope that they would move nearer.

But I waited in vain. The deer is shy of the hommock. It regards the evergreen islet as dangerous ground, and habitually keeps aloof from it. Natural enough, since the creature is oft saluted by the twang of the Indian bow, or the whip-like crack of the hunter's rifle. Thence often reaches it the deadly missile.

Perceiving that the game was getting no nearer, but the contrary, I resolved to course them; and, gliding down from the rock, I descended through the copsewood to the edge of plain.

On reaching the open ground, I rushed forward—at the same time unleashing the dogs, and crying the "view hilloo."

It was a splendid chase—led on by the old buck—the dogs following tail-on-end. I thought I never saw deer run so fleetly; it appeared as if scarcely a score of seconds had transpired while they were crossing the savanna—more than a mile in width. I had a full and perfect view of the whole; there was no obstruction either to run of the animals or the eye of the observer; the grass had been browsed short by the cattle, and not a bush grew upon the green plain; so that it was a trial of pure speed between dogs and deer. So swiftly ran the deer, I began to feel apprehensive about the venison.

My apprehensions were speedily at an end. Just on the farther edge of the savanna, the chase ended—so far at least as the dogs were concerned, and one of the deer. I saw that they had flung a doe, and were standing over her, one of them holding her by the throat.

I hurried forward. Ten minutes brought me to the spot; and after a short struggle, the quarry was killed, and bled.

I was satisfied with my dogs, with the sport, with my own exploits. I was happy at the prospect of being able to redeem my promise; and with the carcass across my shoulders, I turned triumphantly homeward.

As I faced round, I saw the shadow of wings moving over the sunlit savanna. I looked upward. Two large birds were above me in the air; they were at no great height, nor were they endeavouring to mount higher. On the contrary, they were wheeling in spiral rings, that seemed to incline downward at each successive circuit they made around me.

At first glance, the sun's beams were in my eyes, and I could not tell what birds were flapping above me. On facing round, I had the sun in my favour; and his rays, glancing full upon the soft cream-coloured plumage, enabled me to recognise the species—they were *king vultures*—the most beautiful birds of their tribe, I am almost tempted to say the most beautiful birds in creation; certainly they take rank, among those most distinguished in the world of ornithology.

These birds are natives of the flowery land, but stray no farther north. Their haunt is on the green "everglades" and wide savannas of Florida, on the llanos of the Orinoco, and the plains of the Apure. In Florida they are rare, though not in all parts of it; but their appearance in the neighbourhood of the plantations excites an interest similar to that which is occasioned by the flight of an eagle. Not so with the other vultures—*Cathartes aura* and *atratus*—both of which are as common as crows.

In proof that the king vultures are rare, I may state that my sister had never seen one—except at a great distance off; yet this young lady was twelve years of age, and a native of the land. True, she had not gone much abroad—seldom beyond the bounds of the plantation. I remembered her expressing an ardent desire to view more closely one of these beautiful birds. I remembered it that moment; and at once formed the design of gratifying her wish.

The birds were near enough—so near that I could distinguish the deep yellow colour of their throats, the coral red upon their crowns, and the orange lappets that drooped along their beaks. They were near enough—within half reach of my rifle—but moving about as they were, it would have required a better marksman than I to have brought one of them down with a bullet.

I did not think of trying it in that way. Another idea was in my mind; and without farther pause, I proceeded to carry it out.

I saw that the vultures had espied the body of the doe, where it lay across my shoulders. That was why they were hovering above me. My plan was simple enough. I laid the carcass upon the earth; and, taking my rifle, walked away towards the timber.

Trees grew at fifty yards' distance from where I had placed the doe; and behind the nearest of these I took my stand.

I had not long to wait. The unconscious birds wheeled lower and lower, and at length one alighted on the earth. Its companion had not time to join it before the rifle cracked, and laid the beautiful creature lifeless upon the grass.

The other, frighted by the sound, rose higher and higher, and then flew away over the tops of the cypresses.

Again I shouldered my venison; and carrying the bird in my hand started homeward.

My heart was full of exultation. I anticipated a double pleasure—from the double pleasure I was to create. I should make happy the two beings that, of all on earth, were dearest to me—my fond mother, my beautiful sister.

I soon recrossed the savanna, and entered the orangery. I did not stay to go round by the wicket, but climbed over the fence at its lower end. So happy was I that my load felt light as a feather. Exultingly I strode forward, dashing the loaded boughs from my path. I sent their golden globes rolling hither and thither. What mattered a bushel of oranges?

I reached the parterre. My mother was in the verandah; she saw me as I approached, and uttered an exclamation of joy. I flung the spoils of the chase at her feet. I had kept my promise.

"What is that?—a bird?"

"Yes the king vulture—a present for Virgine. Where is she? Not up yet? Ha! the little sluggard—I shall soon arouse her. Still abed and on such a beautiful morning!"

"You wrong her, George; she has been up on hour or more. She has been playing; and has just this moment left off."

"But where is she now? In the drawing-room?"

"No; she has gone to the bath."

"To *the bath*!"

"Yes, she and Viola. What—"

"O mother—mother—"

"Tell me, George—"

"O heavens—*the alligator*!"

Chapter Nine.

The Bath.

"Yellow Jake! the alligator!"

They were all the words I could utter. My mother entreated an explanation; I could not stay to give it. Frantic with apprehension, I tore myself away, leaving her in a state of terror that rivalled my own.

I ran towards the hommock—the bath. I wait not to follow the devious route of the walk, but keep straight on, leaping over such obstacles as present themselves. I spring across the paling, and rush through the orangery, causing the branches to crackle and the fruit to fall. My ears are keenly bent to catch every sound.

Behind are sounds enough: I hear my mother's voice uttered in accents of terror. Already have her cries alarmed the house, and are echoed and answered by the domestics, both females and men. Dogs, startled by the sudden excitement, are baying within the enclosure, and fowls and caged birds screech in concert.

16

From behind come all these noises. It is not for them my ears are bent; I am listening *before* me.

In this direction I now hear sounds. The plashing of water is in my ears, and mingling with the tones of a clear silvery voice—it is the voice of my sister! "Ha, ha, ha!" The ring of laughter! Thank Heaven, she is safe!

I stay my step under the influence of a delicate thought; I call aloud:

"Virgine! Virgine!"

Impatiently I wait the reply. None reaches me; the noise of the water has drowned my voice!

I call again, and louder: "Virgine! sister! Virgine!"

I am heard, and hear:

"Who calls? You, Georgy?"

"Yes; it is I, Virgine."

"And pray, what want you, brother?"

"O sister! come out of the bath."

"For what reason should I? Our friends come? They are early: let them wait, my Georgy. Go you and entertain them. I mean to enjoy myself this most beautiful of mornings; the water's just right—delightful! Isn't it, Viola? Ho! I shall have a swim round the pond: here goes?"

And then there was a fresh plashing in the water, mingled with a cheerful abandon of laughter in the voices of my sister and her maid.

I shouted at the top of my voice:

"Hear me, Virgine, dear sister! For Heaven's sake, come out! come—"

There was a sudden cessation of the merry tones; then came a short sharp ejaculation, followed almost instantaneously by a wild scream. I perceived that neither was a reply to my appeal. I had called out in a tone of entreaty sufficient to have raised apprehension; but the voices that now reached me were uttered in accents of terror. In my sister's voice I heard the words:

"See, Viola! O mercy—the monster! Ha! he is coming this way! O mercy! Help, George, help! Save—save me!"

Well knew I the meaning of the summons; too well could I comprehend the half-coherent words, and the continued screaming that succeeded them.

"Sister, I come, I come!"

Quick as thought, I dashed forward, breaking through the boughs that still intercepted my view.

"Oh, perhaps I shall be too late! She screams in agony; she is already in the grasp of the alligator?"

A dozen bounds carried me clear of the grove; and, gliding along the embankment of the turtle-crawl, I stood by the edge of the tank. A fearful tableau was before me.

My sister was near the centre of the basin, swimming towards the edge. There stood the quadroon—knee deep—screeching and flinging her arms frantically in the air. Beyond, appeared the gigantic lizard; his whole body, arms, hands, and claws clearly traceable in the pellucid water, above the surface of which rose the scaly serrature of his back and shoulders. His snout and tail projected still higher; and with the latter he was lashing the water into white froth, that already mottled the surface of the pond. He was not ten feet from his intended victim. His gaunt jaws almost touched the green baize skirt that floated train-like behind her. At any moment, he might have darted forward and seized her.

My sister was swimming with all her might. She was a capital swimmer; but what could it avail? Her bathing-dress was impeding her; but what mattered that? The alligator might have seized her at any moment; with a single effort, could have caught her, and yet he had not made it.

I wondered why he had not; I wondered that he still held back. I wonder to this hour, for it is not yet explained. I can account for it only on one supposition: that he felt that his victim was perfectly within his power; and as the cat cajoles with the mouse, so was he indulging in the plenitude of his tyrant strength.

17

These observations were made in a single second of time—while I was cocking my rifle.

I aimed, and fired. There were but two places where the shot could have proved fatal—the eye or behind the forearm. I aimed for the eye. I hit the shoulder; but from that hard corrugated skin, my bullet glinted as from a granite rock. Among the rhomboid protuberances it made a whitish score, and that was all.

The play of the monster was brought to a termination. The shot appeared to have given him pain. At all events, it roused him to more earnest action, and perhaps impelled him to the final spring. He made it the instant after.

Lashing the water with his broad tail—as if to gain impetus—he darted forward; his huge jaw hinged vertically upward, till the red throat showed wide agape; and the next moment the floating skirt—and oh! the limbs of my sister, were in his horrid gripe!

I plunged in, and swam towards them. The gun I still carried in my grasp. It hindered me. I dropped it to the bottom, and swam on.

I caught Virgine in my arms. I was just in time, for the alligator was dragging her below.

With all my strength, I held her up. It needed all to keep us above the surface. I had no weapon; and if I had been armed, I could not have spared a hand to strike.

I shouted with all my voice, in the hope of intimidating the assailant, and causing him to let go his hold. It was to no purpose: he still held on.

O Heavens! we shall both be dragged under—drowned—devoured—

A plunge, as of one leaping from a high elevation into the pond—a quick, bold swimmer from the shore—a dark-skinned face, with long black hair that floats behind it on the water—a breast gleaming with bright spangles—a body clad in bead-embroidered garments—a man? a boy!

Who is this strange youth that rushes to our rescue?

He is already by our side—by the side of our terrible antagonist. With all the earnest energy of his look, he utters not a word. He rests one hand upon the shoulder of the huge lizard, and with a sudden spring places himself upon its back. A rider could not have leaped more adroitly to the saddle.

A knife gleams in his uplifted hand. It descends—its blade is buried in the eye of the alligator!

The roar of the saurian betokens its pain. The earth vibrates with the sound; the froth flies up under the lashings of its tail, and a cloud of spray is flung over us. But the monster has now relaxed its gripe, and I am swimming with my sister to the shore.

A glance backward reveals to me a strange sight—I see the alligator diving to the bottom with the bold rider upon its back! He is lost—he is lost!

With painful thoughts, I swim on. I climb out, and place my fainting sister upon the bank. I again look back.

Joy, joy! the strange youth is once more above the surface, and swimming freely to the shore. Upon the further side of the pond, the hideous form is also above water, struggling by the edge—frantic and furious with the agony of its wounds.

Joy, joy! my sister is unharmed. The floating skirt has saved her; scarcely a scratch shows upon her delicate limbs; and now in tender arms, amidst sweet words and looks of kind sympathy, she is borne away from the scene of her peril.

Chapter Ten.

The "Half-Blood."

The alligator was soon clubbed to death, and dragged to the shore—a work of delight to the blacks of the plantation.

No one suspected how the reptile had got to the pond—for I had not said a word to any one. The belief was that it had wandered there from the river, or the lagoons—as others had done before; and Yellow Jake, the most active of all in its destruction, was heard several times repeating this hypothesis! Little did the villain suspect that his secret was known. I thought that besides himself I was the only one privy to it; in this, however, I was mistaken.

The domestics had gone back to the house, "toating" the huge carcass with ropes, and uttering shouts of triumph. I was alone with our gallant preserver. I stayed behind purposely to thank him.

Mother, father, all had given expression to their gratitude; all had signified their admiration of his gallant conduct: even my sister, who had recovered consciousness before being carried away, had thanked him with kind words.

He made no reply, further than to acknowledge the compliments paid him; and this he did either by a smile or a simple inclination of the head. With the years of a boy, he seemed to possess the gravity of a man.

He appeared about my own age and size. His figure was perfectly proportioned, and his face handsome. The complexion was not that of a pure Indian, though the style of his dress was so. His skin was nearer brunette than bronze: he was evidently a "half-blood."

His nose was slightly aquiline, which gave him that fine eagle-look peculiar to some of the North American tribes; and his eye, though mild in common mood, was easily lighted up. Under excitement, as I had just witnessed, it shone with the brilliancy of fire.

The admixture of Caucasian blood had tamed down the prominence of Indian features to a perfect regularity, without robbing them of their heroic grandeur of expression; and the black hair was finer than that of the pure native, though equally shining and luxuriant. In short, the *tout ensemble* of this strange youth was that of a noble and handsome boy that another brace of summers would develop into a splendid-looking man. Even as a boy, there was an individuality about him, that, when once seen, was not to be forgotten.

I have said that his costume was Indian. So was it—purely Indian—not made up altogether of the spoils of the chase, for the buckskin has long, ceased to be the wear of the aborigines of Florida. His moccasins alone were of dressed deer's hide; his leggings were of scarlet cloth; and his tunic of figured cotton stuff—all three elaborately beaded and embroidered. With these he wore a wampum belt, and a fillet encircled his head, above which rose erect three plumes from the tail of the king vulture—which among Indians is an *eagle*. Around his neck were strings of party-coloured beads, and upon his breast three demi-lunes of silver, suspended one above the other.

Thus was the youth attired, and, despite the soaking which his garments had received, he presented an aspect as once noble and picturesque.

"You are sure you have received no injury?" I inquired for the second time.

"Quite sure—not the slightest injury."

"But you are wet through and through; let me offer you a change of clothes: mine, I think, would about fit you."

"Thank you. I should not know how to wear them. The sun is strong: my own will soon be dry again."

"You will come up to the house, and eat something?"

"I have eaten but a short while ago. I thank you. I am not in need."

"Some wine?"

"Again I thank you—water is my only drink."

I scarcely knew what to say to my new acquaintance. He refused all my offers of hospitality, and yet he remained by me. He would not accompany me to the house; and still he showed no signs of taking his departure.

Was he expecting something else? A reward for his services? Something more substantial than complimentary phrases?

The thought was not unnatural. Handsome as was the youth, he was but an Indian. Of compliments he had had enough. Indians care little for idle words. It might be that he waited for something more; it was but natural for one in his condition to do so, and equally natural for one in mine to think so.

In an instant my purse was out; in the next it was in his hands—and in the next it was at the bottom of the pond!

"I did not ask you for money," said he, as he flung the dollars indignantly into the water.

I felt pique and shame; the latter predominated. I plunged into the pond, and dived under the surface. It was not after my purse, but my rifle, which I saw lying upon the rocks at the bottom. I gained the piece, and, carrying it ashore, handed it to him.

The peculiar smile with which he received it, told me that I had well corrected my error, and subdued the capricious pride of the singular youth.

"It is my turn to make reparation," said he. "Permit me to restore you your purse, and to ask pardon for my rudeness."

Before I could interpose, he sprang into the water, and dived below the surface. He soon recovered the shining object, and returning to the bank, placed it in my hands.

"This is a splendid gift," he said, handling the rifle, and examining it—"a splendid gift; and I must return home before I can offer you aught in return. We Indians have not much that the white man values—only *our lands*, I have been told,"—he uttered this phrase with peculiar emphasis. "Our rude manufactures," continued he, "are worthless things when put in comparison with those of your people—they are but curiosities to you at best. But stay—you are a hunter? Will you accept a pair of moccasins and a bullet-pouch? Maümee makes them well—"

"Maümee?"

"My sister. You will find the moccasin better for hunting than those heavy shoes you wear: the tread is more silent."

"Above all things, I should like to have a pair of your moccasins."

"I am rejoiced that it will gratify you. Maümee shall make them, and the pouch too."

"Maümee!" I mentally echoed. "Strange, sweet name! Can it be she?"

I was thinking of a bright being that had crossed my path—a dream—a heavenly vision—for it seemed too lovely to be of the earth.

While wandering in the woods, amid perfumed groves, had this vision appeared to me in the form of an Indian maiden. In a flowery glade, I saw her—one of those spots in the southern forest which nature adorns so profusely. She appeared to form part of the picture.

One glance had I, and she was gone. I pursued, but to no purpose. Like a spirit she glided through the daedalian aisles of the grove, and I saw her no more. But though gone from my sight, she passed not out of my memory; ever since had I been dreaming of that lovely apparition. "Was it Maümee?"

"Your name?" I inquired, as I saw the youth was about to depart.

"I am called Powell by the whites: my father's name—he was white—he is dead. My mother still lives; I need not say she is an Indian."

"I must be gone, sir," continued he after a pause. "Before I leave you, permit me to put a question. It may appear impertinent, but I have good reason for asking it. Have you among your slaves one who is very bad, one who is hostile to your family?"

"There is such a one. I have reason to believe it."

"Would you know his tracks?"

"I should."

"Then follow me!"

"It is not necessary. I can guess where you would lead me. I know all: he lured the alligator hither to destroy my sister."

"Ugh!" exclaimed the young Indian, in some surprise. "How learned you this, sir?"

"From yonder rock, I was a witness of the whole transaction. But how did *you* come to know of it?" I asked in turn.

"Only by following the trail—the man—the dog—the alligator. I was hunting by the swamp. I saw the tracks. I suspected something, and crossed the fields. I had reached the thicket when I heard cries. I was just in time. Ugh!"

"You were in good time, else the villain would have succeeded in his intent. Fear not, friend, he shall be punished."

"Good—he should be punished. I hope you and I may meet again."

A few words more were exchanged between us, and then we shook hands, and parted.

Chapter Eleven.

The Chase.

About the guilt of the mulatto, I had no longer any doubt. The mere destruction of the fish could not have been his design; he would never have taken such pains to accomplish so trifling a purpose. No; his intent was far more horrid; it comprehended a deeper scheme of cruelty and vengeance; its aim was my sister's life!—Viola's!—perhaps both?

Awful as was such a belief, there was no room left to doubt it; every circumstance confirmed it. Even the young Indian had formed the opinion that such was the design. At this season, my sister was in the habit of bathing almost every day; and that this was her custom was known to all upon the plantation. *I* had not thought of it when I went in pursuit of the deer, else I should in all probability have acted in a different manner. But who could have suspected such dire villainy?

The cunning of the act quite equalled its malice. By the merest accident, there were witnesses; but had there been none, it is probable the event would have answered the intention, and my sister's life been sacrificed.

Who could have told the author of the crime? The reptile would have been alone responsible. Even suspicion would not have rested upon the mulatto—how could it? The yellow villain had shown a fiendish craft in his calculation.

I was burning with indignation. My poor innocent sister! Little did she know the foul means that had been made use of to put her in such peril. She was aware that the mulatto liked her not, but never dreamed she that she was the object of such a demoniac spite as this.

The very thoughts of it fired me as I dwelt upon them. I could restrain myself no longer. The criminal must be brought to punishment, and at once. Some severe castigation must be inflicted upon him—something that would place it beyond his power to repeat such dangerous attempts.

How he would be dealt with, I could not tell—that must be left to my elders to determine. The lash had proved of no avail; perhaps the chain-gang would cure him—at all events, he must be banished the plantation.

In my own mind, I had not doomed him to death, though truly he deserved it. Indignant as I felt, I did not contemplate this ultimate punishment of crime; used to my father's mild rule, I did not. The lash—the county prison—the chain-gang at Saint Marks or San Augustine: some of these would likely be his reward.

I knew it would not be left to the lenient disposition of my father to decide. The whole community of planters was interested in a matter of this kind. An improvised jury would soon assemble. No doubt harsher judges than his own master would deal with the guilty man.

I stayed not longer to reflect; I was determined his trial should be immediate. I ran towards the house with the intention of declaring his guilt.

In my haste, as before, I did not follow the usual path, which was somewhat circumambient: I made direct through the grove.

I had advanced only a few paces, when I heard a rustling of the leaves near me. I could see no one, but felt sure that the noise was caused by some person skulking among the trees. Perhaps one of the field-hands, taking advantage of the confusion of the hour, and helping himself to a few oranges.

Compared with my purpose, such slight dereliction was a matter of no importance, and I did not think worth while to stay and hinder it. I only shouted out; but no one made answer, and I kept on.

On arriving at the rear of the house, I found my father in the enclosure by the grand shed—the overseer too. Old Hickman, the alligator-hunter, was there, and one or two other white men, who had casually come upon business.

In the presence of all, I made the disclosure; and, with as much minuteness as the time would permit, described the strange transaction I had witnessed in the morning.

All were thunderstruck. Hickman at once declared the probability of such a manoeuvre, though no one doubted my words. The only doubt was as to the mulatto's intent. Could it have been human lives he designed to sacrifice? It seemed too great a wickedness to be believed. It was too horrible even to be imagined!

At that moment all doubts were set at rest. Another testimony was added to mine, which supplied the link of proof that was wanting. Black Jake had a tale to tell, and told it.

That morning—but half an hour before—he had seen Yellow Jake climb up into a live-oak that stood in one corner of the enclosure. The top of this commanded a view of the pond. It was just at the time that "white missa" and Viola went to the bath. He was quite sure that about that time they must have been going into the water, and that Yellow Jake *must have seen them.*

Indignant at his indecorous conduct, the black had shouted to the mulatto to come down from the tree, and threatened to complain upon him. The latter made answer that he was only gathering acorns—the acorns of the live-oak are sweet food, and much sought after by the plantation-people. Black Jake, however, was positive that this could not be Yellow Jake's purpose; for the former still continuing to threaten, the latter at length came down, and Black Jake saw no acorns—not one!

"Twan't acorn he war arter, Massa Randoff: daat yaller loafa wan't arter no good—daat he wan't sure sartin."

So concluded the testimony of the groom.

The tale produced conviction in the minds of all. It was no longer possible to doubt of the mulatto's intention, horrible as it was. He had ascended the tree to be witness of the foul deed; he had seen them enter the basin; he knew the danger that was lurking in its waters; and yet he had made no movement to give the alarm. On the contrary, he was among the last who had hastened towards the pond, when the screaming of the girls was summoning all the household to their assistance. This was shown by the evidence of others. The case was clear against him.

The tale produced a wild excitement. White men and black men, masters and slaves, were equally indignant at the horrid crime; and the cry went round the yard for "Yellow Jake!"

Some ran one way, some another, in search of him—black, white, and yellow ran together—all eager in the pursuit—all desirous that such a monster should be brought to punishment.

Where was he? His name was called aloud, over and over again, with commands, with threats; but no answer came back. Where was he?

The stables were searched, the shed, the kitchen, the cabins—even the corn-crib was ransacked—but to no purpose. Where had he gone?

He had been observed but the moment before—he had assisted in dragging the alligator. The men had brought it into the enclosure, and thrown it to the hogs to be devoured. Yellow Jake had been with them, active as any at the work. It was but the moment before he had gone away; but where? No one could tell!

At this moment, I remembered the rustling among the orange-trees. It might have been he! If so, he may have overheard the conversation between the young Indian and myself—or the last part of it—and if so, he would now be far away.

I led the pursuit through the orangery: its recesses were searched; he was not there.

The hommock thickets were next entered, and beaten from one end to the other; still no signs of the missing mulatto.

It occurred to me to climb up to the rock, my former place of observation. I ascended at once to its summit, and was rewarded for my trouble. At the first glance over the fields, I saw the fugitive. He was down between the rows of the indigo plants, crawling upon hands and knees, evidently making for the maize.

I did not stay to observe further, but springing back to the ground, I ran after him. My father, Hickman, and others followed me.

The chase was not conducted in silence—no stratagem was used, and by our shouts the mulatto soon learned that he was seen and pursued. Concealment was no longer possible; and rising to his feet, he ran forward with all his speed. He soon entered the maize-field, with the hue and cry close upon his heels.

Though still but a boy, I was the fastest runner of the party. I knew that I could run faster than Yellow Jake, and if I could only keep him in sight, I should soon overtake him. His hopes were to get into the swamp, under cover of the palmetto thickets; once there, he might easily escape by hiding—at all events, he might get off for the time.

To prevent this, I ran at my utmost speed, and with success; for just upon the edge of the woods, I came up with the runaway, and caught hold of the loose flap of his jacket.

It was altogether a foolish attempt upon my part. I had not reflected upon anything beyond getting up with him. I had never thought of resistance, though I might have expected it from a desperate man. Accustomed to be obeyed, I was under the hallucination that, as soon as I should come up, the fellow would yield to me; but I was mistaken.

He at once jerked himself free of my hold, and easily enough. My breath was gone, my strength exhausted—I could not have held a cat.

I expected him to run on as before; but instead of doing so, he stopped in his tracks, turned fiercely upon me, and drawing his knife, he plunged it through my arm. It was my heart he had aimed at; but by suddenly throwing up my arm, I had warded off the fatal thrust.

A second time his knife was upraised—and I should have had a second stab from it—but, just then, another face showed itself in the fray; and before the dangerous blade could descend, the strong arms of Black Jake were around my antagonist.

The fiend struggled fiercely to free himself; but the muscular grasp of his old rival never became relaxed until Hickman and others arrived upon the ground; and then a fast binding of thongs rendered him at once harmless and secure.

Chapter Twelve.

A Severe Sentence.

Such a series of violent incidents of course created excitement beyond our own boundaries. There was a group of plantations upon the river lying side by side, and all having a frontage upon the water; they formed the "settlement." Through these ran the report, spreading like wildfire; and within the hour, white men could be seen coming from every direction. Some were on foot—poor hunters who dwelt on the skirts of the large plantations; others—the planters themselves, or their overseers—on horseback. All carried weapons—rifles and pistols. A stranger might have supposed it the rendezvous of a militia "muster," but the serious looks of those who assembled gave it a different aspect: it more resembled the gathering of the frontier men upon the report of some Indian invasion.

In one hour, more than fifty white men were upon the ground—nearly all who belonged to the settlement.

A jury was quickly formed, and Yellow Jake put upon his trial. There was no law in the proceedings, though legal formality was followed in a certain rude way. These jurors were themselves sovereign—they were the lords of the land, and, in cases like this, could easily *improvise* a judge. They soon found one in planter Ringgold, our adjoining neighbour. My father declined to take part in the proceedings.

The trial was rapidly gone through with. The facts were fresh and clear; I was before their eyes with my arm in a sling, badly cut. The other circumstances which led to this result were all detailed. The chain of guilt was complete. The mulatto had attempted the lives of white people. Of course, death was the decree.

What mode of death? Some voted for hanging; but by most of these men, hanging was deemed too mild. *Burning* met the approbation of the majority. The judge himself cast his vote for the severer sentence.

My father plead mercy—at least so far as to spare the torture—but the stern jurors would not listen to him. They had all lost slaves of late—many runaways had been reported—the proximity of the Indians gave encouragement to defection. They charged my father with too much leniency—the settlement needed an example—they would make one of Yellow Jake, that would deter all who were disposed to imitate him. His sentence was, that he should be *burnt alive*!

Thus did they reason, and thus did they pronounce.

It is a grand error to suppose that the Indians of North America have been peculiar in the habit of torturing their captive foes. In most well-authenticated cases, where cruelty has been practised by them, there has been a provocative deed of anterior date—some grievous wrong—and the torture was but a retaliation. Human nature has yielded to the temptings of revenge in all ages—and ferocity can be charged with as much justice against white skin as against red skin. Had the Indians written the story of border warfare, the world might have modified its belief in their so called cruelty.

It is doubtful if, in all their history, instances of ferocity can be found that will parallel those often perpetrated by white men upon blacks—many of whom have suffered mutilation—torture—death—for the mere offence of a word! certainly often for a blow, since such is a written law!

Where the Indians have practised cruelty, it has almost always been in retaliation; but civilised tyrants have put men to the torture without even the palliating apology of vengeance. If there was revenge, it was not of that natural kind to which the human heart gives way, when it conceives deep wrong has been done; but rather a mean spite, such as is often exhibited by the dastard despot towards some weak individual within his power.

No doubt, Yellow Jake deserved death. His crimes were capital ones; but to *torture* him was the will of his judges.

My father opposed it, and a few others. They were outvoted and overruled. The awful sentence was passed; and they who had decreed it at once set about carrying it into execution.

It was not a fit scene to be enacted upon a gentleman's premises; and a spot was selected at some distance from the house, further down the lake-edge. To this place the criminal was conducted—the crowd of course following.

Some two hundred yards from the bank, a tree was chosen as the place of execution. To this tree the condemned was to be bound, and a log-fire kindled around him.

My father would not witness the execution; I alone of oor family followed to the scene. The mulatto saw me, and accosted me with words of rage. He even taunted me about the wound he had given, glorying in the deed. He was no doubt under the belief that I was one of his greatest foes. I had certainly been the innocent witness of his crime, and chiefly through my testimony, he had been condemned; but I was not revengeful. I would have spared him the terrible fate he was about to undergo—at least its tortures.

We arrived upon the ground. Men were already before us, collecting the logs, and piling them up around the trunk of the tree; others were striking a fire. Some joked and laughed; a few were heard giving utterance to expressions of hate for the whole coloured race.

Young Ringgold was especially active. This was a wild youth—on the eve of manhood, of somewhat fierce, harsh temper—a family characteristic.

I knew that the young fellow affected my sister Virginia; I had often noticed his partiality for her; and he could scarcely conceal his jealousy of others who came near her. His father was the richest planter in the settlement; and the son, proud of this superiority, believed himself welcome everywhere. I did not think he was very welcome with Virgine, though I could not tell. It was too delicate a point upon which to question her, for the little dame already esteemed herself a woman.

Ringgold was neither handsome nor graceful. He was sufficiently intelligent, but overbearing to those beneath him in station—not an uncommon fault among the sons of rich men. He had already gained the character of being resentful. In addition to all, he was dissipated—too often found with low company in the forest cock-pit.

For my part, I did not like him. I never cared to be with him as a companion; he was older than myself, but it was not that—I did not like his disposition. Not so my father and mother. By both was he encouraged to frequent our house. Both probably desired him for a future son-in-law. They saw no faults in him. The glitter of gold has a blinding influence upon the moral eye.

24

This young man, then, was one of the most eager for the punishment of the mulatto, and active in the preparations. His activity arose partly from a natural disposition to be cruel. Both he and his father were noted as hard task-masters, and to be "sold to Mass' Ringgold" was a fate dreaded by every slave in the settlement.

But young Ringgold had another motive for his conspicuous behaviour: he fancied he was playing the knight-errant, by this show of friendship for our family—for Virginia. He was mistaken. Such unnecessary cruelty to the criminal met the approbation of none of us. It was not likely to purchase a smile from my good sister.

The young half-blood, Powell, was also present. On hearing the hue and cry, he had returned, and now stood in the crowd looking on, but taking no part in the proceedings.

Just then the eye of Ringgold rested upon the Indian boy, and I could perceive that it was instantly lit up by a strange expression. He was already in possession of all the details. He saw in the dark-skinned youth, the gallant preserver of Virginia's life, but it was not with gratitude that he viewed him. Another feeling was working in his breast, as could plainly be perceived by the scornful curl that played upon his lips.

More plainly still by the rude speech that followed:

"Hilloa! redskin!" he cried out, addressing himself to the young Indian, "you're sure *you* had no hand in this business? eh, redskin?"

"Redskin!" exclaimed the half-blood in a tone of indignation, at the same time fronting proudly to his insulter—"Redskin you call me? My skin is of better colour than yours, you white-livered lout!"

Ringgold was rather of a sallow complexion. The blow hit home. Not quicker is the flash of powder than was its effect; but his astonishment at being thus accosted by an Indian, combined with his rage, hindered him for some moments from making reply.

Others were before him and cried out:

"O Lordy! such talk from an Injun!"

"Say that again!" cried Ringgold, as soon as he had recovered himself.

"Again if you wish—white-livered lout!" cried the half-blood, giving full emphasis to the phrase.

The words were scarcely out before Ringgold's pistol cracked; but the bullet missed its aim; and next moment the two clinched, seizing each other by the throats.

Both came to the ground, but the half-blood had the advantage. He was uppermost, and no doubt would quickly have despatched his white antagonist—for the ready blade was gleaming in his grasp—but the knife was struck out of his hand; and a crowd of men rushing to the spot, pulled the combatants apart.

Some were loud against the Indian lad, and called for his life; but there were others with finer ideas of fair play, who had witnessed the provocation, and despite the power of the Ringgolds, would not suffer him to be sacrificed. I had resolved to protect him as far as I was able.

What would have been the result, it is difficult to guess; but, at that crisis, a sudden diversion was produced by the cry—that *Yellow Jake had escaped!*

Chapter Thirteen.

The Chase.

I looked around. Sure enough the mulatto was making off.

The rencontre between Ringgold and the Indian monopolised attention, and the criminal was for the moment forgotten. The knife knocked out of Powell's hand had fallen at the feet of Yellow Jake. Unobserved in the confusion he had snatched it up, cut the fastenings from his limbs, and glided off before any one could intercept him. Several clutched at him as he passed through the straggled groups; but, being naked, he was able to glide out of their grasp, and in a dozen bounds he had cleared the crowd, and was running towards the shore of the lake.

It seemed a mad attempt—he would be shot down or overtaken. Even so; it was not madness to fly from certain death—and such a death.

Shots were ringing; at first they were the reports of pistols. The guns had been laid aside, and were leaning against trees and the adjacent fence.

Their owners now ran to seize them. One after another was levelled; and then followed a sharp rapid cracking, like file-firing from a corps of riflemen.

There may have been good marksmen among the party—there were some of the best—but a man running for his life, and bounding from side to side, to avoid the stumps and bushes, offers but a very uncertain mark; and the best shot may miss.

So it appeared on this occasion. After the last rifle rang, the runaway was still seen keeping his onward course, apparently unscathed.

The moment after, he plunged into the water, and swam boldly out from the shore.

Some set to reloading their guns; others, despairing of the time, flung them away; and hastily pulling off hats, coats, boots, rushed down to the lake, and plunged in after the fugitive.

In less than three minutes from the time that the mulatto started off, a new tableau was formed. The spot that was to have been the scene of execution was completely deserted. One half the crowd was down by the shore, shouting and gesticulating; the other half—full twenty in all—had taken to the water, and were swimming in perfect silence—their heads alone showing above the surface. Away beyond—full fifty paces in advance of the foremost—appeared that solitary swimmer—the object of pursuit; his head of black tangled curls conspicuous above the water, and now and then the yellow neck and shoulder, as he forged forward in the desperate struggle for life.

Strange tableau it was; and bore strong resemblance to a deer-hunt—when the stag, close-pressed, takes to the water; and the hounds, in full cry, plunge boldly after—but in this chase were the elements of a still grander excitement—both the quarry and the pack were human.

Not all human—there were dogs as well—hounds and mastiffs mingled among the men—side by side with their masters in the eager purpose of pursuit. A strange tableau indeed!

Stray shots were still fired from the shore. Rifles had been reloaded by those who remained; and now and then the plash of the tiny pellet could be seen, where it struck the water far short of the distant swimmer. He needed no longer have a dread of danger from that source; he was beyond the range of the rifles.

The whole scene had the semblance of a dream. So sudden had been the change of events, I could scarcely give credit to my senses, and believe it a reality. But the moment before, the criminal lay bound and helpless, beside him the pile upon which he was to be burnt—now was he swimming far and free, his executioners a hopeless distance behind him. Rapid had been the transformation—it hardly appeared real. Nevertheless, it *was* real—it was before the eyes.

A long time, too, before our eyes. A chase in the water is a very different affair from a pursuit on dry land; and, notwithstanding there was life and death on the issue, slow was the progress both of pursuers and pursued. For nearly half an hour we who remained upon the shore continued spectators of this singular contest.

The frenzy of the first moments had passed away; but there was sufficient interest to sustain a strong excitement to the last; and some continued to shout and gesticulate, though neither their cries nor actions could in anywise influence the result. No words of encouragement could have increased the speed of the pursuers; no threats were needed to urge forward the fugitive.

We who remained inactive had time enough to reflect; and upon reflection, it became apparent why the runaway had taken to the water. Had he attempted to escape by the fields, he would have been pulled down by the dogs, or else overtaken by swift runners, for there were many swifter than he. There were few better swimmers, however, and he knew it. For this reason, then, had he preferred the water to the woods, and certainly his chances of escape seemed better.

After all, he could *not* escape. The island for which he was making was about half a mile from the shore; but beyond was a stretch of clear water of more than a mile in width. He would arrive at the island before any of his pursuers; but what then? Did he purpose to remain there, in hopes of concealing himself among the bushes? Its surface of several acres was covered with a thick growth of large trees. Some stood close by the shore, their branches draped with silvery tillandsia, overhanging the water. But what of this? There might have been cover enough to have given shelter to a bear or a hunted wolf, but not to a hunted man—not to a slave who had drawn the knife upon his master. No, no. Every inch of the thicket would be searched: to escape by concealing himself he might not.

Perhaps he only meant to use the island as a resting-place; and, after breathing himself, take once more to the water, and swim for the opposite shore. It was possible for a strong swimmer to reach it; but it would not be possible for *him*. There were skiffs and *pirogues* upon the river, both up and down. Men had already gone after them; and, long before he could work his way across that wide reach, half-a-dozen keels would be cutting after him. No, no—he could not escape: either upon the island, or in the water beyond, he would be captured.

Thus reasoned the spectators, as they stood watching the pursuit.

The excitement rose higher as the swimmers neared the island. It is always so at the approach of a crisis; and a crisis was near, though not such a one as the spectators anticipated. They looked to see the runaway reach the island, mount up the bank, and disappear among the trees. They looked to see his pursuers climb out close upon his heels, and perhaps hear of his capture before he could cross through the timber, and take to the water on the other side.

Some such crisis were they expecting; and it could not be distant, for the mulatto was now close into the edge of the island; a few strokes would bring him to the shore; he was swimming under the black shadows of the trees—it seemed as if the branches were over his head—as if he might have thrown up his hands and clutched them.

The main body of his pursuers was still fifty yards in his rear; but some, who had forged ahead of the rest, were within half that distance. From where we viewed them, they seemed far nearer; in fact, it was easy to fancy that they were swimming alongside, and could have laid hands on him at any moment.

The crisis was approaching, but not that which was looked for. The pursuit was destined to a far different ending from that anticipated either by spectators or pursuers. The pursued himself little dreamed of the doom that was so near—a doom awfully appropriate.

The swimmer was cleaving his way across the belt of black shadow; we expected next moment to see him enter among the trees, when all at once he was seen to turn side towards us, and direct his course along the edge of the island!

We observed this manoeuvre with some astonishment—we could not account for it; it was clearly to the advantage of his pursuers, who now swam in a diagonal line to intercept him.

What could be his motive? Had he failed to find a landing-place? Even so, he might have clutched the branches, and by that means drawn himself ashore.

Ha! our conjectures are answered; yonder is the answer; yonder brown log that floats on the black water is *not* the trunk of a dead tree. It is not dead; it has life and motion. See! it assumes a form—the form of the great saurian—the hideous alligator!

Its gaunt jaws are thrown up, its scolloped tail is erect, its breast alone rests upon the water. On this as a pivot it spins round and round, brandishing its tail in the air, and at intervals lashing the spray aloft. Its bellowing is echoed back from the distant shores; the lake vibrates under the hoarse baritone, the wood-birds flutter and cry, and the white crane mounts screaming into the air.

The spectators stand aghast; the pursuers have poised themselves in the water, and advance no farther. One solitary swimmer is seen struggling on; it is he who swims for his life.

It is upon him the eyes of the alligator are fixed. Why upon him more than the others! They are all equally near. Is it the hand of God who takes vengeance?

Another revolution, another sweep of its strong tail, and the huge reptile rushes upon its victim.

I have forgotten his crimes—I almost sympathise with him. Is there no hope of his escape?

See! he has grasped the branch of a live-oak; he is endeavouring to lift himself up—above the water—above the danger. Heaven strengthen his arms!

Ah! he will be too late; already the jaws—That crash?

The branch has broken!

He sinks back to the surface—below it. He is out of sight—he has gone to the bottom! and after him, open-mouthed and eager, darts the gigantic lizard. Both have disappeared from our view.

The froth floats like a blanket upon the waves, clouting the leaves on the broken branch.

We watch with eager eyes. Not a ripple escapes unnoted; but no new movement stirs the surface, no motion is observed, no form comes up; and the waves soon flatten over the spot.

Beyond a doubt the reptile has finished its work.

Whose work? Was it the hand of God who took vengeance?

So they are saying round me.

The pursuers have faced back, and are swimming towards us. None cares to trust himself under the black shadows of those island oaks. They will have a long swim before they can reach the shore, and some of them will scarcely accomplish it. They are in danger; but no—yonder come the skiffs and pirogues that will soon pick them up.

They have seen the boats, and swim slowly, or float upon the water, waiting their approach.

They are taken in, one after another; and all—both dogs and men—are now carried to the island.

They go to continue the search—for there is still some doubt as to the fate of the runaway.

They land—the dogs are sent through the bushes, while the men glide round the edge to the scene of the struggle. They find no track or trace upon the shore.

But there is one upon the water. Some froth still floats—there is a tinge of carmine upon it—beyond a doubt it is the blood of the mulatto.

"All right, boys!" cries a rough fellow; "that's blueskin's blood, I'll sartify. He's gone under an' no mistake. Darn the varmint! it's clean spoilt our sport."

The jest is received with shouts of boisterous laughter.

In such a spirit talked the man-hunters, as they returned from the chase.

Chapter Fourteen.

Ringgold's Revenge.

Only the ruder spirits indulged in this ill-timed levity; others of more refined nature regarded the incident with due solemnity—some even with a feeling of awe.

Certainly it seemed as if the hand of God had interposed, so appropriate had been the punishment—almost as if the criminal had perished by his own contrivance.

It was an awful death, but far less hard to endure than that which had been decreed by man. The Almighty had been more merciful: and in thus mitigating the punishment of the guilty wretch, had rebuked his human judges.

I looked around for the young Indian: I was gratified to find he was no longer among the crowd. His quarrel with Ringgold had been broken off abruptly. I had fears that it was not yet ended. His words had irritated some of the white men, and it was through his being there, the criminal had found the opportunity to get off. No doubt, had the latter finally escaped, there would have been more of it: and even as matters stood, I was not without apprehensions about the safety of the bold half-blood. He was not upon his own ground—the other side of the river was the Indian territory; and, therefore, he might be deemed an intruder. True, we were at peace with the Indians; but for all that, there was enough of hostile feeling between the two races. Old wounds received in the war of 1818 still rankled.

I knew Ringgold's resentful character—he had been humiliated in the eyes of his companions; for, during the short scuffle, the half-blood had the best of it. Ringgold would not be content to let it drop—he would seek revenge.

I was glad, therefore, on perceiving that the Indian had gone away from the ground. Perhaps he had himself become apprehensive of danger, and recrossed the river. There he would be safe from pursuit. Even Ringgold dare not follow him to the other side, for the treaty laws could not have been outraged with impunity. The most reckless of the squatters knew this. An Indian war would have been provoked, and the supreme government, though not over scrupulous, had other views at the time.

I was turning to proceed homeward, when it occurred to me that I would accost Ringgold, and signify to him my disapproval of his conduct. I was indignant at the manner in which he had acted—just angry enough to speak my mind. Ringgold was older than myself, and bigger; but I was not afraid of him. On the contrary, I knew that he was rather afraid of *me*. The insult he had offered to one who, but the hour before, had risked his life for us, had sufficiently roused my blood, and I was determined to reproach him for it. With this intention, I turned back to look for him. He was not there.

"Have you seen Arens Ringgold?" I inquired of old Hickman.

"Yes—jest gone," was the reply.

"In what direction?"

"Up-river. See 'im gallop off wi' Bill Williams an' Ned Spence—desprit keen upon somethin' they 'peered."

A painful suspicion flashed across my mind.

"Hickman," I asked, "will you lend me your horse for an hour?"

"My old critter? Sartin sure will I: a day, if you wants him. But, Geordy, boy, you can't ride wi' your arm that way?"

"O yes; only help me into the saddle."

The old hunter did as desired; and after exchanging another word or two, I rode off in the up-river direction.

Up the river was a ferry; and at its landing it was most likely the young Indian had left his canoe. In that direction, therefore, he should go to get back to his home, and in that direction Ringgold should *not* go to return to his, for the path to the Ringgold plantation led in a course altogether opposite. Hence the suspicion that occurred to me on hearing that the latter had gone up the river. At such a time it did not look well, and in such company, still worse; for I recognised in the names that Hickman had mentioned, two of the most worthless boys in the settlement. I knew them to be associates, or rather creatures, of Ringgold.

My suspicion was that they had gone after the Indian, and of course with an ill intent. It was hardly a conjecture; I was almost sure of it; and as I advanced along the river road, I became confirmed in the belief. I saw the tracks of their horses along the path that led to the ferry, and now and again I could make out the print of the Indian moccasin where it left its wet mark in the dust. I knew that his dress had not yet dried upon him, and the moccasins would still be saturated with water.

I put the old horse to his speed. As I approached the landing, I could see no one, for there were trees all around it; but the conflict of angry voices proved that I had conjectured aright.

I did not stop to listen; but urging my horse afresh, I rode on. At a bend of the road, I saw three horses tied to the trees. I knew they were those of Ringgold and his companions, but I could not tell why they had left them.

I stayed not to speculate, but galloped forward upon the ground. Just as I had anticipated, the three were there—the half-blood was in their hands!

They had crept upon him unawares—that was why their horses had been left behind—and caught him just as he was about stepping into his canoe. He was unarmed—for the rifle I had given him was still wet, and the mulatto had made away with his knife—he could offer no resistance, and was therefore secured at once.

They had been quick about it, for they had already stripped off his hunting-shirt, and tied him to a tree. They were just about to vent their spite on him—by flogging him on the bare back with cowhides which they carried in their hands. No doubt they would have laid them on heavily, had I not arrived in time.

"Shame, Arens Ringgold! shame!" I cried as I rode up. "This is cowardly, and I shall report it to the whole settlement."

Ringgold stammered out some excuse, but was evidently staggered at my sudden appearance.

"The darned Injun desarves it," growled Williams.

"For what, Master Williams?" I inquired.

"For waggin his jaw so imperent to white men."

"He's got no business over here," chimed in Spence; "he has got no right to come this side of the river."

"And you have no right to flog him, whether on this side or the other—no more than you have to flog me."

"Ho, ho! That might be done, too," said Spence, in a sneering tone, that set my blood in a boil.

"Not so easily," I cried, leaping from the old horse, and running forward upon the ground.

My right arm was still sound. Apprehensive of an awkward affair, I had borrowed old Hickman's pistol, and I held it in my hand.

"Now, gentlemen," said I, taking my stand beside the captive, "go on with the flogging; but take my word for it, I shall send a bullet through the first who strikes!"

Though they were but boys, all three were armed with knife and pistol, as was the custom of the time. Of the three, Spence seemed most inclined to carry out his threat; but he and Williams saw that Ringgold, their leader, had already backed out, for the latter had something to lose, which his companions had not. Besides, he had other thoughts, as well as fears for his personal safety.

The result was, that all three, after remonstrating with me for my uncalled-for interference *in a quarrel that did not concern me*, made an angry and somewhat awkward exit from the scene.

The young Indian was soon released from his unpleasant situation. He uttered few words, but his looks amply expressed his gratitude. As he pressed my hand at parting, he said:

"Come to the other side to hunt whenever you please—no Indian will harm you—in the land of the red men *you* will be welcome."

Chapter Fifteen.

Maümee.

An acquaintance thus acquired could not be lightly dropped. Should it end otherwise than in friendship? This half-blood was a noble youth, the germ of a gentleman. I resolved to accept his invitation, and visit him in his forest home.

His mother's *cabin*, he said, was on the other side of the lake, not far off. I should find it on the bank of a little stream that emptied into the main river, above where the latter expands itself.

I felt a secret gratification as I listened to these directions. I knew the stream of which he was speaking; lately, I had sailed up it in my skiff. It was upon its banks I had seen that fair vision—the wood-nymph whose beauty haunted my imagination. Was it Maümee?

I longed to be satisfied. I waited only for the healing of my wound—till my arm should be strong enough for the oar. I chafed at the delay; but time passed, and I was well.

I chose a beautiful morning for the promised visit, and was prepared to start forth. I had no companion—only my dogs and gun.

I had reached my skiff, and was about stepping in, when a voice accosted me; on turning, I beheld my sister.

Poor little Virgine! she had lost somewhat of her habitual gaiety, and appeared much changed of late. She was not yet over the terrible fright—its consequences were apparent in her more thoughtful demeanour.

"Whither goest thou, Georgy?" she inquired as she came near.

"Must I tell, Virgine?"

"Either that or take me with you."

"What! to the woods?"

"And why not? I long for a ramble in the woods. Wicked brother! you never indulge me."

"Why, sister, you never asked me before."

"Even so, you might know that I desired it. Who would not wish to go wandering in the woods? Oh! I wish I were a wild bird, or a butterfly, or some other creature with wings; I should wander all over those beautiful woods, without asking you to guide me, selfish brother."

"Any other day, Virgine, but to-day—"

"Why, but? Why not this very day? Surely it is fine—it is lovely!"

"The truth, then, sister—I am not exactly bound for the woods to-day."

"And whither bound? whither bound, Georgy?—that's what they say in ships."

"I am going to visit young Powell at his mother's cabin. I promised him I should."

"Ha!" exclaimed my sister, suddenly changing colour, and remaining for a moment in a reflective attitude.

The name had recalled that horrid scene. I was sorry I had mentioned it.

"Now, brother," continued she, after a pause; "there is nothing I more desire to see than an Indian cabin—you know I have never seen one. Good Georgy! good Georgy! pray take me along with you!"

There was an earnestness in the appeal I could not resist, though I would rather have gone alone. I had a secret that I would not have trusted even to my fond sister. I had an indefinite feeling, besides, that I ought not to take her with me, so far from home, into a part of the country with which I was so little acquainted.

She appealed a second time.

"If mother will give her consent—"

"Nonsense, Georgy—mamma will not be angry. Why return to the house? You see I am prepared; I have my sun-bonnet. We can be back before we are missed—you've told me it was not far."

"Step in, sis! Sit down in the stern. There—yo ho! we are off!"

There was not much strength in the current, and half an hour's rowing brought the skiff to the mouth of the creek. We entered it, and continued upward. It was a narrow stream, but sufficiently deep to float either skiff or canoe. The sun was hot, but his beams could not reach us; they were intercepted by the tupelo trees that grew upon the banks—their leafy branches almost meeting across the water.

Half a mile from the mouth of the creek, we approached a clearing. We saw fields under cultivation. We noticed crops of maize, and sweet potatoes, with capsicums, melons, and calabashes. There was a dwelling-house of considerable size near the bank, surrounded by an enclosure, with smaller houses in the rear. It was a log structure—somewhat antique in its appearance, with a portico, the pillars of which exhibited a rude carving. There were slaves at work in the field—that is, there were black men, and some red men too—Indians!

It could not be the plantation of a white man—there were none on that side the river. Some wealthy Indian, we conjectured, who is the owner of land and slaves. We were not surprised at this—we knew there were many such.

But where was the cabin of our friend? He had told me it stood upon the bank of the stream not more than half a mile from its mouth. Had we passed without seeing it? or was it still higher up?

"Shall we stop, and inquire, Virgine?"

"Who is it standing in the porch?"

"Ha! your eyes are better than mine, sis—it is the young Indian himself. Surely he does not live *there*? That is not a cabin. Perhaps he is on a visit? But see! he is coming this way."

As I spoke, the Indian stepped out from the house, and walked rapidly towards us. In a few seconds, he stood upon the bank, and beckoned us to a landing. As when seen before, he was gaily dressed, with plumed "toque" upon his head, and garments richly embroidered. As he stood upon the bank above us, his fine form outlined against the sky, he presented the appearance of a miniature warrior. Though but a boy, he looked splendid and picturesque. I almost envied him his wild attire.

My sister seemed to look on him with admiration, though I thought I could trace some terror in her glance. From the manner in which her colour came and went, I fancied that his presence recalled that scene, and again I regretted that she had accompanied me.

He appeared unembarrassed by our arrival. I have known it otherwise among whites; and those, too, making pretensions to *haut ton*. This young Indian was as cool and collected as though he had been expecting us, which he was not. He could not have expected both.

There was no show of coldness in our reception. As soon as we approached near enough, he caught the stem of the skiff, drew her close up to the landing, and with the politeness of an accomplished gentleman, assisted us to debark.

"You are welcome," said he—"welcome!" and then turning to Virginia with an inquiring look, he added:

"I hope the health of the señorita is quite restored. As for yours, sir, I need not inquire: that you have rowed your skiff so far against the current, is a proof you have got over your mishap."

The word "señorita" betrayed a trace of the Spaniards—a remnant of those relations that had erewhile existed between the Seminole Indians and the Iberian race. Even in the costume of our new acquaintance could be observed objects of Andalusian origin—the silver cross hanging from his neck, the sash of scarlet silk around his waist, and the bright triangular blade that was sheathed behind it. The scene, too, had Spanish touches. There were exotic plants, the China orange, the splendid papaya, the capsicums (chilés), and love-apples (tomatoes); almost characteristics of the home of the Spanish colonist. The house itself exhibited traces of Castilian workmanship. The carving was not Indian.

"Is this your home?" I inquired with a little embarrassment.

He had bid us welcome, but I saw no cabin; I might be wrong.

His answer set me at rest. It was his home—his mother's house—his father was long since dead—there were but the three—his mother, his sister, himself.

"And these?" I inquired, pointing to the labourers.

"Our slaves," he replied, with a smile. "You perceive we Indians are getting into the customs of civilisation."

"But these are not all negroes? There are red men; are *they* slaves?"

"Slaves like the others. I see you are astonished. They are not of our tribe—they are *Yamassees*. Our people conquered them long ago; and many of them still remain slaves."

We had arrived at the house. His mother met us by the door—a woman of pure Indian race—who had evidently once possessed beauty. She was still agreeable to look upon—well-dressed, though in Indian costume—maternal—intelligent.

We entered—furniture—trophies of the chase—horse accoutrements in the Spanish style—a guitar—ha! books!

My sister and I were not a little surprised to find, under an Indian roof, these symbols of civilisation.

"Ah!" cried the youth, as if suddenly recollecting himself, "I am glad you are come. Your moccasins are finished. Where are they, mother? Where is she? Where is Maümee?"

He had given words to my thoughts—their very echo.

"Who is Maümee?" whispered Virgine.

"An Indian girl—his sister, I believe."

"Yonder—she comes!"

A foot scarce a span in length; an ankle that, from the broidered flap of the moccasin, exhibits two lines widely diverging upward; a waist of that pleasing flexure that sweeps abruptly inward and out again; a bosom whose prominence could be detected under the coarsest draping; a face of rich golden brown; skin diaphanous; cheeks coral red; lips of like hue; dark eyes and brows; long crescent lashes; hair of deepest black, in wantonness of profusion!

Fancy such a form—fancy it robed in all the picturesque finery that Indian ingenuity can devise—fancy it approaching you with a step that rivals the steed of Arabia, and you may fancy—no, you may not fancy Maümee.

My poor heart—it was she, my wood-nymph!

I could have tarried long under the roof of that hospitable home; but my sister seemed ill at ease—as if there came always recurring to her the memory of that unhappy adventure.

We stayed but an hour; it seemed not half so long—but short as was the time, it transformed me into a man. As I rowed back home, I felt that my boy's heart had been left behind me.

Chapter Sixteen.

The Island.

I longed to revisit the Indian home; and was not slow to gratify my wish. There was no restraint upon my actions. Neither father nor mother interfered with my daily wanderings: I came and went at will; and was rarely questioned as to the direction I had taken. Hunting was supposed to be the purpose of my absence. My dogs and gun, which I always took with me, and the game I usually brought back, answered all curiosity.

My hunting excursions were always in one direction—I need hardly have said so— always across the river. Again and again did the keel of my skiff cleave the waters of the creek—again and again, till I knew every tree upon its banks.

My acquaintance with young Powell soon ripened into a firm friendship. Almost daily were we together—either upon the lake or in the woods, companions in the chase; and many a deer and wild turkey did we slaughter in concert. The Indian boy was already a skilled hunter; and I learned many a secret of woodcraft in his company.

I well remember that hunting less delighted me than before. I preferred that hour when the chase was over, and I halted at the Indian house on my way home—when I drank the honey-sweetened *conti* out of the carved calabash—far sweeter from the hands out of which I received the cup—far sweeter from the smiles of her who gave it—Maümee.

For weeks—short weeks they seemed—I revelled in this young dream of love. Ah! it is true there is no joy in afterlife that equals this. Glory and power are but gratifications— love alone is bliss—purest and sweetest in its virgin bloom.

Often was Virginia my companion in these wild wood excursions. She had grown fond of the forest—she said so—and willingly went along. There were times when I should have preferred going alone; but I could not gainsay her. She had become attached to Maümee. I did not wonder.

Maümee, too, liked my sister—not from any resemblance of character. Physically, they were unlike as two young girls could well be. Virginia was all blonde and gold; Maümee, damask and dark. Intellectually they approached no nearer. The former was timid as the dove; the latter possessed a spirit bold as the falcon. Perhaps the contrast drew closer the ties of friendship that had sprung up between them. It is not an anomaly.

Far more like an anomaly was my feeling in relation to the two. I loved my sister for the very softness of her nature. I loved Maümee for the opposite; but, true, these loves were very distinct in kind—unlike as the objects that called them forth.

While young Powell and I hunted, our sisters stayed at home. They strolled about the fields, the groves, the garden. They played and sang and *read*, for Maümee—despite her costume—was no savage. She had books, a guitar, or rather a bandolin—a Spanish relic— and had been instructed in both. So far as mental cultivation went, she was fit society even for the daughter of a proud Randolph. Young Powell, too; was as well, or better educated than myself. Their father had not neglected his duty.

Neither Virginia nor I ever dreamed of an inequality. The association was by us desired and sought. We were both too young to know aught of *caste*. In our friendships we followed only the prompting of innocent nature; and it never occurred to us that we were going astray.

The girls frequently accompanied us into the forest; and to this we, the hunters, made no objection. We did not always go in quest of the wide-ranging stag. Squirrels and other small game were oftener the objects of our pursuit; and in following these we needed not to stray far from our delicate companions.

As for Maümee, she was a huntress—a bold equestrian, and could have ridden in the "drive." As yet, my sister had scarcely been on horseback.

I grew to like the squirrel-shooting the best; my dogs were often left behind; and it became a rare thing for me to bring home venison.

Our excursions were not confined to the woods. The water-fowl upon the lake, the ibises, egrets, and white cranes, were often the victims of our hunting ardour.

In the lake, there was a beautiful island—not that which had been the scene of the tragedy, but one higher up—near the widening of the river. Its surface was of large extent, and rose to a summit in the centre. For the most part, it was clad with timber, nearly all evergreen—as the live-oak, magnolia, illicium, and the wild orage—indigenous to Florida. There was zanthoxylon trees, with their conspicuous yellow blossoms; the perfumed flowering dogwood, and sweet-scented plants and shrubs—the princely palm towering high over all, and forming, with its wide-spread umbels, a double canopy of verdure.

The timber, though standing thickly, did not form a thicket. Here and there, the path was tangled with epiphytes or parasites—with enormous gnarled vines of the fox-grape—with bignonias—with china and sarsaparilla briers—with bromilias and sweet-scented orchids; but the larger trees stood well apart; and at intervals there were openings—pretty glades, carpeted with grass, and enamelled with flowers.

The fair island lay about half-way between the two homes; and often young Powell and I met upon it, and made it the scene of our sport. There were squirrels among the trees, and turkeys—sometimes deer were found in the glades—and from its covered shores we could do execution among the water-fowl that sported upon the lake.

Several times had we met on this neutral ground, and always accompanied by our sisters. Both delighted in the lovely spot. They used to ascend the slope, and seat themselves under the shade of some tall palms that grew on the summit; while we, the hunters, remained in the game-frequented ground below, causing the woods to ring with the reports of our rifles. Then it was our custom, when satiated with the sport, also to ascend the hill, and deliver up our spoils, particularly when we had been fortunate enough to procure some rare and richly plumed bird—an object of curiosity or admiration.

For my part, whether successful or not, I always left off sooner than my companion. I was not so keen a hunter as he; I far more delighted to recline along the grass where the two maidens were seated: far sweeter than the sound of the rifle was it to listen to the tones of Maümee's voice; far fairer than the sight of game was it to gaze into the eyes of Maümee.

And beyond this, beyond listening and looking, my love had never gone. No love-words had ever passed between us; I even knew not whether I was beloved.

My hours were not all blissful; the sky was not always of rose colour. The doubts that my youthful passion was returned were its clouds; and these often arose to trouble me.

About this time, I became unhappy from another cause. I perceived, or fancied, that Virginia took a deep interest in the brother of Maümee, and that this was reciprocated. The thought gave me surprise and pain. Yet why I should have experienced either, I could not tell. I have said that my sister and I were too young to know ought of the prejudices of rank or caste; but this was not strictly true. I must have had some instinct, that in this free association with our dark-skinned neighbours we were doing wrong, else how could it have made me unhappy? I fancied that Virginia shared this feeling with me. We were both ill at ease, and yet we were not confidants of each other. I dreaded to make known my thoughts even to my sister, and she no doubt felt a like reluctance to the disclosing of her secret.

What would be the result of these young loves if left to themselves? Would they in due time die out? Would there arrive an hour of satiety and change? or, without interruption would they become perpetual? Who knows what might be their fate, if permitted to advance to perfect development. But it is never so—they are always interrupted.

So were ours—the crisis came—and the sweet companionship in which we had been indulging was brought to a sudden close. We had never disclosed it to our father or mother, though we had used no craft to conceal it. We had not been questioned, else should we certainly have avowed it; for we had been taught strictly to regard truth. But no questions had been asked—no surprise had been expressed at our frequent absences. Mine, as a hunter, were but natural; the only wonderment was that Virginia had grown so found of the forest, and so often bore me company; but this slight surprise on the part of my mother soon wore off, and we went freely forth, and as freely returned, without challenge of our motives.

I have said that we used no art to conceal who were our associates in these wild wanderings. That again is not strictly true. Our very silence was craft. We must both have had some secret perception that we were acting wrongly—that our conduct would not meet the approval of our parents—else why should we have cared for concealment.

It was destined that this repose should not be of long continuance. It ended abruptly—somewhat harshly.

One day we were upon the island, all four as usual. The hunt was over, and Powell and I had rejoined our sisters upon the hill. We had stretched ourselves under the shade, and were indulging in trivial conversation, but I far more in the mute language of love. My eyes rested upon the object of my thoughts, too happy that my glances were returned. I saw little besides: I did not notice that there was a similar exchange of ardent looks between the young Indian and my sister. At that moment I cared not; I was indifferent to everything but the smiles of Maümee.

There were those who did observe the exchange of glances, who saw all that was passing. Anxious eyes were bent upon the tableau formed by the four of us, and our words, looks, and gestures were noted.

The dogs rose with a growl, and ran outward among the trees. The rustling branches, and garments shining through the foliage, warned us that there were people there. The dogs had ceased to give tongue, and were wagging their tails. They were friends, then, who were near.

The leaves sheltered them no longer from our view: behold my father—my mother!

Virginia and I were startled by their appearance. We felt some apprehension of evil— arising no doubt, from our own convictions that we had not been acting aright. We observed that the brows of both were clouded. They appeared vexed and angry.

My mother approached first. There was scorn upon her lips. She was proud of her ancestry, even more than the descendant of the Randolphs.

"What!" exclaimed she—"what, my children, these your companions? Indians?"

Young Powell rose to his feet, but said nothing in reply. His looks betrayed what he felt; and that he perfectly understood the slight.

With a haughty glance towards my father and mother, he beckoned to his sister to follow him, and walked proudly away.

Virginia and I were alarmed and speechless. We dared not say adieu.

We were hurried from the spot; and homeward Virginia went with my father and mother. There were others in the boat that had brought them to the island. There were blacks who rowed; but I saw white men there too. The Ringgolds—both father and son— were of the party.

I returned alone in the skiff. While crossing the lake, I looked up. The canoe was just entering the creek. I could see that the faces of the half-blood and his sister were turned towards us. I was watched, and dared not wave an adieu, although there was a sad feeling upon my heart—a presentiment that we were parting for long—perhaps for ever!

Alas! the presentiment proved a just one. In three days from that time I was on my way to the far north, where I was entered as a cadet in the military academy of West Point.

35

My sister, too, was sent to one of those seminaries, in which the cities of the Puritan people abound. It was long, long before either of us again set eyes upon the flowery land.

Chapter Seventeen.

West Point.

The military college of West Point is the finest school in the world. Princes and priests have there no power; true knowledge is taught, and must be learned, under penalty of banishment from the place. The graduate comes forth a scholar, not, as from Oxford and Cambridge, the pert parrot of a dead language, smooth prosodian, mechanic rhymster of Idyllic verse; but a linguist of living tongues—one who has studied science, and not neglected art—a botanist, draughtsman, geologist, astronomer, engineer, soldier—all; in short, a man fitted for the higher duties of social life—capable of supervision and command—equally so of obedience and execution.

Had I been ever so much disinclined to books, in this institution I could not have indulged in idleness. There is no "dunce" in West Point. There is no favour to family and fortune: the son of the President would be ejected, if not able to dress up with the rank; and under the dread of disgrace, I became, perforce, a diligent student—in time a creditable scholar.

The details of a cadet's experience possess but little interest—a routine of monotonous duties—only at West Point a little harder than elsewhere—at times but slightly differing from the slave-life of a common soldier. I bore them bravely—not that I was inspired by any great military ambition, but simply from a feeling of rivalry: I scorned to be the laggard of my class.

There were times, however, when I felt weariness from so much restraint. It contrasted unfavourably with the free life I had been accustomed to; and often did I feel a longing for home—for the forest and the savanna—and far more, for the associates I had left behind.

Long lingered in my heart the love of Maümee—long time unaffected by absence. I thought the void caused by that sad parting would never be filled up. No other object could replace in my mind, or banish from my memory the sweet souvenirs of my youthful love. Morning, noon, and night, was that image of picturesque beauty outlined upon the retina of my mental eye—by day in thoughts, by night in dreams.

Thus was it for a long while—I thought it would never be otherwise! No other could ever interest me, as she had done. No new joy could win me to wander—no Lethe could bring oblivion. Had I been told so by an angel, I would not, I could not, have believed it.

Ah! it was a misconception of human nature. I was but sharing it in common with others, for most mortals have, at some period of life, laboured under a similar mistake. Alas! it is too true—love *is* affected by time and absence. It will not live upon memory alone. The capricious soul, however delighting in the ideal, prefers the real and positive. Though there are but few *lovely* women in the world, there is no one lovelier than all the rest—no man handsomer than all his fellows. Of two pictures equally beautiful, that is the more beautiful upon which the eye is gazing. It is not without reason that lovers dread the parting hour.

Was it books that spoke of lines and angles, of bastions and embrasures—was it drill, drill, drill by day, or the hard couch and harder guard *tour* by night—was it any or all of these that began to infringe upon the exclusivism of that one idea, and at intervals drive it from my thoughts? Or was it the pretty faces that now and then made their appearance at the "Point"—the excursionary belles from Saratoga and Ballston, who came to visit us—or the blonde daughters of the patroons, our nearer neighbours—who came more frequently, and who saw in each coarse-clad cadet the chrysalis of a hero—the embryo of a general?

Which of all these was driving Maümee out of my mind?

It imports little what cause—such was the effect. The impression of my young love became less vivid on the page of memory. Each day it grew fainter and fainter, until it was attenuated to a slim retrospect.

Ah! Maümee! in truth it was long before this came to pass. Those bright smiling faces danced long before my eyes ere thine became eclipsed. Long while withstood I the flattery of those siren tongues; but my nature was human, and my heart yielded too easily to the seduction of sweet blandishments.

It would not be true to say that my first love was altogether gone: it was cold, but not dead. Despite the fashionable flirtations of the hour, it had its seasons of remembrance and return. Oft upon the still night's guard, home-scenes came flitting before me; and then the brightest object in the vision-picture was Maümee. My love for her was cold, not dead. Her presence would have re-kindled it—I am sure it would. Even to have heard from her—of her—would have produced a certain effect. To have heard that she had forgotten me, and given her heart to another, would have restored my boyish passion in its full vigour and entirety; I am sure it would.

I could not have been indifferent then? I must still have been in love with Maümee.

One key pushes out the other; but the fair daughters of the north had not yet obliterated from my heart this dark-skinned damsel of the south.

During all my cadetship, I never saw her—never even heard of her. For five years I was an exile from home—and so was my sister. At intervals during that time we were visited by our father and mother, who made an annual trip to the fashionable resorts of the north—Ballston Spa, Saratoga, and Newport. There, during our holidays, we joined them; and though I longed to spend a vacation at home—I believe so did Virginia—the "mother was steel and the father was stone," and our desires were not gratified.

I suspected the cause of this stern denial. Our proud parents dreaded the danger of a *mésalliance*. They had not forgotten the tableau on the island.

The Ringgolds met us at the watering-places; and Arens was still assiduous in his attentions to Virginia. He had become a fashionable exquisite, and spent his gold freely—not to be outdone by the *ci-devant* tailors and stock-brokers, who constitute the "upper ten" of New York. I liked him no better than ever, though my mother was still his backer.

How he sped with Virginia, I could not tell. My sister was now quite a woman—a fashionable dame, a belle—and had learnt much of the world, among other things, how to conceal her emotions—one of the distinguished accomplishments of the day. She was at times merry to an extreme degree; though her mirth appeared to me a little artificial, and often ended abruptly. Sometimes she was thoughtful—not unfrequently cold and disdainful. I fancied that in gaining so many graces, she had lost much of what was in my eyes more valuable than all, her gentleness of heart. Perhaps I was wronging her.

There were many questions I would have asked her, but our childish confidence was at an end, and delicacy forbade me to probe her heart. Of the past we never spoke: I mean of *that* past—those wild wanderings in the woods, the sailings over the lake, the scenes in the palm-shaded island.

I often wondered whether she had cause to remember them, whether her souvenirs bore any resemblance to mine!

On these points, I had never felt a definite conviction. Though suspicious, at one time even apprehensive—I had been but a blind watcher, a too careless guardian.

Surely my conjectures had been just, else why was she now silent upon themes and scenes that had so delighted us both? was her tongue tied by the after-knowledge that we had been doing wrong—only known to us by the disapproval of our parents? Or, was it that in her present sphere of fashion, she disdained to remember the humble associates of earlier days?

Often did I conjecture whether there had ever existed such a sentiment in her bosom; and, if so, whether it still lingered there? These were points about which I might never be satisfied. The time for such confidences had gone past.

"It is not likely," reasoned I; "or, if there ever was a feeling of tender regard for the young Indian, it is now forgotten—obliterated from her heart, perhaps from her memory. It is not likely it should survive in the midst of her present associations—in the midst of that *entourage* of perfumed beaux who are hourly pouring into her ears the incense of flattery. Far less probable *she* would remember than I; and have not I forgotten?"

Strange, that of the four hearts I knew only my own. Whether young Powell had ever looked upon my sister with admiring eyes, or she on him, I was still ignorant, or rather unconvinced. All I knew was by mere conjecture—suspicion—apprehension. What may appear stranger, I never knew the sentiment of that other heart, the one which interested me more than all. It is true, I had chosen to fancy it in my own favour. Trusting to glances, to gestures, to slight actions, never to words, I had hoped fondly; but often too had I been the victim of doubt. Perhaps, after all, Maümee had never loved me!

Many a sore heart had I suffered from this reflection. I could now bear it with more complacency; and yet, singular to say, it was this very reflection that awakened the memory of Maümee; and, whenever I dwelt upon it, produced the strongest revulsions of my own spasmodic love!

Wounded vanity! powerful as passion itself! thy throes are as strong as love. Under their influence, the chandeliers grow dim, and the fair forms flitting beneath lose half their brilliant beauty. My thoughts go back to the flowery land—to the lake—to the island—to Maümee.

Five years soon flitted past, and the period of my cadetship was fulfilled. With some credit, I went through the ordeal of the final examination. A high number rewarded my application, and gave me the choice of whatever arm of the service was most to my liking. I had a penchant for the rifles, though I might have pitched higher into the artillery, the cavalry, or engineers. I chose the first, however, and was gazetted brevet-lieutenant, and appointed to a rifle regiment, with leave of absence to revisit my native home.

At this time, my sister had also "graduated" at the Ladies' Academy, and carried off her "diploma" with credit; and together we journeyed home.

There was no father to greet us on our return: a weeping and widowed mother alone spoke the melancholy welcome.

Chapter Eighteen.

The Seminoles.

On my return to Florida, I found that the cloud of war was gathering over my native land. It would soon burst, and my first essay in military life would be made in the defence of hearth and home. I was not unprepared for the news. War is always *the* theme of interest within the walls of a military college; and in no place are its probabilities and prospects so folly discussed or with so much earnestness.

For a period of ten years had the United States been at peace with all the world. The iron hand of "Old Hickory" had awed the savage foe of the frontiers. For more than ten years had the latter desisted from his chronic system of retaliation, and remained silent and still. But the pacific *status quo* came to an end. Once more the red man rose to assert his rights, and in a quarter most unexpected. Not on the frontier of the "far west," but in the heart of the flowery land. Yes, Florida was to be the theatre of operations—the stage on which this new drama was to be enacted.

A word historical of Florida, for this writing is, in truth, a history.

In 1821, the Spanish flag disappeared from the ramparts of San Augustine and Saint Marks, and Spain yielded up possession of this fair province—one of her last footholds upon the continent of America. Literally, it was but a foothold the Spaniards held in Florida—a mere nominal possession. Long before the cession, the Indians had driven them from the field into the fortress. Their haciendas lay in ruins—their horses and cattle ran wild upon the savannas; and rank weeds usurped the sites of their once prosperous plantations. During the century of dominion, they had made many a fair settlement, and the ruins of buildings—far more massive than aught yet attempted by their Saxon successors—attest the former glory and power of the Spanish nation.

It was not destined that the Indians should long hold the country they had thus conquered. Another race of white men—their equals in courage and strength—were moving down from the north; and it was easy prophecy to say that the red conquerors must in turn yield possession.

Once already had they met in conflict with the pale-faced usurpers, led on by that stern soldier who now sat in the chair of the president. They were defeated, and forced further south, into the heart of the land—the centre of the peninsula. There, however, they were secured by treaty. A covenant solemnly made, and solemnly sworn to, guaranteed their right to the soil, and the Seminole was satisfied.

Alas! the covenants between the strong and the weak are things of convenience, to be broken whenever the former wills it—in this case, shamefully broken.

White adventurers settled along the Indian border; they wandered over Indian ground—not wandered, but went; they looked upon the land; they saw that it was good—it would grow rice and cotton, and cane and indigo, the olive and orange; they desired to possess it, more than desired—they resolved it should be theirs.

There was a treaty, but what cared they for treaties? Adventurers—ruined planters from Georgia and the Carolinas, "negro traders" from all parts of the south; what were covenants in their eyes, especially when made with redskins? The treaty must be got rid of.

The "Great Father," scarcely more scrupulous than they, approved their plan.

"Yes," said he, "it is good—the Seminoles must be dispossessed; they must remove to another land; we shall find them a home in the west, on the great plains; there they will have wide hunting-grounds, their own for ever."

"No," responded the Seminoles; "we do not wish to move; we are contented here: we love our native land; we do not wish to leave it; we shall stay."

"Then you will not go willingly? Be it so. We are strong, you are weak; we shall force you."

Though not the letter, this is the very spirit of the reply which Jackson made to the Seminoles!

The world has an eye, and that eye requires to be satisfied. Even tyrants dislike the open breach of treaties. In this case, political party was more thought of than the world, and a show of justice became necessary.

The Indians remained obstinate—they liked their own land, they were reluctant to leave it—no wonder.

Some pretext must be found to dispossess them. The old excuse, that they were mere idle hunters, and made no profitable use of the soil, would scarcely avail. It was not true. The Seminole was not exclusively a hunter; he was a husbandman as well, and tilled the land—rudely, it may be, but was this a reason for dispossessing him?

Without this, others were easily found. That cunning commissioner which their "Great Father" sent them could soon invent pretexts. He was one who well knew the art of muddying the stream upwards, and well did he practise it.

The country was soon filled with rumours of Indians—of horses and cattle stolen, of plantations plundered, of white travellers robbed and murdered—all the work of those savage Seminoles.

A vile frontier press, ever ready to give tongue to the popular furor, did not fail in its duty of exaggeration.

But who was to gazette the provocations, the retaliations, the wrongs and cruelties inflicted by the other side? All these were carefully concealed.

A sentiment was soon created throughout the country—a sentiment of bitter hostility towards the Seminole.

"Kill the savage! Hunt him down! Drive him out! Away with him to the west!" Thus was the sentiment expressed. These became the popular cries.

When the people of the United States have a wish, it is likely soon to seek gratification, particularly when that wish coincides with the views of its government; in this case, it did so, the government itself having created it.

It would be easy, all supposed, to accomplish the popular will, to dispossess the savage, hunt him, drive him out. Still there was a treaty. The world had an eye, and there was a thinking minority not to be despised who opposed this clamorous desire. The treaty could not be broken under the light of day; how then, was this obstructive covenant to be got rid of?

Call the head men together, cajole them out of it; the chiefs are human, they are poor, some of them drunkards—bribes will go far, fire-water still farther; make a new treaty with a double construction—the ignorant savages will not understand it; obtain their signatures—the thing is done!

Crafty commissioner! yours is the very plan, and you the man to execute it.

It *was* done. On the 9th of May, 1832, on the banks of the Oclawaha, the chiefs of the Seminole nation in full council assembled bartered away the land of their fathers!

Such was the report given to the world.

It was *not* true.

It was not a full council of chiefs; it was an assembly of traitors bribed and suborned, of weak men flattered and intimidated. No wonder the nation refused to accede to this surreptitious covenant; no wonder they heeded not its terms; but had to be summoned to still another council, for a freer and fuller signification of their consent.

It soon became evident that the great body of the Seminole nation repudiated the treaty. Many of the chiefs denied having signed it. The head chief, Onopa, denied it. Some confessed the act, but declared they had been drawn into it by the influence and advice of others. It was only the more powerful leaders of clans—as the brothers Omatla, Black Clay, and Big Warrior—who openly acknowledged the signing.

These last became objects of jealousy throughout the tribes; they were regarded as traitors, and justly so. Their lives were in danger; even their own retainers disapproved of what they had done.

To understand the position, it is necessary to say a word of the political *status* of the Seminoles. Their government was purely republican—a thorough democracy. Perhaps in no other community in the world did there exist so perfect a condition of freedom; I might add happiness, for the latter is but the natural offspring of the former. Their state has been compared to that of the clans of Highland Scotland. The parallel is true only in one respect. Like the Gael, the Seminoles were without any common organisation. They lived in "tribes" far apart, each politically independent of the other; and although in friendly relationship, there was no power of coercion between them. There was a "head chief"—king he could not be called—for "Mico," his Indian title, has not that signification. The proud spirit of the Seminole had never sold itself to so absurd a condition; they had not yet surrendered up the natural rights of man. It is only after the state of nature has been perverted and abased, that the "kingly" element becomes strong among a people.

The head "mico" of the Seminoles was only a head in name. His authority was purely personal: he had no power over life or property. Though occasionally the wealthiest, he was often one of the poorest of his people. He was more open than any of the others to the calls of philanthropy, and ever ready to disburse with free hand, what was in reality, not his people's, but his own. Hence he rarely grew rich.

He was surrounded by no retinue, girt in by no barbarian pomp or splendour, flattered by no flunkey courtiers, like the rajahs of the east, or, on a still more costly scale, the crowned monarchs of the west. On the contrary, his dress was scarcely conspicuous, often meaner than those around him. Many a common warrior was far more *gaillard* than he.

As with the head chief, so with the chieftains of tribes; they possessed no power over life or property; they could not decree punishment. A jury alone can do this; and I make bold to affirm, that the punishments among these people were in juster proportion to the crimes than those decreed in the highest courts of civilisation.

It was a system of the purest republican freedom, without one idea of the levelling principle; for merit produced distinction and authority. Property was *not* in common, though labour was partially so; but this community of toil was a mutual arrangement, agreeable to all. The ties of family were as sacred and strong as ever existed on earth.

And these were *savages* forsooth—red savages, to be dispossessed of their rights—to be driven from hearth and home—to be banished from their beautiful land to a desert wild—to be shot down and hunted like beasts of the field! The last in its most literal sense, for dogs were to be employed in the pursuit!

Chapter Nineteen.

An Indian Hero.

There were several reasons why the treaty of the Oclawaha could not be considered binding on the Seminole nation. First, it was not signed by a majority of the chiefs. Sixteen chiefs and sub-chiefs appended their names to it. There were five times this number in the nation.

Second, it was, after all, no treaty, but a mere conditional contract—the conditions being that a deputation of Seminoles should first proceed to the lands allotted in the west (upon White River), examine these lands, and bring back a report to their people. The very nature of this condition proves that no contract for removal could have been completed, until the exploration had been first accomplished.

The examination was made. Seven chiefs, accompanied by an agent, journeyed to the far west, and made a survey of the lands.

Now, mark the craft of the commissioner! These seven chiefs are nearly all taken from those friendly to the removal. We find among them both the Omatlas, and Black Clay. True, there is Hoitle-mattee (jumper), a patriot, but this brave warrior is stricken with the Indian curse—he loves the fire-water; and his propensity is well-known to Phagan, the agent, who accompanies them.

A *ruse* is contemplated, and is put in practice. The deputation is hospitably entertained at Fort Gibson, on the Arkansas. Hoitle-mattee is made merry—the contract for removal is spread before the seven chiefs—they all sign it: and the juggle is complete.

But even this was no fulfilment of the terms of the Oclawaha covenant. The deputation was to return with their report, and ask the will of the nation. That was yet to be given; and, in order to obtain it, a new council of all the chiefs and warriors must be summoned.

It was to be a mere formality. It was well-known that the nation as a body disapproved of the facile conduct of the seven chiefs, and would not endorse it. They were not going to "move."

This was the more evident, since other conditions of the treaty were daily broken. One of these was the restoration of runaway slaves, which the signers of the Oclawaha treaty had promised to send back to their owner. No blacks were sent back; on the contrary, they now found refuge among the Indians more secure than ever.

The commissioner knew all this. He was calling the new council out of mere formality. Perhaps he might persuade them to sign—if not, he intended to awe them into the measure, or force them at the point of the bayonet. He had said as much. Troops were concentrating at the agency—Fort King—and others were daily arriving at Tampa Bay. The government had taken its measures; and coercion was resolved upon.

I was not ignorant of what was going on, nor of all that had happened during my long years of absence. My comrades, the cadets, were well versed in Indian affairs, and took a lively interest in them—especially those who expected soon to escape from the college walls. "Black Hawk's war," just terminated in the west, had already given some a chance of service and distinction, and young ambition was now bending its eyes upon Florida.

The idea, however, of obtaining glory in such a war was ridiculed by all. "It would be too easy a war—the foe was not worth considering. A mere handful of savages," asserted they; "scarcely enough of them to stand before a single company. They would be either killed or captured in the first skirmish, one and all of them—there was not the slightest chance of their making any protracted resistance—*unfortunately*, there was not."

Such was the belief of my college companions; and, indeed, the common belief of the whole country, at that time. The army, too, shared it. One officer was heard to boast that he could march through the whole Indian territory with only a corporal's guard at his back; and another, with like bravado, wished that the government would give him a charter of the war, on his own account. He would finish it for 10,000 dollars!

41

These only expressed the sentiments of the day. No one believed that the Indians would or could sustain a conflict with us for any length of time; indeed, there were few who could be brought to think that they would resist at all: they were only holding out for better terms, and would yield before coming to blows.

For my part, I thought otherwise. I knew the Seminoles better than most of those who talked—I knew their country better; and, notwithstanding the odds against them—the apparent hopelessness of the struggle—I had my belief that they would neither yield to disgraceful terms, nor yet be so easily conquered. Still, it was but a conjecture; and I might be wrong. I might be deserving the ridicule which my opposition to the belief of my comrades often brought upon me.

The newspapers made us acquainted with every circumstance. Letters, too, were constantly received at the "Point" from old graduates now serving in Florida. Every detail reached us, and we had become acquainted with the names of many of the Indian chieftains, as well as the internal *politique* of the tribe. It appeared they were not united. There was a party in favour of yielding to the demands of our government, headed by one *Omatla*. This was the traitor party, and a minority. The patriots were more numerous, including the head "mico" himself, and the powerful chiefs Holata, *Coa hajo*, and the negro Abram.

Among the patriots there was one name that, upon the wings of rumour, began to take precedence of all others. It appeared frequently in the daily prints, and in the letters of our friends. It was that of a young warrior, or sub-chief, as he was styled, who by some means or other had gained a remarkable ascendency in the tribe. He was one of the most violent opponents of the "removal;" in fact, the leading spirit that opposed it; and chiefs much older and more powerful were swayed by his counsel.

We cadets much admired this young man. He was described as possessing all the attributes of a hero—of noble aspect, bold, handsome, intelligent. Both his physical and intellectual qualities were spoken of in terms of praise—almost approaching to hyperbole. His form was that of an Apollo, his features Adonis or Endymion. He was first in everything—the best shot in his nation, the most expert swimmer and rider—the swiftest runner, and most successful hunter—alike eminent in peace or war—in short, a Cyrus.

There were Xenophons enough to record his fame. The people of the United States had been long at peace with the red men. The romantic savage was far away from their borders. It was rare to see an Indian within the settlements, or hear aught of them. There had been no late deputations from the tribes to gratify the eyes of gazing citizens; and a real curiosity had grown up in regard to these children of the forest. An Indian hero was wanted, and this young chief appeared to be the man.

His name was Osceola.

Chapter Twenty.

Frontier Justice.

I was not allowed long to enjoy the sweets of home. A few days after my arrival, I received an order to repair to Fort King, the Seminole agency, and head-quarters of the army of Florida. General Clinch there commanded. I was summoned upon his staff.

Not without chagrin, I prepared to obey the order. It was hard to part so soon from those who dearly loved me, and from whom I had been so long separated. Both mother and sister were overwhelmed with grief at my going. Indeed they urged me to resign my commission, and remain at home.

Not unwillingly did I listen to their counsel: I had no heart in the cause in which I was called forth; but at such a crisis I dared not follow their advice: I should have been branded as a traitor—a coward. My country had commissioned me to carry a sword. I must wield it, whether the cause be just or unjust—whether to my liking or not. This is called *patriotism!*

There was yet another reason for my reluctance to part from home. I need hardly declare it. Since my return, my eyes had often wandered over the lake—often rested on that fair island. Oh, I had not forgotten her!

I can scarcely analyse my feelings. They were mingled emotions. Young love triumphant over older passions—ready to burst forth from the ashes that had long shrouded it—young love penitent and remorseful—doubt, jealousy, apprehension. All these were active within me.

Since my arrival, I had not dared to go forth. I observed that my mother was still distrustful. I had not dared even to question those who might have satisfied me. I passed those few days in doubt, and at intervals under a painful presentiment that all was not well.

Did Maümee still live? Was she true? True! Had she reason? Had she ever loved me?

There were those near who could have answered the first question; but I feared to breathe her name, even to the most intimate.

Bidding adieu to my mother and sister, I took the route. These were not left alone: my maternal uncle—their guardian—resided upon the plantation. The parting moments were less bitter, from the belief that I should soon return. Even if the anticipated campaign should last for any considerable length of time, the scene of my duties would lie near, and I should find frequent opportunities of revisiting them.

My uncle scouted the idea of a campaign, as so did every one. "The Indians," he said, "would yield to the demands of the commissioner. Fools, if they didn't!"

Fort King was not distant; it stood upon Indian ground—fourteen miles within the border, though further than that from our plantation. A day's journey would bring me to it; and in company of my cheerful "squire," Black Jake, the road would not seem long. We bestrode a pair of the best steeds the stables afforded, and were both armed *cap-à-pié*.

We crossed the ferry at the upper landing, and rode within the "reserve" (Note 1). The path—it was only a path—ran parallel to the creek, though not near its banks. It passed through the woods, some distance to the rear of Madame Powell's plantation.

When opposite to the clearing, my eyes fell upon the diverging track. I knew it well: I had oft trodden it with swelling heart.

I hesitated—halted. Strange thoughts careered through my bosom; resolves half-made, and suddenly abandoned. The rein grew slack, and then tightened. The spur threatened the ribs of my horse, but failed to strike.

"Shall I go? Once more behold her. Once more renew those sweet joys of tender love? Once more—Ha, perhaps it is too late! I might be no longer welcome—if my reception should be hostile? Perhaps—"

"Wha' you doin' dar, Massr George? Daat's not tha' road to tha fort."

"I know that, Jake; I was thinking of making a call at Madame Powell's plantation."

"Mar'm Powell plantayshun! Gollys! Massr George—daat all you knows 'bout it?"

"About what?" I inquired with anxious heart.

"Dar's no Mar'm Powell da no more; nor hain't a been, since better'n two year—all gone clar 'way."

"Gone away? Where?"

"Daat dis chile know nuffin 'bout. S'pose da gone some other lokayshun in da rezav; made new clarin somewha else."

"And who lives here now?"

"Dar ain't neery one lib tha now: tha ole house am desarted."

"But why did Madame Powell leave it?"

"Ah—daat am a quaw story. Gollys! you nebber hear um, Massr George?"

"No—never."

"Den I tell um. But s'pose, massr, we ride on. I am a gettin' a little lateish, an' 'twont do nohow to be cotch arter night in tha woods."

I turned my horse's head and advanced along the main road, Jake riding by my side. With aching heart, I listened to his narrative.

"You see, Massr George, 'twar all o' Massr Ringgol—tha ole boss (Note 2) daat am—an' I blieve tha young 'un had 'im hand in dat pie, all same, like tha ole 'un. Waal, you see Mar'm Pow'll she loss some niggas dat war ha slaves. Dey war stole from ha, an' wuss dan stole. Dey war tuk, an' by white men, massr. Tha be folks who say dat Mass' Ringgol—he know'd more 'n anybody else 'bout tha whole bizness. But da rubb'ry war blamed on Ned Spence an' Bill William. Waal, Mar'm, Powell she go to da law wi' dis yar Ned an' Bill; an' she 'ploy Massr Grubb tha big lawyer dat lib down tha ribba. Now Massr Grubb, he great friend o' Massr Ringgol, an' folks *do* say dat boaf de two put tha heads together to cheat dat ar Indyen 'ooman."

"How?"

"Dis chile don't say for troof, Massr George; he hear um only from da black folks: tha white folks say diffrent. But I hear um from Mass' Ringgol's own nigga woodman— Pomp, you know Massr, George? an' he say that them ar two bosses *did* put tha heads together to cheat dat poor Indyen 'ooman."

"In what way, Jake?" I asked impatiently.

"Waal, you see, Massr George, da lawya he want da Indyen sign ha name to some paper—power ob 'turney, tha call am, I believe. She sign; she no read tha writin. Whuch! daat paper war no power ob 'turney: it war what tha lawyas call a 'bill ob sale'."

"Ha!"

"Yes, Massr George, dat's what um war; an' by dat same bill ob sale all Mar'm Pow'll's niggas an' all ha plantation-clarin war made ober to Massr Grubb."

"Atrocious scoundrel?"

"Massr Grubb he swar he bought 'em all, an' paid for 'em in cash dollar. Mar'm Pow'll she swar he berry contr'y. Da judge he decide for Massr Grubb, 'kase great Massr Ringgoh he witness; an' folks *do* say Massr Ringgol now got dat paper in um own safe keeping an' war at tha bottom ob tha whole bizness."

"Atrocious scoundrels! oh, villains! But tell me, Jake, what became of Madame Powell?"

"Shortly arter, tha all gone 'way—nob'dy know wha. Da mar'm haself an' dat fine young fellur you know, an' da young Indyen gal dat ebbery body say war so good-lookin'— yes, Massr George, tha all gone 'way."

At that moment an opening in the woods enabled me to catch a glimpse of the old house. There it stood in all its grey grandeur, still embowered in the midst of beautiful groves of orange and olive. But the broken fence—the tall weeds standing up against the walls—the shingles here and there missing from the roof—all told the tale of ruin.

There was ruin in my heart, as I turned sorrowing away.

Note 1. That portion of Florida *reserved* for the Seminoles by the treaty of Moultrie Creek made in 1823. It was a large tract, and occupied the central part of the peninsula.

Note 2. Master or proprietor; universally in use throughout the Southern States. From the Dutch "baas."

Chapter Twenty One.

Indian Slaves.

It never occurred to me to question the genuineness of Jake's story. What the "black folks" said was true; I had no doubt of it. The whole transaction was redolent of the Ringgolds and lawyer Grubbs—the latter a half planter, half legal practitioner of indifferent reputation.

Jake further informed me that Spence and Williams had disappeared during the progress of the trial. Both afterwards returned to the settlement, but no ulterior steps were taken against them, as there was no one to prosecute!

As for the stolen negroes, they were never seen again in that part of the country. The robbers had no doubt carried them to the slave-markets of Mobile or New Orleans, where a sufficient price would be obtained to remunerate Grubbs for his professional services, as also Williams and Spence for theirs. The land would become Ringgold's, as soon as the Indians could be got out of the country—and this was the object of the "bill of sale."

A transaction of like nature between white man and white man would have been regarded as a grave swindle, an atrocious crime. The whites affected not to believe it; but there were some who knew it to be true, and viewed it only in the light of a clever *ruse*!

That it was true, I could not doubt. Jake gave me reasons that left no room for doubt; in fact it was only in keeping with the general conduct of the border adventures towards the unfortunate natives with whom they came in contact.

Border adventures did I say? Government agents, members of the Florida legislature, generals, planters, rich as Ringgold, all took part in similar speculations. I could give names. I am writing truth, and do not fear contradiction.

It was easy enough, therefore, to credit the tale. It was only one of twenty similar cases of which I had heard. The acts of Colonel Gad Humphreys, the Indian agent—of Major Phagan, another Indian agent—of Dexter, the notorious negro-stealer—of Floyd—of Douglass—of Robinson and Millburn, are all historic—all telling of outrages committed upon the suffering Seminole. A volume might be filled detailing such swindles as that of Grubbs and Ringgold. In the mutual relations between white man and red man, it requires no skillful advocate to shew on which side must lie the wrongs unrepaired and unavenged. Beyond all doubt, the Indian has ever been the victim.

It is needless to add that there were retaliations: how could it be otherwise?

One remarkable fact discloses itself in these episodes of Floridian life. It is well-known that slaves thus stolen from the Indians *always returned to their owners whenever they could.* To secure them from finding their way back, the Dexters and Douglasses were under the necessity of taking them to some distant market, to the far "coasts" of the Mississippi—to Natchez or New Orleans.

There is but one explanation of this social phenomenon; and that is, that the slaves of the Seminole were *not* slaves. In truth they were treated with an indulgence to which the helot of other lands is a stranger. They were the agriculturists of the country, and their Indian master was content if they raised him a little corn—just sufficient for his need—with such other vegetable products as his simple *cuisine* required. They lived far apart from the dwellings of their owners. Their hours of labour were few, and scarcely compulsory. Surplus product was their own; and in most cases they became rich—far richer than their own masters, who were less skilled in economy. Emancipation was easily purchased, and the majority were actually free—though from such claims it was scarcely worth while to escape. If slavery it could be called, it was the mildest form ever known upon earth—far differing from the abject bondage of Ham under either Shem or Japheth.

It may be asked how the Seminoles became possessed of these black slaves? Were they "runaways" from the States—from Georgia and the Carolinas, Alabama, and the plantations of Florida? Doubtless a few were from this source; but most of the runaways were not claimed as property; and, arriving among the Indians, became free. There was a time when by the stern conditions of the Camp Moultrie Covenant these "absconding" slaves were given up to their white owners; but it is no discredit to the Seminoles, that they were always *remiss* in the observance of this disgraceful stipulation. In fact, it was not always possible to surrender back the fugitive negro. Black communities had concentrated themselves in different parts of the Reserve, who under their own leaders were socially free, and strong enough for self-defence. It was with these that the runaways usually found refuge and welcome. Such a community was that of "Harry" amidst the morasses of Pease Creek—of "Abram" at Micosauky—of "Charles" and the "mulatto king."

No; the negro slaves of the Seminoles were *not* runaways from the plantations; though the whites would wish to make it appear so. Very few were of this class. The greater number was the "genuine property" of their Indian owners, so far as a slave can be called *property.* At all events, they were *legally* obtained—some of them from the Spaniards, the original settlers, and some by fair purchase from the American planters themselves.

How purchased? you will ask. What could a tribe of savages give in exchange for such a costly commodity? The answer is easy. Horses and horned cattle. Of both of these the Seminoles possessed vast herds. On the evacuation by the Spaniards the savannas swarmed with cattle, of Andalusian race—half-wild. The Indians caught and reclaimed them—became their owners.

This, then, was the *quid pro quo*—quadrupeds in exchange for bipeds!

The chief of the crimes charged against the Indians was the *stealing of cattle*—for the white men had their herds as well. The Seminoles did not deny that there were bad men amongst them—lawless fellows difficult to restrain. Where is the community without scamps?

One thing was very certain. The Indian chiefs, when fairly appealed to, have always evinced an earnest desire to make restoration: and exhibited an energy in the cause of justice, entirely unknown upon the opposite side of their border.

It differed little how they acted, so far as regarded their character among their white neighbours. These had made up their mind that the dog should be hanged; and it was necessary to give him a bad name. Every robbery, committed upon the frontier was of course the act of an Indian. White burglars had but to give their faces a coat of Spanish brown, and justice could not see through the paint.

Chapter Twenty Two.

A Circuitous Transaction.

Such were my reflections as I journeyed on—suggested by the sad tale to which I had been listening.

As if to confirm their correctness, an incident at that moment occurred exactly to the point.

We had not ridden far along the path, when we came upon the tracks of cattle. Some twenty head must have passed over the ground going in the same direction as ourselves—*towards* the Indian "Reserve."

The tracks were fresh—almost quite fresh. I was tracker enough to know that they must have passed within the hour. Though cloistered so long within college walls, I had not forgotten all the forest craft taught me by young Powell.

The circumstance of thus coming upon a cattle-trail, fresh or old, would have made no impression upon me. There was nothing remarkable about it. Some Indian herdsmen had been driving home their flock; and that the drivers *were* Indians, I could perceive by the moccasin prints in the mud. It is true, some frontiersmen wear the moccasin; but these were not the foot-prints of white men. The turned-in toes, (Note 1) the high instep, other trifling signs which, from early training, I knew how to translate, proved that the tracks were Indian.

So were they agreed my groom, and Jake was no "slouch" in the ways of the woods. He had all his life been a keen 'coon-hunter—a trapper of the swamp-hare, the "possum," and the "gobbler." Moreover, he had been my companion upon many a deer-hunt—many a chase after the grey fox, and the rufous "cat." During my absence he had added greatly to his experiences. He had succeeded his former rival in the post of woodman, which brought him daily in contact with the denizens of the forest, and constant observation of their habits had increased his skill.

It is a mistake to suppose that the negro brain is incapable of that acute reasoning which constitutes a cunning hunter. I have known black men who could read "sign" and lift a trail with as much intuitive quickness as either red or white. Black Jake could have done it.

I soon found that in this kind of knowledge he was now my master; and almost on the instant I had cause to be astonished at his acuteness.

I have said that the sight of the cattle-tracks created no surprise in either of us. At *first* it did not; but we had not ridden twenty paces further, when I saw my companion suddenly rein up, at the same instant giving utterance to one of those ejaculations peculiar to the negro thorax, and closely resembling the "wugh" of a startled hog.

I looked in his face. I saw by its expression that he had some revelation to make.

"What is it, Jake?"

"Golly! Massr George, d'you see daat?"

"What?"

"Daat down dar."

"I see a ruck of cow-tracks—nothing more."

"Doant you see dat big 'un?"

"Yes—there is one larger than the rest."

"By Gosh! it am de big ox Ballface—I know um track anywha—many's tha load o' cypress log dat ar ox hab toated for ole massr."

"What? I remember Baldface. You think the cattle are ours?"

"No, Massr George—I 'spect tha be da lawya Grubb's cattle. Ole massr sell Ballface to Massr Grubb more'n a year 'go. Daat am Bally's track for sartin."

"But why should Mr Grubb's cattle be here in Indian ground, and so far from his plantation?—and with Indian drivers, too?"

"Dat ere's just what dis chile can't clarly make out, Massr George."

There was a singularity in the circumstance that induced reflection. The cattle could not have strayed so far of themselves. The voluntary swimming of the river was against such a supposition. But they were not *straying*. They were evidently *concluded*—and by Indians. Was it a *raid*?—were the beeves being stolen?

It had the look of a bit of thievery, and yet it was not crafty enough. The animals had been driven along a frequented path, certain to be taken by those in quest of them; and the robbers—if they were such—had used no precaution to conceal their tracks.

It looked like a theft, and it did not; and it was just this dubious aspect that stimulated the curiosity of my companion and myself—so much so that we made up our minds to follow the trail, and if possible ascertain the truth.

For a mile or more the trail coincided with our own route; and then turning abruptly to the left, it struck off towards a track of "hommock" woods.

We were determined not to give up our intention lightly. The tracks were so fresh, that we knew the herd must have passed within the hour—within the quarter—they could not be distant. We could gallop back to the main road, through some thin pine timber we saw stretching away to the right; and with these reflections, we turned head along the cattle-trail.

Shortly after entering the dense forest, we heard voices of men in conversation, and at intervals the routing of oxen.

We alit, tied our horses to a tree, and moved forward afoot.

We walked stealthily and in silence, guiding ourselves by the sounds of the voices, that kept up an almost continual clatter. Beyond a doubt, the cattle whose bellowing we heard were those whose tracks we had been tracing; but equally certain was it, that the voices we now listened to were *not* the voices of those who had driven them!

It is easy to distinguish between the intonation of an Indian and a white man. The men whose conversation reached our ears were whites—their language was our own, with all its coarse embellishments. My companion's discernment went beyond this—he recognised the individuals.

"Golly! Massr George, it ar tha two dam ruffins—Spence and Bill William!"

Jake's conjecture proved correct. We drew closer to the spot. The evergreen trees concealed us perfectly. We got up to the edge of an opening; and there saw the herd of beeves, the two Indians who had driven them, and the brace of worthies already named.

We stood under cover watching and listening; and in a very short while, with the help of a few hints from my companion, I comprehended the whole affair.

Each of the Indians—worthless outcasts of their tribe—was presented with a bottle of whisky and a few trifling trinkets. This was in payment for their night's work—the plunder of lawyer Grubb's pastures.

Their share of the business was now over; and they were just in the act of delivering up their charge as we arrived upon the ground. Their employers, whose droving bout was here to begin, had just handed over their rewards. The Indians might go home and get drunk: they were no longer needed. The cattle would be taken to some distant part of the country—where a market would be readily found—or, what was of equal probability, they would find their way back to lawyer Grubb's own plantation, having been rescued by the gallant fellows Spence and Williams from a band of Indian rievers! This would be a fine tale for the plantation fireside—a rare chance for a representation to the police and the powers.

Oh, those savage Seminole robbers! they must be got rid of—they must be "moved" out.

47

As the cattle chanced to belong to lawyer Grubbs, I did not choose to interfere. I could tell my tale elsewhere; and, without making our presence known, my companion and I turned silently upon our heels, regained our horses, and went our way reflecting.

I entertained no doubt about the justness of our surmise—no doubt that Williams and Spence had employed the drunken Indians—no more that lawyer Grubbs had employed Williams and Spence, in this circuitous transaction.

The stream must be muddied upward—the poor Indian must be driven to desperation.

Note 1. It is art, not nature, that causes this peculiarity; it is done in the cradle.

Chapter Twenty Three.

Reflections by the Way.

At college, as elsewhere, I had been jeered for taking the Indian side of the question. Not unfrequently was I "twitted" with the blood of poor old Powhatan, which, after two hundred years of "whitening," must have circulated very sparsely in my veins. It was said I was not *patriotic*, since I did not join in the vulgar clamour, so congenial to nations when they talk of an enemy.

Nations are like individuals. To please them, you must be as wicked as they—feel the same sentiment, or speak it—which will serve as well—affect like loves and hates; in short, yield up independence of thought, and cry "crucify" with the majority.

This is the world's man—the patriot of the times.

He who draws his deductions from the fountain of truth, and would try to stem the senseless current of a people's prejudgments, will never be popular during life. Posthumously he may, but not this side the grave. Such need not seek the "living Fame" for which yearned the conqueror of Peru: he will not find it. If the true patriot desire the reward of glory, he must look for it only from posterity—long after his "mouldering bones" have rattled in the tomb.

Happily there is another reward. The *mens conscia recti* is not an idle phrase. There are those who esteem it—who have experienced both sustenance and comfort from its sweet whisperings.

Though sadly pained at the conclusions to which I was compelled—not only by the incident I had witnessed, but by a host of others lately heard of—I congratulated myself on the course I had pursued. Neither by word nor act, had I thrown one feather into the scale of injustice. I had no cause for self-accusation. My conscience cleared me of all ill-will towards the unfortunate people, who were soon to stand before me in the attitude of enemies.

My thoughts dwelt not long on the general question—scarcely a moment. That was driven out of my mind by reflections of a more painful nature—by the sympathies of friendship, of love. I thought only of the ruined widow, of her children, of Maümee. It were but truth to confess that I thought only of the last; but this thought comprehended all that belonged to her. All of hers were endeared, though she was the centre of the endearment.

And for all I now felt sympathy, sorrow—ay, a far more poignant bitterness than grief—the ruin of sweet hopes. I scarcely hoped ever to see them again.

Where were they now? Whither had they gone? Conjectures, apprehensions, fears, floated upon my fancy. I could not avoid giving way to dark imaginings. The men who had committed that crime were capable of any other, even the highest known to the calendar of justice. What had become of these friends of my youth?

My companion could throw no light on their history after that day of wrong. He "'sposed tha had move off to some oder clarin in da Indyen rezav, for folks nebba heern o' um nebber no more arterward."

Even this was a conjecture. A little relief to the heaviness of my thoughts was imparted by the changing scene.

Hitherto we had been travelling through a pine forest. About noon we passed from it into a large tract of hommock, that stretched right and left of our course. The road or path we followed ran directly across it.

The scene became suddenly changed as if by a magic transformation. The soil under our feet was different, as also the foliage over our heads. The pines were no longer around us. Our view was interrupted on all sides by a thick frondage of evergreen trees—some with broad shining coriaceous leaves, as the magnolia, that here grew to its full stature. Alongside it stood the live-oak, the red mulberry, the Bourbon laurel, iron-wood, *Halesia* and *Callicarpa*, while towering above all rose the cabbage-palm, proudly waving its plumed crest in the breeze, as if saluting with supercilious nod its humbler companions beneath.

For a long while we travelled under deep shadow—not formed by the trees alone, but by their parasites as well—the large grape-vine loaded with leaves—the coiling creepers of *smilax* and *hedera*—the silvery tufts of *tillandsia* shrouded the sky from our sight. The path was winding and intricate. Prostrate trunks often carried it in a circuitous course, and often was it obstructed by the matted trellis of the muscadine, whose gnarled limbs stretched from tree to tree like the great stay-cables of a ship.

The scene was somewhat gloomy, yet grand and impressive. It chimed with my feelings at the moment; and soothed me even more than the airy open of the pine-woods.

Having crossed this belt of dark forest, near its opposite edge we came upon one of these singular ponds already described—a circular basin surrounded by hillocks and rocks of testaceous formation—an extinct water volcano. In the barbarous jargon of the Saxon settler, these are termed sinks, though most inappropriately, for where they contain water, it is always of crystalline brightness and purity.

The one at which we had arrived was nearly full of the clear liquid. Our horses wanted drink—so did we. It was the hottest hour of the day. The woods beyond looked thinner and less shady. It was just the time and place to make a halt; and, dismounting, we prepared to rest and refresh ourselves.

Jake carried a capacious haversack, whose distended sides—with the necks of a couple of bottles protruding from the pouch—gave proof of the tender solicitude we had left behind us.

The ride had given me an appetite, the heat had caused thirst; but the contents of the haversack soon satisfied the one, and a cup of claret, mingled with water from the cool calcareous fountain, gave luxurious relief to the other.

A cigar was the natural finish to this *al fresco* repast; and, having lighted one, I lay down upon my back, canopied by the spreading branches of an umbrageous magnolia.

I watched the blue smoke as it curled upward among the shining leaves, causing the tiny insects to flutter away from their perch.

My emotions grew still—thought became lull within my bosom—the powerful odour from the coral cones and large wax-like blossoms added its narcotic influences; and I fell asleep.

Chapter Twenty Four.

A Strange Apparition.

I had been but a few minutes in this state of unconsciousness, when I was awakened by a plunge, as of some one leaping into the pond. I was not startled sufficiently to look around, or even to open my eyes.

"Jake is having a dip," thought I; "an excellent idea—I shall take one myself presently."

It was a wrong conjecture. The black had not leaped into the water, but was still upon the bank near me, where he also had been asleep. Like myself, awakened by the noise, he had started to his feet; and I heard his voice, crying out:

"Lor, Massr George! lookee dar!—ain't he a big un? Whugh!"

I raised my head and looked towards the pond. It was not Jake who was causing the commotion in the water—it was a large alligator.

It had approached close to the bank where we were lying; and, balanced upon its broad breast, with muscular arms and webbed feet spread to their full extent, it was resting upon the water, and eyeing us with evident curiosity. With head erect above the surface, and tail stiffly "cocked" upward, it presented a comic, yet hideous aspect.

"Bring me my rifle, Jake!" I said, in a half whisper. "Tread gently, and don't alarm it!"

Jake stole off to fetch the gun; but the reptile appeared to comprehend our intentions—for, before I could lay hands upon the weapon, it revolved suddenly on the water, shot off with the velocity of an arrow, and dived into the dark recesses of the pool.

Rifle in hand, I waited for some time for its re-appearance; but it did not again come to the surface. Likely enough, it had been shot at before, or otherwise attacked; and now recognised in the upright form a dangerous enemy. The proximity of the pond to a frequented road rendered probable the supposition.

Neither my companion nor I would have thought more about it, but for the similarity of the scene to one well-known to us. In truth, the resemblance was remarkable—the pond, the rocks, the trees that grew around, all bore a likeness to those with which our eyes were familiar. Even the reptile we had just seen—in form, in size, in fierce ugly aspect—appeared the exact counterpart to that one whose story was now a legend of the plantation.

The wild scenes of that day were recalled; the details starting fresh into our recollection, as if they had been things of yesterday—the luring of the amphibious monster—the perilous encounter in the tank—the chase—the capture—the trial and fiery sentence—the escape—the long lingering pursuit across the lake, and the abrupt awful ending—all were remembered at the moment with vivid distinctness. I could almost fancy I heard that cry of agony—that half-drowned ejaculation, uttered by the victim as he sank below the surface of the water. They were not pleasant memories either to my companion or myself, and we soon ceased to discourse of them.

As if to bring more agreeable reflections, the cheerful "gobble" of a wild turkey at that moment sounded in our ears; and Jake asked my permission to go in search of the game. No objection being made, he took up the rifle, and left me.

I re-lit my "havanna"—stretched myself as before along the soft sward, watched the circling eddies of the purple smoke, inhaled the narcotic fragrance of the flowers, and once more fell asleep.

This time I dreamed, and my dreams appeared to be only the continuation of the thoughts that had been so recently in my mind. They were visions of that eventful day; and once more its events passed in review before me, just as they had occurred.

In one thing, however, my dream differed from the reality. I dreamt that I saw the mulatto rising back to the surface of the water, and climbing out upon the shore of the island. I dreamt that he had escaped unscathed, unhurt—that he had returned to revenge himself—that by some means he had got me in his power, and was about to kill me!

At this crisis in my dream, I was again suddenly awakened—this time not by the plashing of water, but by the sharp "spang" of a rifle that had been fired near.

"Jake has found the turkeys," thought I. "I hope he has taken good aim. I should like to carry one to the fort. It might be welcome at the mess-table, since I hear that the larder is not overstocked. Jake is a good shot, and not likely to miss. If—"

My reflections were suddenly interrupted by a second report, which, from its sharp detonation, I knew to be also that of a rifle.

"My God! what can it mean? Jake has but one gun, and but one barrel—he cannot have reloaded since? he has not had time. Was the first only a fancy of my dream? Surely I heard a report? surely it was that which awoke me? There were two shots—I could not be mistaken."

In surprise, I sprang to my feet. I was alarmed as well. I was alarmed for the safety of my companion. Certainly I had heard two reports. Two rifles must have been fired, and by two men. Jake may have been one, but who was the other? We were upon dangerous ground. Was it an enemy?

I shouted out, calling the black by name.

I was relieved on hearing his voice. I heard it at some distance off in the woods; but I drew fresh alarm from it as I listened. It was uttered, not in reply to my call, but in accents of terror.

Mystified, as well as alarmed, I seized my pistols, and ran forward to meet him. I could tell that he was coming towards me, and was near; but under the dark shadow of the trees his black body was not yet visible. He still continued to cry out, and I could now distinguish what he was saying.

"Gorramighty! gorramighty!" he exclaimed in a tone of extreme terror. "Lor! Massa George, are you hurt?"

"Hurt! what the deuce should hurt me?"

But for the two reports, I should have fancied that he had fired the rifle in my direction, and was under the impression he might have hit me.

"You are not shot? Gorramighty be thank you are not shot, Massr George."

"Why, Jake, what does it all mean?"

At this moment he emerged from the heavy timber, and in the open ground I had a clear view of him.

His aspect did not relieve me from the apprehension that something strange had occurred.

He was the very picture of terror, as exhibited in a negro. His eyes were rolling in their sockets—the whites oftener visible than either pupil or iris. His lips were white and bloodless; the black skin upon his face was blanched to an ashy paleness; and his teeth chattered as he spoke. His attitudes and gestures confirmed my belief that he was in a state of extreme terror.

As soon as he saw me, he ran hurriedly up, and grasped me by the arm—at the same time casting fearful glances in the direction whence he had come, as if some dread danger was behind him!

I knew that under ordinary circumstances Jake was no coward—Quite the contrary. There must have been peril then—what was it?

I looked back; but in the dark depths of the forest shade, I could distinguish no other object than the brown trunks of the trees.

I again appealed to him for an explanation.

"O Lor! it wa-wa-war *him*, I'se sure it war *him*."

"Him? who?"

"O Massr George; you—you—you shure you not hurt. He fire at you. I see him t-t-take aim; I fire at *him*—I fire after; I mi-mi-miss; he run away—way—way."

"Who fired? who ran away?"

"O Gor! it wa-wa-war him; him or him go-go-ghost."

"For heaven's sake, explain! what him? what ghost? Was it the devil you have seen?"

"Troof, Massr George; dat am the troof. It wa-wa-war de debbel I see; it war *Yell' Jake!*"

"Yellow Jake?"

Chapter Twenty Five.

Who Fired the Shot?

"Yellow Jake?" I repeated in the usual style of involuntary interrogative—of course without the slightest faith in my companion's statement. "Saw Yellow Jake, you say?"

"Yes, Massr George," replied the groom, getting a little over his fright: "sure as the sun, I see 'im—eytha 'im or 'im ghost."

"Oh, nonsense! there are no ghosts: your eyes deceived you under the shadow of a tree. It must have been an illusion."

"By Gor! Massr George," rejoined the black with emphatic earnestness, "I swar I see 'im—'twant no daloosyun, I see—'twar eytha Yell' Jake or 'im ghost."

"Impossible!"

"Den, massr, ef't be impossible, it am de troof. Sure as da gospel, I see Yell' Jake; he fire at you from ahind tha gum tree. Den I fire at 'im. Sure, Massr George, you hear boaf de two shot?"

"True; I heard two shots, or fancied I did."

"Gollys! massr, da wa'nt no fancy 'bout 'em. Whugh! no—da dam raskel he fire, sure. Lookee da, Massr George! What I say? Lookee da!"

We had been advancing towards the pond, and were now close to the magnolia under whose shade I had slept. I observed Jake in a stooping attitude under the tree, and pointing to its trunk. I looked in the direction indicated. Low down, on the smooth bark, I saw the score of a bullet. It had creased the tree, and passed onward. The wound was green and fresh, the sap still flowing. Beyond doubt, I had been fired at by some one, and missed only by an inch. The leaden missile must have passed close to my head where it rested upon the valise—close to my ears, too, for I now remembered that almost simultaneously with the first report, I had heard the "wheep" of a bullet.

"Now, you b'lieve um, Massr George?" interposed the black, with an air of confident interrogation. "Now you b'lieve dat dis chile see no daloosyun?"

"Certainly I believe that I have been shot at by some one—"

"Yell' Jake, Massr George! Yell' Jake, by Gor!" earnestly asseverated my companion. "I seed da yaller raskel plain's I see dat log afore me."

"Yellow skin or red skin, we can't shift our quarters too soon. Give me the rifle: I shall keep watch while you are saddling. Haste, and let us be gone!"

I speedily reloaded the piece; and placing myself behind the trunk of a tree, turned my eyes in that direction whence the shot must have come. The black brought the horses to the rear of my position, and proceeded with all despatch to saddle them, and buckle on our *impedimenta*.

I need not say that I watched with anxiety—with fear. Such a deadly attempt proved that a deadly enemy was near, whoever he might be. The supposition that it was Yellow Jake was too preposterous, I of course, ridiculed the idea. I had been an eye-witness of his certain and awful doom; and it would have required stronger testimony than even the solemn declaration of my companion, to have given me faith either in a ghost or a resurrection. I had been fired at—that fact could not be questioned—and by some one, whom my follower—under the uncertain light of the gloomy forest, and blinded by his fears—had taken for Yellow Jake. Of course this was a fancy—a mistake as to the personal identity of our unknown enemy. There could be no other explanation.

Ha! why was I at that moment dreaming of him—of the mulatto? And why such a dream? If I were to believe the statement of the black, it was the very realisation of that unpleasant vision that had just passed before me in my sleep.

A cold shuddering came over me—my blood grew chill within my veins—my flesh crawled, as I thought over this most singular coincidence. There was something awful in it—something so damnably probable, that I began to think there was truth in the solemn allegation of the black; and the more I pondered upon it, the less power felt I to impeach his veracity.

Why should an Indian, thus unprovoked, have singled *me* out for his deadly aim? True, there was hostility between red and white, but not war. Surely it had not yet come to this? The council of chiefs had not met—the meeting was fixed for the following day; and, until its result should be known, it was not likely that hostilities would be practised on either side. Such would materially influence the determinations of the projected assembly. The Indians were as much interested in keeping the peace as their white adversaries—ay, far more indeed—and they could not help knowing that an ill-timed demonstration of this kind would be to their disadvantage—just the very pretext which the "removal" party would have wished for.

Could it, then, have been an Indian who aimed at my life? And if not, who in the world besides had a motive for killing *me*? I could think of no one whom I had offended—at least no one that I had provoked to such deadly retribution.

The drunken drovers came into my mind. Little would they care for treaties or the result of the council. A horse, a saddle, a gun, a trinket, would weigh more in their eyes than

52

the safety of their whole tribe. Both were evidently true bandits—for there are robbers among red skins as well as white ones.

But no; it could not have been they? They had not seen us as we passed, or, even if they had, they could hardly have been upon the ground so soon? We had ridden briskly, after leaving them; and they were afoot.

Spence and Williams were mounted; and from what Jake had told me as we rode along in regard to the past history of these two "rowdies," I could believe them capable of anything—even of that.

But it was scarcely probable either; they had not seen us: and besides they had their hands full.

Ha! I guessed it. At last; at all events I had hit upon the most probable conjecture. The villain was some runaway from the settlements, some absconding slave—perhaps ill-treated—who had sworn eternal hostility to the whites; and who was thus wreaking his vengeance on the first who had crossed his path. A mulatto, no doubt; and maybe bearing some resemblance to Yellow Jake—for there is a general similarity among men of yellow complexion, as among blacks.

This would explain the delusion under which my companion was labouring! at all events, it rendered his mistake more natural; and with this supposition, whether true or false, I was forced to content myself.

Jake had now got everything in readiness; and, without staying to seek any further solution of the mystery we leaped to our saddles, and galloped away from the ground.

We rode for some time with the "beard on the shoulder;" and, as our path now lay through thin woods, we could see for a long distance behind us.

No enemy, white or black, red or yellow, made his appearance, either on our front, flank, or rear. We encountered not a living creature till we rode up to the stockade of Fort King (Note); which we entered just as the sun was sinking behind the dark line of the forest horizon.

Note. Called after a distinguished officer in the American army. Such is the fashion in naming the frontier posts.

Chapter Twenty Six.

A Frontier Fort.

The word "fort" calls up before the mind a massive structure, with angles and embrasures, bastions and battlements, curtains, casemates, and glacis—a place of great strength, for this is its essential signification. Such structures have the Spaniards raised in Florida as elsewhere—some of which (Note 1) are still standing, while others, even in their ruins, bear witness to the grandeur and glory that enveloped them at that time, when the leopard flag waved proudly above their walls.

There is a remarkable dissimilarity between the colonial architecture of Spain and that of other European nations. In America the Spaniards built without regard to pains or expense, as if they believed that their tenure would be eternal. Even in Florida, they could have no idea their lease would be so short—no forecast of so early an ejectment.

After all, these great fortresses served them a purpose. But for their protection, the dark Yamassee, and, after him, the conquering Seminole, would have driven them from the flowery peninsula long before the period of their actual rendition.

The United States has its great stone fortresses; but far different from these are the "forts" of frontier phraseology, which figure in the story of border wars, and which, at this hour, gird the territory of the United States as with a gigantic chain. In these are no grand battlements of cut rock, no costly casemates, no idle ornaments of engineering. They are rude erections of hewn logs, of temporary intent, put up at little expense, to be abandoned with as little loss—ready to follow the ever-flitting frontier in its rapid recession.

Such structures are admirably adapted to the purpose which they are required to serve. They are types of the utilitarian spirit of a republican government, not permitted to squander national wealth on such costly toys as Thames Tunnels and Britannia Bridges, at the expense of an overtaxed people. To fortify against an Indian enemy, proceed as follows:

Obtain a few hundred trees; cut them into lengths of eighteen feet; split them up the middle; set them in a quadrangle, side by side, flat faces inward; batten them together; point them at the tops; loophole eight feet from the ground; place a staging under the loopholes; dig a ditch outside; build a pair of bastions at alternate corners, in which plant your cannon; hang a strong gate and you have a "frontier fort."

It may be a triangle, a quadrangle, or any other polygon best suited to the ground.

You need quarters for your troops and stores. Build strong blockhouses within the enclosure—some at the angles, if you please; loophole them also—against the contingency of the stockade being carried; and, this done, your fort is finished.

Pine trees serve well. Their tall, branchless stems are readily cut and split to the proper lengths; but in Florida is found a timber still better for the purpose—in the trunk of the "cabbage-palm" (*Chamaerops palmetto*). These, from the peculiarity of their endogenous texture, are less liable to be shattered by shot, and the bullet buries itself harmlessly in the wood. Of such materials was Fort King.

Fancy, then, such a stockade fort. People it with a few hundred soldiers—some in jacket uniforms of faded sky-colour, with white facings, sadly dimmed with dirt (the infantry); some in darker blue, bestriped with red (artillery); a few adorned with the more showy yellow (the dragoons); and still another few in the sombre green of the rifles. Fancy these men lounging about or standing in groups, in slouched attitudes, and slouchingly attired—a few of tidier aspect, with pipe-clayed belts and bayonets by their sides, on sentry, or forming the daily guard—some half-score of slattern women, their laundress-wives, mingling with a like number of brown-skinned squaws—a sprinkling of squalling brats—here and there an officer hurrying along, distinguished by his dark-blue undress frock (Note 2)—half-a-dozen gentlemen in civilian garb—visitors, or non-military *attachés* of the fort—a score less gentle-looking—sutlers, beef-contractors, drovers, butchers, guides, hunters, gamblers, and idlers—some negro servants and friendly Indians—perhaps the pompous commissioner himself—fancy all these before you, with the star-spangled flag waving above your head, and you have the *coup d'oeil* that presented itself as I rode into the gateway of Fort King.

Of late not much used to the saddle, the ride had fatigued me. I heard the *reveille*, but not yet being ordered on duty, I disregarded the call, and kept my bed till a later hour.

The notes of a bugle bursting through the open window, and the quick rolling of drums, once more awoke me. I recognised the parade music, and sprang from my couch. Jake at this moment entered to assist me in my toilet.

"Golly, Massr George!" he exclaimed, pointing out by the window; "lookee dar! darts tha whole Indyen ob tha Seminole nayshun—ebbery red skin dar be in ole Floridy. Whugh!"

I looked forth. The scene was picturesque and impressive. Inside the stockade, soldiers were hurrying to and fro—the different companies forming for parade. They were no longer, as on the evening before, slouched and loosely attired; but, with jackets close buttoned, caps jauntily cocked, belts pipe-clayed to a snowy whiteness, guns, bayonets, and buttons gleaming under the sunlight, they presented a fine military aspect. Officers were moving among them, distinguished by their more splendid uniforms and shining epaulets; and a little apart stood the general himself, surrounded by his staff, conspicuous under large black chapeaux with nodding plumes of cock's feathers, white and scarlet. Alongside the general was the commissioner—himself a general—in full government uniform.

This grand display was intended for effect on the minds of the Indians.

There were several well-dressed civilians within the enclosure, planters from the neighbourhood, among whom I recognised the Ringgolds.

So far the impressive. The picturesque lay beyond the stockade.

On the level plain that stretched to a distance of several hundred yards in front, were groups of tall Indian warriors, attired in their savage finery—turbaned, painted, and plumed. No two were dressed exactly alike, and yet there was a similarity in the style of all. Some wore hunting-shirts of buckskin, with leggings and moccasins of like material—all profusely fringed, beaded, and tasselled; others were clad in tunics of printed cotton stuff, checked or flowered, with leggings of cloth, blue, green, or scarlet, reaching from hip to ankle, and girt below the knee with bead-embroidered gaiters, whose tagged and tasselled ends hung down the outside of the leg. The gorgeous wampum belt encircled their waists, behind which were stuck their long knives, tomahawks, and, in some instances, pistols, glittering with a rich inlay of silver—relics left them by the Spaniards. Some, instead of the Indian wampum, encircled their waists with the Spanish scarf of scarlet silk, its fringed extremities hanging square with the skirt of the tunic, adding gracefulness to the garment. A picturesque head-dress was not wanting to complete the striking costume; and in this the variety was still greater. Some wore the beautiful coronet of plumes—the feathers stained to a variety of brilliant hues; some the "toque" of checked "bandanna;" while others wore shako-like caps of fur—of the black squirrel, the bay lynx, or raccoon—the face of the animal often fantastically set to the front. The heads of many were covered with broad fillets of embroidered wampum, out of which stood the wing plumes of the king vulture, or the gossamer feathers of the sand-hill crane. A few were still further distinguished by the nodding plumes of the great bird of Afric.

All carried guns—the long rifle of the backwoods hunter, with horns and pouches slung from their shoulders. Neither bow nor arrow was to be seen, except in the hands of the youth—many of whom were upon the ground, mingling with the warriors.

Further off, I could see tents, where the Indians had pitched their camp. They were not together, but scattered along the edge of the wood, here and there, in clusters, with banners floating in front—denoting the different clans or sub-tribes to which each belonged.

Women in their long frocks could be seen moving among the tents, and little dark-skinned "papooses" were playing over the grassy sward in front of them.

When I first saw them, the warriors were assembling in front of the stockade. Some had already arrived, and stood in little crowds, conversing, while others strode over the ground, passing from group to group, as if bearing words of council from one to the other.

I could not help observing the upright carriage of these magnificent men. I could not help admiring their full, free port, and contrasting it with the gingerly step of the drilled soldier! No eye could have looked upon them without acknowledging this superiority of the *savage*.

As I glanced along the line of Saxon and Celtic soldiery—starched and stiff as they stood, shoulder to shoulder, and heel to heel—and then looked upon the plumed warriors without, as they proudly strode over the sward of their native soil, I could not help the reflection, that to conquer these men we must needs *outnumber* them!

I should have been laughed at had I given expression to the thought. It was contrary to all experience—contrary to the burden of many a boasting legend of the borders. The Indian had always succumbed; but was it to the superior strength and courage of his white antagonist? No: the inequality lay in numbers—oftener in arms. This was the secret of our superiority. What could avail the wet bowstring and ill-aimed shaft against the death-dealing bullet of the rifle?

There was no inequality now. Those hunter warriors carried the fire-weapon, and could handle it as skillfully as we.

The Indians now formed into a half-circle in front of the fort. The chiefs, having aligned themselves so as to form the concave side of the curve, sat down upon the grass. Behind them the sub-chiefs and more noted warriors took their places, and still further back, in rank after rank, stood the common men of the tribes. Even the women and boys drew near, clustering thickly behind, and regarding the movements of the men with quiet but eager interest.

Contrary to their usual habits, they were grave and silent. It is not their character to be so; for the Seminole is as free of speech and laughter as the clown of the circus ring; even the light-hearted negro scarcely equals him in joviality.

It was not so now, but the very reverse. Chiefs, warriors and women—even the boys who had just forsaken their play—all wore an aspect of solemnity.

No wonder. That was no ordinary assemblage—no meeting upon a trivial matter— but a council at which was to be decided one of the dearest interests of their lives—a council whose decree might part them forever from their native land. No wonder they did not exhibit their habitual gaiety.

It is not correct to say that all looked grave. In that semi-circle of chiefs were men of opposite views. There were those who wished for the removal—who had private reasons to desire it—men bribed, suborned, or tampered with—traitors to their tribe and nation.

These were neither weak nor few. Some of the most powerful chiefs had been bought over, and had agreed to sell the rights of their people. Their treason was known or suspected, and this it was that was causing the anxiety of the others. Had it been otherwise—had there been no division in the ranks—the patriot party might easily have obtained a triumphant decision; but they feared the defection of traitors.

The band had struck up a march—the troops were in motion, and filing through the gate.

Hurrying on my uniform, I hastened out; and took my place among the staff of the general.

A few minutes after we were on the ground, face to face with the assembled chiefs.

The troops formed in line, the general taking his stand in front of the colours, with the commissioner by his side. Behind these were grouped the officers of the staff with clerks, interpreters, and some civilians of note—the Ringgolds, and others—who by courtesy were to take part in the proceedings.

Hands were shaken between the officers and chiefs; the friendly calumet was passed round; and the council at length inaugurated.

Note 1. Forts Piscolata on the Saint Johns, Fort San Augustine, and others, at Pensacola, Saint Marks, and elsewhere.

Note 2. An American officer is rarely to be seen in full uniform—still more rarely when on campaigning service, as in Florida.

Chapter Twenty Seven.

The Council.

First came the speech of the commissioner.

It is too voluminous to be given in detail. Its chief points were, an appeal to the Indians to conform peaceably to the terms of the Oclawaha treaty—to yield up their lands in Florida—to move to the west—to the country assigned them upon the White River of Arkansas—in short, to accept all the terms which the government had commissioned him to require.

He took pains to specify the advantages which would accrue from the removal. He painted the new home as a perfect paradise—prairies covered with game, elk, antelopes, and buffalo—rivers teeming with fish—crystal waters and unclouded skies. Could he have found credence for his words, the Seminole might have fancied that the happy hunting-grounds of his fancied heaven existed in reality upon the earth.

On the other hand, he pointed out to the Indians the consequences of their non-compliance. White men would be settling thickly along their borders. Bad white men would enter upon their lands; there would be strife and the spilling of blood; the red man would be tried in the court of the white man, where, according to law, his oath would be of no avail; and *therefore he must suffer injustice!*

Such were in reality the sentiments of Mr Commissioner Wiley Thompson (historically true), uttered in the council of Fort King, in April, 1835. I shall give them in his own words; they are worthy of record, as a specimen of *fair dealing* between white and red. Thus spoke he:

"Suppose—what is, however impossible—that you could be permitted to remain here for a few years longer, what would be your condition? This land will soon be surveyed, sold to, and settled by the whites. *There is now a surveyor in the country.* The jurisdiction of the government will soon be extended over you. Your laws will be set aside—your chiefs will cease to be chiefs. Claims for debt and for your negroes would be set up against you by bad white men; or you would perhaps be charged with crimes affecting life. You would be haled before the white man's court. The claims and charges would be decided by the white man's law. White men would be witnesses against you. Indians would not be permitted to give evidence. Your condition in a few years would be hopeless wretchedness. You would be reduced to abject poverty, and when urged by hunger to ask—perhaps from the man who had thus ruined you—for a crust of bread, you might be called an Indian dog, and spurned from his presence. For this reason it is that your 'Great Father' (!) wishes to remove you to the west—to save you from all these evils."

And this language in the face of a former treaty—that of Camp Moultrie—which guaranteed to the Seminoles their right to remain in Florida, and the third article of which runs thus:

"The United States will take the Florida Indians under their care and patronage; *and will afford them protection against all persons whatsoever.*"

O tempora, O mores!

The speech was a mixture of sophistry and implied menace—now uttered in the tones of a petitioner, anon assuming the bold air of the bully. It was by no means clever— both characters being overdone.

The commissioner felt no positive hostility towards the Seminoles. He was indignant only with those chiefs who had already raised opposition to his designs, and one, in particular, he *hated*; but the principal *animus* by which he was inspired, was a desire to do the work for which he had been delegated—an ambition to carry out the wish of his government and nation and thus gain for himself credit and glory. At this shrine he was ready—as most officials are—to sacrifice his personal independence of thought, with every principle of morality and honour. What matters the cause so long as it is the king's? Make it "congress" instead of "king's" and you have the motto of our Indian agent.

Shallow as was the speech, it was not without its effects. The weak and wavering were influenced by it. The flattering sketch of their new home, with the contrasted awful picture of what might be their future condition, affected the minds of many. During that spring the Seminoles had planted but little corn. The summons of war had been sounding in their ears; and they had neglected seed time: there would be no harvest—no maize, nor rice, nor yams. Already were they suffering from their improvidence. Even then were they collecting the roots of the China briar (Note 1), and the acorns of the live-oak. How much worse would be their condition in the winter?

It is not to be wondered at that they gave way to apprehension; and I noticed many whose countenances bore an expression of awe. Even the patriot chiefs appeared to evince some apprehension for the result.

They were not dismayed, however. After a short interval, Hoitle-mattee, one of the strongest opponents of the removal, rose to reply. There is no order of precedence in such matters. The tribes have their acknowledged orators, who are usually permitted to express the sentiments of the rest. The head chief was present, seated in the middle of the ring, with a British crown upon his head—a relic of the American Revolution. But "Onopa" was no orator, and waived his right to reply in favour of Hoitle-mattee—his son-in-law.

The latter had the double reputation of being a wise councillor and brave warrior; he was, furthermore, one of the most eloquent speakers in the nation. He was the "prime-minister" of Onopa, and, to carry the comparison into classic times, he might be styled the Ulysses of his people. He was a tall, spare man, of dark complexion, sharp aquiline features, and somewhat sinister aspect. He was not of the Seminole race, but, as he stated himself, a descendant of one of the ancient tribes who peopled Florida in the days of the early Spaniards. Perhaps he was a Yamassee, and his dark skin would favour this supposition.

His powers of oratory may be gathered from his speech:

"At the treaty of Moultrie, it was engaged that we should rest in peace upon the land allotted to us for twenty years. All difficulties were buried, and we were assured that if we died, it should not be by the violence of the white man, but in the course of nature. The lightning should not rive and blast the tree, but the cold of old age should dry up the sap, and the leaves should wither and fall, and the branches drop, and the trunk decay and die.

"The deputation stipulated at the talk on the Oclawaha to be sent on the part of the nation, was only authorised to *examine* the country to which it was proposed to remove us, and bring back its report to the nation. We went according to agreement, and saw the land.

It is no doubt good land, and the fruit of the soil may smell sweet, and taste well, and be healthy, but it is surrounded with bad and hostile neighbours, and the fruit of bad neighbourhood is blood that spoils the land, and fire that dries up the brook. Even of the horses we carried with us, some were stolen by the Pawnees, and the riders obliged to carry their packs on their backs. You would send us among bad Indians, with whom we could never be at rest.

"When we saw the land, we said nothing; but the agents of the United States made us sign our hands to a paper which *you* say signified our consent to remove, but *we considered* we did no more than say we liked the land, and when we returned, the *nation would decide*. We had no authority to do more.

"Your talk is a good one, but my people cannot say they will go. The people differ in their opinions, and must be indulged with time to reflect. They cannot consent now; they are not willing to go. If their tongues say yes, their hearts cry no, and call them liars. We are not hungry for other lands—why should we go and hunt for them? We like our own land, we are happy here. If suddenly we tear our hearts from the homes round which they are twined, our heart-strings will snap. We cannot consent to go—*we will not go!*"

A chief of the removal party spoke next. He was "Omatla," one of the most powerful of the tribe, and suspected of an "alliance" with the agent. His speech was of a pacific character, recommending his red-brothers not to make any difficulty, but act as honourable men, and comply with the treaty of the Oclawaha.

It was evident this chief spoke under restraint. He feared to show too openly his partiality for the plans of the commissioner, dreading the vengeance of the patriot warriors. These frowned upon him as he stood up, and he was frequently interrupted by Arpiucki, Coa Hajo, and others.

A bolder speech, expressing similar views, was delivered by Lusta Hajo (the Black Clay). He added little to the argument; but by his superior daring, restored the confidence of the traitorous party and the equanimity of the commissioner, who was beginning to exhibit signs of impatience and excitement.

"Holata Mico" next rose on the opposite side—a mild and gentlemanly Indian, and one of the most regarded of the chiefs. He was in ill health, as his appearance indicated; and in consequence of this, his speech was of a more pacific character than it might otherwise have been; for he was well-known to be a firm opponent of the removal.

"We come to deliver our talk to-day. We are all made by the same Great Father; and are all alike his children. We all came from the same mother; and were suckled at the same breast. Therefore, we are brothers; and, as brothers, should not quarrel, and let our blood rise up against each other. If the blood of one of us, by each other's blow, should fall upon the earth, it would stain it, and cry aloud for vengeance from the land wherever it had sunk, and call down the frown and the thunder of the Great Spirit. I am not well. Let others who are stronger speak, and declare their minds."

Several chiefs rose successively and delivered their opinions. Those for removal followed the strain of Omatla and the Black Clay. They were "Obala" (the big warrior), the brothers Itolasse and Charles Omatla, and a few others of less note.

In opposition to those, spoke the patriots "Acola," "Yaha Hajo" (mad wolf), "Echa Matta" (the water-serpent), "Poshalla" (the dwarf), and the negro "Abram." The last was an old "refugee," from Pensacola; but now chief of the blacks living with the Micosauc tribe (Note 2), and one of the counsellors of Onopa, over whom he held supreme influence. He spoke English fluently; and at the council—as also that of the Oclawaha—he was the principal interpreter on the part of the Indians. He was a pure negro, with the thick lips, prominent cheek-bones, and other physical peculiarities of his race. He was brave, cool, and sagacious; and though only an adopted chief, he proved to the last the true friend of the people who had honoured him by their confidence. His speech was brief and moderate; nevertheless it evinced a firm determination to resist the will of the agent.

As yet, the "king" had not declared himself, and to him the commissioner now appealed. Onopa was a large, stout man, of somewhat dull aspect, but not without a considerable expression of dignity. He was not a man of great intellect, nor yet an orator; and although the head "mico" of the nation, his influence with the warriors was not equal to that of several chiefs of inferior rank. His decision, therefore, would by no means be regarded as definitive, or binding upon the others; but being nominally "mico-mico," or chief-chief, and actually head of the largest clan—the Micosaucs—his vote would be likely to turn the scale, one way or the other. If he declared for the removal, the patriots might despair.

There was an interval of breathless silence. The eyes of the whole assemblage, of both red men and white men, rested upon the king. There were only a few who were in the secret of his sentiments; and how he would decide, was to most of those present a matter of uncertainty. Hence the anxiety with which they awaited his words.

At this crisis, a movement was observed among the people who stood behind the king. They were making way for some one who was passing through their midst. It was evidently one of authority, for the crowd readily yielded him passage.

The moment after, he appeared in front—a young warrior, proudly caparisoned, and of noble aspect. He wore the insignia of a chief; but it needed not this to tell that he was one; there was that in his look and bearing which at once pronounced him a leader of men.

His dress was rich, without being frivolous or gay. His tunic, embraced by the bright wampum sash, hung well and gracefully; and the close-fitting leggings of scarlet cloth displayed the perfect sweep of his limbs. His form was a model of strength—terse, well-knit, symmetrical. His head was turbaned with a shawl of brilliant hues; and from the front rose three black ostrich-plumes, that drooped backward over the crown till their tips almost touched his shoulders. Various ornaments were suspended from his neck; but one upon his breast was conspicuous. It was a circular plate of gold, with lines radiating from a common centre. It was a representation of the Rising Sun.

His face was stained of a uniform vermilion red: but despite the levelling effect of the dye, the lineaments of noble features could be traced. A well-formed mouth and chin, thin lips, a jawbone expressive of firmness, a nose slightly aquiline, a high, broad forehead, with eyes that, like the eagle's, seemed strong enough to gaze against the sun.

The appearance of this remarkable man produced an electric effect upon all present. It was similar to that exhibited by the audience in a theatre on the *entrée* of the great tragedian for whom they have been waiting.

Not from the behaviour of the young chief himself—withal right modest—but from the action of the others, I perceived that he was in reality the hero of the hour. The *dramatis personae*, who had already performed their parts, were evidently but secondary characters; and this was the man for whom all had been waiting.

There followed a movement—a murmur of voices—an excited tremor among the crowd—and then, simultaneously, as if from one throat, was shouted the name, "Osceola!"

Note 1. *Smilax pseudo-China.* From its roots the Seminoles make the *conti*, a species of jelly—a sweet and nourishing food.

Note 2. The Micosauc (Micosaukee) or tribe of the "redstick," was the largest and most warlike of the nation. It was under the immediate government of the head chief Onopa—usually called "Miconopa."

Chapter Twenty Eight.

The Rising Sun.

Yes, it was Osceola, "the Rising Sun" (Note 1)—he whose fame had already reached to the farthest corner of the land—whose name had excited such an interest among the cadets at college—outside the college—in the streets—in the fashionable drawing-room—everywhere; he it was who had thus unexpectedly shown himself in the circle of chiefs.

A word about this extraordinary young man.

Suddenly emerging from the condition of a common warrior—a sub-chief, with scarcely any following—he had gained at once, and as if by magic, the confidence of the nation. He was at this moment the hope of the patriot party—the spirit that was animating them to resistance, and every day saw his influence increasing. Scarcely more appropriate could have been his native appellation.

One might have fancied him less indebted to accident than design for the name, had it not been that which he had always borne among his own people. There was a sort of prophetic or typical adaptation in it, for at this time he was in reality the Rising Sun of the Seminoles. He was so regarded by them.

I noticed that his arrival produced a marked effect upon the warriors. He may have been present upon the ground all the day, but up to that moment he had not shown himself in the front circle of the chiefs. The timid and wavering became reassured by his appearance, and the traitorous chiefs evidently cowered under his glance. I noticed that the Omatlas, and even the fierce Lusta Hajo regarded him with uneasy looks.

There were others besides the red men who were affected by his sudden advent. From the position in which I stood, I had a view of the commissioner's face; I noticed that his countenance suddenly paled, and there passed over it a marked expression of chagrin. It was clear that with him the "Rising Sun" was anything but welcome. His hurried words to Clinch reached my ears—for I stood close to the general, and could not help overhearing them.

"How unfortunate!" he muttered in a tone of vexation. "But for him, we should have succeeded. I was in hopes of nailing them before he should arrive. I told him a wrong hour, but it seems to no purpose. Deuce take the fellow! he will undo all. See! he is earwigging Onopa, and the old fool listens to him like a child. Bah!—he will obey him like a great baby, as he is. It's all up, general; we must come to blows."

On hearing this half-whispered harangue, I turned my eyes once more upon him who was the subject of it, and regarded him more attentively. He was still standing behind the king, but in a stooping attitude, and whispering in the ear of the latter—scarcely whispering, but speaking audibly in their native language. Only the interpreters could have understood what he was saying, and they were too distant to make it out. His earnest tone, however—his firm yet somewhat excited manner—the defiant flash of his eye, as he glanced toward the commissioner—all told that he himself had no intention to yield; and that he was counselling his superior to like bold opposition and resistance.

For some moments there was silence, broken only by the whisperings of the commissioner on one side, and the muttered words passing between Osceola and the mico on the other. After a while even these sounds were hushed, and a breathless stillness succeeded.

It was a moment of intense expectation, and one of peculiar interest. On the words which Onopa was about to utter, hung events of high import—important to almost every one upon the ground. Peace or war, and therefore life or death, was suspended over the heads of all present. Even the soldiers in the lines were observed with outstretched necks in the attitude of listening; and upon the other side, the Indian boys, and the women with babes in their arms, clustered behind the circle of warriors, their anxious looks betraying the interest they felt in the issue.

The commissioner grew impatient; his face reddened again. I saw that he was excited and angry—at the same time he was doing his utmost to appear calm. As yet he had taken no notice of the presence of Osceola, but was making pretence to ignore it, although it was evident that Osceola was at that moment the main subject of his thoughts. He only looked at the young chief by side-glances, now and again turning to resume his conversation with the general.

This by-play was of short duration. Thompson could endure the suspense no longer. "Tell Onopa," said he to the interpreter, "that the council awaits his answer."

The interpreter did as commanded.

"I have but one answer to make," replied the taciturn king, without deigning to rise from his seat; "I am content with my present home; I am not going to leave it."

A burst of applause from the patriots followed this declaration. Perhaps these were the most popular words that old Onopa had ever uttered. From that moment he was possessed of real kingly power, and might command in his nation.

I looked round the circle of the chiefs. A smile lit up the gentlemanly features of Holata Mico; the grim face of Hoitle-mattee gleamed with joy: the "Alligator," "Cloud," and Arpiucki exhibited more frantic signs of their delight; and even the thick lips of Abram were drawn flat over his gums, displaying his double tier of ivories in a grin of triumphant satisfaction.

On the other hand, the Omatlas and their party wore black looks. Their gloomy glances betokened their discontent; and from their gestures and attitudes, it was evident that one and all of them were suffering under serious apprehension.

They had cause. They were no longer suspected, no longer traitors only attainted; their treason was now patent—it had been declared.

It was fortunate for them that Fort King was so near—well that they stood in the presence of that embattled line. They might need its bayonets to protect them.

The commissioner had by this time lost command of his temper. Even official dignity gave way, and he now descended to angry exclamations, threats, and bitter invective.

In the last he was personal, calling the chiefs by name, and charging them with faithlessness and falsehood. He accused Onopa of having already signed the treaty of the Oclawaha; and when the latter denied having done so, the commissioner told him he *lied*. (Again historically true—the very word used!) Even the savage did not reciprocate the vulgar accusation, but treated it with silent disdain.

After spending a portion of his spleen upon various chiefs of the council, he turned towards the front and in a loud, angry tone cried out: "It is *you* who have done this—*you*, Powell!"

I started at the word. I looked to see who was addressed—who it was that bore that well-known name.

The commissioner guided my glance both by look and gesture. He was standing with arm outstretched, and finger pointed in menace. His eye was bent upon the young warchief—upon Osceola!

All at once a light broke upon me. Already strange memories had been playing with my fancy; I thought that through the vermilion paint I saw features I had seen before.

Now I recognised them. In the young Indian hero, I beheld the friend of my boyhood—the preserver of my life—the brother of Maümee.

Note 1. Osceola—written Oçeola, Asseola, Assula, Hasseola, and in a dozen other forms of orthography—in the Seminole language, signifies the Rising Sun.

Chapter Twenty Nine.

The Ultimatum.

Yes—Powell and Osceola were one; the boy, as I had predicted, now developed into the splendid man—a hero.

Under the impulsive influences of former friendship and present admiration, I could have rushed forward and flung my arms around him; but it was neither time nor place for the display of such childish enthusiasm. Etiquette—duty forbade it; I kept my ground, and, as well as I could, the composure of my countenance, though I was unable to withdraw my eyes from what had now become doubly an object of admiration.

There was little time for reflection. The pause created by the rude speech of the commissioner had passed; the silence was again broken—this time by Osceola himself.

The young chief, perceiving that it was he who had been singled out, stepped forth a pace or two, and stood confronting the commissioner, his eye fixed upon him, in a glance, mild, yet firm and searching.

"Are you addressing me?" he inquired in a tone that evinced not the slightest anger or excitement.

"Who else than you?" replied the commissioner abruptly. "I called you by name—Powell."

"My name is *not* Powell."

"Not Powell?"

"No!" answered the Indian, raising his voice to its loudest pitch, and looking with proud defiance at the commissioner. "You may call me Powell, if you please, *you, General Wiley Thompson*,"—slowly and with a sarcastic sneer, he pronounced the full titles of the agent; "but know, sir, that I scorn the white man's baptism. I am an Indian; I am the child of my mother (Note 1); my name is Osceola."

The commissioner struggled to control his passion. The sneer at his plebeian cognomen stung him to the quick, for Powell understood enough of English nomenclature to know that "Thompson" was not an aristocratic appellation; and the sarcasm cut keenly.

He was angry enough to have ordered the instant execution of Osceola, had it been in his power; but it was not. Three hundred warriors trod the ground, each grasping his ready rifle, quite a match for the troops at the post; besides the commissioner knew that such rash indulgence of spleen might not be relished by his government. Even the Ringgolds—his dear friends and ready advisers—with all the wicked interest they might have in the downfall of the Rising Sun, were wiser than to counsel a proceeding like that.

Instead of replying, therefore to the taunt of the young chief, the commissioner addressed himself once more to the council.

"I want no more talking," said he with the air of a man speaking to inferiors; "we have had enough already. Your talk has been that of children, of men without wisdom or faith: I will no longer listen to it.

"Hear, then, what your Great Father says, and what he has sent me to say to you. He has told me to place before you this paper." The speaker produced a fold of parchment, opening it as he proceeded: "It is the treaty of Oclawaha. Most of you have already signed it. I ask you now to step forward and confirm your signatures."

"I have not signed it," said Onopa, urged to the declaration by Osceola, who stood by behind him. "I shall not sign it now. Others may act as they please; I shall not go from my home. I shall not leave Florida."

"Nor I," added Hoitle-mattee, in a determined tone. "I have fifty kegs of powder: so long as a grain of it remains unburned, I shall not be parted from my native land."

"His sentiments are mine," added Holata.

"And mine!" exclaimed Arpiucki.

"And mine?" echoed Poshalla (the dwarf), Coa Hajo, Cloud, and the negro Abram.

The patriots alone spoke; the traitors said not a word. The signing was a test too severe for them. They had all signed it before at the Oclawaha; but now, in the presence of the nation, they dared not confirm it. They feared even to advocate what they had done. They remained silent.

"Enough!" said Osceola, who had not yet publicly expressed his opinion, but who was now expected to speak, and was attentively regarded by all. "The chiefs have declared themselves; they refuse to sign. It is the voice of the nation that speaks through its chiefs, and the people will stand by their word. The agent has called us children and fools; it is easy to give names. We know that there are fools among us, and children too, and worse than both—*traitors*. But there are men, and some as true and brave as the agent himself. He wants no more talk with us—be it so; we have no more for *him*—he has our answer. He may stay or go.

"Brothers!" continued the speaker, facing to the chiefs and warriors, and as if disregarding the presence of the whites, "you have done right; you have spoken the will of the nation, and the people applaud. It is false that we wish to leave our homes and go west. They who say so are deceivers, and do not speak our mind. We have no desire for this *fine land* to which they would send us. It is not as fair as our own. It is a wild desert, where in summer the springs dry up and water is hard to find. From thirst the hunter often dies by the way. In winter, the leaves fall from the trees, snow covers the ground, frost stiffens the clay, and chills the bodies of men, till they shiver in pain—the whole country looks as though the earth were dead. Brothers! we want no cold country like that; we like our own land better. If it be too hot, we have the shade of the live-oak, the big laurel (Note 2), and the noble palm-tree. Shall we forsake the land of the palm? No! Under its shadow have we lived: under its shadow let us die!"

Up to this point the interest had been increasing. Indeed, ever since the appearance of Osceola, the scene had been deeply impressive—never to be effaced from the memory, though difficult to be described in words. A painter, and he alone, might have done justice to such a picture.

It was full of points, thoroughly and thrillingly dramatic; the excited agent on one side, the calm chiefs on the other; the contrast of emotions; the very women who had left their unclad little ones to gambol on the grass and dally with the flowers, while they themselves, with the warriors pressed closely around the council, under the most intense, yet subdued, interest; catching every look as it gleamed from the countenance, and hanging on every word as it fell from the lips of Osceola. The latter—his eye calm, serious, fixed—his attitude manly, graceful, erect—his thin, close-pressed lip, indicative of the "mind made up"—his firm, yet restrained, tread, free from all stride or swagger—his dignified and composed bearing—his perfect and solemn silence, except during his sententious talk—the head thrown backward, the arms firmly folded on the protruding chest—all, all instantaneously changing, as if by an electric shock, whenever the commissioner stated a proposition that he knew to be false or sophistic. At such times the fire-flash of his indignant eye—the withering scorn upon his upcurled lip—the violent and oft repeated stamping of his foot—his clenched hand, and the rapid gesticulation of his uplifted arm—the short, quick breathing and heaving of his agitated bosom, like the rushing wind and swelling wave of the tempest-tossed ocean, and these again subsiding into the stillness of melancholy, and presenting only that aspect and attitude of repose wherewith the ancient statuary loved to invest the gods and heroes of Greece.

The speech of Osceola brought matters to a crisis. The commissioner's patience was exhausted. The time was ripe to deliver the dire threat—the ultimatum—with which the president had armed him; and, not bating one jot of his rude manner, he pronounced the infamous menace:

"You will not sign?—you will not consent to go? I say, then you *must*. War will be declared against you—troops will enter your land—you will be forced from it at the point of the bayonet."

"Indeed!" exclaimed Osceola, with a derisive laugh. "Then be it so!" he continued. "Let war be declared! Though we love peace, we fear not war. We know your strength: your people outnumber us by millions; but were there as many more of them, they will not compel us to submit to injustice. We have made up our minds to endure death before dishonour. Let war be declared! Send your troops into our land; perhaps they will not force us from it so easily as you imagine. To your muskets we will oppose our rifles, to your bayonets, our tomahawks; and your starched soldiers will be met, face to face, by the warriors of the Seminole. Let war be declared! We are ready for its tempest. The hail may rattle, and the flowers be crushed; but the strong oak of the forest will lift its head to the sky and the storm, towering and unscathed."

A yell of defiance burst from the Indian warriors at the conclusion of this stirring speech; and the disturbed council threatened a disruption. Several of the chiefs, excited by the appeal, had risen to their feet, and stood with lowering looks, and arms stretched forth in firm, angry menace.

The officers of the line had glided to their places, and in an undertone ordered the troops into an attitude of readiness; while the artillerists on the bastions of the fort were seen by their guns, while the tiny wreath of blue smoke told that the fuse had been kindled.

For all this, there was no danger of an outbreak. Neither party was prepared for a collision at that moment. The Indians had come to the council with no hostile designs, else they would have left their wives and children at home. With them by their sides, they would not dream of making an attack; and their white adversaries dared not, without better pretext. The demonstration was only the result of a momentary excitement, and soon subsided to a calm.

The commissioner had stretched his influence to its utmost. His threats were now disregarded as had been his wheedling appeal; and he saw that he had no longer the power to effect his cherished purpose.

But there was still hope in time. There were wiser heads than his upon the ground, who saw this: the sagacious veteran Clinch and the crafty Ringgolds saw it.

These now gathered around the agent, and counselled him to the adoption of a different course.

"Give them time to consider," suggested they. "Appoint to-morrow for another meeting. Let the chiefs discuss the matter among themselves in private council, and not as now, in presence of the people. On calmer reflection, and when not intimidated by the crowd of warriors, they may decide differently, particularly now that they know the alternative; and perhaps," added Arens Ringgold—who, to other bad qualities, added that of a crafty diplomatist—"perhaps the more hostile of them will not stay for the council of to-morrow: you do not want *all* their signatures."

"Right," replied the commissioner, catching at the idea. "Right—it shall be done;" and with this laconic promise, he faced once more to the council of chiefs.

"Brothers!" he said, resuming the tone in which he had first addressed them, "for, as the brave chief Holata has said, we are all brothers. Why, then, should we separate in anger? Your Great Father would be sad to hear that we had so parted from one another. I do not wish you hastily to decide upon this important matter. Return to your tents—hold your own councils—discuss the matter freely and fairly among yourselves, and let us meet again to-morrow; the loss of a day will not signify to either of us. To-morrow will be time enough to give your decision; till then, let us be friends and brothers."

To this harangue, several of the chiefs replied. They said it was "good talk," and they would agree to it; and then all arose to depart from the ground.

I noticed that there was some confusion in the replies. The chiefs were not unanimous in their assent. Those who agreed were principally of the Omatla party; but I could hear some of the hostile warriors, as they strode away from the ground, declare aloud their intention to return no more.

Note 1. The child follows the fortunes of the mother. The usage is not Seminole only, but the same with all the Indians of America.

Note 2. *Magnolia grandiflora.* So styled in the language of the Indians.

Chapter Thirty.

Talk over the Table.

Over the mess-table I gathered much knowledge. Men talk freely while the wine is flowing, and under the influence of champagne, the wisest grow voluble.

The commissioner made little secret either of his own designs or the views of the President, but most already guessed them.

He was somewhat gloomed at the manner in which the day's proceedings had ended, and by the reflection that his diplomatic fame would suffer—a fame ardently aspired to by all agents of the United States government. Personal slights, too, had he received from Osceola and others—for the calm cold Indian holds in scorn the man of hasty temper; and this weakness had he displayed to their derision throughout the day. He felt defeated, humiliated, resentful against the men of red skin. On the morrow, he flattered himself that he would make them feel the power of his resentment—teach them that, if passionate, he was also firm and daring.

As the wine warmed him, he said as much in a half boasting way; he became more reckless and jovial.

As for the military officers, they cared little for the *civil* points of the case, and took not much part in the discussion of its merits. Their speculations ran upon the probability of strife—war, or no war? That was the question of absorbing interest to the men of the sword. I heard much boasting of *our* superiority, and decrying of the strength and the courage of the prospective enemy. But to this, there were dissentient opinions expressed by a few old "Indian fighters" who were of the mess.

It is needless to say that Oceola's character was commented upon; and about the young chief, opinions were as different as vice from virtue. With some, he was the "noble savage" he seemed; but I was astonished to find the majority dissent from this view. "Drunken savage," "cattle thief," "impostor," and such-like appellations were freely bestowed upon him.

I grew irate; I could not credit these accusations. I observed that most of those who made them were comparative strangers—new comers—to the country, who could not know much of the past life of him with whose name they were making so free.

The Ringgolds joined in the calumny, and they must have known him well; but I comprehended *their* motives.

I felt that I owed the subject of the conversation a word of defence; for two reasons: he was absent—he had saved my life. Despite the grandeur of the company, I could not restrain my tongue.

"Gentlemen," I said, speaking loud enough to call the attention of the talkers, "can any of you prove these accusations against Osceola?"

The challenge produced an awkward silence. No one could exactly prove either the drunkenness, the cattle-stealing, or the imposture.

"Ha?" at length ejaculated Arens Ringgold, in his shrill squeaky voice, "you are his defender, are you, Lieutenant Randolph?"

"Until I hear better evidence than mere assertion, that he is not worthy of defence."

"Oh! that may be easily obtained," cried one; "everybody knows what the fellow is, and has been—a regular cow-stealer for years."

"You are mistaken there," I replied to this confident speaker; "I do not know it—do you, sir?"

"Not from personal experience, I admit," said the accuser, somewhat taken aback by the sudden interrogation.

"Since you are upon the subject of cattle-stealing, gentlemen, I may inform you that I met with a rare incident only yesterday, connected with the matter. If you will permit me, I shall relate it."

"Oh! certainly—by all means, let us have it."

Being a stranger, I was indulged with a patient hearing. I related the episode of lawyer Grubb's cattle, omitting names. It created some sensation. I saw that the commander-in-chief was impressed with it, while the commissioner looked vexed, as if he would rather I had held my tongue. But the strongest effect was produced upon the Ringgolds—father and son. Both appeared pale and uneasy; perhaps no one noticed this except myself, but I observed it with sufficient distinctness to be left under the full impression, that both knew more of the matter than I myself!

The conversation next turned upon "runaways"—upon the number of negroes there might be among the tribes—upon the influence they would exert against us in case of a conflict.

These were topics of serious importance. It was well-known there were large numbers of black and yellow men "located," in the reserve: some as agriculturists—some graziers—not a few wandering through the savannas and forests, rifle in hand—having adopted the true style of Indian hunter-life.

The speakers estimated their numbers variously: the lowest put them at 500, while some raised their figure to a 1000.

All these would be against us to a man. There was no dissent to that proposition.

Some alleged they would fight badly; others, bravely; and these spoke with more reason. All agreed that they would greatly aid the enemy, and give us trouble, and a few went so far as to say, that we had more to fear from the "black runaways" than the "red runaways." In this expression, there was a latent jest.

(The Seminoles were originally of the great tribe of Muscogees (Creeks). Seceding from these, for reasons not known, the Seminoles passed southward into Florida; and obtained from their former kindred the name they now bear, which in their own tongue has the signification of "runaway.")

65

There could be no doubt that the negroes would take up arms in the pending struggle; and no more, that they would act with efficiency against us. Their knowledge of the white man's "ways" would enable them to do so. Besides, the negro is no coward; their courage has been ofttimes proved. Place him in front of a *natural* enemy—a thing of flesh, bone, and blood, armed with gun and bayonet—and the negro is not the man to flinch. It is otherwise if the foe be not physical, but belonging to the world of Obeah. In the soul of the unenlightened child of Afric, superstition is strong indeed; he lives in a world of ghosts, ghouls, and goblins, and his dread of these supernatural spirits is real cowardice.

As the conversation continued on the subject of the blacks, I could not help noticing the strong animus that actuated the speakers—especially the planters in the civilian garb. Some waxed indignant—even wroth to vulgarity—threatening all sorts of punishment to such runaways as might be captured. They gloated over the prospect of restoration, but as much at the idea of a not distant revenge. Shooting, hanging, burning, *barbecuing*, were all spoken of, besides a variety of other tortures peculiar to this southern land. Rare punishments—no lack of them—were promised in a breath to the unfortunate absconder who should chance to get caught.

You who live far away from such sentiments can but ill comprehend the moral relations of caste and colour. Under ordinary circumstances, there exists between white and black no feeling of hostility—quite the contrary. The white man is rather kindly disposed towards his coloured *brother*, but only so long as the latter opposes not his will. Let the black but offer resistance—even in the slightest degree—and then hostility is quickly kindled, justice and mercy are alike disregarded—vengeance is only felt.

This is a general truth; it will apply to every one who owns a slave.

Exceptionally, the relation is worse. There are white my in the southern States who hold the life of a black at but slight value—just the value of his market price. An incident in the history of young Ringgold helps me to an illustration. But the day before, my "squire," Black Jake had given me the story.

This youth, with some other boys of his acquaintance, and of like dissolute character, was hunting in the forest. The hounds had passed beyond hearing, and no one could tell the direction they had taken. It was useless riding further, and the party halted, leaped from their saddles, and tied their horses to the trees.

For a long time the baying of the beagles was not heard, and the time hung heavily on the hands of the hunters. How were they to pass it?

A negro boy chanced to be near "chopping" wood. They knew the boy well enough—one of the slaves on a neighbouring plantation.

"Let's us have some sport with the darkie," suggested one.

"What sport?"

"Let us hang him for sport."

The proposal of course produced a general laugh.

"Joking apart," said the first speaker, "I should really like to try how much hanging a nigger *could* bear without being killed outright."

"So should I," rejoined a second.

"And so I, too," added a third.

The idea took; the experiment promised to amuse them.

"Well, then, let us make trial; that's the best way to settle the point."

The trial *was* made—I am relating a *fact*—the unfortunate boy was seized upon, a noose was adjusted round his neck, and he was triced up to the branch of a tree.

Just at that instant, a stag broke past with the hounds in full cry. The hunters ran to their horses, and in the excitement, forgot to cut down the victim of their deviltry. One left the duty to another, and all neglected it!

When the chase was ended, they returned to the spot; the negro was still hanging from the branch—he was dead!

There was a trial—the mere mockery of a trial. Both judge and jury were the relatives of the criminals; and the sentence was, that the negro *should be paid for*! The owner of the slave was contented with the price; justice was satisfied, or supposed to be; and Jake had heard hundreds of white Christians, *who knew the tale to be true*, laughing at it as a capital joke. As such, Arens Ringgold was often in the habit of detailing it!

You on the other side of the Atlantic hold up your hands and cry "Horror!" You live in the fancy you have no slaves—no cruelties like this. You are sadly in error. I have detailed an exceptional case—an individual victim. Land of the workhouse and the jail! your victims are legion.

Smiling Christian! you parade your compassion, but you have made the misery that calls it forth. You abet with easy concurrence the *system* that begets all this suffering; and although you may soothe your spirit by assigning crime and poverty to *natural causes*, nature will not be impugned with impunity. In vain may you endeavour to shirk your individual responsibility. For every cry and canker, you will be held responsible in the sight of God.

The conversation about runaways naturally guided my thoughts to the other and more mysterious adventure of yesterday; having dropped a hint about this incident, I was called upon to relate it in detail. I did so—of course scouting the idea that my intended assassin could have been Yellow Jake. A good many of those present knew the story of the mulatto, and the circumstances connected with his death.

Why was it, when I mentioned his name, coupled with the solemn declaration of my sable groom—why was it that Arens Ringgold started, turned pale, and whispered some words in the ear of his father?

Chapter Thirty One.

The Traitor Chiefs.

Soon after, I retired from the mess-table, and strolled out into the stockade.

It was now after sunset. Orders had been issued for no one to leave the fort; but translating these as only applicable to the common soldier, I resolved to sally forth.

I was guided by an impulse of the heart. In the Indian camp were the wives of the chiefs and warriors—their sisters and children—why not she among the rest?

I had a belief that she was there—although, during all that day, my eyes had been wandering in vain search. She was not among those who had crowded around the council: not a face had escaped my scrutiny.

I resolved to seek the Seminole camp—to go among the tents of the Micosaucs— there, in all likelihood, I should find Powell—there I should meet with Maümee.

There would be no danger in entering the Indian camp—even the hostile chiefs were yet in relations of friendship with us; and surely Powell was still *my* friend? He could protect me from peril or insults.

I felt a longing to grasp the hand of the young warrior, that of itself would have influenced me to seek the interview. I yearned to renew the friendly confidence of the past— to talk over those pleasant times—to recall those scenes of halcyon brightness. Surely the sterner duties of the chief and war-leader had not yet indurated a heart, once mild and amiable? No doubt the spirit of my former friend was embittered by the white man's injustice; no doubt I should find him rancorous against our race; he had reason—still I had no fears that I myself was not an exception to this wholesale resentment.

Whatever the result, I resolved to seek him, and once more extend to him the hand of friendship.

I was on the eve of setting forth, when a summons from the commander-in-chief called me to his quarters. With some chagrin, I obeyed the order.

I found the commissioner there, with the officers of higher rank—the Ringgolds and several other civilians of distinction.

On entering, I perceived that they were in "caucus," and had just ended the discussion of some plan of procedure.

"The design is excellent," observed General Clinch, addressing himself to the others; "but how are Omatla and 'Black Dirt' (Note 1) to be met? If we summon them hither, it may create suspicion; they could not enter the fort without being observed."

67

"General Clinch," said the elder Ringgold—the most cunning diplomatist of the party—"if you and General Thompson were to meet the friendly chiefs outside?"

"Exactly so," interrupted the commissioner. "I have been thinking of that. I have sent a messenger to Omatla, to inquire if he can give us a secret meeting. It will be best to see them outside. The man has returned—I hear him."

At this moment, a person entered the room, whom I recognised as one of the interpreters who had officiated at the council. He whispered something to the commissioner, and then withdrew.

"All right, gentlemen!" exclaimed the latter, as the interpreter went out; "Omatla will meet us within the hour. Black Dirt will be with him. They have named the 'Sink' as the place. It lies to the north of the fort. We can reach it without passing the camp, and there will be no risk of our being observed. Shall we go, General?"

"I am ready," replied Clinch, taking up his cloak, and throwing it over his shoulders; "but, General Thompson," said he, turning to the commissioner, "how about your interpreters? Can they be intrusted with a secret of so much importance?"

The commissioner appeared to hesitate. "It might be imprudent," he replied at length, in a half soliloquy.

"Never mind, then—never mind," said Clinch; "I think we can do without them. Lieutenant Randolph," continued he, turning to me, "you speak the Seminole tongue fluently?"

"Not fluently, General; I speak it, however."

"You could interpret it fairly."

"Yes, General; I believe so."

"Very well, then; that will do. Come with us!"

Smothering my vexation, at being thus diverted from my design, I followed in silence—the commissioner leading the way, while the General, disguised in cloak and plain forage cap, walked by his side.

We passed out of the gate, and turned northward around the stockade. The tents of the Indians were upon the southwest, placed irregularly along the edge of a broad belt of "hommocky" woods that extended in that direction. Another tract of hommock lay to the north, separated from the larger one by savannas and open forests of pine timber. Here was the "Sink." It was nearly half a mile distant from the stockade; but in the darkness we could easily reach it without being observed from any part of the Seminole camp.

We soon arrived upon the ground. The chiefs were before us. We found them standing under the shadows of the trees by the edge of the pond.

My duty now began. I had little anticipation that it was to have been so disagreeable.

"Ask Omatla what is the number of his people—also those of Black Dirt, and the other chiefs who are for us."

I put the question as commanded.

"One-third of the whole Seminole nation," was the ready reply.

"Tell them that ten thousand dollars shall be given to the friendly chiefs, on their arrival in the west, to be shared among them as they deem best—that this sum is independent of the appropriation to the whole tribe."

"It is good," simultaneously grunted the chiefs, when the proposition was explained to them.

"Does Omatla and his friends think that all the chiefs will be present to-morrow?"

"No—not all."

"Which of them are likely to be absent?"

"The mico-mico will not be there."

"Ha! Is Omatla sure of that?"

"Sure. Onopa's tents are struck: he has already left the ground."

"Whither has he gone?"

"Back to his town."

"And his people?"

"Most of them gone with him."

For some moments the two generals communicated together in a half whisper. They were apart from me: I did not not hear what they said. The information just acquired was of great importance, and seemed not to discontent them.

"Any other chief likely to be absent to-morrow?" they asked, after a pause.

"Only those of the tribe of 'redsticks.'" (Note 2.)

"Hoitle-mattee?"

"No—he is here—he will remain."

"Ask them if they think *Osceola* will be at the council to-morrow."

From the eagerness with which the answer was expected, I could perceive that this was the most interesting question of all. I put it directly.

"What!" exclaimed the chiefs, as if astonished at the interrogatory. "The Rising Sun! He is sure to be present: he will *see it out!*"

"Good!" involuntarily ejaculated the commissioner, and then turning to the General, he once more addressed him in a low tone. This time, I overheard what passed between them.

"It seems, General, as if Providence was playing into our hands. My plan is almost sure to succeed. A word will provoke the impudent rascal to some rudeness—perhaps worse—at all events, I shall easily fix a pretext for shutting him up. Now that Onopa has drawn off his following, we will be strong enough for any contingency. The hostiles will scarcely outnumber the friendly, so that there will no chance of the rascals making resistance."

"Oh! that we need not fear."

"Well—with *him* once in our power the opposition will be crushed—the rest will yield easily—for, beyond doubt, it is that now intimidates and hinders them from signing."

"True," replied Clinch in a reflective tone; "but how about the government, eh? Will it endorse the act, think you?"

"It will—it must—my latest dispatch from the President almost suggests as much. If you agree to act, I shall take the risk."

"Oh, I place myself under your orders," replied the commander-in-chief, evidently inclined to the commissioner's views, but still not willing to share the responsibility. "It is but my duty to carry out the will of the executive. I am ready to coöperate with you."

"Enough then—it shall be done as we have designed it. Ask the chiefs," continued the speaker, addressing himself to me, "ask them, if they have any fear of signing to-morrow."

"No—not of the signing, but *afterwards.*"

"And what afterwards?"

"They dread an attack from the hostile party—their lives will be in danger."

"What would they have us do?"

"Omatla says, if you will permit him and the other head chiefs to go on a visit to their friends at Tallahassee, it will keep them out of danger. They can stay there till the removal is about to take place. They give their promise that they will meet you at Tampa, or elsewhere, whenever you summon them."

The two generals consulted together—once more in whispers. This unexpected proposal required consideration.

Omatla added:

"If we are not allowed to go to Tallahassee, we cannot, we dare not, stay at home; we must come under the protection of the fort."

"About your going to Tallahassee," replied the commissioner, "we shall consider it, and give you an answer to-morrow. Meanwhile, you need not be under any apprehension. This is the war-chief of the whites; he will protect you."

"Yes," said Clinch, drawing himself proudly up. "My warriors are numerous and strong. There are many in the fort, and many more on the way. You have nothing to fear."

"It is good!" rejoined the chiefs. "If troubles arise, we shall seek your protection; you have promised it—it is good."

"Ask the chiefs," said the commissioner, to whom a new question had suggested itself—"ask them if they know whether Holata Mico will remain for the council of to-morrow."

"We cannot tell now. Holata Mico has not declared his intention. We shall soon know it. If he designs to stay his tents will stand till the rising of the sun; if not, they will be struck before the moon goes down. The moon is sinking—we shall soon know whether Holata Mico will go or stay."

"The tents of this chief are not within sight of the fort?"

"No—they are back among the trees."

"Can you send word to us?"

"Yes, but only to this place; our messenger would be seen entering the fort. We can come back here ourselves, and meet one from you."

"True—it is better so," replied the commissioner, apparently pleased with the arrangement.

A few minutes passed, during which the two generals communicated with each other in while whispers, the chiefs stood apart, silent and immobile as a pair of statues.

The commander-in-chief at length broke the silence:

"Lieutenant! you will remain upon the ground till the chiefs return. Get their report, and bring it direct to my quarters."

Salutations were exchanged; the two generals walked off on the path that led to the fort, while the chiefs glided silently away in the opposite direction. I was left alone.

Note 1. So Lusta Hajo was called by the Americans. His full name was Fuchta-Lusta-Hajo, which signifies "Black Crazy Clay."

Note 2. A name given to the Micosaucs, from their custom of setting up red poles in front of their houses when going to war. A similar custom exists among other tribes; hence the name "Baton Rouge," applied by the French colonists.

Chapter Thirty Two.

Shadows in the Water.

Alone with my thoughts, and these tainted with considerable acerbity. More than one cause contributed to their bitterness. My pleasant purpose thwarted—my heart aching for knowledge—for a renewal of tender ties—distracted with doubts—wearied with protracted suspense.

In addition to these, my mind was harassed by other emotions I experienced disgust at the part I had been playing. I had been made the mouth-piece of chicanery and wrong; aiding conspiracy had been the first act of my warlike career; and although it was not the act of my own will, I felt the disagreeableness of the duty—a sheer disgust in its performance.

Even the loveliness of the night failed to soothe me. Its effect was contrary; a storm would have been more congenial to my spirit.

And it was a lovely night. Both the earth and the air were at peace.

Here and there the sky was fleeced with white cirrhi, but so thinly, that the moon's disk, passing behind them, appeared to move under a transparent gauze-work of silver, without losing one ray of her effulgence. Her light was resplendent in the extreme; and, glancing from the glabrous leaves of the great laurels, caused the forests to sparkle, as though beset with a million of mirrors. To add to the effect, fire-flies swarmed under the shadows of the trees, their bodies lighting up the dark aisles with a mingled coruscation of red, blue and gold—now flitting in a direct line, now curving, or waving upward and downward, as though moving through the mazes of some intricate *cotillon*.

In the midst of all this glittering array, lay the little tarn, shining, too, but with the gleam of plated glass—a mirror in its framework of fretted gild.

The atmosphere was redolent of the most agreeable perfumes. The night was cool enough for human comfort, but not chill. Many of the flowers refused to close their corollas—for not all of them were brides of the sun. The moon had its share of the sweets.

The sassafras and bay-trees were in blossom, and dispensed their odours around, that, mingling with the aroma of the aniseed and the orange, created a delicious fragrance in the air.

There was a stillness in the atmosphere, but not silence. It is never silent in the southern forests by night. Tree-frogs and cicadas utter their shrillest notes after the sun has gone out of sight, and there is a bird that makes choice melody during the moonlight hours—the famed mimic of the American woods. One, perched upon a tall tree that grew over the edge of the pond, appeared trying to soothe my chafed spirit with his sweet notes.

I heard other sounds—the hum of the soldiery in the fort, mingling with the more distant noises from the Indian camp, now and then some voice louder than the rest, in oath, exclamation, or laughter, broke forth to interrupt the monotonous murmur.

How long should I have to wait the return of the chiefs? It might be an hour, or two hours, or more? I had a partial guide in the moon. They said that Holata would depart before the shining orb went down, or not at all. About two hours, then, would decide the point, and set me free.

I had been standing for half the day. I cared not to keep my feet any longer; and choosing a fragment of rock near the water's edge, I sat down upon it:

My eyes wandered over the pond. Half of its surface lay in shadow; the other half was silvered by the moonbeams, that, penetrating the pellucid water, rendered visible the white shells and shining pebbles at the bottom. Along the line where the light and darkness met, were outlined several noble palms, whose tall stems and crested crowns appeared stretching towards the nadir of the earth—as though they belonged to another and a brighter firmament beneath my feet. The trees, of which these were but the illusory images, grew upon the summit of a ridge, which, trending along the western side of the pond, intercepted the rays of the moon.

I sat for some time gazing into this counterpart of heaven's canopy, with my eyes mechanically tracing the great fan-like fronds.

All at once, I was startled at perceiving a new image upon the aqueous reflector. A form, or rather the shadow of one, suddenly appeared among the trunks of the palms. It was upright, and evidently human, though of magnified proportions—beyond a doubt, a human figure, yet not that of a man.

The small head, apparently uncovered, the gentle rounding of the shoulders, the soft undulation of the waist, and the long, loose draping which reached nearly to the ground, convinced me that the shadow was that of a woman.

When I first observed it, it was moving among the stems of the palm-trees; presently it stopped, and for some seconds remained in a fixed attitude. It was then I noted the peculiarities that distinguish the sex.

My first impulse was to turn round, and, if possible, get a sight of the figure that cast this interesting shadow. I was myself on the western edge of the pond, and the ridge was behind me. Facing round I could not see the summit nor yet the palms. Rising to my feet, I still could not see them: a large live-oak, under which I had seated myself, intercepting my view.

I stepped hastily to one side, and then both the outline of the ridge and the palm-trees were before my eyes; but I could see no figure, neither of man nor woman.

I scanned the summit carefully, but no living thing was there; some fronds of the saw-palmetta, standing along the crest, were the only forms I could perceive.

I returned to where I had been seated; and, placing myself as before, again looked upon the water. The palm shadows were there, just as I had left them; but the image was gone.

There was nothing to be astonished at. I did not for a moment believe myself under any delusion. Some one had been upon the ridge—a woman, I supposed—and had passed down under the cover of the trees. This was the natural explanation of what I had seen, and of course contented me.

At the same time, the silent apparition could not fail to arouse my curiosity; and instead of remaining seated, and giving way to dreamy reflections, I rose to my feet, and stood looking and listening with eager expectation.

71

Who could the woman be? An Indian, of course. It was not probable that a white woman should be in such a place, and at such an hour. Even the peculiar outlines of the shadow were not those that would have been cast by one habited in a garb of civilisation: beyond a doubt, the woman was an Indian.

What was she doing in that solitary place, and alone?

These questions were not so easily answered; and yet there was nothing so remarkable about her presence upon the spot. To the children of the forest, time is not as with us. The hours of the night are as those of the day—often the hours of action or enjoyment. She might have many a purpose in being there. She might be on her way to the pond for water—to take a bath; or it might be some impassioned maiden, who, under the secret shadows of this secluded grove, was keeping assignation with her lover.

A pang, like a poisoned arrow, passed through my heart: "*might it be Maümee?*"

The unpleasantness which this conjecture caused me is indescribable. I had been all day the victim of dire suspicions, arising from some half-dozen words, casually dropped from the lips of a young officer, and which I had chanced to overhear. They had reference to a beautiful girl among the Indians, apparently well-known at the fort; and I noticed that the tone of the young fellow was that of one either triumphant or boasting. I listened attentively to every word, and watched not only the countenance of the speaker, but those of his auditory—to make out in which of the two categories I should place him. His vanity appeared to have had some sacrifice made to it—at least by his own statement; and his listeners, or most of them, agreed to concede to him the happiness of a *bonne fortune*. There was no name given—no hint that would enable me to connect the subject of the conversation with that of my own thoughts; but that the girl was an Indian, and a "beauty," were points, that my jealous heart almost accepted as sufficient for identification.

I might easily have become satisfied. A word, a simple question, would have procured me the knowledge I longed for; and yet I dared not say that word. I preferred passing long hours—a whole day—upon the rack of uncertainty and suspicion.

Thus, then, was I prepared for the painful conjectures that sprang into my thoughts on beholding that mirrored form.

The pain was of short duration; almost instantaneous was the relief. A shadowy figure was seen gliding around the edge of the pond; it emerged into the open moonlight, not six paces from where I stood. I had a full and distinct view of it. It was a woman—an Indian woman. It was *not* Maümee.

Chapter Thirty Three.

Haj-Ewa.

I saw before me a woman of middle age—somewhere between thirty and forty—a large woman, who once possessed beauty—beauty that had been abused. She was the wreck of a grand loveliness, whose outlines could not be effaced—like the statue of some Grecian goddess, broken by Vandal hands, but whose very fragments are things of priceless value.

Not that her charms had departed. There are men who affect to admire this ripe maturity; to them, she would have been a thing of peerless splendour. Time had made no inroad upon those large rounded arms, none upon the elliptical outlines of that noble bust. I could judge of this—for it was before my eyes, in the bright moonlight, nude, from neck to waist, as in the hour of infancy. Alone the black hair, hanging in wild dishevelment over the shoulders, formed a partial shrouding. Nor had time laid a finger upon this: amidst all that profusion of rich raven clusters, not a strand of silver could be detected.

Time could not affect, nor had it, that fine facial outline. The moulding of the chin; the oval of those lips; the aquiline nose, with its delicate spirally curved nostril; the high, smooth front; the eye—the eye—what is it? why that unearthly flash? that wild unmeaning glance? Ha! that eye—Merciful heavens! *the woman is mad!*

Alas! it was true—she was mad. Her glance would have satisfied even a casual observer, that reason was no longer upon its throne. But I needed not to look at her eye; I knew the story of her misfortunes, of her wrongs. It was not the first time I had looked upon that womanly form—more than once I had stood face to face with Haj-Ewa (Note 1), the mad queen of the Micosaucs.

Beautiful as she was, I might have felt fear at her presence—still worse than fear, I might have been terrified or awed—the more so on perceiving that her necklace was a green serpent; that the girdle around her waist, that glittered so conspicuously in the light of the moon, was the body of an enormous rattlesnake, living and writhing!

Yes, both were alive—the smaller serpent wound about her neck, with its head resting upon her bosom; the more dangerous reptile knotted around her waist, its vertebrated tail hanging by her side, while its head, held in her hand, protruding through her fingers, exhibited a pair of eyes that scintillated like diamonds.

On the head of Haj-Ewa was no other covering than that which nature had provided for it; but those thick black clusters afforded ample protection against sun and storm. On her feet she wore moccasins, but those were hidden by the long "hunna," that reached to the ground. This was the only garment she wore. It was profusely adorned with beads and embroidery—with the bright plumage of the green parroquet—the skin of the summer-duck, and the for of various wild animals. It was fastened round her waist, though not by the girdle already described.

Truly, I might have felt terror, had this singular appearance been new to me. But I had seen all before—the green snake, and the crotalus, the long hanging tresses, the wild flash of that maniac eye—all before, all harmless, all innocuous—at least to me. I knew it, and had no fear.

"Haj-Ewa!" I called out, as she advanced to where I was standing.

"I-e-ela!" (an expression of astonishment, usually lengthened out into a sort of drawl) exclaimed she with a show of surprise.

"Young Randolph! war-chief among the pale-faces! You have not then forgotten poor Haj-Ewa?"

"No, Ewa, I have not. What seek you here?"

"Yourself, little mico."

"Seek *me*?"

"No—I have found you."

"And what want you with me?"

"Only to save your life, your young of life, pretty mico—your fair life—your precious life—ah! precious to her, poor bird of the forest! Ah! there was one precious to me—long, long ago. Ho, ho, ho!

"O why did I trust in a pale-faced lover?

Ho, ho, ho! (Literally, Yes, yes, yes!)
Why did I meet him in the wild woods' cover?
Ho, ho, ho!
Why did I list to his lying tongue,
That poisoned my heart when my life was young?
Ho, ho, ho!

"Down, *chitta mico!*" (Note 1) she cried, interrupting the strain, and addressing herself to the rattlesnake, that at my presence had protruded his head, and was making demonstrations of rage—"down, great king of the serpents! 'tis a friend, though in the garb of an enemy—quiet, or I crush your head!"

"I-e-ela!" she exclaimed again, as if struck by some new thought; "I waste time with my old songs; he is gone, he is gone! they cannot bring him back. Now, young mico, what came I for? what came I for?"

As she uttered these interrogatives, she raised her hand to her head, as if to assist her memory.

"Oh! now I remember. *Hulwak* (it is bad). I lose time. You may be killed, young mico—you may be killed, and then—Go! begone, begone, begone! back to the topekee (fort). Shut yourself up; keep among your people: do not stray from your blue soldiers; do not wander in the woods! Your life is in danger."

All this was spoken in a tone of earnestness that astonished me. More than astonished, I began to feel some slight alarm, since I had not forgotten the attempted assassination of yesterday. Moreover, I knew that there were periods when this singular woman was not positively insane. She had her lucid intervals, during which she both talked and acted rationally, and often with extraordinary intelligence. This might be one of those intervals. She might be privy to some scheme against my life, and had come, as she alleged, to defeat it.

But who was my enemy or enemies? and how could she have known of their design?

In order to ascertain this, I said to her:

"I have no enemy, Ewa; why should my life be in danger?"

"I tell you, pretty mico, it is—you have enemies. I-e-ela! you do not know it?"

"I never wronged a red man in my life."

"Red—did I say red man? *Cooree* (boy), pretty Randolph, there is not a red man in all the land of the Seminoles that would pluck a hair from your head. Oh! if they did, what would say the Rising Sun? He would consume them like a forest fire. Fear not the red men—your enemies are not of that colour."

"Ha! not red men? What, then?"

"Some white—some yellow."

"Nonsense, Ewa! I have never given a white man cause to be my enemy."

"*Chepawnee* (fawn) you are but a young fawn, whose mother has not told it of the savage beasts that roam the forest. There are wicked men who are enemies without a cause. There are some who seek your life, though you never did them wrong."

"But who are they? And for what reason?"

"Do not ask, chepawnee! There is not time. Enough if I tell you, you are owner of a rich plantation, where black men make the blue dye. You have a fair sister—very fair. Is she not like a beam from yonder moon? And I was fair once—so he said. Ah! it is bad to be beautiful Ho, ho, ho!

"Why did I trust in a pale-faced lover?

Ho, ho, ho! Why did I meet him—

"*Hulwak!*" she exclaimed, again suddenly breaking off the strain: "I am mad; but I remember. Go! begone! I tell you, go: you are but an *echochee* (fawn), and the hunters are upon your trail. Back to the topekee—go! go!"

"I cannot, Ewa; I am here for a purpose; I must remain till some one comes."

"Till some one comes! *hulwak! they* will come soon."

"Who?"

"Your enemies—they who would kill you; and then the pretty doe will bleed—her poor heart will bleed: she will go mad—she will be like Haj-Ewa."

"Whom do you speak of?"

"Of—Hush! hush! hush! It is too late—they come—they come! see their shadows upon the water!"

I looked, as Haj-Ewa pointed. Sure enough there were shadows upon the pond, just where I had seen hers. They were the figures of men—four of them. They were moving among the palm-trees, and along the ridge.

In a few seconds the shadows disappeared. They who had been causing them had descended the slope, and entered among the timber.

"It is too late now," whispered the maniac, evidently at that moment in full possession of her intellect. "You dare not go out into the open woods. They would see you—you must stay in the thicket. There!" continued she, grasping me by the wrist, and, with a powerful jerk, bringing me close to the trunk of the live-oak: "this is your only chance. Quick—ascend! Conceal yourself among the moss. Be silent—stir not till I return. *Hinklas!*" (It is good—it is well.)

And so saying, my strange counsellor stepped back under the shadow of the tree; and, gliding into the umbrageous covert of the grove, disappeared from my sight.

I had followed her directions, and was now ensconced upon one of the great limbs of the live-oak—perfectly hidden from the eyes of any one below by festoons of the silvery *tillandsia*. These, hanging from branches still higher up, draped around me like a set of gauze curtains, and completely enveloped my whole body; while I myself had a view of the

74

pond—at least, that side of it on which the moon was shining—by means of a small opening between the leaves.

At first I fancied I was playing a very ridiculous *rôle*. The story about enemies, and my life being in danger, might, after all, be nothing more than some crazy fancy of the poor maniac's brain. The men, whose shadows I had seen, might be the chiefs on their return. They would reach the ground where I had appointed to meet them, and not finding me there, would go back. What kind of report should I carry to head-quarters? The thing was ridiculous enough—and for me, the result might be worse than ridiculous.

Under these reflections, I felt strongly inclined to descend, and meet the men—whoever they might be—face to face.

Other reflections, however, hindered me. The chiefs were only *two*—there were *four* shadows. True, the chiefs might be accompanied by some of their followers—for better security to themselves on such a traitorous mission—but I had noticed, as the shadows were passing over the pond—and notwithstanding the rapidity with which they moved—that the figures were not *those of Indians*. I observed no hanging drapery, nor plumes. On the contrary, I fancied there were *hats* upon their heads, such as are worn only by white men. It was the observation of this peculiarity that made me so ready to yield obedience to the solicitations of Haj-ewa.

Other circumstances had not failed to impress me: the strange assertions made by the Indian woman—her knowledge of events, and the odd allusions to well-known persons—the affair of yesterday: all these, commingling in my mind, had the effect of determining me to remain upon my perch, at least for some minutes longer. I might be relieved from my unpleasant position sooner than I expected.

Without motion, almost without breathing, I kept my seat, my eyes carefully watching, and ears keenly bent to catch every sound.

My suspense was brief. The acuteness of my eyes was rewarded by a sight, and my ears by a tale, that caused my flesh to creep, and the blood to run cold in my veins. In five minutes' time, I was inducted into a belief in the wickedness of the human heart, exceeding in enormity all that I had ever read or heard of.

Four demons filed before me—demons, beyond a doubt: their looks, which I noted well—their words, which I heard—their gestures, which I saw—their designs, with which I in that hour became acquainted—fully entitled them to the appellation.

They were passing around the pond. I saw their faces, one after another, as they emerged into the moonlight.

Foremost appeared the pale, thin visage of Arens Ringgold; next, the sinister aquiline features of Spence; and, after him, the broad brutal face of the bully Williams.

There were *four*—who was the fourth?

"Am I dreaming?—Do my eyes deceive me? Is it real? Is it an illusion? Are my senses gone astray—or is it only a resemblance, a counterpart? No—no—no! It is no counterpart, but the man himself!—that black curling hair, that tawny skin, the form, the gait—all, all are his. O God! it is Yellow Jake!"

Note 1. Literally, "crazy wife," from *Haja*, crazy, and *Ewa* or *Awa*, wife. Philologists have remarked the resemblance of this Muscogee word to the Hebraic name of the mother of mankind.

Note 2. "Chief of the snakes"—the rattlesnake is so styled by the Seminoles, being the most remarkable serpent in their country. They have a superstitions dread of this reptile.

Chapter Thirty Four.

A Pretty Plot.

To dispute the identity was to doubt the evidence of my senses. The mulatto was before me—just as I remembered him—though with changed apparel, and perhaps grown a little bigger in body. But the features were the same—that *tout ensemble* the same as that presented by Yellow Jake, the *ci-devant* woodman of our plantation.

And yet how could it *possibly* be he? And in the company of Arens Ringgold too, one of the most active of his intended executioners? No, no, no! altogether improbable—utterly impossible! Then must I be deluded—my eyes deceiving me—for as certain as I looked upon man, I was looking upon Jake the mulatto! He was not twenty feet from where I lay hidden; his face was full towards me; the moon was shining upon it with a brilliancy scarcely inferior to the light of day. I could note the old expression of evil in his eyes, and mark the play of his features. It *was* Yellow Jake.

To confirm the impression, I remembered that, notwithstanding all remonstrance and ridicule, the black pertinaciously adhered to his story. He would listen to no compromise, no hypothesis founded upon resemblance. He had seen Yellow Jake, or his ghost. This was his firm belief, and I had been unable to shake it.

Another circumstance I now remember: the strange behaviour of the Ringgolds during the postprandial conversation—the action of Arens when I mentioned the mulatto's name. It had attracted my attention at the time, but what was I to think now? Here was a man supposed to be dead, in company of three others who had been active in assisting at his death—one of them the very keenest of his executioners, and all four now apparently as thick as thieves! How was I to explain, in one moment, this wonderful resurrection and reconciliation?

I could not explain it—it was too complicated a mystery to be unravelled by a moment's reflection; and I should have failed, had not the parties themselves soon after aided me to an elucidation.

I had arrived at the only natural conclusion, and this was, that the mulatto, notwithstanding the perfect resemblance, *could not be* Yellow Jake. This, of course, would account for everything, after a manner; and had the four men gone away without parley, I should have contented myself with this hypothesis.

But they went not, until after affording me an opportunity of overhearing a conversation, which gave me to know, that, not only was Yellow Jake *still in the land of the living*, but that Haj-Ewa had spoken the truth, when she told me *my life was in danger.*

"Damn! he's not here, and yet where can he have gone?"

The ejaculation and interrogative were in the voice of Arens Ringgold, uttered in a tone of peevish surprise. Some one was sought for by the party who could not be found. Who that was, the next speaker made manifest.

There was a pause, and then reached my ears the voice of Bill Williams—which I easily recognised, from having heard it but the day before.

"You are sartint, Master Arens, he didn't sneak back to the fort 'long wi' the ginral?"

"Sure of it," replied Master Arens; "I was by the gate as they came in. There were only the two—the general and the commissioner. But the question is, did he leave the hommock along with them? There's where we played devil's fool with the business—in not getting here in time, and watching them as they left. But who'd have thought he was going to stay behind them; if I had only known that—You say," he continued, turning to the mulatto—"you say, *Jake*, you came direct from the Indian camp? He couldn't have passed you on the path."

"*Carajo! Señor* Aren! No?"

The voice, the old Spanish expression of profanity, just as I had heard them in my youth. If there had been doubt of the identity, it was gone. The testimony of my ears confirmed that of my eyes. The speaker was Yellow Jake.

"Straight from Seminole come. Cat no pass me on the road; I see her. Two chiefs me meet. I hide under the palmettoes; they no me see. *Carrambo!* no."

"Deuce take it! where can he have gone! There's no signs of him here. I know he *might have a reason* for paying a visit to the Indians—that I know; but how has he got round there without Jake seeing him!"

"What's to hinder him to hev goed round the tother road?"

"By the open plain?"

"Yes—that away."

76

"No—he would not be likely. There's only one way I can explain it: he must have come as far as the gate along with the general, and then kept down the stockade, and past the sutler's house—that's likely enough."

This was said by Ringgold in a sort of half soliloquy.

"Devils?" he exclaimed in an impatient tone, "we'll not get such a chance soon again."

"Ne'er a fear, Master Arens," said Williams—"ne'er a fear. Plenty o' chances, I kalkerlate—gobs o' chances sech times as these."

"We'll make chances," pithily added Spence, who now spoke for the first time in my hearing.

"Ay, but here was a chance for *Jake*—*he* must do it, boys; neither of you must have a hand in it. It *might leak out*; and then we'd all be in a pretty pickle. Jake can do it, and not harm himself, for *he's dead*, you know, and the law can't reach him! Isn't it so, my yellow boy?"

"*Carrambo! si, señor.* No fear have, Don Aren Ringgol; 'for long, I opportunity find. Jake you get rid of enemy—never hear more of him; soon Yellow Jake good chance have. Yesterday miss. She bad gun, Don Aren—not worth shuck gun."

"He has not yet returned inside the fort," remarked Ringgold, again speaking in a half soliloquy. "I think he has not. If no, then he should be at the camp. He must go back to-night. It may be after the moon goes down. He must cross the open ground in the darkness. You hear, Jake, what I am saying?"

"Si, señor; Jake hear all."

"And you know how to profit by the hint, eh?"

"*Carrambo*! si, señor. Jake know."

"Well, then, we must return. Hear me, Jake—if—"

Here the voice of the speaker fell into a half whisper, and I could not hear what was said. Occasionally there were phrases muttered so loudly that I could catch their sound, and from what had already transpired, was enabled to apprehend something of their signification. I heard frequently pronounced the names of Viola the quadroon, and that of my own sister; the phrases—"only one that stands in our way,"—"mother easily consent,"—"when I am master of the plantation,"—"pay you two hundred dollars."

These, with others of like import, satisfied me that between the two fiends some contract for the taking of my life had already been formed; and that this muttered dialogue was only a repetition of the terms of the hideous bargain!

No wonder that the cold sweat was oozing from my temples, and standing in bead-like drops upon my brow. No wonder that I sat upon my perch shaking like an aspen—far less with fear than with horror at the contemplated crime—absolute horror. I might have trembled in a greater degree, but that my nerves were to some extent stayed by the terrible indignation that was swelling up within my bosom.

I had sufficient command of my temper to remain silent; it was prudent I did so; had I discovered myself at that moment, I should never have left the ground alive. I felt certain of this, and took care to make no noise that might betray my presence.

And yet it was hard to hear four men coolly conspiring against one's life—plotting and bargaining it away like a piece of merchandise—each expecting some profit from the speculation!

My wrath was as powerful as my fears—almost too strong for prudence. There were four of them, all armed. I had sword and pistols; but this would not have made me a match for four desperadoes such as they. Had there been only two of them—only Ringgold and the mulatto—so desperate was my indignation, at that moment, I should have leaped from the tree and risked the encounter *coûte qui coûte*.

But I disobeyed the promptings of passion, and remained silent till they had moved away.

I observed that Ringgold and his brace of bullies went towards the fort, while the mulatto took the direction of the Indian camp.

Chapter Thirty Five.

Light after Darkness.

I stirred not till they were gone—till long after. In fact, my mind was in a state of bewilderment, that for some moments hindered me either from acting or thinking; and I sat as if glued to the branch. Reflection came at length, and I began to speculate upon what I had just heard and seen.

Was it a farce to frighten me? No, no—they were not the characters of a farce—not one of the four; and the re-appearance of Yellow Jake, partaking as it did of the wild and supernatural, was too dramatic, too serious to form an episode in comedy.

On the contrary, I had just listened to the prologue of an intended tragedy, of which I was myself to be the victim. Beyond doubt, these men had a design upon my life!

Four men, too, not one of whom could charge me with ever having done him a serious injury. I knew that all four disliked me, and ever had—though Spence and Williams could have no other cause of offence than what might spring from boyish grudge—long-forgotten by me; but doubtless their motive was Ringgold's. As for the mulatto, I could understand his hostility; though mistaken, it was of the deadliest kind.

But what was I to think of Arens Ringgold, the leader in this designed assassination? A man of some education—my equal in social rank—a gentleman!

O Arens Ringgold—Arens Ringgold! How was I to explain it? How account for conduct so atrocious, so fiendish?

I knew that this young man liked me but little—of late less than ever. I knew the cause too. I stood in the way of his relations with my sister—at least so thought he. And he had reason; for, since my father's death, I had spoken more freely of family affairs. I had openly declared that, with my consent, he should never be my brother; and this declaration had reached him. I could easily believe, therefore, that he was angry with me; but anger that would impel a man to such demoniac purpose, I could not comprehend.

And what meant those half-heard phrases—"one that stands in our way," "mother easily consent," "master of the plantation," coupled with the names of Viola and my sister? What meant they?

I could give them but one, and that a terrible interpretation—too fearful to dwell upon.

I could scarcely credit my senses, scarcely believe that I was not labouring under some horrid hallucination, some confusion of the brain produced by my having been *en rapport* with the maniac!

But no; the moon had been over them—my eyes open upon them—my ears open, and could not have deceived me. I saw what they did—I heard what they said. They designed to kill me!

"Ho, ho, young mico, you may come down. The *honowaw-hulwa* (bad men) are gone. *Hinklas!* Come down, pretty mico—down, down, down!"

I hastened to obey, and stood once more in the presence of the mad queen.

"Now you believe Haj-Ewa? Have an enemy, young mico? Ho—four enemies. Your life in danger? Ho? ho?"

"Ewa, you have saved my life; how am I to thank you for the service you have done me?"

"Be true to *her*—true—true—true."

"To whom?"

"Great Spirit! he has forgotten her! False young mico! false pale-face! Why did I save him? Why did I not let his blood fall to the ground?"

"Ewa!"

"*Hulwak, hulwak!* Poor forest-bird! the beauty-bird of all; her heart will sicken and die, her head will go mad."

"Ewa, explain."

"*Hulwak!* better he should die than desert her. Ho, ho! false pale-face, would that he had died before he broke poor Ewa's heart; then Ewa would have lost only her heart; but her head—her head, that is worse. Ho, ho, ho!

"Why did I trust in a pale-faced lover?

Ho, ho, ho!

Why did I meet him—"

"Ewa," I exclaimed with an earnestness that caused the woman to leave off her wild song, "tell me! of whom do you speak?"

"Great Spirit, hear what he asks! Of whom?—of whom? there is more than one. Ho, ho! there is more than one, and the true one forgotten. *Hulwak, hulwak!* what shall Ewa say? What tale can Ewa tell? Poor bird! her heart will bleed, and her brain be crushed. Ho, ho! There will be two Haj-Ewas—two mad queens of the Micosaucs."

"For Heaven's sake! keep me not in suspense. Tell me, Ewa, good Ewa, of whom are you speaking? Is it—"

The name trembled upon my tongue; I hesitated to pronounce it. Notwithstanding that my heart was full of delightful hope, from the confidence I felt of receiving an affirmative answer, I dreaded to put the question.

Not a great while did I hesitate; I had gone too far to recede. I had long waited to satisfy the wish of a yearning heart; I could wait no longer. Ewa might give me the satisfaction. I pronounced the words:

"Is it—Maümee?"

The maniac gazed upon me for some moments without speaking. The expression of her eye I could not read; for the last few minutes, it had been one of reproach and scorn. As I uttered the name, it changed to a look of bewilderment; and then her glance became fixed upon me, as if searching my thoughts.

"If it be Maümee," I continued, without awaiting her reply—for I was now carried away by the ardour of my resuscitated passion—"if it be she, know, Ewa, that her I love—Maümee I love."

"You love Maümee? You still love Maümee?" interrogated the maniac with startling quickness.

"Ay, Ewa—by my life—by my—"

"*Cooree, cooree!* swear not—*his* very oath. *Hulwak!* and he was false. Speak again, young mico? say you love Maümee—say you are true, but do not swear."

"True—true?"

"Hinklas!" cried the woman in a loud and apparently joyful tone—"*Hinklas!* the mico is true—the pretty pale-faced mico is true, and the *haintclitz* (the pretty one) will be happy."

Ho, ho!

Now for the love, the sweet young love

Under the tala tree (Palm, *Chamaerops palmetto*).

Who would not be like yonder dove—

The wild little dove—

The soft little dove—

Sitting close by his mate in the shade of the grove—

Co-cooing to his mate in the shade of the grove,

With none to hear or see?

"Down, *chitta mico!*" she exclaimed, once more addressing the rattlesnake; "and you, *ocola chitta!* (Green snake.) Be quiet both. It is *not* an enemy. Quiet, or I crush your heads!"

"Good Ewa—"

"Ho! you call me good Ewa. Some day, you may call me bad Ewa. Hear me!" she continued, raising her voice, and speaking with increased earnestness—"hear me, George Randolph! If ever you are bad—false like *him*, like *him*, then Haj-Ewa will be your enemy; *chitta mico* will destroy you. You will, my king of serpents? you will? Ho, ho, ho!"

As she spoke the reptile appeared to comprehend her, for its head was suddenly raised aloft, its bright basilisk eyes gleamed as though emitting sparks of fire—its forked, glittering tongue was protruded from its mouth, and the "skirr-rr" of the rattles could be heard for some moments sounding continuously.

"Quiet! now quiet!" said she, with a motion of her fingers, causing the serpent to resume its attitude of repose. "Not he, *chitta!* not he, thou king of the crawlers! Quiet, I say!"

"Why do you threaten me, Ewa? You have no cause."

"*Hinklas!* I believe it, fair mico, gallant mico; true, I believe it."

"But, good Ewa, explain to me—tell me of—"

"*Cooree, cooree!* not now, not to-night. There is no time, *chepawnee!* See! look yonder to the west! *Netle-hasse* (the night sun—the moon) is going to bed. You must be gone. You dare not walk in the darkness. You must get back to the *topekee* before the moon is hid—go, go, go!"

"But I told you, Ewa, I had business here. I dare not leave till it is done."

"*Hulwak!* there is danger then. What business, mico! Ah! I guess. See! they come for whom you wait?"

"True—it is they, I believe."

I said this, as I perceived the tall shadows of the two chiefs flitting along the further edge of the pond.

"Be quick, then: do what you must, but waste not time. In the darkness you will meet danger. Haj-Ewa must be gone. Good night, young mico: good night."

I returned the salutation; and facing round to await the arrival of the chiefs, lost sight of my strange companion.

The Indians soon came upon the ground, and briefly delivered their report.

Holata Mico had struck his tents, and was moving away from the encampment.

I was too much disgusted with these traitorous men to spend a moment in their company; and, as soon as I had gained the required information, I hurried away from their presence.

Warned by Haj-Ewa, as well as by the words of Arens Ringgold, I lost no time in returning to the fort. The moon was still above the horizon; and I had the advantage of her light to protect me from being surprised by any sudden onset.

I walked hastily, taking the precaution to keep in the open ground, and giving a wide berth to any covert that might shelter an assassin.

I saw no one on the way, nor around the back of the stockade. On arriving opposite the gate of the fort, however, I perceived the figure of a man—not far from the sutler's store—apparently skulking behind some logs. I fancied I knew the man; I fancied he was the mulatto.

I would have gone after him, and satisfied myself; but I had already hailed the sentinel, and given the countersign; and I did not desire to cause a flurry among the guard—particularly as I had received injunctions to pass in as privately as possible.

Another time, I should likely encounter this Jacob *redivius,* when I should be less embarrassed, and perhaps have a better opportunity of calling him and his diabolical associates to an account. With this reflection, I passed through the gate, and carried my report to the quarters of the commander-in-chief.

Chapter Thirty Six.

In Need of a Friend.

To pass the night under the same roof with a man who intends to murder you is anything but pleasant, and repose under the circumstance, is next to impossible. I slept but little, and the little sleep I did obtain was not tranquil.

Before retiring for the night, I had seen nothing of the Ringgolds, neither father nor son; but I knew they were still in the fort, where they were to remain as guests a day or two longer. They had either gone to bed before my return, or were entertained in the quarters of some friendly officer. At all events, they did not appear to me during the remainder of the night.

Neither saw I aught of Spence and Williams. These worthies, if in the fort, would find a lodgment among the soldiers, but I did not seek them.

Most of the night I lay awake, pondering on the strange incidents of the day, or rather upon that one episode that had made me acquainted with such deadly enemies.

I was in a state of sad perplexity as to what course I should pursue—uncertain all night long; and when daylight shone through the shutters, still uncertain.

My first impulse had been to disclose the whole affair at head-quarters, and demand an investigation—a punishment.

On reflection, this course would not do. What proofs could I offer of so grave an accusation? Only my own assertions, unbacked by any other evidence—unsustained even by probability—for who would have given credence to crime so unparalleled in atrocity?

Though certain the assassins referred to me, I could not assert that they had even mentioned my name. My story would be treated with ridicule, myself perhaps with something worse. The Ringgolds were mighty men—personal friends both of the general and commissioner—and though known to be a little scoundrelly and unscrupulous in worldly affairs, still holding the rank of gentlemen. It would need better evidence than I could offer to prove Arens Ringgold a would-be murderer.

I saw the difficulty, and kept my secret.

Another plan appeared more feasible—to accuse Arens Ringgold openly before all, and challenge him to mortal combat. This, at least, would prove that I was sincere in my allegations.

But duelling was against the laws of the service. It would require some management to keep clear of an arrest—which of course would frustrate the scheme before satisfaction could be obtained. I had my own thoughts about Master Arens Ringgold. I knew his courage was but slippery. He would be likely enough to play the poltroon; but whether so or not, the charge and challenge would go some way towards exposing him.

I had almost decided on adopting this course, though it was morning before I had come to any determination.

I stood sadly in need of a friend; not merely a second—for this I could easily procure—but a companion in whom I could confide, and who might aid me by his counsel. As ill luck would have it, every officer in the fort was a perfect stranger to me. With the Ringgolds alone had I any previous acquaintance.

In my dilemma, I thought of one whose advice might stand me in good stead, and I determined to seek it. Black Jake was the man—he should be my counsellor.

Shortly after daylight the brave fellow was by my side. I told him all. He appeared very little surprised. Some suspicion of such a plot had already taken possession of his mind, and it was his intention to have revealed it to me that very morning. Least of all did he express surprise about Yellow Jake. That was but the confirmation of a belief, which he entertained already, without the shadow of a doubt. He knew positively that the mulatto was living—still more, he had ascertained the mode by which the latter had made his almost miraculous escape.

And yet it was simple enough. The alligator had seized him, as was supposed; but the fellow had the adroitness to "job" its eyes with the knife, and thus cause it to let go its hold. He had followed the example of the young Indian, using the same weapon!

This occurred under water, for the mulatto was a good diver. His limbs were lacerated—hence the blood—but the wounds did not signify, nor did they hinder him from making further efforts to escape.

He took care not to rise to the surface until after swimming under the bank; there, concealed by the drooping branches, he had glided out, and climbed up into a live-oak— where the moss sheltered him from the eyes of his vengeful pursuers. Being entirely naked, there was no sign left by dripping garments, to betray him; besides, the blood upon the water had proved his friend. On seeing that, the hunters were under the full belief that he had "gone under," and therefore took but little pains to search further.

Such was Black Jake's account of this affair. He had obtained it the evening before from one of the friendly Indians at the fort, who professed to have the narration from the mulatto's own lips.

There was nothing improbable in the story, but the contrary. In all likelihood, it was strictly true; and it at once dispersed the half-dozen mysteries that had gathered in my mind. The black had received other information. The runaway had taken refuge with one of the half-negro tribes established amid the swamps that envelop the head-waters of the Amazura. He had found favour among his new associates, had risen to be a chief, and now passed under the cognomen of the "Mulatto-mica."

There was still a little mystery: how came he and Arens Ringgold in "cahoot?"

After all, there was not much puzzle in the matter. The planter had no particular cause for hating the runaway. His activity during the scene of the baffled execution was all a sham. The mulatto had more reason for resentment; but the loves or hates of such men are easily set aside—where self-interest interferes—and can, at any time, be commuted for gold.

No doubt, the white villain had found the yellow one of service in some base undertaking, and *vice versâ*. At all events, it was evident that the "hatchet had been buried" between them, and their present relations were upon the most friendly footing.

"Jake!" said I, coming to the point on which I desired to hear his opinion, "what about Arens Ringgold—shall I call him out?"

"Golly, Massr George, he am out long 'go—I see um 'bout, dis two hour an' more— dat ar bossy doant sleep berry sound—he hant got de good conscience, I reck'n."

"Oh! that is not what I mean, my man."

"Wha—what massr mean?"

"To call him out—challenge him to fight me."

"Whaugh! massr, d'you mean to say a dewel ob sword an' pistol?"

"Swords, pistols, or rifles—I care not which weapon he may choose."

"Gorramity! Massr George, don't talk ob such a thing. O Lordy! no—you hab moder—you hab sister. 'Spose you get kill—who know—tha bullock he sometime kill tha butcha—den, Massr George, no one lef—who lef take care on ya moder?—who be guardium ob ya sister Vagin? who 'tect Viola—who 'tect all ob us from dese bad bad men? Gorramity! massr, let um lone—doant call 'im out!"

At that moment, I was myself called out. The earnest appeal was interrupted by the braying of bugles and the rolling of drums, announcing the assembling of the council; and without waiting to reply to the disinterested remonstrance of my companion, I hastened to the scene of my duties.

Chapter Thirty Seven.

The Final Assembly.

The spectacle of yesterday was repeated: the troops in serried lines of blue and steel— the officers in full uniform with shining epaulettes—in the centre the staff grouped around the general, close buttoned and of brilliant sheen; fronting these the half-circle of chiefs, backed by concentric lines of warriors, plumed, painted, and picturesque—horses standing near, some neighing under ready saddles, some picketed and quietly browsing—Indian women in their long *hunnas*, hurrying to and fro—boys and babes at play upon the grass— flags waring above the soldiers—banners and pennons floating over the heads of the red warriors—drums beating—bugles braying; such was the array.

Again the spectacle was imposing, yet scarcely so much as that of the preceding day. The eye at once detected a deficiency in the circle of the chiefs, and nearly half of the warriors were wanting. The assemblage no longer impressed you with the idea of a multitude—it was only a respectable crowd, with room enough for all to gather close around the council.

The absence of many chiefs was at once perceived. King Onopa was not there. The coronet of British brass—lacquered symbol of royalty, yesterday conspicuous in the centre— was no longer to be seen. Holato Mico was missing, with other leaders of less note; and the thinness in the ranks of the common warriors showed that these chiefs had taken their followers along with them. Most of the Indians on the ground appeared to be of the clans of Omatla, "Black Dirt," and Ohala.

Notwithstanding the fewness of their following, I saw that Hoitle-mattee, Arpiucki, negro Abram, and the dwarf were present. Surely these stayed not to sign?

I looked for Osceola. It was not difficult to discover one so conspicuous, both in figure and feature. He formed the last link in the now contracted curve of the chiefs. He was lowest in rank, but this did not signify, as regarded his position. Perhaps he had placed himself there from a feeling of modesty—a well-known characteristic of the man. He was in truth the very youngest of the chiefs, and by birthright entitled to a smaller command than any present; but, viewing him as he stood—even at the bottom of the rank—one could not help fancying that he was the head of all.

As upon the preceding day, there was no appearance of bravado about him. His attitude, though stately and statuesque, was one of perfect ease. His arms were folded over his full chest—his weight resting on one limb, the other slightly retired—his features in repose, or now and then lit up by an expression rather of gentleness. He seemed the impersonation of an Apollo—or, to speak less mythologically, a well-behaved gentleman waiting for some ceremony, of which he was to be a simple spectator. As yet, nothing had transpired to excite him; no words had been uttered to rouse a spirit that only *seemed* to slumber.

Ere long, that attitude of repose would pass away—that soft smile would change to the harsh frown of passion.

Gazing upon his face, one could hardly fancy such a transformation possible, and yet a close observer might. It was like the placid sky that precedes the storm—the calm ocean that in a moment may be convulsed by the squall—the couchant lion that on the slightest provocation may be roused to ungovernable rage.

During the moments that preceded the inauguration of the council, I kept my eyes upon the young chief. Other eyes were regarding him as well; he was the cynosure of many, but mine was a gaze of peculiar interest.

I looked for some token of recognition, but received none—neither nod nor glance. Once or twice, his eye fell upon me, but passed on to some one else, as though I was but one among the crowd of his pale-faced adversaries. He appeared not to remember me. Was this really so? or was it, that his mind, preoccupied with great thoughts, hindered him from taking notice?

I did not fail to cast my eyes abroad—over the plain—to the tents—towards the groups of loitering women. I scanned their forms, one after another.

I fancied I saw the mad queen in their midst—a centre of interest. I had hopes that her *protégée* might be near, but no. None of the figures satisfied my eye: they were all too *squaw-like*—too short or too tall—too corpulent or too *maigre*. She was not there. Even under the loose *hunna* I should have recognised her splendid form—*if still unchanged*.

If—the hypothesis excites your surprise. Why changed, you ask? Growth?—development?—maturity? Rapid in this southern clime is the passage from maiden's form to that of matron.

No; not that, not that. Though still so young, the undulating outlines had already shown themselves. When I last looked upon her, her stature had reached its limits; her form exhibited the bold curve of Hogarth, so characteristic of womanhood complete. Not that did I fear.

And what then? The contrary? Change from attenuation—from illness or grief? Nor this.

I cannot explain the suspicions that racked me—sprung from a stray speech. That jay bird, that yestreen chattered so gaily, had poured poison into my heart. But no; it could not be Maümee! She was too innocent. Ah! why do I rave? There is no guilt in love. If true—if she—hers was not crime; he alone was the guilty one.

I have ill described the torture I experienced, consequent upon my unlucky "eavesdropping." During the whole of the preceding days it had been a source of real suffering. I was in the predicament of one who had, heard too much, and to little.

You will scarcely wonder that the words of Haj-Ewa cheered me; they drove the unworthy suspicion out of my mind, and inspired me with fresh hopes. True, she had mentioned no name till I myself had pronounced it; but to whom could her speech refer?

"Poor bird of the forest—her heart will bleed and break." She spoke of the "Rising Sun:" that was Osceola, who could the "haintclitz" be? who but Maümee?

It might be but a tale of bygone days—a glimpse of the past deeply impressed upon the brain of the maniac, and still living in her memory. This was possible. Haj-Ewa had known us in these days, had often met us in our wild wood rambles, had even been with us upon the island—for the mad queen could paddle her canoe with skill, could ride her wild steed, could go anywhere, went everywhere.

It might only be a souvenir of these happy days that caused her to speak as she had done—in the chaos of her intellect, mistaking the past for the present. Heaven forbid!

The thought troubled me, but not long; for I did not long entertain it. I clung to the pleasanter belief. Her words were sweet as honey, and formed a pleasing counterpoise to the fear I might otherwise have felt, on discovering the plot against my life. With the knowledge that Maümee once loved—still loved me—I could brave dangers a hundred-fold greater than that. It is but a weak heart that would not be gallant under the influence of love. Encouraged by the smiles of a beautiful mistress, even cowards can be brave. Arens Ringgold was standing by my side. Entrained in the crowd, our garments touched; we conversed together!

He was even more polite to me than was his wont—more *friendly*! His speech scarcely betrayed the habitual cynicism of his nature; though, whenever I looked him in the face, his eye quailed, and his glance sought the ground.

For all that, he had no suspicion—not the slightest—that I knew I was side by side with the man who designed to murder me.

Chapter Thirty Eight.

Cashiering the Chiefs.

To-day the commissioner showed a bolder front. A bold part had he resolved to play, but he felt sure of success; and consequently there was an air of triumph in his looks. He regarded the chiefs with the imperious glance of one determined to command them; confident they would yield obedience to his wishes.

At intervals his eye rested upon Osceola with a look of peculiar significance, at once sinister and triumphant. I was in the secret of that glance: I guessed its import; I knew that it boded no good to the young Seminole chief. Could I have approached him at that moment, I should have held duty but lightly, and whimpered in his ear a word of warning.

I was angry with myself that I had not thought of this before. Haj-Ewa could have borne a message on the previous night; why did I not send it? My mind had been too full. Occupied with my own thoughts, I had not thought of the danger that threatened my friend—for in this light I still regarded Powell.

I had no exact knowledge of what was meant; though, from the conversation I had overheard, I more than half divined the commissioner's purpose. Upon some plea, *Osceola was to be arrested.*

A plea was needed; the outrage could not be perpetrated without one. Even the reckless agent might not venture upon such a stretch of power without plausible pretext; and how was this pretext to be obtained?

The withdrawal of Onopa and the "hostiles," while Omatla with the "friendlies" remained, had given the agent the opportunity. *Osceola himself was to furnish the plea.*

Would that I could have whispered in his ear one word of caution!

It was too late: the toils had been laid—the trap set; and the noble game was about to enter it. It was too late for me to warn him. I must stand idly by—spectator to an act of injustice—a gross violation of right.

A table was placed in front of the ground occupied by the general and staff; the commissioner stood immediately behind it. Upon this table was an inkstand with pens; while a broad parchment, exhibiting the creases of many folds, was spread out till it occupied nearly the whole surface. This parchment was the treaty of the Oclawaha.

"Yesterday," began the commissioner, without further preamble, "we did nothing but talk—to-day we are met to act. This," said he, pointing to the parchment, "is the treaty of

Payne's Landing. I hope you have all considered what I said yesterday, and are ready to sign it?"

"We have considered," replied Omatla for himself and those of his party. "We are ready to sign."

"Onopa is head chief," suggested the commissioner; "let him sign first. Where is Miconopa?" he added, looking around the circle with feigned surprise.

"The mico-mico is not here."

"And why not here? He should have been here. Why is he absent?"

"He is sick—he is not able to attend the council."

"That is a *lie*, Jumper. Miconopa is shamming—you know he is."

The dark brow of Hoitle-mattee grew darker at the insult, while his body quivered with rage. A grunt of disdain was all the reply he made, and folding his arms, he drew back into his former attitude.

"Abram! you are Miconopa's private counsellor—you know his intentions. Why has he absented himself?"

"O Massr Ginral!" replied the black in broken English, and speaking without much show of respect for his interrogator, "how shed ole Abe know the 'tention of King Nopy? The mico no tell me ebberting—he go he please—he come he please—he great chief; he no tell nobody his 'tention."

"Does he intend to sign? Say yes or no."

"No, den!" responded the interpreter, in a firm voice, as if forced to the answer. "That much ob his mind Abe *do* know. He no 'tend to sign that ar dockament. He say no, no."

"Enough!" cried the commissioner in a loud voice—"enough! Now hear me, chiefs and warriors of the Seminole nation! I appear before you armed with a power from your Great Father the President—he who is chief of us all. That power enables me to punish for disloyalty and disobedience; and I now exercise that right upon Miconopa. *He is no longer king of the Seminoles!*"

This unexpected announcement produced an effect upon the audience similar to that of an electric shock. It started the chiefs and warriors into new attitudes, and all stood looking eagerly at the speaker. But the expression upon their faces was not of like import—it varied much. Some showed signs of anger as well as surprise. A few appeared pleased, while the majority evidently received the announcement with incredulity.

Surely the commissioner was jesting? How could *he* make or unmake a king of the Seminoles? How could the Great Father himself do this? The Seminoles were a free nation; they were not even tributary to the whites—under no political connection whatever. They themselves could alone elect their king—they only could depose him. Surely the commissioner was jesting?

Not at all. In another moment, they perceived he was in earnest. Foolish as was the project of deposing King Onopa, he entertained it seriously. He had resolved to carry it into execution; and as far as decrees went, he did so without further delay.

"Omatla! you have been faithful to your word and your honour; you are worthy to head a brave nation. From this time forth, *you* are King of the Seminoles! Our Great Father, and the people of the United States, hail you as such; they will acknowledge no other. Now—let the signing proceed."

At a gesture from the commissioner, Omatla stepped forward to the table, and taking the pen in his hand, wrote his name upon the parchment.

The act was done in perfect silence. But one voice broke the deep stillness—one word only was heard uttered with angry aspirate; it was the word "traitor."

I looked round to discover who had pronounced it; the hiss was still quivering upon the lips of Osceola; while his eye was fixed on Omatla with a glance of ineffable scorn.

"Black Crazy Clay" next took the pen, and affixed his signature, which was done by simply making his "mark."

After him follower Ohala, Itolasse Omatla, and about a dozen—all of whom were known as the chiefs that favoured the scheme of removal.

The hostile chiefs—whether by accident or design I know not—stood together, forming the left wing of the semi-circle. It was now their turn to declare themselves.

Hoitle-mattee was the first about whose signing the commissioner entertained any doubt. There was a pause, significant of apprehension.

"It is your turn, Jumper," said the latter at length, addressing the chief by his English name.

"You may *jump* me, then," replied the eloquent and witty chief, making a jest of what he meant for earnest as well.

"How? you refuse to sign?"

"Hoitle-mattee does not write."

"It is not necessary; your name is already written; you have only to place your finger upon it."

"I might put my finger on the wrong place."

"You can sign by making a cross," continued the agent, still in hopes that the chief would consent.

"We Seminoles have but little liking for the cross; we had enough of it in the days of the Spaniards. *Hulwak!*"

"Then you positively refuse to sign?"

"Ho! Mister Commissioner does it surprise you?"

"Be it so, then. Now hear what I have to say to you."

"Hoitle-mattee's ears are as open as the commissioner's mouth," was the sneering rejoinder.

"I depose Hoitle-mattee from the chieftainship of his clan. The Great Father will no longer recognise him as chief of the Seminoles."

"Ha, ha, ha!" came the scornful laugh in reply. "Indeed—indeed! And tell me," he asked, still continuing to laugh, and treating with derision the solemn enunciation of the commissioner, "of whom am I to be chief, General Thompson."

"I have pronounced," said the agent, evidently confused and nettled by the ironical manner of the Indian; "you are no more a chief—we will not acknowledge you as one."

"But my people?—what of them?" asked the other in a fine tone of irony; "have they nothing to say in this matter?"

"Your people will act with reason. They will listen to their Great Father's advice. They will no longer obey a leader who has acted without faith."

"You say truly, agent," replied the chief, now speaking seriously. "My people will act with reason, but they will also act with patriotism and fidelity. Do not flatter yourself on the potency of our Great Father's advice. If it be given as a father's counsel, they will listen to it; if not, they will shut their ears against it. As to your disposal of myself, I only laugh at the absurdity of the act. I treat both act and agent with scorn. I have no dread of your power. I have no fear of the loyalty of my people. Sow dissension among them as you please; you have been successful elsewhere in making traitors,"—here the speaker glared towards Omatla and his warriors—"but I disregard your machinations. There is not a man in my tribe that will turn his back upon Hoitle-mattee—not one."

The orator ceased speaking, and, folding his arms, fell back into an attitude of silent defiance. He saw that the commissioner had done with him, for the latter was now appealing to Abram for his signature.

The black's first answer was a decided negative—simply "No." When urged to repeat his refusal, he added:

"No—by Jovah! I nebber sign the damned paper—nebber. Dat's enuf—aint it, Bossy Thompson?"

Of course, this put an end to the appeal, and Abram was "scratched" from the list of chiefs.

Arpiucki followed next, and "Cloud" and the "Alligator," and then the dwarf Poshalla. All these refused their signatures, and were in turn formally deposed from their dignities. So, likewise, were Holata Mico and others who were absent.

Most of the chiefs only laughed as they listened to the wholesale cashiering. It was ludicrous enough to hear this puny office holder of an hour pronounce edicts with all the easy freedom of an emperor! (Note 1.)

Poshala, the last who had been disgraced, laughed like the others; but the dwarf had a bitter tongue, and could not refrain from a rejoinder.

"Tell the fat agent," cried he to the interpreter—"tell him that I shall be chief of the Seminoles when the rank weeds are growing over his great carcass—ha, ha!"

The rough speech was not carried to the ears of the commissioner. He did not even hear the scornful cachinnation that followed it, for his attention was now entirely occupied with one individual—the youngest of the chiefs—the last in the line—Osceola.

Note 1. The United States government afterwards disapproved of this absurd dethronement of the chiefs; but there is no doubt that Thompson acted under secret instructions from the President.

Chapter Thirty Nine.

The Signature of Osceola.

Up to this moment the young chief had scarcely spoken; only when Charles Omatla took hold of the pen he had hissed out the word traitor.

He had not remained all the time in the same attitude, neither had his countenance shown him indifferent to what was passing. There was no constraint either in his gestures or looks—no air of affected stoicism—for this was not his character. He had laughed at the wit of Jumper, and applauded the patriotism of Abram and the others, as heartily as he had frowned disapproval of the conduct of the traitors.

It was now his turn to declare himself, and he stood, with modest mien, in the expectation of being asked. All the others had been appealed to by name—for the names of all were well-known to the agent and his interpreters.

I need hardly state that at this crisis silence was on tiptoe. Throughout the ranks of the soldiery—throughout the crowd of warriors—everywhere—there was a moment of breathless expectancy, as if every individual upon the ground was imbued with the presentiment of a scene.

For my part I felt satisfied that an explosion was about to take place; and, like the rest, I stood spell-bound with expectation.

The commissioner broke the silence with the words:

"At last we have come to you, *Powell*. Before proceeding further, let me ask—Are you acknowledged as a *chief?*"

There was insult in the tone, the manner, the words. It was direct and intended, as the countenance of the speaker clearly showed. There was malice in his eye—malice mingled with the confidence of prospective triumph.

The interrogation was irrelevant, superfluous. Thompson knew well that Powell was a chief—a sub-chief, it is true, but still a chief—a war-chief of the Redsticks, the most warlike tribe of the nation. The question was put for mere provocation. The agent tempted an outburst of that temper that all knew to be none of the gentlest.

Strange to say, the insult failed in its effect, or it seemed so. They who expected an angry answer were doomed to disappointment. Osceola made no reply. Only a peculiar smile was observed upon his features. It was not of anger, nor yet of scorn: it was rather a smile of silent, lordly contempt—the look which a gentleman would bestow upon a blackguard who is abusing him. Those who witnessed it were left under the impression that the young chief regarded his insulter as beneath the dignity of a reply, and the insult too gross, as it really was, to be answered. Such impression had I, in common with others around me.

Osceola's look, might have silenced the commissioner, or, at least, have caused him to have changed his tactics, had he been at all sensitive to derision. But no—the vulgar soul of the plebeian official was closed against shame, as against justice; and without regarding the repulse, he pressed on with his plan.

87

"I ask, are you a chief?" continued he, repeating the interrogatory in a still more insulting tone. "Have you the right to sign?"

This time his questions were answered, and by a dozen voices at once. Chieftains in the ring, and warriors who stood behind it; shouted in reply:

"The Rising Sun?—a chief! He *is* a chief. He has the right to sign."

"Why call his right in question?" inquired Jumper, with a sneering laugh. "Time enough when he wishes to exercise it. He is not likely to do that now."

"But I am," said Osceola, addressing himself to the orator, and speaking with marked emphasis. "I have the right to sign—*I shall sign*."

It is difficult to describe the effect produced by this unexpected avowal. The entire audience—white men as well as red men—was taken by surprise; and for some moments there was a vibratory movement throughout the assembly, accompanied by a confused murmur of voices. Exclamations were heard on all sides—cries of varied import, according to the political bias of those who uttered them. All, however, betokened astonishment; with some, in tones of joy; with others, in the accents of chagrin or anger. Was it Osceola who had spoken? Had they heard aright? Was the "Rising Sun" so soon to sink behind the clouds? After all that had transpired—after all he had promised—was *he* going to turn traitor?

Such questions passed rapidly among the hostile chiefs and warriors; while those of the opposite party could scarcely conceal their delight. All knew that the signing of Osceola would end the affair; and the removal become a matter of coarse. The Omatlas would have nothing more to fear; the hostile warriors, who had sworn it might still resist; but there was no leader among them who could bind the patriots together as Osceola had done. With this defection the spirit of resistance would become a feeble thing; the patriots might despair.

Jumper, Cloud, Coa Hajo, and Abram, Arpiucki and the dwarf, seemed all equally stricken with astonishment. Osceola—he on whom they had reposed their fullest confidence—the bold designer of the opposition—the open foe to all who had hitherto advocated the removal—he, the pure patriot in whom all had believed—whom all had trusted, was now going to desert them—now, in the eleventh hour, when his defection would be fatal to their cause.

"He has been bribed," said they. "His patriotism has been all a sham: his resistance a cheat. He has been bought by the agent! He has been acting for him all along.*Holy-waugus! Iste-hulwa-stchay.* (bad man—villain). 'Tis a treason blacker than Omatla's!"

Thus muttered the chiefs to one another, at the same time eyeing Osceola with the fierce look of tigers.

With regard to Powell's defection, I did not myself know what to make of it. He had declared his resolution to sign the treaty; what more was needed? That he was ready to do so was evident from his attitude; he seemed only to wait for the agent to invite him.

As to the commissioner being a party to this intention, I knew he was nothing of the kind. Any one who looked in his face, at that moment, would have acquitted him of all privity to the act. He was evidently as much astonished by Osceola's declaration as any one upon the ground, or even more so; in fact, he seemed bewildered by the unexpected avowal; so much so, that it was some time before he could make rejoinder.

He at length stammered out:

"Very well, Osceola! Step forward here, and sign then."

Thompson's tone was changed; he spoke soothingly. A new prospect was before him. Osceola would sign, and thus agree to the removal. The business upon which the supreme government had deputed him would thus be accomplished, and with a dexterity that would redound to his own credit. "Old Hickory" would be satisfied; and then what next? what next? Not a mission to a mere tribe of savages, but an embassy to some high court of civilisation. He might yet be ambassador? perhaps to Spain?

Ah! Wiley Thompson! thy castles in the air (*châteaux en Espagne*) were soon dissipated. They fell as suddenly as they had been built; they broke down like a house of cards.

Osceola stepped forward to the table, and bent over it, as if to scan the words of the document. His eyes ran rapidly across the parchment; he seemed to be searching for some particular place.

He found it—it was a name—he read it aloud: "Charles Omatla."

Raising himself erect, he faced the commissioner; and, in a tone of irony, asked the latter if he still desired him to sign.

"You have promised, Osceola."

"Then will I keep my promise."

As he spoke the words, he drew his long Spanish knife from its sheath, and raising it aloft, struck the blade through the parchment till its point was deep buried in the wood.

"That is my signature!" cried he, as he drew forth the steel. "See, Omatla! it is through *your* name. Beware, traitor! Undo what you have done, or its blade may yet pass through your heart!"

"Oh! that is what he meant," cried the commissioner, rising in rage. "Good. I was prepared for this insolence—this outrage. General Clinch!—I appeal to you—your soldiers—seize upon him—arrest him!"

These broken speeches I heard amidst the confusion of voices. I heard Clinch issue some hurried orders to an officer who stood near. I saw half a dozen files separate from the ranks, and rush forward; I saw them cluster around Osceola—who the next moment was in their grasp.

Not till several of the blue-coated soldiers were sent sprawling over the ground; not till guns had been thrown aside, and a dozen strong men had fixed their gripe upon him, did the young chief give over his desperate struggles to escape; and then apparently yielding, he stood rigid and immobile, as if his frame had been iron.

It was an unexpected *dénouement*—alike unlooked for by either white men or Indians. It was a violent proceeding, and altogether unjustifiable. This was no court whose judge had the right to arrest for contempt. It was a council, and even the insolence of an individual could not be punished without the concurrence of both parties. General Thompson had exceeded his duty—he had exercised a power arbitrary as illegal.

The scene that followed was so confused as to defy description. The air was rent with loud ejaculations; the shouts of men, the screams of the women, the cries of children, the yells of the Indian warriors, fell simultaneously upon the ear. There was no attempt at rescue—that would have been impossible in the presence of so many troops—so many traitors; but the patriot chiefs, as they hurried away from the ground, gave out their wild 'Yo-ho-ehee'—the gathering war-word of the Seminole nation—that in every utterance promised retaliation and revenge.

The soldiers commenced dragging Osceola inside the fort.

"Tyrant!" cried he, fixing his eye upon the commissioner, "you have triumphed by treachery; but fancy not that this is the end of it. You may imprison Osceola—hang him, if you will—but think not that his spirit will die. No; it will live, and cry aloud for vengeance. It speaks! Hear ye yonder sounds? Know ye the 'war-cry' of the Redsticks? Mark it well; for it is not the last time it will ring in your ears. *Ho—yo-ho-ehee! yo-ho-ehee!* Listen to it, tyrant! it is your death-knell—it is your death-knell!"

While giving utterance to these wild threats, the young chief was drawn through the gate, and hurried off to the guard-house within the stockade.

As I followed amid the crowd, some one touched me on the arm, as if to draw my attention. Turning, I beheld Haj-Ewa.

"To-night, by the we-wa," (spring, pond, water) said she, speaking so as not to be heard by those around. "There will be shadows—more shadows upon the water. Perhaps—"

I did not hear more; the crowd pressed us apart; and when I looked again, the mad queen had moved away from the spot.

Chapter Forty.

"Fighting Gallagher."

The prisoner was confined in a strong, windowless blockhouse. Access to him would be easy enough, especially to those who wore epaulets. It was my design to visit him; but, for certain reasons, I forbore putting it in execution, so long as daylight lasted. I was desirous that my interview should be as private as possible and therefore waited for the night.

I was influenced by other reasons; my hands were full of business; I had not yet done with Arens Ringgold.

I had a difficulty in deciding how to act. My mind was a chaos of emotions; hatred for the conspirators—indignation at the unjust behaviour of the agent towards Osceola—love for Maümee—now fond and trusting—anon doubting and jealous. Amid such confusion, how could I think with clearness?

Withal, one of these emotions had precedence—anger against the villain who intended to take my life was at that moment the strongest passion in my breast.

Hostility so heartless, so causeless, so deadly, had not failed to imbue me with a keen desire for vengeance; and I resolved to punish my enemy at all hazards.

He only, whose life has been aimed at by an assassin, can understand the deadly antipathy I felt towards Arens Ringgold. An open enemy, who acts under the impulse of anger, jealousy, or fancied wrong, you may respect. Even the two white wretches, and the yellow runaway, I regarded only with contempt, as tools pliant for any purpose; but the arch-conspirator himself I now both hated and despised. So acute was my sense of injury, that I could not permit it to pass without some act of retaliation, some effort to punish my wronger.

But how? Therein lay the uncertainty! How? A duel?

I could think of no other way. The criminal was still inside the law. I could not reach him, otherwise than by my own arm.

I well weighed the words of my sable counsellor; but the faithful fellow had spoken in vain, and I resolved to act contrary to his advice, let the hazard fall as it might. I made up my mind to the challenge.

One consideration still caused me to hesitate: *I must give Ringgold my reasons.*

He should have been welcome to them as a dying souvenir; but if I succeeded in only *half-killing* him, or he in half-killing me, how about the future? I should be showing my hand to him, by which he would profit; whereas, unknown to him, I now knew his, and might easily foil his designs.

Such calculations ran rapidly through my mind, though I considered them with a coolness that in after-thought surprises me. The incidents that I had lately encountered—combined with angry hatred of this plausible villain—had made me fierce, cold and cruel. I was no longer myself; and, wicked as it may appear, I could not control my longings for vengeance.

I needed a friend to advise me. Who could I make the confidant of my terrible secret?

Surely my ears were not deceiving me? No; it was the voice of my old school-fellow, Charley Gallagher. I heard it outside, and recognised the ring of his merry laugh. A detachment of rifles had just entered the fort with Charley at their head. In another instant we had "embraced."

What could have been more opportune? Charley had been my "chum" at college—my bosom companion. He deserved my confidence, and almost upon the instant, I made known to him the situation of affairs.

It required much explanation to remove his incredulity; he was disposed to treat the whole thing as a joke—that is, the conspiracy against my life. But the rifle shot was real, and Black Jake was by to confirm my account of it: so that my friend was at length induced to take a serious view of the matter.

"Bad luck to me!" said he, in Irish accent: "it's the quarest case that ever came accrast your humble frind's experience. Mother o' Moses! the fellow must be the divil incarnate. Geordie, my boy, have ye looked under his instip?"

Despite the name and "brogue," Charley was not a Hibernian—only the son of one. He was a New-Yorker by birth, and could speak good English when he pleased; but from some freak of eccentricity or affectation, he had taken to the brogue, and used it habitually, when among friends, with all the rich garniture of a true Milesian, fresh from the "sod."

90

He was altogether an odd fellow, but with a soul of honour, and a heart true as steel. He was no dunce either, and the man above all others upon whose coat tail it would not have been safe to "trid." He was already notorious for having been engaged in two or three "affairs," in which he had played both principal and second, and had earned the bellicose appellation of "Fighting Gallagher." I knew what *his* advice would be before asking it—"Call the schoundrel out by all manes."

I stated the difficulty as to my reasons for challenging Ringgold.

"Thrue, *ma bohil!* You're right there; but there need be no throuble about the matther."

"How?"

"Make the spalpeen challenge you. That's betther—besides, it gives you the choice of waypons."

"In what way can I do this?"

"Och! my innocent gossoon! Shure that's as asy as tumblin' from a haycock. Call him a liar; an' if that's not sufficiently disagraable, twake his nose, or squirt your tobacco in his ugly countenance. That'll fetch him out, I'll be bail for ye."

"Come along, my boy!" continued my ready counsellor, moving towards the door. "Where is this Mister Ringgowld to be sarched for? Find me the gint, and I'll shew you how to scratch his buttons. Come along wid ye!"

Not much liking the plan of procedure, but without the moral strength to resist, I followed this impetuous son of a Celt through the doorway.

Chapter Forty One.

Provoking a Duel.

We were scarcely outside before we saw him for whom we were searching. He was standing at a short distance from the porch, conversing with a group of officers, among whom was the dandy already alluded to, and who passed under the appropriate appellation of "Beau Scott." The latter was aide-de-camp to the commander-in-chief, of whom he was also a relative.

I pointed Ringgold out to my companion.

"He in the civilian dress," I said.

"Och! man, ye needn't be so purticular in your idintification. That sarpint-look spakes for itself. Be my sowl! it's an unwholesome look altogither. That fellow needn't fear wather—the say'll niver drown *him*. Now, look here, Geordy, boy," continued Gallagher, facing towards me and speaking in a more earnest tone: "Follow my advice to the letther! First trid upon his toes, an' see how he takes it. The fellow's got corns; don't ye see, he wears a tight boot? Give him a good scrouge; make him sing out. Ov course, he'll ask you to apologise—he must—you won't. Shurely that'll do the bizness without farther ceremony? If it don't, then, by Jabus! hit him a kick in the latter end."

"No, Gallagher," said I, disliking the programme, "it will never do."

"Bad luck to it, an' why not? You're not going to back out, are ye? Think man! a villain who would murdher you! an' maybe will some day, if you let him escape."

"True—but—"

"Bah! no buts. Move up, an' let's see what they're talking about, anyhow. I'll find ye a chance, or my name's not Gallagher."

Undetermined how to act, I walked after my companion, and joined the group of officers.

Of course, I had no thoughts of following Gallagher's advice. I was in hopes that some turn in the conversation might give me the opportunity I desired, without proceeding to such rude extremes.

My hopes did not deceive me. Arens Ringgold seemed to tempt his fate, for I had scarcely entered among the crowd, before I found cause sufficient for my purpose.

"Talking of Indian beauties," said he, "no one has been so successful among them as Scott here. He has been playing Don Giovanni ever since he came to the fort."

91

"Oh," exclaimed one of the newly arrived officers, "that does not surprise us. He has been a lady-killer ever since I knew him. The man who is irresistible among the belles of Saratoga, will surely find little difficulty in carrying the heart of an Indian maiden."

"Don't be so confident about that, Captain Roberts. Sometimes these forest damsels are very shy of us pale-faced lovers. Lieutenant Scott's present sweetheart cost him a long siege before he could conquer her. Is it not so, lieutenant?"

"Nonsense," replied the dandy with a conceited smirk.

"But she yielded at last?" said Roberts, turning interrogatively towards Scott.

The dandy made no reply, but his simpering smile was evidently intended to be taken in the affirmative.

"Oh yes," rejoined Ringgold, "she yielded at last: and is now the 'favourite,' it is said."

"Her name—her name?"

"Powell—Miss Powell."

"What! That name is not Indian?"

"No, gentlemen; the lady is no savage, I assure you; she can play and sing, and read and write too—such pretty *billets-doux*. Is it not so, lieutenant?"

Before the latter could make reply, another spoke:

"Is not that the name of the young chief who has just been arrested?"

"True," answered Ringgold; "it is the fellow's name. I had forgotten to say that she is his sister."

"What! the sister of Osceola?"

"Neither more nor less—half-blood like him too. Among the whites they are known by the name of Powell, since that was the cognomen of the worthy old gentleman who begot them. Osceola, which signifies 'the Rising Sun,' is the name by which he is known among the Seminoles; and *her* native appellation—ah, that is a very pretty name indeed."

"What is it? Let us hear it; let us judge for ourselves."

"Maümee."

"Very pretty indeed!"

"Beautiful! If the damsel be only as sweet as her name, then Scott is a fortunate fellow."

"Oh, she is a very wonder of beauty; eyes liquid and full of fiery love—long lashes: lips luscious as honeycombs; figure tall; bust full and firm; limbs like those of the Cyprian goddess; feet like Cinderella's—in short, perfection."

"Wonderful. Why, Scott, you are the luckiest mortal alive. But say, Ringgold! are you speaking in seriousness. Has he really conquered this Indian divinity? Honour bright—*has he succeeded?* You understand what I mean?"

"*Most certainly,*" was the prompt reply.

Up to this moment I had not interfered. The first words of the conversation had bound me like a spell, and I stood as if glued to the ground. My brain was giddy, and my heart felt as if the blood passing through it was molten lead. The bold enunciations had so staggered me, that it was some time before I could draw my breath; and more than one of the bystanders noticed the effect which the dialogue was producing on me.

After a little, I grew calmer, or rather more resolute. The very despair that had passed into my bosom had the effect of steeling my nerves; and just as Ringgold uttered the flippant affirmative, I was ready for him.

"Liar!" I exclaimed; and before the red could mount into his cheek, I gave it a slap with the back of my hand, that no doubt helped to heighten the colour.

"Nately done!" cried Gallagher; "there can be no mistake about the maynin of that."

Nor was there. My antagonist accepted the act for what it was meant—a deadly insult. In such company, he could not do otherwise; and, muttering some indistinct threats, he walked away from the ground, attended by his especial friend, the lady-killer, and two or three others.

The incident, instead of gathering a crowd, had the contrary effect; it scattered the little group who had witnessed it; the officers retiring in-doors to discuss the motives, and speculate as as to when and where "the affair would come off."

Gallagher and I also left the ground; and, closeted in my quarters, commenced preparing for the event.

Chapter Forty Two.

The Challenge.

At the time of which I write duelling was not uncommon in the United States army. In *war-time*, it is not uncommon yet, as I can testify from late experience. It is contrary to the regulations of the American service—as I believe it is of every other in the civilised world. Notwithstanding, an infringement of the *code militaire* in this regard, is usually looked upon with leniency—more often "winked at" than punished. This much I can affirm—that any officer in the American army who has received the "lie direct," will find more honour in the breach of this military rule than in its observance.

After all that has been said and written about duelling, the outcry against it is a sad sham, at least in the United States of America—nothing less than a piece of superb hypocrisy. Universal as has been this condemnation, I should not like to take shelter under it. I well know that it would not protect me from being called by that ugly appellation, "poltroon." I have noticed over and over again, that the newspapers loudest in their declamations against duelling, are the first to fling "coward" in the teeth of him who refuses to fight.

It is even so. In America, moral courage, though much be-praised, does not find ready credence. A refusal to meet the man who may challenge you is not thus explained. It is called "backing out," "shewing the white feather;" and he who does this, need look no more upon his ladye-love; she would "flog him with her garters."

More than once have I heard this threat, spoken by pretty lips, and in the centre of a brilliant circle. His moral courage must be great who would provoke such chastisement. With such a sentiment over the land, then, I had nailed Arens Ringgold for a meeting; and I joyed to think I had done so without compromising my secret.

But ah! it was a painful provocation he had given me; and if he had been the greatest coward in the world, he could not have been more wretched than I, as I returned to my quarters.

My jovial companion could no longer cheer me, though it was not fear for the coming fight that clouded my spirits. Far from it—far otherwise. I scarcely thought of that. My thoughts were of Maümee—of what I had just heard. She was false—false—betraying, herself betrayed—lost—lost forever!

In truth was I wretched. One thing alone could have rendered me more so—an obstacle to the anticipated meeting—anything to hinder my revenge. On the duel now rested my hopes. It might enable me to disembarrass my heart of the hot blood that was burning it. Not all—unless he too stood before me—he, the seducer who had made this misery. Would I could find pretext for challenging him. I should do so yet. Why had I not? Why did I not strike him for that smile? I could have fought them both at the same time, one after the other.

Thus I raved, with Gallagher by my side. My friend knew not all my secret. He asked what I had got "aginst the aide-de-cong."

"Say the word, Geordie, boy, an' we'll make a four-handed game ov it. Be Saint Pathrick! I'd like mightily to take the shine out of that purty paycock!"

"No, Gallagher, no. It's not your affair; you could not give *me* satisfaction for that. Let us wait till we know more. I cannot believe it—I cannot believe it."

"Believe what?"

"Not now, my friend. When it is over I shall explain."

"All right, my boy! Charley Gallagher's not the man to disturb your saycrets. Now let's look to the bull-dogs, an' make shure they're in barking condition. I hope the scamps won't blab at head-quarters, an' disappoint us after all."

It was my only fear. I knew that arrest was possible—probable—certain, if my adversary wished it. Arrest would put an end to the affair; and I should be left in a worse position than ever. Ringgold's father was gone—I had ascertained this favourable circumstance; but no matter. The commander-in-chief was the friend of the family—a word in his ear would be sufficient. I feared that the aide-de-camp Scott, instructed by Arens, might whisper that word.

"After all, he daren't," said Gallagher; "you driv the nail home, an' clinched it. He daren't do the dhirty thing—not a bit of it; it might get wind, an' thin he'd have the kettle to his tail; besides, *ma bohill*, he wants to kill you anyhow; so he ought to be glad of the fine handy chance you've given him. He's not a bad shot, they say. Never fear, Geordie, boy! he won't back out this time; he must fight—he will fight. Ha! I told you so. See, yonder comes Apollo Belvidare! Holy Moses! how Phoebus shines!"

A knock—"Come in,"—the door was opened, and the aide-de-camp appeared in full uniform.

"To arrest me," thought I, and my heart fell.

But no; the freshly written note spoke a different purpose, and I was relieved. It was the challenge.

"Lieutenant Randolph, I believe," said the gentleman, advancing towards me.

I pointed to Gallagher, but made no reply.

"I am to understand that Captain Gallagher is your friend."

I nodded assent.

The two faced each other, and the next instant were *en rapport*; talking the matter over as cool as cucumbers and sweet as sugar-plums.

From observation, I hazard this remark—that the politeness exhibited between the seconds in a duel cannot be surpassed by that of the most accomplished courtiers in the world.

The time occupied in the business was brief. Gallagher well knew the routine, and I saw that the other was not entirely unacquainted with it. In five minutes, everything was arranged—place, weapons, and distance.

I nodded; Gallagher made a sweeping salaam; the aide-de-camp bowed stiffly and withdrew.

I shall not trouble you with my reflections previous to the duel, nor yet with many details of the affair itself. Accounts of these deadly encounters are common enough in books, and their sameness will serve as my excuse for not describing one.

Ours differed only from the ordinary kind in the weapon used. We fought with *rifles*, instead of swords or pistols. It was my choice—as the challenged party, I had the right—but it was equally agreeable to my adversary, who was as well skilled in the use of the rifle as I. I chose this weapon because it was the *deadliest*.

The time arranged was an hour before sunset. I had urged this early meeting in fear of interruption; the place, a spot of level ground near the edge of the little pond where I had met Haj-Ewa; the distance, ten paces.

We met—took our places, back to back—waited for the ominous signal, "one, two, three,"—received it—faced rapidly round—and fired at each other.

I heard the "hist" of the leaden pellet as it passed my ear, but felt no stroke.

The smoke puffed upward. I saw my antagonist upon the ground: he was not dead; he was writhing and groaning.

The seconds, and several spectators who were present, ran up to him, but I kept my ground.

"Well, Gallagher?" I asked, as my friend came back to me.

"Winged, by japers! You've spoilt the use ov his dexter arm—bone broke above the ilbow-joint."

"That all?"

"Arrah, sowl! aren't it enough? Hear how the hound whimpers!"

I felt as the tiger is said to feel after tasting blood, though I cannot now account for my ferocity. The man had sought my life—I thirsted for his. This combined with the other thought had nigh driven me mad.

I was not satisfied, and would make no apology; but my antagonist had had enough; he was eager to be taken from the ground on any terms, and thus the affair ended.

It was my first duel, but not my last.

Chapter Forty Three.

The Assignation.

Our opponents passed silently away—the spectators along with them—leaving my second and myself upon the ground.

It was my intention to stay by the pond. I remembered the invitation of Haj-Ewa. By remaining, I should avoid the double journey. Better to await her coming.

A glance to the western horizon shewed me that the sun had already sunk below the tree-tops. The twilight would be short. The young moon was already in the heavens. It might be only a few minutes before Haj-Ewa should come. I resolved to stay.

I desired not that Gallagher should be with me; and I expressed the wish to be left alone.

My companion was a little surprised and puzzled at the request; but he was too well bred not to yield instant compliance.

"Why, Geordie, boy!" said he, about to retire, "shurely there's something the matther wid ye? It isn't this thrifling spurt we've been engaged in? Didn't it ind intirely to your satisfaction? Arrah, man! are ye sorry you didn't kill him dead? Be my trath, you look as milancholic and down-hearted as if he had killed _you!_"

"Dear friend, leave me alone. On my return to quarters, you shall know the cause of my melancholy, and why I now desire to part from your pleasant company."

"Oh, that part I can guess," rejoined he with a significant laugh; "always a petticoat where there's shots exchanged. Niver mind, my boy, no saycrets for Charley Gallagher; I'm bad at keepin' them. Ov coorse, you're going to meet betther company than mine; but laste you might fall in with worse—an' by my sowl! from what ye've towld me, that same isn't beyond the bounds of probability—take this little cheeper. I'm a great dog-braker, you know." Here the speaker handed me a silver call, which he had plucked from his button. "If any thing inconvenient or disagraable should turn up, put that between your lips, an' Charley Gallagher will be at your side in the mention of Jack Robison's name. Cupid spade ye with your lady-love. I'll go an' kill time over a tumbler ov nagus till ye come."

So saying, my warm-hearted friend left me to myself.

I ceased to think of him ere he was gone out of sight—even the bloody strife, in which I had been so recently engaged, glided out of my mind. Maümee—her falsehood and her fall—alone occupied my thoughts.

For a long while, I made no doubt of what I had heard. How could I, with proofs so circumstantial?—the testimony of those cognisant of the scandal—of the chief actor in it, whose silent smile spoke stronger than words. That smile of insolent triumph—why had I permitted it to pass without challenge, without rebuke? It was not too late—I should call upon him to speak plainly and point blank—yes or no. If yes, then for a second duel more deadly than the first.

Notwithstanding these resolves to make my rival declare himself, I doubted not the damning truth; I endeavoured to resign myself to its torture.

For a long while was my soul upon the rack—more than an hour. Then, as my blood grew more cool, reflections of a calmer nature entered my mind; and at intervals, I experienced the soothing influence of hope; this especially when I recalled the words of Haj-Ewa, spoken on the preceding night. Surely the maniac had not been mocking me? Surely it was not a dream of her delirious brain? a distorted _mirage_ of memory—the memory of some far-away, long-forgotten scene, by her only remembered? No, no; her tale was not distorted—her thoughts were not delirious—her words were not mockeries!

How sweet it was to think so!

Yes—I began to experience intervals of placid thought: more than placid—pleasant.

Alas! they were evanescent. The memory of those bold meretricious phrases, those smiling innuendoes, dissipated or darkened them, as cumuli darken the sun. "He *had*succeeded." She was now his favourite. "Most certainly"—words worse than death. Withal it was a foul testimony on which to build a faith.

I longed for light, that true light—the evidence of the senses—that leaves nought uncertain. I should seek it with rash directness, reckless of the result, till it illumined her whole history, proving the past a disgrace, the future a chaos of utter despair. I longed for light; I longed for the coming of Haj-Ewa.

I knew not what the maniac wanted—something, I supposed, concerning the captive. Since noon, I had little thought of him. The mad queen went everywhere, knew every one; she must know all, understand all—ay, well understand; she, too, had been betrayed.

I repaired to our place of meeting on the preceding night; there I might expect her. I crossed the little ridge among the stems of the palmettoes; it was the direct route to the shadowy side of the tank. I descended the slope, and stood as before under the spreading arms of the live-oak.

Haj-Ewa was before me. A single moonbeam slanting athwart the leaves, shone upon her majestic figure. Under its light the two serpents glittered with a metallic lustre, as though her neck and waist were encircled with precious gems.

"*Hinklas*! pretty mico! you are come. Gallant mico! where was thine eye and thine arm that thou didst not kill the *Iste-hulwa*?" (Literally bad man—villain.)

"Ah! the hunter of the deer—
He was stricken so with fear
When he stood before the wolf,
The gaunt wicked wolf,
When he saw the snarling wolf,
He trembled so with fear,
That unharmed the fierce wolf ran away.

"Ha, ha, ha! was it not so, brave mico?"

"It was not fear that hindered me, Ewa. Besides, the wolf did not go unscathed."

"Ho! the wolf has a wounded leg—he will lick himself well again; he will soon be strong as ever. *Hulwak*! you should have killed him, fair mico, ere he bring the pack upon you."

"I could not help my ill luck. I am unfortunate every way."

"*Cooree, cooree*—no. You shall be happy, young mico; you *shall* be happy, friend of the red Seminole. Wait till you see—"

"See what?"

"Patience, *chepawnee*! To-night under this very tree, you will see what is fair—you will hear what is sweet—and perchance Haj-Ewa will be revenged."

This last phrase was spoken with an earnest emphasis, and in a tone that shewed a strong feeling of resentment against some one unknown. I could not comprehend the nature of the expected vengeance.

"His son—yes," continued the maniac, now in soliloquy, "it must be—it must: his eyes, his hair, his form, his gait, his *name*; *his* son and *hers*. Oh, Haj-Ewa will have revenge."

Was I myself the object of this menace? Such a thought entered my mind.

"Good Ewa! of whom are you speaking?"

Roused by my voice, she looked upon me with a bewildered stare, and then broke out into her habitual chant:

"Why did I trust to a pale-faced lover?
Ho, ho, ho!" etc.

Suddenly stopping, she seemed once more to remember herself, and essayed a reply to my question.

"Whom, young mico? Of him the fair one—the wicked one—the *Wykomé hulwa* (the spirit of evil). See! he comes, he comes! Behold him in the water. Ho, ho! it is he. Up, young mico! up into thy leafy bower; stay till Ewa comes! Hear what you may hear—see what you may see; but, for your life, stir not till I give you the signal. Up, up, up!"

Just as on the preceding night, half lifting me into the live-oak, the maniac glided away amidst the shadows.

I lost no time in getting into my former position, where I sat silent and expecting.

The shadow had grown shorter, but there was still enough to shew me that it was the form of a man. In another moment, it vanished.

Scarcely an instant had elapsed, ere a second was flung upon the water, advancing over the ridge, and as if following the track of the former one, though the two persons did not appear to be in company.

That which followed I could trace in full outline. It was the figure of a woman, one whose upright bearing and free port proved her to be young.

Even the shadow exhibited a certain symmetry of form and gracefulness of motion, incompatible with age. Was it still Haj-Ewa? Had she gone round through the thicket, and was now following the footsteps of the man?

For a moment I fancied so; but I soon perceived that my fancy was astray.

The man advanced under the tree. The same moonbeam, that but a moment before had shone upon Haj-Ewa, now fell upon him, and I saw him with sufficient distinctness; he was the aide-de-camp.

He stopped, took out his watch, held it up to the light, and appeared to be inquiring the hour.

But I heeded him no further. Another face appeared under that silvery ray—false and shining as itself: it was the face that to me seemed the loveliest in the world—the face of Maümee.

Chapter Forty Four.

An Eclaircissement.

These were the shadows upon the water promised by Haj-Ewa—black shadows upon my heart.

Mad queen of the Micosaucs! what have I done to deserve this torture? Thou too my enemy! Had I been thy deadliest foe, thou couldst scarcely have contrived a keener sting for thy vengeance.

Face to face stood Maümee and her lover—seduced and seducer. I had no doubt as to the identity of either. The moonbeam fell upon both—no longer with soft silvery light, but gleaming rude and red, like the chandeliers of a bagnio. It may have been but a seeming—the reflection of an inflamed imagination that influenced me from within; but my belief in her innocence was gone—hopelessly gone; the very air seemed tainted with her guilt—the world appeared a chaos of debauchery and ruin.

I had no other thought than that I was present at a scene of assignation. How could I think otherwise? No signs of surprise were exhibited by either, as they came together. They met as those who have promised to come—who have often met before.

Evidently each expected the other. Though other emotions declared themselves, there was not the slightest sign of novelty in the encounter.

For me, it was a terrible crisis. The anguish of a whole life compressed into the space of a single moment could not have been more unendurable. The blood seemed to scald my heart as it gushed through. So acute was the pang, I could scarcely restrain myself from crying aloud.

An effort—a stern determined effort—and the throe was over. Firmly bracing my nerves—firmly grasping the branches—I clung to my seat, resolved to know more.

That was a fortunate resolution. Had I at that moment given way to the wild impulse of passion, and sought a reckless revenge, I should in all likelihood have carved out for myself a long lifetime of sorrow. Patience proved my guardian angel, and the end was otherwise.

Not a word—not a motion—not a breath. What will they say?—what do?

My situation was like his of the suspended sword. On second thoughts, the simile is both trite and untrue: the sword had already fallen; it could wound me no more. I was as one paralysed both in body and soul—impervious to further pain.

Not a word—not a motion—not a breath. What will they say?—what do?

The light is full upon Maümee; I can see her from head to foot. How large she has grown—a woman in all her outlines, perfect, entire. And her loveliness has kept pace with her growth. Larger, she is lovelier than ever. Demon of jealousy! art thou not content with what thou hast already done? Have I not suffered enough? Why hast thou presented her in such witching guise? O that she were scarred, hideous, hag-like—as she shall yet become! Even thus to see her, would be some satisfaction—an anodyne to my chafed soul.

But it is not so. Her face is sweetly beautiful—never so beautiful before. Soft and innocent as ever—not a line of guilt can be traced on those placid features—not a gleam of evil in that round, rolling eye! The angels of heaven are beautiful; but they are good. Oh, who could believe in crime concealed under such loveliness as hers?

I expected a more meretricious mien. There was a scintillation of cheer in the disappointment.

Do not suppose that these reflections occupied time. In a few seconds they passed through my mind, for thought is quicker than the magnetic shock. They passed while I was waiting to hear the first words that, to my surprise, were for some moments unspoken. To my surprise; *I* could not have met her in such fashion. My heart would have been upon my tongue, and lips—

I see it now. The hot burst of passion is past—the springs tide of love has subsided—such an interview is no longer a novelty—perhaps he grows tired of her, foul libertine that he is! See! they meet with some shyness. Coldness has risen between them—a love quarrel—fool is he as villain—fool not to rush into those arms, and at once reconcile it. Would that his opportunities were mine!—not all the world could restrain me from seeking that sweet embrace.

Bitter as were my thoughts, they were less bitter on observing this attitude of the lovers. I fancied it was half-hostile.

Not a word—not a motion—not a breath. What will they say;—what do.

My suspense came to an end. The aide-de-camp at length found his tongue.

"Lovely Maümee, you have kept your promise."

"But you, sir, have not yours? No—I read it in your looks. You have yet done nothing for us?"

"Be assured, Maümee, I have not had an opportunity. The general has been so busy, I have had no chance to press the matter upon him. But do not be impatient. I shall be certain to persuade him; and your property shall be restored to you in due time. Tell your mother not to feel uneasy: for *your* sake, beautiful Maümee, I shall spare no exertion. Believe me, I am as anxious as yourself; but you must know the stern disposition of my uncle; and, moreover, that he is on the best 'most friendly terms with the Ringgold family. In this will lie the main difficulty, but I fear not that I shall be able to surmount it."

"O sir, your words are fine, but they have little worth with us now. We have waited long upon your promise to befriend us. We only wished for an investigation; and you might easily have obtained it ere this. We no longer care for our lands, for greater wrongs make us forget the less. I should not have been here to-night, had we not been in sad grief at the misfortune—I should rather say outrage—that has fallen upon my poor brother. You have professed friendship to our family. I come to seek it now, for now may you give proof of it. Obtain my brother's freedom, and we shall then believe in the fair words you have so often spoken. Do not say it is impossible; it cannot even be difficult for you who hold so much authority among the white chiefs. My brother may have been rude; but he has committed no crime that should entail severe punishment. A word to the great war-chief, and he would be set free. Go, then, and speak that word."

"Lovely Maümee! you do not know the nature of the errand upon which you send me. Your brother is a prisoner by orders of the agent, and by the act of the commander-in-chief. It is not with us as among your people. I am only a subordinate in rank, and were I to offer the counsel you propose, I should be rebuked—perhaps punished."

"Oh, you fear rebuke for doing an act of justice?—to say naught of your much offered friendship? Good, sir! I have no more to say, except this—we believe you no longer. You need come to our humble dwelling no more."

She was turning away with a scornful smile. How beautiful seemed that scorn!

"Stay, Maümee!—fair Maümee, do not part from me thus—doubt not that I will do all in my power—"

"Do what I have asked you. Set my brother free—let him return to his home."

"And if I should—"

"Well, sir."

"Know, Maümee, that for me to do so would be to risk everything. I might be degraded from my rank—reduced to the condition of a common soldier—disgraced in the eyes of my country—ay, punished, perhaps, by imprisonment worse than that which your brother is likely to endure. All this would I risk by the act."

The girl paused in her step, but made no reply. "And yet all these chances shall I undergo—ay, the danger of death itself—if you, fair Maümee,"—here the speaker waxed passionate and insinuating—"if you will only consent."

"Consent—to what, sir?"

"Lovely Maümee, need I tell you? Surely you understand my meaning. You cannot be blind to the love—to the passion—to the deep devotion with which your beauty has inspired me—"

"Consent to what, sir?" demanded she, repeating her former words, and in a soft tone, that seemed to promise compliance. "Only to love me, fair Maümee—*to become my mistress.*" For some moments, there was no reply. The grand woman seemed immobile as a statue. She did not even start on hearing the foul proposal, but, on the contrary, stood as if turned to stone.

Her silence had an encouraging effect upon the ardent lover; he appeared to take it for assent. He could not have looked into her eye, or he would there have read an expression that would have hindered him from pressing his suit farther. No—he could not have observed that glance, or he would hardly have made such a mistake.

"Only promise it, fair Maümee; your brother shall be free before the morning, and you shall have everything—"

"Villain, villain, villain! Ha, ha! ha, ha! Ha, ha! ha, ha, ha!"

In all my life, I never heard aught so delightful as that laugh. It was the sweetest sound that ever fell upon my ears. Not all the wedding-bells that ever rang—not all the lutes that ever played—not all the harps and hautboys—the clarions and trumpets—in the world, could have produced such melodious music for me.

The moon seemed to pour silver from the sky—the stars had grown bigger and brighter—the breeze became filled with delicious odours, as if a perfumed censer had been spilled from heaven, and the whole scene appeared suddenly transformed into an Elysium.

Chapter Forty Five.

Two Duels in One Day.

The crisis might have been my cue to come down; but I was overpowered with a sense of delightful happiness, and could not stir from my seat. The arrow had been drawn out of my breast, leaving not a taint of its poison—the blood coursed pleasantly through my veins—my pulse throbbed firm and free—my soul was triumphant. I could have cried out for very joy.

With an effort, I held my peace, and waited for the *dénouement*—for I saw that the scene was not yet at an end.

"Mistress, indeed!" exclaimed the bold beauty in scornful accent. "And this is the motive of your proffered friendship. Vile wretch! for what do you mistake me? a camp-wench, or a facile squaw of the Yamassee? Know, sir, that I am your equal in blood and race; and though your pale-faced friends have robbed me of my inheritance, there is that which neither they nor you can take from me—the honour of my name. Mistress, indeed! Silly fellow! No—not even your *wife*. Sooner than sell myself to such base love as yours, I should wander naked through the wild woods, and live upon the acorns of the oak. Rather than redeem him at such a price, my brave brother would spend his lifetime in your chains. Oh, that he were here! Oh, that he were witness of this foul insult! Wretch! he would smite thee like a reed to the earth."

The eye, the attitude, the foot firmly planted, the fearless determined bearing—all reminded me of Osceola while delivering himself before the council. Maümee was undoubtedly his sister.

The *soi-disant* lover quailed before the withering reproach, and for some time stood shrinking and abashed.

He had more than one cause for abasement. He might feel regret at having made a proposal so ill received; but far more at the disappointment of his hopes, and the utter discomfiture of his designs.

Perhaps, the moment before, he would have smothered his chagrin, and permitted the girl to depart without molestation; but the scornful apostrophe had roused him to a sort of frenzied recklessness; and probably it was only at that moment that he formed the resolve to carry his rudeness still further, and effect his purpose by force.

I could not think that he had held such design, anterior to his coming on the ground. Professed libertine though he was, he was not the man for such perilous emprise. He was but a speck of vain conceit, and lacked the reckless daring of the ravisher. It was only when stung by the reproaches of the Indian maiden, that he resolved upon proceeding to extremes.

She had turned her back upon him, and was moving away.

"Not so fast!" cried he, rushing after, and grasping her by the wrist; "not so fast, my brown-skinned charmer! Do you think you can cast me off so lightly? I have followed you for months, and, by the god of Phoebus, I shall make you pay for the false smiles you have treated me to. You needn't struggle; we are alone here; and ere we part, I shall—"

I heard no more of this hurried speech—I had risen from my perch, and was hurrying down to the rescue; but before I could reach the spot, another was before me.

Haj-Ewa—her eyes glaring fiercely—with a wild maniac laugh upon her lips—was rushing forward. She held the body of the rattlesnake in her extended hands, its head projected in front, while its long neck was oscillating from side to side, showing that the reptile was angry, and eager to make an attack. Its hiss, and the harsh "skirr-rr" of its rattles could be heard sounding at intervals as it was carried forward.

In another instant, the maniac was face to face with the would-be ravisher—who, startled by her approach, had released his hold of the girl, and falling back a pace, stood gazing with amazement at this singular intruder.

"Ho, ho!" screamed the maniac, as she glided up to the spot. "His son, his son! Ho! I am sure of it, just like his false father—just as he on the day he wronged the trusting Ewa. Hulwak! It is the hour—the very hour—the moon in the same quarter, horned and wicked—smiling upon the guilt. Ho, ho! the hour of the deed—the hour of vengeance! The father's crime shall be atoned by the son. Great Spirit! give me revenge! *Chitta mico!* give me revenge!"

As she uttered these apostrophic appeals, she sprang forward, holding the snake far outstretched—as if to give it the opportunity of striking the now terrified man.

The latter mechanically drew his sword, and then, as if inspired by the necessity of defending himself, cried out:

"Hellish sorceress! if you come a step nearer, I shall run you through the body. Back, now! Keep off, or, by — I shall do it!"

The resolution expressed by his tone proved that the speaker was in earnest; but the appeal was unheeded. The maniac continued to advance despite the shining blade that menaced her, and within reach of whose point she had already arrived.

I was now close to the spot; I had drawn my own blade, and was hurrying forward to ward off the fatal blow which I expected every moment would be struck. It was my design to save Haj-Ewa, who seemed recklessly rushing upon her destruction.

In all probability, I should have been too late, had the thrust been given; but it was not.

Whether from terror at the wild unearthly aspect of his assailants, or, what is more likely, fearing that she was about to fling the snake upon him, the man appeared struck with a sudden panic, and retreated backward.

A step or two brought him to the edge of the water. There were loose stones strewed thickly along the shore; among these his feet became entangled; and, balancing backward, he fell with a plash upon the pond!

The water deepened abruptly, and he sank out of sight. Perhaps the sudden immersion was the means of saving his life; but the moment after, he rose above the surface, and clambered hastily up on the bank.

He was now furious, and with his drawn sword, which he had managed to retain hold of, he rushed towards the spot where Haj-Ewa still stood. His angry oaths told his determination to slay her.

It was not the soft, yielding body of a woman, nor yet of a reptile, that his blade was to encounter. It struck against steel, hard and shining as his own.

I had thrown myself between him and his victims, and had succeeded in restraining Haj-Ewa from carrying out her vengeful design. As the assailant approached, his rage, but more, the water half-blinding him, hindered him from seeing me; and it was not till our blades had rasped together, that he seemed aware of my presence.

There was a momentary pause, accompanied by silence.

"You, Randolph!" at length he exclaimed in a tone of surprise.

"Ay, Lieutenant Scott—Randolph it is. Pardon my intrusion, but your pretty love-scene changing so suddenly to a quarrel, I deemed it my duty to interfere."

"You have been listening?—you have heard?—and pray, sir, what business have you either to play the spy on my actions, or interfere in my affairs?"

"Business—right—duty—the duty which all men have to protect weak innocence from the designs of such a terrible Blue Beard as you appear to be."

"By —, you shall rue this."

"Now?—or when?"

"Whenever you please."

"No time like the present. Come on."

Not another word was spoken between us; but, the instant after, our blades were clinking in the fierce game of thrust and parry.

The affair was short. At the third or fourth lunge, I ran my antagonist through the right shoulder, disabling his arm. His sword fell jingling among the pebbles.

"You have wounded me!" cried he; "I am disarmed," he added, pointing to the fallen blade. "Enough, sir; I am satisfied."

"But not I—not till you have knelt upon these stones, and asked pardon from her whom you have so grossly insulted."

"Never!" cried he; "never!"—and as he uttered these words, giving, as I presumed, a proof of determined courage, he turned suddenly; and, to my utter astonishment, commenced running away from the ground!

I ran after, and soon overtook him. I could have thrust him in the back, had I been sanguinarily inclined; but instead, I contented myself with giving him a foot-salute, in what Gallagher would have termed his "postayriors," and with no other adieu, left him to continue his shameful flight.

Chapter Forty Six.

A Silent Declaration.

"Now for the love, the sweet young love,
Under the *tala* tree," etc.

It was the voice of Haj-Ewa, chanting one of her favourite melodies. Far sweeter the tones of another voice pronouncing my own name:

"George Randolph!"

"Maümee!"

"*Ho, ho!* you both remember?—still remember? *Hinklas!* The island—that fair island—fair to you, but dark in the memory of Haj-Ewa. *Hulwak!* I'll think of't no more—no, no!

"Now for the love, the sweet young love,
Under—

"It was once mine—it is now yours, mico! yours, *haintclitz!* Pretty creatures! enjoy it alone; you wish not the mad queen for a companion? Ha, ha! *Cooree, cooree!* I go; fear not the rustling wind, fear not the whispering trees; none can approach while Haj-Ewa watches. She will be your guardian. *Chitta mico,* too. Ho, *chitta mico!*

"Now for the love, the sweet young love."

And again renewing her chant, the strange woman glided from the spot, leaving me alone with Maümee.

The moment was not without embarrassment to me—perhaps to both of us. No profession had ever passed between us, no assurance, not a word of love. Although I loved Maümee with all my heart's strength, although I now felt certain that she loved me, there had been no mutual declaration of our passion. The situation was a peculiar one, and the tongue felt restraint.

But words would have been superfluous in that hour. There was an electricity passing between us—our souls were *en rapport,* our hearts in happy communion, and each understood the thoughts of the other. Not all the words in the world could have given me surer satisfaction that the heart of Maümee was mine.

It was scarcely possible that *she* could misconceive. With but slight variation, my thoughts were hers. In all likelihood, Haj-Ewa had carried to her ears my earnest declaration. Her look was joyful—assured. She did not doubt me.

I extended my arms, opening them widely. Nature prompted me, or perhaps passion—all the same. The silent signal was instantly understood, and the moment after, the head of my beloved was nestling upon my bosom.

Not a word was spoken. A low fond cry alone escaped her lips as she fell upon my breast, and twined her arms in rapturous compression around me.

For some moments we exchanged not speech; our hearts alone held converse.

Soon the embarrassment vanished, as a light cloud before the summer sun: not a trace of shyness remained; and we conversed in the confidence of mutual love.

I am spared the writing of our love-speeches. You have yourself heard or uttered them. If too common-place to be repeated, so also are they too sacred. I forbear to detail them.

We had other thoughts to occupy us. After a while, the transport of our mutual joys, though still sweet, assumed a more sober tinge; and, half-forgetting the present, we talked of the past and the future.

I questioned Maümee much. Without guile, she gave me the history of that long interval of absence. She confessed, or rather declared—for there was no coquettish hesitation in her manner—that she had loved me from the first—even from that hour when I first saw and loved her: through the long silent years, by night as by day, had the one thought held possession of her bosom. In her simplicity, she wondered I had not known of it!

I reminded her that her love had never been declared. It was true, she said; but she had never dreamt of concealing it. She thought I might have perceived it. Her instincts were keener: she had been *conscious of mine!*

So declared she, with a freedom that put me off my guard.

If not stronger, her passion was nobler than my own.

She had never doubted me during the years of separation. Only of late; but the cause of this doubt was explained: the pseudo-lover had poured poison into her ears. Hence the errand of Haj-Ewa.

Alas! my story was not so guileless. Only part of the truth could I reveal; and my conscience smote me as I passed over many an episode that would have given pain.

But the past was past, and could not be re-enacted. A more righteous future was opening before me; and silently in my heart did I register vows of atonement. Never more should I have cause to reproach myself—never would my love—never could it wander away from the beautiful being I held in my embrace.

Proudly my bosom swelled as I listened to the ingenuous confession of her love, but sadly when other themes became the subject of our converse. The story of family trials, of wrongs endured, of insults put upon them—and more especially by their white neighbours, the Ringgolds—caused my blood to boil afresh.

The tale corresponded generally with what I had already learned; but there were other circumstances unknown to public rumour. He, too—the wretched hypocrite—had *made love to her.* He had of late desisted from his importunities, through fear of her brother, and dared no longer come near.

The other, Scott, had made his approaches under the guise of friendship. He had learned, what was known to many, the position of affairs with regard to the Indian widow's plantation. From his relationship in high quarters, he possessed influence, and had promised to exert it in obtaining restitution. It was a mere pretence—a promise made without any intention of being kept; but, backed by fair words, it had deceived the generous, trusting heart of Osceola. Hence the admission of this heartless cur into the confidence of a family intimacy.

For months had the correspondence existed, though the opportunities were but occasional. During all this time had the *soi-disant* seducer been pressing his suit—though not very boldly, since he too dreaded the frown of that terrible brother—neither successfully: he had *not* succeeded.

Ringgold well knew this when he affirmed the contrary. His declaration had but one design—to sting *me.* For such purpose, it could not have been made in better time.

There was one thing I longed to know. Surely Maümee, with her keen quick perception, from the girlish confidence that had existed between them—surely she could inform me. I longed to know the relations that had existed between my sister and her brother.

Much as I desired the information, I refrained from asking it.

And yet we talked of both—of Virginia especially, for Maümee remembered my sister with affection, and made many inquiries in relation to her. Virginia was more beautiful than ever, she had heard, and accomplished beyond all others. She wondered if my sister would remember those walks and girlish amusements—those happy hours upon the island.

"Perhaps," thought I, "*too well.*"

It was a theme that gave me pain.

The future claimed our attention; the past was now bright as heaven, but there were clouds in the sky of the future.

We talked of that nearest and darkest—the imprisonment of Osceola. How long would it last? What could be done to render it as brief as possible?

I promised to do everything in my power; and I purposed as I promised. It was my firm resolve to leave no stone unturned to effect the liberation of the captive chief. If right should not prevail, I was determined to try stratagem. Even with the sacrifice of my commission—even though personal disgrace should await me—the risk of life itself—I resolved he should be free.

I needed not to add to my declaration the emphasis of an oath; I was believed without that. A flood of gratitude was beaming from those liquid orbs; and the silent pressure of love-burning lips was sweeter thanks than words could have uttered.

It was time for parting; the moon told the hour of midnight.

On the crest of the hill, like a bronze statue outlined against the pale sky, stood the mad queen. A signal brought her to our side; and after another embrace, one more fervid pressure of sweet lips, Maümee and I parted.

Her strange but faithful guardian led her away by some secret path, and I was left alone.

I could scarcely take myself away from that consecrated ground; and I remained for some minutes longer, giving full play to triumphant and rapturous reflections.

The declining moon again warned me; and, crossing the crest of the hill, I hastened back to the Fort.

Chapter Forty Seven.

The Captive.

Late as was the hour, I determined to visit the captive before going to rest. My design would not admit of delay; besides, I had a suspicion that, before another day passed, my own liberty might be curtailed. Two duels in one day—two antagonists wounded, and both friends to the commander-in-chief—myself comparatively friendless—it was hardly probable I should escape "scot free." Arrest I expected as certain—perhaps a trial by court-martial, with a fair chance of being cashiered the service.

Despite my lukewarmness in the cause in which we had become engaged, I could not contemplate this result without uneasiness. Little did I care for my commission: I could live without it; but whether right or wrong, few men are indifferent to the censure of their fellows, and no man likes to bear the brand of official disgrace. Reckless as one may be of self, kindred and family have a concern in the matter not to be lightly ignored.

Gallagher's views were different.

"Let them arrist and cashear, an' be hanged! What need you care? Divil a bit, my boy. Sowl, man, if I were in your boots, with a fine plantation and a whole regiment of black nagers, I'd snap my fingers at the sarvice, and go to raisin' shugar and tobaccay. Be Saint Pathrick! that's what I'd do."

My friend's consolatory speech failed to cheer me; and, in no very joyous mood, I walked towards the quarters of the captive, to add still further to my chances of "cashierment."

Like an eagle freshly caught and caged—like a panther in a pentrap—furious, restless, at intervals uttering words of wild menace, I found the young chief of the *Baton Rouge*.

The apartment was quite dark; there was no window to admit even the grey lustre of the night; and the corporal who guided me in carried neither torch nor candle. He went back to the guard-house to procure one, leaving me in darkness.

I heard the footfall of a man. It was the sound of a moccasined foot, and soft as the tread of a tiger; but mingling with this was the sharp clanking of a chain. I heard the breathing of one evidently in a state of excitement, and now and then an exclamation of fierce anger. Without light, I could perceive that the prisoner was pacing the apartment in rapid, irregular strides. At least his limbs were free.

I had entered silently, and stood near the door, I had already ascertained that the prisoner was alone; but waited for the light before addressing him. Preoccupied as he appeared to be, I fancied that he was not conscious of my presence.

My fancy was at fault. I heard him stop suddenly in his tracks—as if turning towards me—and the next moment his voice fell upon my ear. To my surprise, it pronounced my name. He must have seen through the darkness.

"You, Randolph!" he said, in a tone that expressed reproach; "you, too, in the ranks of our enemies? Armed—uniformed—equipped—ready to aid in driving us from our homes!"

"Powell!"

"Not Powell, sir; my name is Osceola."

"To me, still Edward Powell—the friend of my youth, the preserver of my life. By that name alone do I remember you."

There was a momentary pause. The speech had evidently produced a conciliating effect; perhaps memories of the past had come over him.

He replied:

"Your errand? Come you as a friend? or only like others, to torment me with idle words? I have had visitors already; gay, gibbering fools, with forked tongues, who would counsel me to dishonour. Have *you* been sent upon a like mission?"

From this speech I concluded that Scott—the pseudo-friend—had already been with the captive—likely on some errand from the agent.

"I come of my own accord—as a friend."

"George Randolph, I believe you. As a boy, you possessed a soul of honour. The straight sapling rarely grows to a crooked tree. I will not believe that you are changed, though enemies have spoken against you. No—no; your hand, Randolph—your hand! forgive me for doubting you."

I reached through the darkness to accept the proffered salute. Instead of one, I grasped both hands of the prisoner. I felt that they were manacled together: for all that, the pressure was firm and true; nor did I return it with less warmth.

Enemies had spoken against me. I needed not to ask who these were: that had been already told me; but I felt it necessary to give the captive assurance of my friendship. I needed his full confidence to insure the success of the plan which I had conceived for his liberation; and to secure this, I detailed to him what had transpired by the pond—only a portion of what had passed. There was a portion of it I could not intrust even to the ears of a brother.

I anticipated a fresh paroxysm of fury, but was agreeably disappointed. The young chief had been accustomed to harsh developments, and could outwardly control himself; but I saw that my tale produced an impression that told deeply, if not loudly, upon him. In the darkness, I could not see his face; but the grinding teeth and hissing ejaculations were expressive of the strong passions stirring within.

"Fool!" he exclaimed at length—"blind fool that I have been! And yet I suspected this smooth-tongued villain from the first. Thanks, noble Randolph! I can never repay this act of chivalric friendship; henceforth you may command Osceola!"

"Say no more, Powell; you have nothing to repay; it was I who was the debtor. But come, we lose time. My purpose in coming here is to counsel you to a plan for procuring your release from this awkward confinement. We must be brief, else my intentions may be suspected."

"What plan, Randolph?"

"You must sign the treaty of the Oclawaha."

Chapter Forty Eight.

The War-Cry.

A single "Ugh!" expressive of contemptuous surprise, was all the reply; and then a deep silence succeeded.

I broke the silence by repeating my demand.

"You must sign it."

"Never!" came the response, in a tone of emphatic determination. "Never! Sooner than do that, I will linger among these logs till decay has worn the flesh from my bones, and dried up the blood in my veins. Sooner than turn traitor to my tribe, I will rush against the bayonets of my jailers, and perish upon the spot. Never!"

"Patience, Powell, patience! You do not understand me—you, in common with other chiefs, appear to misconceive the terms of this treaty. Remember, it binds you to a mere conditional promise—to surrender your lands and move west, only in case a *majority of your nation agree to it*. Now, to-day a majority has *not* agreed, nor will the addition of your name make the number a majority."

"True, true," interrupted the chief, beginning to comprehend my meaning.

"Well, then, you may sign, and not feel bound by your signature, since the most essential condition still remains unfulfilled. And why should you not adopt this ruse? Ill-used as you certainly have been, no one could pronounce it dishonourable in you. For my part, I believe you would be justified in any expedient that would free you from so wrongful an imprisonment."

Perhaps my principles were scarcely according to the rules of moral rectitude; but at that moment they took their tone from strong emotions; and to the eyes of friendship and love the wrong was not apparent.

Osceola was silent. I observed that he was meditating on what I had urged.

"Why, Randolph," said he, after a pause, "you must have dwelt in Philadelphia, that famed city of lawyers. I never took this view before. You are right; signing would *not* bind me—it is true. But think you that the agent would be satisfied with my signature? He hates me; I know it, and his reasons. I hate *him*, for many reasons; for this is not the first outrage I have suffered at his hands. Will he be satisfied if I sign?"

"I am almost certain of it. Simulate submission, *if you can*. Write your name to the treaty, and you will be at once set free."

I had no doubt of this. From what I had learned since Osceola's arrest, I had reason to believe that Thompson repented his conduct. It was the opinion of others that he had acted rashly, and that his act was likely to provoke evil consequences. Whispers of this nature had reached him; and from what the captive told me of the visit of the aide-de-camp, I could perceive that it was nothing else than a mission from the agent himself. Beyond doubt, the latter was tired of his prisoner, and would release him on the easiest terms.

"Friend! I shall act as you advise. I shall sign. You may inform the commissioner of my intention."

"I shall do so at the earliest hour I can see him. It is late: shall I say good night?"

"Ah, Randolph! it is hard to part with a friend—the only one with a white skin now left me. I could have wished to talk over other days, but, alas! this is neither the place nor the time."

The haughty mien of the proud chief was thrown aside, and his voice had assumed the melting tenderness of early years.

"Yes," he continued, "the only white friend left—the only one I have any regard for—one other whom I—"

He stopped suddenly, and with an embarrassed air, as if he had found himself on the eve of disclosing some secret, which on reflection he deemed it imprudent to reveal.

I awaited the disclosure with some uneasiness, but it came not. When he spoke again, his tone and manner were completely changed.

"The whites have done us much wrong," he continued, once more rousing himself into an angry attitude—"wrongs too numerous to be told; but, by the Great Spirit! I shall seek revenge. Never till now have I sworn it; but the deeds of this day have turned my blood into fire. Ere you came, I had vowed to take the lives of two, who have been our especial enemies. You have not changed my resolution, only strengthened it; you have added a third to the list of my deadly foes: and once more I swear—by Wykomé, I swear—that I shall take no rest till the blood of these three men has reddened the leaves of the forest—three white villains, and one red traitor. Ay, Omatla! triumph in your treason—it will not be for long— soon shalt thou feel the Vengeance of a patriot—soon shalt thou shrink under the steel of Osceola!"

I made no reply, but waited in silence till this outburst of passion had passed.

In a few moments the young chief became calm, and again addressed me in the language of friendship.

"One word," said he, "before we part. Circumstances may hinder us—it may be long ere we meet again. Alas! our next meeting may be as foes in the field of fight—for I will not attempt to conceal from you that I have no intention to make peace. No—never! I wish to make a request; I know, Randolph, you will accede to it without asking an explanation. Accept this token, and if you esteem the friendship of the giver, and would honour him, wear it conspicuously upon your breast. That is all."

As he spoke, he took from around his neck a chain, upon which was suspended the image of the Rising Sun—already alluded to. He passed the chain over my head, until the glistening symbol hung down upon my breast.

I made no resistance to this offering of friendship, but promising to comply with his request, presented my watch in return, and, after another cordial pressure of hands, we parted.

106

As I had anticipated, there was but little difficulty in obtaining the release of the Seminole chief. Though the commissioner entertained a personal hatred against Osceola—for causes to me unknown—he dared not indulge his private spite in an official capacity. He had placed himself in a serious dilemma by what he had already done; and as I communicated the purposed submission of the prisoner, I saw that Thompson was but too eager to adopt a solution of his difficulty, easy as unexpected. He therefore lost no time in seeking an interview with the captive chief.

The latter played his part with admirable tact; the fierce, angry attitude of yesterday had given place to one of mild resignation. A night in the guard-house, hungered and manacled, had tamed down his proud spirit, and he was now ready to accept any conditions that would restore him to liberty. So fancied the commissioner.

The treaty was produced. Osceola signed it without saying a word. His chains were taken off—his prison-door thrown open—and he was permitted to depart without further molestation. Thompson had triumphed, or fancied so.

It was but fancy. Had he noticed, as I did, the fine satirical smile that played upon the lips of Osceola as he stepped forth from the gate, he would scarcely have felt confidence in his triumph.

He was not allowed to exult long in the pleasant hallucination.

Followed by the eyes of all, the young chief walked off with a proud step towards the woods.

On arriving near the edge of the timber, he faced round to the fort, drew the shining blade from his belt, waved it above his head, and in defiant tones shouted back the war-cry, "Yo-ho-ehee!"

Three times the wild signal pealed upon our ears; and at the third repetition, he who had uttered it turned again, sprang forward into the timber, and was instantly lost to our view.

There was no mistaking the intent of that demonstration; even the self-glorifying commissioner was convinced that it meant "war to the knife," and men were hurriedly ordered in pursuit.

An armed crowd rushed forth from the gate, and flung themselves on the path that had been taken by the *ci-devant* captive.

The chase proved bootless and fruitless; and after more than an hour spent in vein search, the soldiers came straggling back to the fort.

Gallagher and I had stayed all the morning in my quarters, expecting the order that would confine me there. To our astonishment it came not: there was no arrest.

In time, we obtained the explanation. Of my two duelling antagonists, the first had not returned to the fort after his defeat, but had been carried to the house of a friend—several miles distant. This partially covered the scandal of that affair. The other appeared with his arm in a sling; but it was the impression, as Gallagher learned outside, that his horse had carried him against a tree. For manifest reasons the interesting invalid had not disclosed the true cause of his being "crippled," and I applauded his silence. Except to my friend, I made no disclosure of what had occurred, and it was long before the affair got wind.

Upon duty, the aide-de-camp and I often met afterwards, and were frequently compelled to exchange speech; but it was always of an official character, and, I need not add, was spoken in the severest reserve.

It was not long before circumstances arose to separate us; and I was glad to part company with a man for whom I felt a profound contempt.

Chapter Forty Nine.

War to the Knife.

For some weeks following the council at Fort King, there appeared to be tranquillity over the land. The hour of negotiation had passed—that for action was nigh; and among the white settlers the leading topic of conversation was how the Indians would act? Would they fight, or give in? The majority believed they would submit.

Some time was granted them to prepare for the removal—runners were sent to all the tribes, appointing a day for them to bring in their horses and cattle to the fort. These were to be sold by auction, under the superintendence of the agent; and their owners were to receive a fair value for them on their arrival at their new home in the west. Their plantations or "improvements" were to be disposed of in a similar manner.

The day of auction came round; but, to the chagrin of the commissioner, the expected flocks did not make their appearance, and the sale had to be postponed.

The failure on the part of the Indians to bring in their cattle was a hint of what might be expected; though others, of a still more palpable nature, were soon afforded.

The tranquillity that had reigned for some weeks was but the ominous silence that precedes the storm. Like the low mutterings of the distant thunder, events now began to occur, the sure harbingers of an approaching conflict.

As usual, the white man was the aggressor. Three Indians were found hunting outside the boundary of the "reserve." They were made captives by a party of white men, and, fast bound with raw-hide ropes, were confined in a log-stable belonging to one of the party. In this situation they were kept three days and nights, until a band of their own tribe hearing of their confinement, hastened to their rescue. There was a skirmish, in which some Indians were wounded; but the white men fled, and the captives were released.

"On bringing them forth to the light, their friends beheld a most pitiable sight,"—I am quoting from a faithful history—"the rope with which these poor fellows were tied had worn through the flesh: they had temporarily lost the use of their limbs, being unable to stand or walk. They had bled profusely, and had received no food during their confinement; so it may readily be imagined that they presented a horrible picture of suffering."

Again: "Six Indians were at their camp near Kanapaha Pond, when a party of whites came upon them, took their guns from them, examined their packs, and commenced whipping them. While in the act, two other Indians approached, and seeing what was going on, fired upon the whites. The latter returned the fire, killed one of the Indians, and severely wounded the other."

Exasperation was natural—retaliation certain. On the other side, read:

"On the 11th of August, Dalton, the mail-carrier between Fort King and Fort Brooke, was met within six miles of the latter place by a party of Indians, who seized the reins of his horse, and dragging him from the saddle, shot him dead. The mangled body was discovered some days afterwards concealed in the woods."

"A party of fourteen mounted men proceeded on a scout towards Wacahonta—the plantation of Captain Gabriel Priest—and when within one mile of the place, they came upon a small hommock, through which some of the party declined passing. Four of them, however, dashed into it, when the Indians suddenly arose from ambush, and fired upon them. The two in advance were wounded. A Mr Foulke received a bullet in his neck, but was picked up by those in his rear, and borne off. The other, a son of Captain Priest, had his arm broken, and his horse shot dead under him. He fled, and sinking his body in a swamp, succeeded in eluding the search of the pursuers."

"About the same time, a party of Indians attacked a number of men who were employed cutting live-oak timber on an island in Lake George. The men escaped by taking to their boats, though two of their number were wounded."

"At New River, on the south-east side of the peninsula, the Indians attacked the house of a Mr Cooley—murdered his wife, children, and a tutor engaged in the family. They carried off twelve barrels of provisions, thirty hogs, three horses, one keg of powder, over two hundred pounds of lead, seven hundred dollars in silver, and two negroes. Mr Cooley was absent at the time. On his return, he found his wife shot through the heart with her infant child in her arms, and his two oldest children also shot in the same place. The girl still held her book in her hands, and the boy's lay by his side. The house was in flames."

"At Spring Garden, on the Saint Johns, the extensive plantation of Colonel Rees was laid waste, and his buildings burnt to the ground. Sugar-cane, sufficient to manufacture ninety hogsheads, was destroyed; besides thirty hogsheads of sugar, and *one hundred and sixty-*

two negroes were carried off. The mules and horses were also taken. The same Indians destroyed the buildings of M. Depeyster, with *whose negroes they formed a league;* and being supplied with a boat, they crossed the river and fired the establishment of Captain Dummett. Major Heriot's plantation was laid waste, and *eighty of his negroes moved off with the Indians.* Then on towards San Augustine, where the extensive plantations of General Hernandez were reduced to a ruin; next, Bulow's, Dupont's of Buen Retiro, Dunham's, McRae's of Tomoka Creek, the plantations of Bayas, General Herring, and Bartalone Solano, with nearly every other from San Augustine southward."

Simple historic facts. I quote them as illustrating the events that ushered in the Seminole war. Barbarous though they be, they were but acts of retaliation—the wild outburst of a vengeance long pent up—a return for wrongs and insults patiently endured.

As yet, no general engagement had taken place; but marauding parties sprang up simultaneously in different places. Many of those who had inflicted outrage upon the Indians were forthwith repaid; and many barely escaped with their lives. Conflagration succeeded conflagration, until the whole country was on fire. Those who lived in the interior, or upon the borders of the Indian reserve, were compelled to abandon their crops, their stock, their implements of husbandly, their furniture, and indeed every article of value, and seek shelter within the forts, or concentrate themselves in the neighbouring villages, around which stockades were erected for their better security.

The friendly chiefs—the Omatlas and others—with about four hundred followers, abandoned their towns, and fled to Fort Brooke for protection.

The strife was no longer hypothetical, no longer doubtful; it was declared in the wild *Yo-ho-ehee!* that night and day was heard ringing in the woods.

Chapter Fifty.

Tracing a Strange Horseman.

As yet but few troops had reached Florida, though detachments were on the way from New Orleans, Fort Moultrie, Savannah, Mobile, and other dépôts, where the soldiers of the United States are usually stationed. Corps of volunteers, however, were being hastily levied in the larger towns of Georgia, Carolina, and Florida itself; and every settlement was mustering its quota to enter upon the campaign.

It was deemed advisable to raise a force in the settlements of the Suwanee—my native district—and on this duty my friend Gallagher was dispatched, with myself to act as his lieutenant.

Right gladly did I receive this order. I should escape from the monotonous duties of the fort garrison, of which I had grown weary enough; but what was a still more pleasant prospect, I should have many days at home—for which I was not without longing.

Gallagher was as overjoyed as myself. He was a keen sportsman; though, having spent most of his life within the walls of cities, or in forts along the Atlantic seaboard, he had found only rare opportunities of enjoying either the "fox-chase" or "deer-drive." I had promised him both to his heart's content, for both the game and the "vermin" were plenteous in the woods of the Suwanee.

Not unwillingly, therefore, did we accept our recruiting commission; and, bidding adieu to our companions at the fort, set out with light hearts and pleasant anticipations. Equally joyous was Black Jake to get back once more to the "ole plantayshun."

In the quarter of the Suwanee settlements, the Indian marauders had not yet shown themselves. It lay remote from the towns of most of the hostile tribes, though not too distant for a determined foray. In a sort of lethargic security, the inhabitants still remained at their houses—though a volunteer force had already been mustered—and patrols were kept in constant motion.

I had frequent letters from my mother and Virginia; neither appeared to feel any alarm: my sister especially declared her confidence that the Indians would not molest them.

Withal, I was not without apprehension; and with so much the greater alacrity did I obey the order to proceed to the settlements.

Well mounted, we soon galloped over the forest road, and approached the scenes of my early life. This time, I encountered no ambuscade, though I did not travel without caution. But the order had been given us within the hour; and having almost immediately set forth, my assassin-enemies could have had no warning of my movements. With the brave Gallagher by my side, and my stout henchman at my back, I dreaded no open attack from white men.

My only fear was, that we might fall in with some straggling party of red men—now our declared enemies. In this there was a real danger; and we took every precaution to avoid such an encounter.

At several places we saw traces of the Indians nearly fresh. There were moccasin prints, in the mud, and the tracks of horses that had been mounted. At one place we observed the débris of a fire still smouldering, and around it were signs of the red men. A party had there bivouacked.

But we saw no man, red or white, until we had passed the deserted plantation upon the creek, and were approaching the banks of the river. Then for the first time during our journey a man was in sight.

He was a horseman, and at a glance we pronounced him an Indian. He was at too great a distance for us to note either his complexion or features; but the style of dress, his attitude in the saddle, the red sash and leggings, and above all, the ostrich-plumes waving over his head, told us he was a Seminole. He was mounted upon a large black horse; and had just emerged from the wood into the opening, upon which we had ourselves entered. He appeared to see us at the same time we caught sight of him, and was evidently desirous of avoiding us.

After scanning us a moment, he wheeled his steed, and dashed back into the timber.

Imprudently enough, Gallagher put spurs to his horse and galloped after. I should have counselled a contrary course; but that the belief was in my mind that the horseman was Osceola. In that case, there could be no danger; and from motives of friendship, I was desirous of coming up with the young chief, and exchanging a word with him. With this view I followed my friend at a gallop—Jake coming on in the rear.

I was almost sure the strange horseman was Osceola. I fancied I recognised the ostrich-plumes; and Jake had told me that the young chief rode a fine black horse. In all likelihood, then it was he; and in order to hail, and bring him to a halt, I spurred ahead of Gallagher—being better mounted.

We soon entered the timber, where the horseman had disappeared. I saw the fresh tracks, but nothing more. I shouted aloud, calling the young chief by name, and pronouncing my own; but there was no reply, save the echo of my voice.

I followed the trail for a short distance, continuing to repeat my cries; but no heed was given to them. The horseman did not wish to answer my hail, or else had ridden too far away to understand its intent.

Of course, unless he made a voluntary halt, it was vain to follow. We might ride on his trail for a week without coming up with him. Gallagher saw this as well as myself; and abandoning the pursuit, we turned once more towards the road, with the prospect of soon ending our journey.

A cross-path, which I remembered, would bring us by a shorter route to the landing; and for this we now headed.

We had not ridden far, when we again struck upon the tracks of a horse—evidently those made by the horseman we had just pursued, but previously to our having seen him. They led in a direct line from the river, towards which we were steering.

Some slight thought prompted me to an examination of the hoof-prints. I perceived that they were *wet*—water was oozing into them from the edges; there was a slight sprinkling of water upon the dead leaves that lay along the trail. The horseman had been swimming—he had been across the river!

This discovery led me into a train of reflection. What could he—an Indian—want on the other side? If Osceola, as I still believed, what could *he* be doing there? In the excited state of the country, it would have been risking his life for an Indian to have approached the settlement—and to have been discovered and captured would have been certain death. This

Indian, then, whoever he was, must have some powerful-motive for seeking the other side. What motive? If Osceola, what motive?

I was puzzled—and reflected; I could think of no motive, unless that the young chief had been playing the spy—no dishonourable act on the part of an Indian.

The supposition was not improbable, but the contrary; and yet I could not bring myself to believe it true. A cloud had swept suddenly over my soul, a presentiment scarcely defined or definable was in my thoughts, a demon seemed to whisper in my ears: *It is not that.*

Certainly had the horseman been across the river? Let us see!

We rode rapidly along the trail, tracing it backwards.

In a few minutes it guided us to the bank, where the tracks led out from the water's edge. No corresponding trail entered near. Yes, he had been across.

I plied the spur, and plunging in, swam for the opposite shore. My companion followed without asking any questions.

Once more out of the river, I rode up the bank. I soon discovered the hoof-marks of the black horse where he had sprung off into the stream.

Without pausing, I continued to trace them backwards, still followed by Gallagher and Jake.

The former wondered at my eagerness, and put some questions, which I scarcely answered coherently. My presentiment was each moment growing darker—my heart throbbed in my bosom with a strange indescribable pain.

The trail brought us to a small opening in the heart of a magnolia grove. It went no further. We had arrived at its end.

My eyes rested upon the ground with a sort of mechanical gaze. I sat in the saddle in a kind of stupor. The dark presentiment was gone, but a far darker thought occupied its place.

The ground was covered with hoof-tracks, as if horses had been halted there. Most of the tracks were those of the black horse; but there were others of not half their dimensions. There was the tiny shoe-mark of a small pony.

"Golly! Mass'r George," muttered Jake, coming forward in advance of the other, and bending his eyes upon the ground; "lookee dar—dat am tha track ob de leetle White Fox. Missa Vaginny's been hya for sartin."

Chapter Fifty One.

Who was the Rider?

I felt faint enough to have reeled from the saddle; but the necessity of concealing the thoughts that were passing within me, kept me firm. There are suspicions that even a bosom friend may not share; and mine were of this character, if suspicions they could be called. Unhappily, they approached the nature of convictions.

I saw that Gallagher was mystified; not, as I supposed, by the tracks upon the ground, but by my behaviour in regard to them. He had observed my excited manner on taking up the trail, and while following it; he could not have failed to do so; and now, on reaching the glade, he looked upon a pallid face, and lips quivering with emotions to him unintelligible.

"What is it, Geordie, my boy? Do you think the ridskin has been after some dhirty game? Playing the spy on your plantation, eh?"

The question aided me in my dilemma. It suggested a reply which I did not believe to be the truth.

"Likely enough," I answered, without displaying any embarrassment; "an Indian spy, I have no doubt of it; and evidently in communication with some of the negroes, since this is the track of a pony that belongs to the plantation. Some of them have ridden thus far to meet him; though for what purpose it is difficult to guess."

"Massa George," spoke out my black follower, "dar's no one ebber ride da White Fox, 'ceptin'—"

"Jake!" I shouted, sharply interrupting him, "gallop forward to the house, and tell them we are coming. Quick, my man!"

My command was too positive to be obeyed with hesitation; and, without finishing his speech, the black put spurs to his cob, and rode rapidly past us.

It was a manoeuvre of mere precaution. But the moment before, I had no thought of dispatching an *avant courier* to announce us. I knew what the simple fellow was about to say: "No one ebber ride da White Fox, 'ceptin' Missa Vaginny;" and I had adopted this ruse to stifle his speech.

I glanced towards my companion, after Jake had passed out of sight. He was a man of open heart and free of tongue, with not one particle of the secretive principle in his nature. His fine florid face was seldom marked by a line of suspicion; but I observed that it now wore a puzzled expression, and I felt uneasy. No remark, however, was made by either of us; and turning into the path which Jake had taken, we rode forward.

The path was a cattle-track—too narrow to admit of our riding abreast; and Gallagher permitting me to act as pilot, drew his horse into the rear. In this way we moved silently onward.

I had no need to direct my horse. It was an old road to him: he knew where he was going. I took no heed of him, but left him to stride forward at his will.

I scarcely looked at the path—once or twice only—and then I saw the tracks of the pony—backward and forward; but I heeded them no more; I knew whence and whither they led.

I was too much occupied with thoughts within, to notice aught without or around me.

Could it have been any other than Virginia? Who else? It was true what Jake had intended to say—that no one except my sister ever rode "White Fox"—no one upon the plantation being permitted to mount this favourite miniature of a steed.

Yes—there was an exception. I had seen Viola upon him. Perhaps Jake would have added this exception, had I allowed him to finish his speech. Might it have been Viola?

But what could be her purpose in meeting the Seminole chief? for that the person who rode the pony had held an interview with the latter, there could not be the shadow of a doubt; the tracks told that clearly enough.

What motive could have moved the quadroon to such a meeting? Surely none. Not surely, either; how could *I* say so? I had been long absent; many strange events had transpired in my absence—many changes. How could I tell but that Viola had grown "tired" of her sable sweetheart, and looked kindly upon the dashing chieftain? No doubt there had been many opportunities for her seeing the latter; for, after my departure for the north, several years had elapsed before the expulsion of the Powells from their plantation. And now, that I thought of it, I remembered something—a trifling circumstance that had occurred on that very day when young Powell first appeared among us: Viola had expressed admiration of the handsome youth. I remembered that this had made Black Jake very angry; that my sister, too, had been angry, and scolded Viola, as I thought at the time, for mortifying her faithful lover. Viola was a beauty, and like most beauties, a coquette. My conjecture might be right. It was pleasant to think so; but, alas, poor Jake!

Another slight circumstance tended to confirm this view. I had observed of late a change in my henchman; he was certainly not as cheerful as of yore; he appeared more reflective—serious—dull.

God grant that this might be the explanation!

There was another conjecture that offered me a hope; one that, if true, would have satisfied me still better, for I had a strong feeling of friendship for Black Jake.

The other hypothesis was simply what Gallagher had already suggested—although White Fox was not allowed to be ridden, some of the people might have *stolen him for a ride*. It was possible, and not without probability. There might be disaffected slaves on our plantation—there were on almost every other—who were in communication with hostile Indians. The place was more than a mile from the house. Riding would be pleasanter than walking; and taking the pony from its pastures might be easily accomplished, without fear of observation. A great black negro may have been the rider after all. God grant that *this* might be the true explanation!

The mental prayer had scarcely passed my thoughts, when an object came under my eyes, that swept my theories to the wind, sending a fresh pang through my heart.

A locust tree grew by the side of the path, with its branches extending partially across. A strip of ribbon had caught on one of the spines, and was waving in the breeze. It was silk, and of fine texture—a bit of the trimming of a lady's dress torn off by the thorn.

To me it was a sad token. My fabric of hopeful fancies fell into ruin at the sight. No negro—not even Viola—could have left such evidence as that; and I shuddered as I spurred past the fluttering relic.

I was in hopes my companion would not observe it; but he did. It was too conspicuous to be passed without notice. As I glanced back over my shoulder, I saw him reach out his arm, snatch the fragment from the branch, and gaze upon it with a puzzled and inquiring look.

Fearing he might ride up and question me, I spurred my horse into a rapid gallop, at the same time calling to him to follow.

Ten minutes after, we entered the lawn and pulled up in front of the house. My mother and sister had come out into the verandah to receive us; and we were greeted with words of welcome.

But I heard, or heeded them not; my gaze was riveted on Virginia—upon her dress. It was a *riding-habit*: the plumed chapeau was still upon her head!

My beautiful sister—never seemed she more beautiful than at that moment; her cheeks were crimsoned with the wind, her golden tresses hanging over them. But it joyed me not to see her so fair: in my eyes, she appeared a fallen angel.

I glanced at Gallagher as I tottered out of my saddle: I saw that he comprehended all. Nay, more—his countenance wore an expression indicative of great mental suffering, apparently as acute as my own. My friend he was—tried and true; he had observed my anguish—he now guessed the cause; and his look betokened the deep sympathy with which my misfortune inspired him.

Chapter Fifty Two.

Cold Courtesy.

I received my mother's embrace with filial warmth; my sister's in silence—almost with coldness. My mother noticed this, and wondered. Gallagher also shewed reserve in his greeting of Virginia; and neither did this pass unobserved.

Of the four, my sister was the least embarrassed; she was not embarrassed at all. On the contrary, her lips moved freely, and her eyes sparkled with a cheerful expression, as if really joyed by our arrival.

"You have been on horseback, sister?" I said, in a tone that affected indifference as to the reply.

"Say, rather, pony-back. My little Foxey scarcely deserves the proud title of horse. Yes, I have been out for an airing."

"Alone?"

"Quite alone—*solus bolus*, as the black people have it."

"Is it prudent, sister?"

"Why not? I often do it. What have I to fear? The wolves and panthers are hunted out, and White Fox is too swift either for a bear or an alligator."

"There are creatures to be encountered in the woods more dangerous than wild beasts."

I watched her countenance as I made the remark, but I saw not the slightest change.

"What creatures, George?" she asked in a drawling tone, imitating that in which I had spoken.

"Redskins—Indians," I answered abruptly.

"Nonsense, brother; there are no Indians in this neighbourhood—at least," added she with marked hesitation, "none that *we* need fear. Did I not write to tell you so? You are fresh from the hostile ground, where I suppose there is an Indian in every bush; but remember,

Geordy, you have travelled a long way, and unless you have brought the savages with you, you will find none here. So, gentlemen, you may go to sleep to-night without fear of being awakened by the *Yo-ho-ehee.*"

"Is that so certain, Miss Randolph?" inquired Gallagher, now joining in the conversation, and no longer "broguing" it. "Your brother and I have reason to believe that some, who have already raised the war-cry, are not so far off from the settlements of the Suwanee."

"*Miss* Randolph! Ha, ha, ha! Why *Mister* Gallagher, where did you learn that respectful appellative? It is so distant you must have fetched it a long way. *It* used to be Virginia, and Virgine, and Virginny, and simple 'Gin—for which last I could have spitted you, *Mister* Gallagher, and would, had you not given up calling me so. What's the matter? It is just three months since we—that is, you and I, Mister Gallagher—met last; and scarcely two since Geordy and I parted; and now you are both here—one talking as solemnly as Solon, the other as soberly as Socrates! George, I presume, after another spell of absence, will be styling me *Miss* Randolph—I suppose that's the fashion at the fort. Come, fellows," she added, striking the balustrade with her whip, "your minds and your mouths, and give me the reason of this wonderful 'transmogrification,' for by my word, you shall not eat till you do!"

The relation in which Gallagher stood to my sister requires a little explanation. He was not new either to her or my mother. During their sojourn in the north, he had met them both; but the former often. As my almost constant companion, he had ample opportunity of becoming acquainted with Virginia; and he had, in reality, grown well acquainted with her. They met on the most familiar terms—even to using the diminutives of each other's names; and I could understand why my sister regarded "Miss Randolph" as a rather distant mode of address; but I understood, also, why he had thus addressed her.

There was a period when I believed my friend in love with Virginia; that was shortly after their introduction to each other. But as time wore on, I ceased to have this belief. Their behaviour was not that of lovers—at least, according to my notion. They were too *friendly* to be in love. They used to romp together, and read comic books, and laugh, and chatter by the hour about trivial things, and call each other jack-names, and the like. In fact, it was a rare thing to hear them either talk or act soberly when in each other's company. All this was so different from my ideas of how two lovers *would* act—so different from the way in which *I* should have acted—that I gave up the fancy I had held, and afterwards regarded them as two beings whose characters had a certain correspondence, and whose hearts were in unison for friendship, but not for love.

One other circumstance confirmed me in this belief: I observed that my sister, during Gallagher's absence, had little relish for gaiety, which had been rather a characteristic of her girlish days; but the moment the latter would make his appearance, a sudden change would come over her, and she would enter with *abandon* into all the idle bagatelle of the hour.

Love, thought I, does not so exhibit itself. If there was one in whom she felt a heart-interest, it was not he who was present. No—Gallagher was not the man; and the play that passed between them was but the fond familiarity of two persons who esteemed each other, without a spark of love being mixed up in the affection.

The dark suspicion that now rested upon his mind, as upon my own, had evidently saddened him—not from any feeling of jealousy, but out of pure friendly sympathy for me—perhaps, too, for her. His bearing towards her, though within the rules of the most perfect politeness, *was* changed—much changed; no wonder she took notice of it—no wonder she called for an explanation.

"Quick!" cried she, cutting the vine-leaves with her whip. "Is it a travesty, or are you in earnest? Unbosom yourselves both, or I keep my vow—you shall have no dinner. I shall myself go to the kitchen, and countermand it."

Despite the gloomy thoughts passing within, her manner and the odd menace compelled Gallagher to break into laughter—though his laugh was far short of the hearty cachinnation she had been accustomed to hear from him.

I was myself forced to smile; and, seeing the necessity of smothering my emotions, I stammered forth what might pass for an explanation. It was not the time for the true one.

"Verily, sister," said I, "we are too tired for mirth, and too hungry as well. Consider how far we have ridden, and under a broiling sun! Neither of us has tasted a morsel since leaving the fort, and our breakfast there was none of the most sumptuous—corncakes and weak coffee, with pickled pork. How I long for some of Aunt Sheba's Virginia biscuits and 'chicken fixings.' Pray, let us have our dinner, and then you shall see a change in us! We shall both be as merry as sand-boys after it."

Satisfied with this explanation, or affecting to be so—for her response was a promise to let us have our dinner—accompanied by a cheerful laugh—my sister retired to make the necessary change in her costume, while my friend and I were shown to our separate apartments.

At dinner, and afterwards, I did my utmost to counterfeit ease—to appear happy and cheerful. I noticed that Gallagher was enacting a similar *métier*.

Perhaps this seeming may have deceived my mother, but not Virginia. Ere many hours had passed, I observed signs of suspicion—directed equally against Gallagher as myself. She suspected that all was not right, and began to show pique—almost spitefulness—in her conversation with us both.

Chapter Fifty Three.

My Sister's Spirit.

For the remainder of that day and throughout the next, this unsatisfactory state of things continued, during which time the three of us—my friend, my sister, and myself—acted under a polite reserve. It was triangular, for I had not made Gallagher my confidant, but left him entirely to his conjectures. He was a true gentleman; and never even hinted at what he must have well-known was engrossing the whole of my thoughts. It was my intention to unbosom myself to him, and seek his friendly advice, but not until a little time had elapsed—not till I had obtained a full *éclaircissement* from Virginia.

I waited for an opportunity to effect this. Not but that many a one offered—many a time might I have found her alone; but, on each occasion, my resolution forsook me. I actually dreaded to bring her to a confession.

And yet I felt that it was my duty. As her brother—the nearest male relative, it was mine to guard her honour—to preserve the family escutcheon pure and untarnished.

For days was I restrained from this fraternal duty—partly through a natural feeling of delicacy—partly from a fear of the disclosure I might draw forth. I dreaded to know the truth. That a correspondence had passed between my sister and the Indian chief—that it was in all probability still going on—that a clandestine meeting had taken place—more than one, mayhap—all this I knew well enough. But to what length had these proceedings been carried? How far had my poor sister compromised herself? These were the interrogatories to which I dreaded the answer.

I believed she would tell me the truth—that is, if entreated; if commanded, *no*.

Of the last, I felt satisfied. I knew her proud spirit—prouder of late. When roused to hostility, she could be capable of the most obstinate resistance—firm and unyielding. There was much of my mother's nature in her, and little of my father's. Personally, as already stated, she resembled her mother; intellectually, there was also a similitude. She was one of those women—for she now deserved the title—who have never known the restraint of a severe discipline, and who grow up in the belief that they have no superior, no master upon earth. Hence the full development of a feeling of perfect independence, which, among American women, is common enough, but, in other lands, can only exist among those of the privileged classes. Uncontrolled by parent, guardian, or teacher—for this last had not been allowed to "rule by the rod"—my sister had grown to the age of womanhood, and she felt herself as masterless as a queen upon her throne.

She was independent in another sense—one which exerts a large influence over the freedom of the spirit—her fortune was her own.

In the States of America, the law of entail is not allowed; it is even provided against by statute. Those statesmen presidents who in long line succeeded the Father of the Republic, were wise legislators. They saw lurking under this wicked law—which, at most, appears only to affect the family relations—the strong arm of the political tyrant; and, therefore, took measures to guard against its introduction to the land. Wisely did they act, as time will show, or, indeed, has shown already; for had the congress of Washington's day but sanctioned the law of entail, the great American republic would long since have passed into an oligarchy.

Untrammelled by any such unnatural statute, my father had acted as all men of proper feeling are likely to do; he had followed the dictates of the heart, and divided his property in equal shares between his children. So far as independence of fortune went, my sister was my equal.

Of course, our mother had not been left unprovided for, but the bulk of the patrimonial estate now belonged to Virginia and myself.

My sister, then, was an heiress—quite independent of either mother or brother—bound by no authority to either, except that which exists in the ties of the heart—in filial and sororal affection.

I have been minute with these circumstances, in order to explain the delicate duty I had to perform, in calling my sister to an account.

Strange that I reflected not on my own anomalous position. At that hour, it never entered my thoughts. Here was I affianced to the sister of this very man, with the sincere intention of making her my wife.

I could perceive nothing unnatural, nothing disgraceful in the alliance—neither would society. Such, in earlier times, had done honour to Rolfe, who had mated with a maiden of darker skin, less beauty, and far slighter accomplishments than Maümee. In later days, hundreds of others had followed his example, without the loss either of *caste* or character; and why should not I? In truth, the question had never occurred to me, for it never entered my thoughts that my purpose in regard to *my* Indian *fiancée* was otherwise than perfectly *en règle*.

It would have been different had there been a taint of *African blood* in the veins of my intended. Then, indeed, might I have dreaded the frowns of society—for in America it is not the colour of the skin that condemns, but the blood—the blood. The white gentleman may marry an Indian wife; she may enter society without protest—if beautiful, become a belle.

All this I knew, while, at the same time, I was slave to a belief in the monstrous anomaly that where the blood is mingled from the other side—where the woman is white and the man red—the union becomes a *mésalliance*, a disgrace. By the friends of the former, such a union is regarded as a misfortune—a fall; and when the woman chances to be a *lady*—ah! then, indeed—

Little regard as I had for many of my country's prejudices, regarding race and colour, I was not free from the influence of this social maxim. To believe my sister in love with an Indian, would be to regard her as lost—fallen! No matter how high in rank among his own people—no matter how brave—how accomplished he might be—no matter if it were Osceola himself!

Chapter Fifty Four.

Asking an Explanation.

Suspense was preying upon me; I could endure it no longer. I at length resolved upon demanding an explanation from my sister, as soon as I should find her alone.

The opportunity soon offered. I chanced to see her in the lawn, down near the edge of the lake. I saw that she was in a mood unusually cheerful.

"Alas!" thought I, as I approached full of my resolutions—"these smiles! I shall soon change them to tears. Sister."

She was talking to her pets, and did not hear me, or pretended she did not.

"Sister!" I repeated, in a louder voice.

"Well, what is it?" she inquired, drily, without looking up.

"Pray, Virginia, leave off your play, and talk to me."

"Certainly, that is an inducement. I have had so little of your tongue of late, that I ought to feel gratified by your proposal. Why don't you bring your friend, and let him try a little in that line too. You have been playing double dummy long enough to get tired of it, I should think. But go on with the game, if it please you; it don't trouble me, I assure you.

"A Yankee ship and a Yankee crew,
Tally high ho, you know!
Won't strike to the foe while the sky it is blue,
And a tar's aloft or alow.

"Come now, little Fan! Fan! don't go too near the bank, or you may get a ducking, do you hear?"

"Pray, sister Virginia, give over this badinage: I have something of importance to say to you."

"Importance! What! are you going to get married? No, that can't be it—your face is too portentous and lugubrious; you look more like one on the road to be hanged—ha, ha, ha!"

"I tell you, sister, I am in earnest."

"Who said you wasn't? In earnest? I believe you, my boy."

"Listen to me, Virginia. I have something important—very important to talk about. I have been desirous of breaking the subject to you ever since my return."

"Well, why did you not? you have had opportunities enough. Have I been hid from you?"

"No—but—the fact is—"

"Go on, brother; you have an opportunity now. If it be a petition, as your looks appear to say, present it; I am ready to receive it."

"Nay, Virginia; it is not that. The subject upon which I wish to speak—"

"What subject, man? Out with it!"

I was weary with so much circumlocution, and a little piqued as well; I resolved to bring it to an end. A word, thought I, will tame down her tone, and render her as serious as myself, I answered:

"Osceola."

I looked to see her start, to see her cheek turn alternately red and pale; but to my astonishment no such symptoms displayed themselves; not the slightest indication of any extraordinary emotion betrayed itself either in her look or manner.

She replied almost directly and without hesitation:

"What! the young chief of the Seminoles? our old playfellow, Powell? He is to be the subject of our discourse? You could not have chosen one more interesting to *me*. I could talk all day long about this brave fellow!"

I was struck dumb by her reply, and scarcely knew in what way to proceed.

"But what of him, brother George?" continued my sister, looking me more soberly in the face. "I hope no harm has befallen him?"

"None that I know of: the harm has fallen upon those nearer and dearer."

"I do not understand you, my mysterious brother."

"But you shall. I am about to put a question to you—answer me, and answer me truly, as you value my love and friendship."

"Your question, sir, without these insinuations. I can speak the truth, I fancy, without being scared by threats."

"Then speak it, Virginia. Tell me, is Powell—is Osceola—your lover?"

"Ha, ha, ha, ha, ha, ha!"

"Nay, Virginia, this is no laughing matter."

"By my faith, I think it is—a very capital joke—ha, ha, ha!"

"I want no trifling, Virginia; an answer."

"You shall get no answer to such an absurd question."

"It is not absurd. I have good reasons for putting it."

"Reasons—state them, pray!"

"You cannot deny that something has passed between you? You cannot deny that you have given him a meeting, and in the forest too? Beware how you make answer, for I have the proofs. We encountered the chief on his return. We saw him at a distance. He shunned us—no wonder. We followed his trail—we saw the tracks of the pony—oh! you met: it was all clear enough."

"Ha, ha, ha! What a pair of keen trackers—you and your friend—astute fellows! You will be invaluable on the warpath. You will be promoted to be chief spies to the army. Ha, ha, ha! And so, this is the grand secret, is it? this accounts for the demure looks, and the odd-fashioned airs that have been puzzling me. My honour, eh? that was the care that was cankering you. By Diana! I have reason to be thankful for being blessed with such a chivalric brace of guardians.

"In England, the garden of beauty is kept
By the dragon of prudery, placed within call;
But so oft this unamiable dragon has slept,
That the garden was carelessly watched after all.

"And so if, I have not the dragon prudery to guard me, I am to find a brace of dragons in my brother and his friend. Ha, ha, ha!"

"Virginia, you madden me—this is no answer. Did you meet Osceola?"

"I'll answer that directly: after such sharp espionage, denial would not avail me. I *did* meet him."

"And for what purpose? Did you meet as lovers?"

"That question is impertinent; I won't answer *it.*"

"Virginia! I implore you—"

"And cannot two people encounter each other in the woods, without being charged with love-making? Might we not have come together by chance? or might I not have had other business with the Seminole chief? You do not know all my secrets, nor do I intend you shall either."

"Oh, it was no chance encounter—it was an appointment—a love-meeting: you could have had no other affair with *him.*"

"It is natural for you to think so—very natural, since I hear you practise such *duettos* yourself. How long, may I ask, since you held your last *tête-à-tête* with your own fair charmer—the lovely Maümee? Eh! brother?"

I started as if stung. How could my sister have gained intelligence of this? Was she only guessing? and had chanced upon the truth?

For some moments I could not make reply, nor did I make any to her last interrogatory. I paid no heed to it, but, becoming excited, pressed my former inquiries with vehemence.

"Sister! I must have an explanation; I insist upon it—I demand it!"

"Demand! Ho! that is your tone, is it? That will scarcely serve you. A moment ago, when you put yourself in the imploring attitude, I had well-nigh taken pity on you, and told you all. But, *demand,* indeed! I answer no demands; and to show you that I do not, I shall now go and shut myself in my room. So, my good fellow, you shall see no more of me for this day, nor to-morrow either, unless you come to your senses. Good-by, Geordy—and *au revoir,* only on condition you behave yourself like a gentleman.

"A Yankee ship and a Yankee crew, Tally high ho, you know! Won't strike to the foe, etc, etc."

And with this catch pealing from her lips, she passed across the parterre, entered the verandah, and disappeared within the doorway.

Disappointed, mortified, sad, I stood riveted to the spot, scarcely knowing in what direction to turn myself.

Chapter Fifty Five.

The Volunteers.

118

My sister kept her word. I saw no more of her for that day, nor until noon of the next. Then she came forth from her chamber in full riding costume, ordered White Fox to be saddled, and mounting, rode off alone.

I felt that I had no power over this capricious spirit. It was idle to attempt controlling it. She was beyond the dictation of fraternal authority—her own mistress—and evidently determined upon having her will and her way.

After the conversation of yesterday, I felt no inclination to interfere again. She was acquainted with my secret; and knowing this, any counsel from me would come with an ill grace, and be as ill received. I resolved, therefore, to withhold it, till some crisis should arrive that would render it more impressive.

For several days this coolness continued between us—at which my mother often wondered, but of which she received no explanation. Indeed, I fancied that even *her* affection towards me was not so tender as it used to be. Perhaps I was wronging her. She was a little angry with me about the duel with Ringgold, the first intelligence of which had gravely affected her. On my return I had received her reproaches, for it was believed that I alone was to blame in bringing the affair about. "Why had I acted so rudely towards Arens Ringgold? And all about nothing? A trumpery Indian belle? What mattered it to me what may have been said about the girl? Likely what was said was nothing more than the truth. I should have behaved with more prudence."

I perceived that my mother had been informed upon most of the material points connected with the affair. Of one, however, she was ignorant: she knew not who the "trumpery Indian belle" was—she had not heard the name of Maümee. Knowing her to be ignorant of this, I listened with more calmness to the aspersive remarks.

For all that, I was somewhat excited by her reproaches, and several times upon the point of declaring to her the true cause why I had called Ringgold to an account. For certain reasons I forbore. My mother would not have believed me.

As for Ringgold himself, I ascertained that a great change in his fortunes had lately taken place. His father was dead—had died in a fit of passion, whilst in the act of chastising one of his slaves. A blood-vessel had burst, and he had fallen, as if by a judgment of God.

Arens, the only son, was now master of his vast, ill-gotten wealth—a plantation with some three hundred slaves upon it; and it was said that this had only made him more avaricious than ever.

His aim was—as it had been that of the older Ringgold—to become owner of everybody and everything around him—a grand money-despot. The son was a fit successor to the father.

He had played the invalid for a while—carrying his arm in a sling—and, as people said, not a little vain of having been engaged in a duel. Those who understood how that affair had terminated, thought he had little reason to be proud of it.

It seemed the hostility between him and myself had brought about no change in his relations with our family. I learned that he had been a constant visitor at the house; and the world still believed him the accepted suitor of Virginia. Moreover, since his late accession to wealth and power, he had grown more than ever a favourite with my ambitious mother. I learned all this with regret.

The old home appeared to have undergone a change. There was not the same warmth of affection as of yore. I missed my kind, noble father. My mother at times appeared cold and distant, as if she believed me undutiful. My uncle was her brother, and like her in everything; even my fond sister seemed for the moment estranged.

I began to feel as a stranger in my own house, and, feeling so, stayed but little at home. Most of the day was I abroad, with Gallagher as my companion. Of course, my friend remained our guest during our stay on the Suwanee.

Our time was occupied partly with the duties upon which we had been commanded, and partly in following the amusement of the chase. Of deer-hunting and fox running we had an abundance; but I did not enjoy it as formerly; neither did my companion—ardent sportsman though he was—seem to take the delight in it which he had anticipated.

Our military duties were by no means of an arduous nature, and were usually over before noon. Our orders had been, not so much to recruit volunteers as to superintend the organisation of those already raised; and "muster them into service." A corps had already advanced some length towards formation, having elected its own officers and enrolled most of its rank and file. Our part was to inspect, instruct, and govern them.

The little church, near the centre of the settlement, was the head-quarters of the corps; and there the drill was daily carried on.

The men were mostly of the poorer class of white settlers—small renting planters—and squatters who dwelt along the swamp-edges, and who managed to eke out a precarious subsistence partly by the use of their axes, and partly from the product of their rifles. The old hunter Hickman was among the number; and what did not much surprise me, I found the worthies Spence and Williams enrolled in the corps. Upon these scamps I was determined to keep a watchful eye, and hold them at a wary distance.

Many of the privates were men of a higher class—for the common danger had called all kinds into the field.

The officers were usually planters of wealth and influence; though there were some who, from the democratic influence of elections, were but ill qualified to wear epaulettes.

Many of these gentlemen bore far higher official titles than either Gallagher or myself. Colonels and majors appeared to be almost as numerous as privates. But for all this, they did not demur to our exercising authority over them. In actual war-time, it is not uncommon for a lieutenant of the "line," or the lowest subaltern of the regular army, to be placed in command of a full colonel of militia or volunteers!

Here and there was an odd character, who, perhaps, in earlier life had "broken down" at West Point, or had gone through a month of campaigning service in the Greek wars, under "Old Hickory." These, fancying themselves *au fait* in the military art, were not so pleasant to deal with; and at times it required all Gallagher's determined firmness to convince them that *he* was commander-in-chief upon the Suwanee.

My friend's reputation as a "fire eater," which had preceded him, had as much weight in confirming his authority as the commission which he brought with him from "head-quarters."

Upon the whole, we got along smoothly enough with these gentlemen—most of whom seemed desirous of learning their duty, and submitted to our instructions with cheerfulness.

There was no lack of champagne, brandy, and cigars. The neighbouring planters were hospitable; and had my friend or myself been inclined towards dissipation, we could not have been established in better quarters for indulging the propensity.

To this, however, neither of us gave way; and our moderation no doubt caused us to be held in higher esteem, even among the hard drinkers by whom we were surrounded.

Our new life was by no means disagreeable; and but for the unpleasantness that had arisen at home, I could have felt for the time contented and happy.

At home—at home—there was the canker: it appeared no longer a home.

Chapter Fifty Six.

Mysterious Changes.

Not many days had elapsed before I observed a sudden change in the conduct of Gallagher; not towards myself or my mother, but in his manner towards Virginia.

It was the day after I had held the conversation with her, that I first noticed this. I noticed at the same time that her manner towards him was equally altered.

The somewhat frosty politeness that had hitherto been observed between them, appeared to have suddenly thawed, and their old genial friendship to become reestablished on its former footing.

They now played, and sang, and laughed together, and read, and chattered nonsense, as they had been used to do in times past.

"Ah!" thought I, "it is easy for him to forget; he is but a friend, and, of course, cannot have the feelings of a brother. Little matters it to him what may be her secret relations, or with whom. What need he care about her improprieties? She is good company, and her winning way has beguiled him from dwelling upon that suspicion, which he must have entertained as well as myself. He has either forgotten, forgiven, or else found some explanation of her conduct that seems to satisfy him. At all events, *I* appear to have lost his sympathy, while *she* has regained his confidence and friendship."

I was at first astonished at this new phase in the relations of our family circle—afterwards puzzled by it.

I was too proud and piqued to ask Gallagher for an explanation; and, as he did not volunteer to give one, I was compelled to abide in ignorance.

I perceived that my mother also regarded this altered behaviour with surprise, and also with a feeling of a somewhat different kind—suspicion.

I could guess the reason of this. She fancied that they were growing too fond of each other—that, notwithstanding he had no fortune but his pay-roll, Virginia might fancy the dashing soldier for a husband.

Of course my mother, having already formed designs as to the disposal of her daughter, could not calmly contemplate such a destiny as this. It was natural enough, then, she should look with a jealous eye upon the gay confidence that had been established between them.

I should have been glad if I could have shared my mother's suspicions; happy if my sister had but fixed her affections there. My friend would have been welcome to call me brother. Fortuneless though he might be, I should have made no opposition to that alliance.

But it never entered my thoughts that there was aught between the two but the old rollicking friendship; and love acts not in that style. So far as Captain Gallagher was concerned, I could have given my mother assurance that would have quieted her fears.

And yet to a stranger they might have appeared as lovers—almost to any one except myself. They were together half the day and half the night: they rode together into the woods, and were sometimes absent for hours at a time. I perceived that my comrade began to care little for *my* company, and daily less. Stranger still, the chase no longer delighted him! As for duty, this he sadly neglected, and had not the "lieutenant" been on the ground, I fear the "corps" would have stood little chance of instruction.

As days passed on, I fancied that Gallagher began to relapse into a more sober method. He certainly seemed more thoughtful. This was when my sister was out of sight. It was not the air he had worn after our arrival—but very different.

It certainly resembled the bearing of a man in love. He would start on hearing my sister's voice from without—his ear was quick to catch every word from her, and his eyes expressed delight whenever she came into the room. Once or twice, I saw him gazing at her with an expression upon his countenance that betokened more than friendship.

My old suspicions began to return to me. After all, he *might* be in love with Virginia?

Certainly, she was fair enough to impress the heart even of this adamantine soldier. Gallagher was no lady's man—had never been known to seek conquests over the sex—in fact, felt some awkwardness in their company. My sister seemed the only one before whom he could converse with fluency or freedom.

Notwithstanding, and after all, he *might* be in love!

I should have been pleased to know it, could I only have insured him a reciprocity of his passion; but alas! that was not in my power.

I wondered whether *she* ever thought of him as a lover; but no—she could not—not if she was thinking of—

And yet her behaviour towards him was at times of such a character, that a stranger to her eccentricities would have fancied she loved him. Even I was mystified by her actions. She either had some feeling for him, beyond that of mere friendship, or made show of it. If he loved her, and she knew it, then her conduct was cruel in the extreme.

I indulged in such speculations, though, only when I could not restrain myself from dwelling upon them. They were unpleasant; at times, even painful.

I lived in a maze of doubt, puzzled and perplexed at what was passing around me; but at this time there turned up a new chapter in our family history, that, in point of mystery, eclipsed all others. A piece of information reached me, that, if true, must sweep all these new-sprung theories out my mind.

121

I learned that my sister was *in love with Arens Ringgold*—in other words, that she was "listening to his addresses!"

<h2>Chapter Fifty Seven.</h2>

<h3>My Informant.</h3>

This I had upon the authority of my faithful servant, Black Jake. Upon almost any other testimony, I should have been incredulous; but his was unimpeachable. Negro as he was, his perceptions were keen enough; while his earnestness proved that he believed what he said. He had reasons, and he gave them.

I received the strange intelligence in this wise:

I was seated by the bathing-pond, alone, busied with a book, when I heard Jake's familiar voice pronouncing my name: "Massr George."

"Well, Jake?" I responded, without withdrawing my eyes from the page.

"Ise wanted all da mornin to git you 'lone by yarself; Ise want to hab a leetle bit ob a convasayshun, Massr George."

The solemn tone, so unusual in the voice of Jake, awoke my attention. Mechanically closing the book, I looked up in his face: it was solemn as his speech.

"A conversation with me, Jake?"

"Ye, massr—dat am if you isn't ingage?"

"Oh, by no means, Jake. Go on: let me hear what you have to say."

"Poor fellow!" thought I—"he has his sorrows too. Some complaint about Viola. The wicked coquette is torturing him with jealousy; but what can I do? I cannot *make* her love him—no. 'One man may lead a horse to the water, but forty can't make him drink.' No; the little jade will act as she pleases in spite of any remonstrance on my part. Well, Jake?"

"Wa, Massr George, I doant meself like to intafere in tha 'fairs ob da family—daat I doant; but ye see, massr, things am a gwine all wrong—all wrong, by golly!"

"In what respect?"

"Ah, massr, dat young lady—dat young lady."

Polite of Jake to call Viola a young lady.

"You think she is deceiving you?"

"More dan me, Massr George—more dan me."

"What a wicked girl! But perhaps, Jake, you only fancy these things? Have you had any proofs of her being unfaithful? Is there any one in particular who is now paying her attentions?"

"Yes, massr; berry partickler—nebber so partickler before—nebber."

"A white man?"

"Gorramighty, Massr George!" exclaimed Jake in a tone of surprise; "you do talk kewrious: ob coorse it am a white man. No odder dan a white man dar shew 'tention to tha young lady."

I could not help smiling. Considering Jake's own complexion, he appeared to hold very exalted views of the unapproachableness of his charmer by those of her own race. I had once heard him boast that he was the "only man ob colour dat could shine *thar*." It was a white man, then, who was making his misery.

"Who is he, Jake?" I inquired.

"Ah, massr, he am dat ar villain debbil, Arens Ringgol!"

"What! Arens Ringgold?—he making love to Viola!"

"Viola! Gorramighty, Massr George!" exclaimed the black, staring till his eyes shewed only the whites—"Viola! Gorramighty, I nebber say Viola!—nebber!"

"Of whom, then, are you speaking?"

"O massr, did I not say da young lady? dat am tha young Missa—Missa Vaginny."

"Oh! my sister you mean. Poh, poh! Jake. That is an old story. Arens Ringgold has been paying his addresses to my sister for many years; but with no chance of success. You needn't trouble yourself about that, my faithful friend; there is no danger of their getting married. She doesn't like him, Jake—I wonder who does or could—and even if she did, I would not permit it. But there's no fear, so you may make your mind easy on that score."

My harangue seemed not to satisfy the black. He stood scratching his head, as if he had something more to communicate. I waited for him to speak.

"'Scoose me, Massr George, for da freedom, but dar you make mighty big mistake. It am true dar war a time when Missa Vaginny she no care for dat ar snake in da grass. But de times am change: him father—da ole thief—he am gone to tha udda world? tha young un he now rich—he big planter—tha biggest on da ribber: ole missa she 'courage him come see Missa Vaginny—'cause he rich, he good spec."

"I know all that, Jake: my mother always wished it; but that signifies nothing—my sister is a little self-willed, and will be certain to have her own way. There is no fear of her giving her consent to marry, Arens Ringgold."

"'Scoose me, Massr George, scoose me 'gain—I tell you, massr, you make mistake: she a'most consent now."

"Why, what has put this notion into your head, my good fellow?"

"Viola, massr. Dat ere quadroon tell me all."

"So, you are friends with Viola again?"

"Ye, Massr George, we good friend as ebber. 'Twar only my s'picion—I wor wrong. She good gal—she true as de rifle. No more s'picion o' her, on de part ob Jake—no."

"I am glad of that. But pray, what has she told you about Arens Ringgold and my sister?"

"She tell me all: she see somethin' ebbery day."

"Every day! Why, it is many days since Arens Ringgold has visited here?"

"No, massr; dar you am mistake 'gain: Mass Arens he come to da house ebbery day— a'most ebbery day."

"Nonsense; I never saw him here. I never heard of his having been, since my return from the fort."

"But him hab been, for all dat, massr; I see him meseff. He come when you gone out. He be here when we goes a huntin'. I see um come yest'day, when you any Mass Garger wor away to tha volunteers—dat he war sat'n."

"You astonish me."

"Dat's not all, massr. Viola she say dat Missa Vaginny she 'have different from what she used to: he talk love; she not angry no more; she listen to him talk. Oh, Massr George, Viola think she give her consent to marry him: dat would be dreadful thing—berry, berry dreadful."

"Jake," said I, "listen to me. You will stay by the house when I am absent. You will take note of every one who comes and goes; and whenever Arens Ringgold makes his appearance on a visit to the family, you will come for me as fast as horse can carry you."

"Gollys! dat I will, Massr George: you nebber fear, I come fass enuff—like a streak ob de greased lightnin'."

And with this promise the black left me.

With all my disposition to be incredulous, I could not disregard the information thus imparted to me. Beyond doubt, there was truth in it. The black was too faithful to think of deceiving me, and too astute to be himself deceived. Viola had rare opportunities for observing all that passed within our family circle; and what motive could she have for inventing a tale like this?

Besides Jake had himself seen Ringgold on visits—of which I had never been informed. This confirmed the other—confirmed all.

What was I to make of it? Three who appear as lovers—the chief, Gallagher, Arens Ringgold! Has she grown wicked, abandoned, and is coquetting with all the world?

Can she have a thought of Ringgold? No—it is not possible. I could understand her having an affection for the soldier—a romantic passion for the brave and certainly handsome chief; but for Arens Ringgold—a squeaking conceited snob, with nought but riches to recommend him—this appeared utterly improbable.

Of course, the influence was my mother's; but never before had I entertained a thought that Virginia would yield. If Viola spoke the truth, she had yielded, or was yielding.

"Ah, mother, mother! little knowest thou the fiend you would introduce to your home, and cherish as your child."

Chapter Fifty Eight.

Old Hickman.

The morning after, I went as usual to the recruiting quarters. Gallagher was along with me, as upon this day the volunteers were to be "mustered into service," (Note 1) and our presence was necessary at the administering of the oath.

A goodly company was collected, forming a troop more respectable in numbers than appearance. They were "mounted volunteers;" but as each individual had been his own quartermaster, no two were either armed or mounted alike. Nearly all carried rifles, though there were a few who shouldered the old family musket—a relic of revolutionary times—and were simply armed with single or double barrelled shot-guns. These, however, loaded with heavy buck-shot, would be no contemptible weapons in a skirmish with Indians. There were pistols of many sorts—from the huge brass-butted holsters to small pocket-pistols—single and double barrelled—but no revolvers, for as yet the celebrated "Colt" (Note 2) had not made its appearance in frontier warfare. Every volunteer carried his knife—some, dagger-shaped with ornamented hafts; while the greater number were long, keen blades, similar to those in use among butchers. In the belts of many were stuck small hatchets, an imitation of the Indian tomahawk. These were to serve the double purpose of cutting a way through the brushwood, or breaking in the skull of a savage, as opportunity might offer.

The equipments consisted of powder-horns, bullet-pouches, and shot-belts—in short, the ordinary sporting gear of the frontiersman or amateur hunter when out upon the "still-hunt," of the fallow deer.

The "mount" of the troop was as varied as the arms and accoutrements: horses from thirteen hands to seventeen; the tall, raw-boned steed; the plump, cob-shaped roadster; the tight, wiry native of the soil, of Andalusian race (Note 3); the lean, worn-out "critter," that carried on his back the half-ragged squatter, side by side with the splendid Arabian charger, the fancy of some dashing young planter who bestrode him, with no slight conceit in the grace and grandeur of his display. Not a few were mounted upon mules, both of American and Spanish origin; and these, when well trained to the saddle, though they may not equal the horse in the charge, are quite equal to him in a campaign against an Indian foe. Amid thickets—through forests of heavy timber, where the ground is a marsh, or strewn with logs, fallen branches, and matted with protrate parasites, the hybrid will make way safely, when the horse will sink or stumble. Some of the most experienced backwoods hunters, while following the chase, prefer a mule to the high-mettled steed of Arabia.

Motley were the dresses of the troop. There were uniforms, or half-uniforms, worn by some of the officers; but among the men no two were dressed in like fashion. Blanket-coats of red, blue, and green; linsey woolseys of coarse texture, grey or copper-coloured; red flannel shirts; jackets of brown linen, or white—some of yellow nankin cotton—a native fabric; some of sky-blue cottonade; hunting-shirts of dressed deer-skin, with moccasins and leggins; boots of horse or alligator hide, high-lows, brogans—in short, every variety of *chaussure* known throughout the States.

The head-gear was equally varied and fantastic. No stiff shakos were to be seen there; but caps of skin, and hats of wool and felt, and straw and palmetto-leaf, broad-brimmed, scuffed, and slouching. A few had forage-caps of blue cloth, that gave somewhat of a military character to the wearers.

In one respect, the troop had a certain uniformity; they were all eager for the fray—burning for a fight with the hated savages, who were committing such depredations throughout the land. When were they to be led against them? This was the inquiry constantly passing through the ranks of the volunteer array.

Old Hickman was among the most active. His age and experience had procured him the rank of sergeant by free election; and I had many opportunities of conversing with him. The alligator-hunter was still my true friend, and devoted to the interests of our family. On this very day I chanced to be with him alone, when he gave proof of his attachment by volunteering a conversation I little expected from him. Thus he began:

"May a Injun sculp me, lootenant, if I can bar the thought o' that puke a marrin' yur sister."

"Marrying my sister—who?" I inquired in some surprise. Was it Gallagher he meant?

"Why, in coorse the fellar as everybody sez is a goin' to—that cussed polecat o' a critter, Ary Ringgold."

"Oh! him you mean? Everybody says so, do they?"

"In coorse—it's the hul talk o' the country. Durn me, George Randolph, if I'd let him. Yur sister—the putty critter—she ur the finest an' the hansomest gurl in these parts; an' for a durned skunk like thet, not'ithstandin' all his dollars, to git her, I can't a bear to hear o't. Why, George, I tell you, he'll make her mis'able for the hul term o' her nat'ral life—that ere's whet he'll be sartint to do—durnation to him!"

"You are kind to counsel me, Hickman; but I think the event you dread is not likely ever to come to pass."

"Why do people keep talkin' o't, then? Everybody says it's a goin' to be. If it wan't thet I'm an old friend o' yur father, George, I wudn't ha' tuk sich a liberty; but I war his friend, an' I'm *yur* friend; an' thurfor it be I hev spoke on the matter. We may talk o' Injuns; but thur ain't ne'er a Injun in all Floridy is as big a thief as them Ringgolds—father an' son, an' the hul kit o' them. The old un' he's clurred out from hyar, an' whar he's gone to 'tain't hard to tell. Ole Scratch hez got hold o' him, an' I reck'n he'll be catchin' it by this time for the deviltries he carried on while about hyar. He'll git paid up slick for the way he treated them poor half-breeds on tother side the crik."

"The Powells?"

"Ye-es—that wur the durndest piece o' unjustice I ever know'd o' in all my time. By —, it wur!"

"You know what happened them, then?"

"Sartinly I do; every trick in the hul game. Twur a leetle o' the meanest transackshun I ever know'd a white—an' a white that called himself a gentleman—to have a hand in. By —, it wur!"

Hickman now proceeded, at my request, to detail with more minuteness than I had yet heard them, the facts connected with the robbery of the unfortunate family.

It appeared by his account that the Powells had not voluntarily gone away from the plantation; that, on the contrary, their removal had been to the friendless widow the most painful thing of all. Not only was the land of great value—the best in the whole district—but it had been to her the scene of a happy life—a home endeared by early love, by the memory of a kind husband, by every tie of the heart's affection; and she had only parted from it when driven out by the strong arm of the law—by the staff of the sheriff's officer.

Hickman had been present at the parting scene, and described it in rough but feeling terms. He told me of the sad unwillingness which the family exhibited at parting; of the indignant reproaches of the son—of the tears and entreaties of mother and daughter—how the persecuted widow had offered everything left her—her personal property—even the trinkets and jewels—souvenirs given her by her departed husband—if the ruffians would only allow her to remain in possession of the house—the old homestead, consecrated to her by long happy years spent under its roof.

Her appeals were in vain. The heartless persecutor was without compassion, and she was driven forth.

Of all these things, the old hunter spoke freely and feelingly; for although a man of somewhat vulgar speech and rough exterior, he was one whose heart beat with humanity, and who hated injustice. He had no friendship for mere wrong-doers, and he heartily detested the whole tribe of the Ringgolds. His narration re-kindled within me the indignant emotions I had experienced on first hearing of this monstrous act of cruelty; and my sympathy for Osceola—interrupted by late suspicions—was almost restored, as I stood listening to the story of his wrongs.

Note 1. In the United States, a volunteer corps or regiment "raises itself." When the numbers are complete, and the officers are elected, if the government accept its services, both officers and men are then "mustered in"—In other words, sworn to serve for a fixed period, under exactly the same regulations as the regular troops, with like pay, rations, etc.

Note 2. The military corps first armed with Colt's pistols was the regiment of Texan Rangers. Its first trial in actual warfare occurred in the war between the United States and Mexico in a skirmish with the guerilla band of Padre Jaranta. 125 guerrilleros were put *hors de combat* in less than fifteen minutes by this effective weapon.

Note 3. The horse was introduced into Florida by the Spaniards; hence the breed.

Chapter Fifty Nine.

A Hasty Messenger.

In the company of Hickman, I had walked off to some distance from the crowd, in order that our conversation should be unrestrained.

As the moments passed, the old hunter warmed into greater freedom of speech, and from his manner I fancied he had still other developments to make. I had firm faith in his devotion to our family—as well as in his personal friendship for myself—and once or twice I was on the eve of revealing to him the thoughts that rendered me unhappy. In experience, he was a sage, and although a rude one, he might be the best counsellor I could find. I knew no other who possessed half his knowledge of the world—for Hickman had not always lived among the alligators; on the contrary, he had passed through various phases of life. I could safely trust to his devotedness: with equal safety I might confide in the resources of his judgment.

Under this belief, I should have unburdened myself of the heavy secrets weighing upon my mind—of some of them at least—had it not been that I fancied he already knew some of them. With the re-appearance of Yellow Jake I knew him to be acquainted: he alleged that he had never felt sure about the mulatto's death, and had heard long ago that he was alive; but it was not of him I was thinking, but of the designs of Arens Ringgold. Perhaps Hickman knew something of these. I noticed that when his name was mentioned in connection with those of Spence and Williams, he glanced towards me a look of strange significance, as if he had something to say of these wretches.

I was waiting for him to make a disclosure, when the footfall of a fast-going horse fell upon my ear. On looking up, I perceived a horseman coming down the bank of the river, and galloping as earnestly as if riding a "quarter-race."

The horse was white, and the rider black; I recognised both at a glance; Jake was the horseman.

I stepped out from among the trees, in order that he should see me, and not pass on to the church that stood a little beyond. I hailed him as he advanced.

He both saw and heard me; and abruptly turning his horse, came galloping up to the spot where the old hunter and I were standing.

He was evidently upon an errand; but the presence of Hickman prevented him from declaring it aloud. It would not keep, however, and throwing himself from the saddle, he drew near me, and whispered it into my ear. It was just what I was expecting to hear—Arens Ringgold was at the house.

"That dam nigga am thar, Massr George."

Such was literally Jake's muttered announcement.

I received the communication with as much show of tranquillity as I could assume; I did not desire that Hickman should have any knowledge of its nature, nor even a suspicion that there was anything extraordinary upon the *tapis*; so dismissing the black messenger with a word, I turned away with the hunter; and walking back to the church enclosure, contrived to lose him in the crowd of his comrades.

126

Soon after, I released my horse from his fastening; and, without saying a word to any one—not even to Gallagher—I mounted, and moved quietly off.

I did not take the direct road that led to our plantation, but made a short circuit through some woods that skirted close to the church. I did this to mislead old Hickman or any other who might have noticed the rapid arrival of the messenger; and who, had I gone directly back with him, might have held guesses that all was not right at home. To prevent this, I appeared to curious eyes, to have gone in an opposite direction to the right one.

A little rough riding through the bushes brought me out into the main up-river road; and then, sinking the spur, I galloped as if life or death were staked upon the issue. My object in making such haste was simply to get to the house in time, before the clandestine visitor—welcome guest of mother and sister—should make his adieus.

Strong reasons as I had for hating this man, I had no sanguinary purpose; it was not my design to kill Arens Ringgold—though such might have been the most proper mode to dispose of a reptile so vile and dangerous as he. Knowing him as I did, freshly spurred to angry passion by Hickman's narrative of his atrocious behaviour, I could at that moment have taken his life without fear of remorse.

But although I felt fierce indignation, I was yet neither mad nor reckless. Prudential motives—the ordinary instinct of self-safety—still had their influence over me; and I had no intention to imitate the last act in the tragedy of Samson's life.

The programme I had sketched out for myself was of a more rational character.

My design was to approach the house—if possible, unobserved—the drawing-room as well—where of course the visitor would be found—an abrupt *entrée* upon the scene—both guest and hosts taken by surprise—the demand of an explanation from all three—a complete clearing-up of this mysterious *imbroglio* of our family relations, that was so painfully perplexing me. Face to face, I should confront the triad—mother, sister, wooer—and force all three to confession.

"Yes!" soliloquised I, with the eagerness of my intention driving the spur into the flanks of my horse—"Yes—confess they shall—they must—one and all, or—"

With the first two I could not define the alternative; though some dark design, based upon the slight of filial and fraternal love, was lurking within my bosom.

For Ringgold, should he refuse to give the truth, my resolve was first to "cowhide" him, then kick him out of doors, and finally command him never again to enter the house—the house, of which henceforth I was determined to be master.

As for etiquette, that was out of the question; at that hour, my soul was ill attuned to the observance of delicate ceremony. No rudeness could be amiss, in dealing with the man who had tried to murder me.

Chapter Sixty.

A Lover's Gift.

As I have said, it was my design to make an entrance unobserved; consequently, it was necessary to observe caution in approaching the house. To this end, as I drew near the plantation, I turned off the main road into a path that led circuitously by the rear. This path would conduct me by the hommock, the bathing-pond, and the orange-groves, without much danger of my approach being noticed by any one. The slaves at work within the enclosures could see me as I rode through the grounds; but these were the "field-hands." Unless seen by some of the domestics, engaged in household affairs, I had no fear of being announced.

My messenger had not gone directly back; I had ordered him to await me in an appointed place, and there I found him.

Directing him to follow me, I kept on; and having passed through the fields, we rode into the thick underwood of the hommock, where halting, we dismounted from our horses. From this point I proceeded alone.

As the hunter steals upon the unexpecting game, or the savage upon his sleeping foe, did I approach the house—my home, my father's home, the home of mother and sister. Strange conduct in a son and a brother—a singular situation.

My limbs trembled under me as I advanced, my knees knocked together, my breast was agitated by a tumult of wild emotions. Once I hesitated and halted. The prospect of the unpleasant scene I was about to produce stayed me. My resolution was growing weak and undecided.

Perhaps I might have gone back—perhaps I might have waited another opportunity, when I might effect my purpose by a less violent development—but just then voices fell upon my ear, the effect of which was to strengthen my wavering resolves. My sister's voice was ringing in laughter, that sounded light and gay. There was another—only one. I easily recognised the squeaking treble of her despicable suitor. The voices remaddened me—the tones stung me, as if they had been designedly uttered in mockery of myself. How could she behave thus? how riot in joy, while I was drooping under dark suspicions of her misbehaviour?

Piqued as well as pained, I surrendered all thought of honourable action; I resolved to carry through my design, but first—to play the listener.

I drew nearer, and heard clearer. The speakers were not in the house, but outside, by the edge of the orange grove. Softly treading, gently parting the boughs, now crouching beneath them, now gliding erect, I arrived unobserved within six paces of where they stood—near enough to perceive their dresses glistening through the leaves—to hear every word that passed between them.

Not many had been spoken, before I perceived that I had arrived at a peculiar moment—a crisis. The lover had just offered himself for a husband—had, perhaps for the first time, seriously made his declaration. In all probability it was this had been eliciting my sister's laughter.

"And really, Mr Ringgold, you wish to make me your wife? You are in earnest in what you have said?"

"Nay, Miss Randolph, do not mock me; you know for how many years I have been devoted to you."

"Indeed, I do not. How could I know that?"

"By my words. Have I not told you so a hundred times?"

"Words! I hold words of little value in a matter of this kind. Dozens have talked to me as you, who, I suppose, cared very little about me. The tongue is a great trifler, Mr Arens."

"But my actions prove my sincerity. I have offered you my hand and my fortune; is not that a sufficient proof of devotion?"

"No, silly fellow; nothing of the sort. Were I to become your wife, the fortune would still remain your own. Besides, I have some little fortune myself, and that would come under your control. So you see the advantage would be decidedly in your favour. Ha, ha, ha!"

"Nay, Miss Randolph; I should not think of controlling yours; and if you will accept my hand—"

"Your hand, sir? If you would win a woman, you should offer your *heart*—hearts, not hands, for me."

"You know that is yours already; and has been for long years: all the world knows it."

"You must have told the world, then; and I don't like it a bit."

"Really, you are too harsh with me: you have had many proofs of how long and devotedly I have admired you. I would have declared myself long since, and asked you to become my wife—"

"And why did you not?"

Ringgold hesitated.

"The truth is, I was not my own master—I was under the control of my father."

"Indeed?"

"That exists no longer. I can now act as I please; and, dearest Miss Randolph, if you will but accept my hand—"

"Your hand again! Let me tell you, sir, that this hand of yours has not the reputation of being the most open one. Should I accept it, it might prove sparing of pin-money. Ha, ha, ha!"

"I am aspersed by enemies. I swear to you, that in that sense you should have no cause to complain of my liberality."

"I am not so sure of that, notwithstanding the oath you would take. Promises made before marriage are too often broken after. I would not trust you, my man—not I, i' faith."

"But you can trust me, I assure you."

"You cannot assure me; besides, I have had no proofs of your liberality in the past. Why, Mr Ringgold, you never made me a present in your life. Ha, ha, ha!"

"Had I known you would have accepted one—it would gratify me—Miss Randolph, I would give you anything I possess."

"Good! Now, I shall put you to the test: you shall make me a gift."

"Name it—it shall be yours."

"Oh, you fancy I am going to ask you for some trifling affair—a horse, a poodle, or some bit of glittering *bijouterie*. Nothing of the sort, I assure you."

"I care not what. I have offered you my whole fortune, and therefore will not hesitate to give you a part of it. Only specify what you may desire, and I shall freely give it."

"That sounds liberal indeed. Very well, then, you have something I desire to possess—and very much desire it—in truth, I have taken a fancy to be its owner, and had some designs of making offers to you for the purchase of it."

"What can you mean, Miss Randolph?"

"A plantation."

"A plantation!"

"Exactly so. Not your own, but one of which you are the proprietor."

"Ah!"

"I mean that which formerly belonged to a family of half-bloods upon Tupelo Creek. Your father *purchased* it from them, I believe!"

I noted the emphasis upon the word "purchased." I noted hesitation and some confusion in the reply.

"Yes—yes," said he; "it was so. But you astonish me, Miss Randolph. Why care you for this, when you shall be mistress of all I possess?"

"That is my affair. I *do* care for it. I may have many reasons. That piece of ground is a favourite spot with me; it is a lovely place—I often go there. Remember, my brother is owner here—he is not likely to remain a bachelor all his life—and my mother may desire to have a home of her own. But no; I shall give you no reasons; make the gift or not, as you please."

"And if I do, you will—"

"Name conditions, and I will not accept it—not if you ask me on your knees. Ha, ha, ha!"

"I shall make none, then: if you will accept it, it is yours."

"Ah, that is not all, Master Arens. You might take it back just as easily as you have given it. How am I to be sure that you would not? I must have the *deeds*."

"You shall have them."

"And when?"

"Whenever you please—within the hour, if you desire it."

"I do, then. Go, get them! But remember, sir, *I make no conditions—remember that?*"

"Oh," exclaimed the overjoyed lover, "I make none. I have no fears: I leave all to you. In an hour, you shall have them. Adieu!"

And so saying, he made a hurried departure.

I was so astonished by the nature of this dialogue—so taken by surprise at its odd ending—that for a time I could not stir from the spot. Not until Ringgold had proceeded to some distance did I recover self-possession; and then I hesitated what course to pursue—whether to follow him, or permit him to depart unmolested.

Virginia had gone away from the ground, having glided silently back into the house. I was even angrier with her than with him; and, obedient to this impulse, I left Ringgold to go free, and went straight for an explanation with my sister.

It proved a somewhat stormy scene. I found her in the drawing-room in company with my mother. I stayed for no circumlocution; I listened to no denial or appeal, but openly announced to both the character of the man who had just left the house—openly declared him my intended murderer.

"Now, Virginia! sister! will you marry this man?" "Never, George—never! I never intended it—Never!" she repeated emphatically, as she sank upon the sofa, burying her face in her hands.

My mother was incredulous—even yet incredulous!

I was proceeding to the proofs of the astounding declaration I had made, when I heard my name loudly pronounced outside the window: some one was calling me in haste.

I ran out upon the verandah to inquire what was wanted.

In front was a man on horseback, in blue uniform, with yellow facings—a dragoon. He was an orderly, a messenger from the fort. He was covered with dust, his horse was in a lather of sweat and foam. The condition of both horse and man showed that they had been going for hours at top-speed.

The man handed me a piece of paper—a dispatch hastily scrawled. It was addressed to Gallagher and myself. I opened and read:

"Bring on your men to Fort King as fast as their horses can carry them. The enemy is around us in numbers; every rifle is wanted—lose not a moment. Clinch."

Chapter Sixty One.

The Route.

The dispatch called for instant obedience. Fortunately my horse was still under the saddle, and in less than five minutes I was upon his back, and galloping for the volunteer camp.

Among these eager warriors, the news produced a joyous excitement, expressed in a wild *hurrah*. Enthusiasm supplied the place of discipline; and, in less than half an hour, the corps was accoutred and ready for the road.

There was nothing to cause delay. The command to march was given; the bugle sounded the "forward," and the troop filing "by twos," into a long somewhat irregular line, took the route for Fort King.

I galloped home to say adieu. It was a hurried leave-taking—less happy than my last—but I rode away with more contentment, under the knowledge that my sister was now warned, and there was no longer any danger of an alliance with Arens Ringgold.

The orderly who brought the dispatch rode back with the troop. As we marched along, he communicated the camp-news, and rumours in circulation at the fort. Many events had occurred, of which we had not heard. The Indians had forsaken their towns, taking with them their wives, children, cattle, and chattels. Some of their villages they had themselves fired, leaving nothing for their pale-faced enemies to destroy. This proved a determination to engage in a general war, had other proofs of this disposition been wanting. Whither they had gone, even our spies had been unable to find out. It was supposed by some that they had moved farther south, to a more distant part of the peninsula. Others alleged that they had betaken themselves to the great swamp that stretches for many leagues around the head-waters of the Amazura river, and known as the "Cove of the Ouithlacoochee."

This last conjecture was the more likely, though so secretly and adroitly had they managed their migration, that not a trace of the movement could be detected. The spies of the friendly Indians—the keenest that could be employed—were unable to discover their retreat. It was supposed that they intended to act only on the defensive—that is, to make plundering forays on whatever quarter was left unguarded by troops, and then retire with their booty to the fastnesses of the swamp. Their conduct up to this time had rendered the supposition probable enough. In such case, the war might not be so easily brought to a termination! in other words, there might be no war at all, but a succession of fruitless marches and pursuits; for it was well enough understood that if the Indians did not choose to stand before us in action, we should have but little chance of overhauling them in their retreat.

The fear of the troops was, that their adversaries would "take to the cover," where it would be difficult, if not altogether impossible, to find them.

However, this state of things could not be perpetual; the Indians could not always subsist upon plunder, where the booty must be every day growing less. They were too numerous for a mere band of robbers, though there existed among the whites a very imperfect idea of their numbers. Estimates placed them at from one to five thousand souls—runaway negroes included—and even the best informed frontiersmen could give only rude guesses on this point. For my part, I believed that there were more than a thousand warriors, even after the defection of the traitor clans; and this was the opinion of one who knew them well—old Hickman the hunter.

How, then, were so many to find subsistence in the middle of a morass? Had they been provident, and there accumulated a grand commissariat? No: this question could at once be answered in the negative. It was well-known that the contrary was the case—for in this year the Seminoles were without even their usual supply. Their removal had been urged in the spring; and, in consequence of the doubtful prospect before them, many had planted little—some not at all. The crop, therefore, was less than in ordinary years; and previous to the final council at Fort King, numbers of them had been both buying and begging food from the frontier citizens.

What likelihood, then, of finding subsistence throughout a long campaign? They would be starved out of their fortresses—they must come out, and either stand fight, or sue for peace. So people believed.

This topic was discoursed as we rode along. It was one of primary interest to all young warriors thirsting for fame—inasmuch as, should the enemy determine to pursue so inglorious a system of warfare, where were the laurels to be plucked? A campaign in the miasmatic and pestilential climate of the swamps was more likely to yield a luxuriant crop of cypresses.

Most hoped, and hence believed, that the Indians would soon grow hungry, and shew themselves in a fair field of fight.

There were different opinions as to the possibility of their subsisting themselves for a lengthened period of time. Some—and these were men best acquainted with the nature of the country—expressed their belief that they could. The old alligator-hunter was of this way of thinking.

"Thuv got," said he, "that ere durned brier wi' the big roots they calls 'coonty' (*Smilax pseudo-china*); it grows putty nigh all over the swamp, an' in some places as thick as a cane-brake. It ur the best o' eatin', an' drinkin' too, for they make a drink o' it. An' then thar's the acorns o' the live-oak—them ain't such bad eatin', when well roasted i' the ashes. They may gather thousands of bushels, I reckon. An' nixt thar's the cabbidge in the head o' the big palmetter; thet ere'll gi' them greens. As to their meat, thar's deer, an' thar's bar—a good grist o' them in the swamp—an' thares allaygatur, a tol'ably goodish wheen o' them varmint, I reckon—to say nothin o' turtle, an' turkey, an' squirrels an' snakes, an' sandrats, for, durn a red skin! he kin eat anythin' that crawls—from a punkin to a polecat. Don't you b'lieve it, fellars. Them ere Injuns aint a gwine to starve, s'easy as you think for. Thu'll hold out by thar teeth an' toe-nails, jest so long as thar's a eatable thing in the darnationed swamp—that's what thu'll do."

This sage reasoning produced conviction in the minds of those who heard it. After all, the dispersed enemy might not be so helpless as was generally imagined.

The march of the volunteers was not conducted in a strict military style. It was so commenced; but the officers soon found it impossible to carry out the "tactics." The men, especially the younger ones, could not be restrained from occasionally falling out of the lines—to help themselves to a pull out of some odd-looking flask; and at intervals one would gallop off into the woods, in hopes of getting a shot at a deer or a turkey he had caught a glimpse of through the trees.

131

Reasoning with these fellows, on the part of their officers, proved rather a fruitless affair; and getting angry with them was only to elicit a sulky rejoinder.

Sergeant Hickman was extremely wroth with some of the offenders.

"Greenhorns!" he exclaimed; "darnationed greenhorns! let 'em go on at it. May a allaygatur eet me, if they don't behave diff'rent by-'m-by. I'll stake my critter agin any hoss in the crowd, that some o' them ere fellars'll get sculped afore sundown; durned if they don't."

No one offered to take the old hunter's bet, and fortunately for them, as his words proved prophetic.

A young planter, fancying himself as safe as if riding through his own sugar-canes, had galloped off from the line of march. A deer, seen browsing in the savanna, offered an attraction too strong to be resisted.

He had not been gone five minutes—had scarcely passed out of sight of his comrades—when two shots were heard in quick succession; and the next moment, his riderless horse came galloping back to the troop.

The line was halted, and faced in the direction whence the shots had been heard. An advance party moved forward to the ground. No enemy was discovered, nor the traces of any, except those exhibited in the dead body of the young planter, that lay perforated with a brace of bullets just as it had fallen out of the saddle.

It was a lesson—though an unpleasant one to his comrades—and after this, there were no more attempts at deer-stalking. The man was buried on the spot where he lay, and with the troop more regularly and compactly formed—now an easier duty for its officers—we continued the march unmolested, and before sunset were within the stockade of the fort.

Chapter Sixty Two.

A Knock on the Head.

Excepting the memory of one short hour, Fort King had for me no pleasant reminiscences. There had been some new arrivals in my absence, but none of them worthy of companionship. They only rendered quarters more crowded, and accommodation more difficult to obtain. The sutlers and the blacklegs were rapidly making their fortunes; and these, with the quartermaster, the commissary (Note 1), and the "beef-contractor," appeared to be the only prosperous men about the place.

The "beau" was still chief aide-de-camp, gaily caparisoned as ever; but of him I had almost ceased to think.

It was not long before I was ordered upon duty—almost the moment after my arrival—and that, as usual, of a disagreeable kind. Before I had time to obtain a moment's rest after the long ride—even before I could wash the road-dust from my skin—I was summoned to the head-quarters of the commander-in-chief.

What could he want with me, in such hot haste? Was it about the duels? Were these old scores going to be reckoned up?

Not without some apprehension did I betake myself into the presence of the general.

It proved however, to be nothing concerning the past; though, when I learned the duty I was to perform, I half regretted that it was not a reprimand.

I found the agent closeted with the commander-in-chief. They had designed another interview with Omatla and "Black Dirt." I was merely wanted as an interpreter.

The object of this fresh interview with the chiefs was stated in my hearing. It was to arrange a plan for concerted action between the troops and the friendly Indians, who were to act as our allies against their own countrymen; the latter—as was now known by certain information—being collected in large force in the "Cove of the Ouithlacoochee." Their actual position was still unknown; but that, it was confidently hoped, would be discovered by the aid of the friendly chiefs, and their spies, who were constantly on the run.

The meeting had been already pre-arranged. The chiefs—who, as already stated, had gone to Fort Brooke, and were there living under protection of the garrison—were to make a secret journey, and meet the agent and general at an appointed place—the old ground, the hommock by the pond.

132

The meeting had been fixed for that very night—as soon as it should be dark enough to hide the approach of both tempters and traitors.

It was dark enough almost the moment the sun went down—for the moon was in her third quarter, and would not be in the sky until after sunset.

Shortly after twilight, therefore, we three proceeded to the spot—the general, the agent, and the interpreter, just as we had done on the former occasion.

The chiefs were not there, and this caused a little surprise. By the noted punctuality with which an Indian keeps his assignation, it was expected they would have been on the ground, for the hour appointed had arrived.

"What is detaining them? What can be detaining them?" mutually inquired the commissioner and general.

Scarcely an instant passed till the answer came. It came from afar, and in a singular utterance; but it could be no other than a reply to the question—so both my companions conjectured.

Borne upon the night-breeze was the sound of strife—the sharp cracking of rifles and pistols; and distinctly heard above all, the shrill Yo-ho-ehee.

The sounds were distant—away amid the far woods; but they were sufficiently distinct to admit of the interpretation, that a life-and-death struggle was going on between two parties of men.

It could be no feint, no false alarm to draw the soldiers from the fort, or terrify the sentinel on his post. There was an earnestness in the wild treble of those shrill cries, that convinced the listener that human blood was being spilled.

My companions were busy with conjectures. I saw that neither possessed a high degree of courage, for that is not necessary to become a general. In my warlike experience, I have seen more than one hiding behind a tree or piece of a wall. One, indeed, who was afterwards elected the chief of twenty millions of people, I have seen skulking in a ditch to screen himself from a stray shot, while his lost brigade, half a mile in the advance, was gallantly fighting under the guidance of a sub-lieutenant.

But why should I speak of these things here? The world is full of such heroes.

"It is they, by —," exclaimed the commissioner. "They have been waylaid; they are attacked by the others; that rascal Powell for a thousand!"

"It is extremely probable," replied the other, who seemed to have a somewhat steadier nerve, and spoke more coolly. "Yes, it must be. There are no troops in that direction; no whites either—not a man. It must therefore be an affair among the Indians themselves; and what else than attack upon the friendly chiefs? You are right, Thompson; it is as you say."

"If so, general, it will be of no use our remaining here. If they have waylaid Omatla, they will of course have superior numbers, and he must fall. We need not expect him."

"No; he is not likely to come, neither he nor Lusta. As you say, it is idle for us to remain here. I think we may as well return to the fort."

There was a moment's hesitation, during which I fancied both generals were debating in their own minds whether it would be *graceful* thus to give up their errand and purpose.

"If they should come,"—continued the soldier.

"General," said I, taking the liberty to interrupt him, "if you desire it, I will remain upon the ground for a while, and see. If they should come," I added, in continuation of the broken sentence, "I can proceed to the fort, and give you notice."

I could not have made a proposition more agreeable to the two. It was instantly accepted, and the brace of official heroes moved away, leaving me to myself.

It was not long ere I had cause to regret my generous rashness. My late companions could scarcely have reached the fort when the sounds of the strife suddenly ceased, and I heard the *caha-queené*—the Seminole shout of triumph. I was still listening to its wild intonations, when half-a-dozen men—dark-bodied men—rushed out of the bushes, and surrounded me where I stood.

Despite the poor light the stars afforded, I could see shining blades, guns, pistols, and tomahawks. The weapons were too near my eyes to be mistaken for the fire-flies that had been glittering around my head, besides, the clink of steel was in my ears.

My assailants made no outcry, perhaps because they were too near the fort; and my own shouts were soon suppressed by a blow that levelled me to the earth, depriving me as well of consciousness as of speech.

Note 1. In the United States army, these two offices are quite distinct. A "commissary" caters only for the inner man; a quartermaster's duty is to shelter, clothe, arm, and equip. A wise regulation.

Chapter Sixty Three.

An Indian Executioner.

After a short spell of obliviousness, I recovered my senses. I perceived that the Indians were still around me, but no longer in the menacing attitude in which I had seen them before being struck down; on the contrary, they appeared to be treating me with kindness. One of them held my head upon his knee, while another was endeavouring to staunch the blood that was running freely from a wound in my temples. The others stood around regarding me with interest, and apparently anxious about my recovery.

Their behaviour caused me surprise, for I had no other thought than that they had intended to kill me; indeed, as I sank under the stroke of the tomahawk, my senses had gone out, under the impression that I *was* killed. Such a reflection is not uncommon to those whom a blow has suddenly deprived of consciousness.

My surprise was of an agreeable character. I felt that I still lived—that I was but little hurt; and not likely to receive any further damage from those who surrounded me.

They were speaking to one another in low tones, pronouncing the prognosis of my wound, and apparently gratified that they had not killed me.

"We have spilled your blood, but it is not dangerous," said one, addressing himself to me in his native tongue. "It was I who gave the blow. *Hulwak*! it was dark. Friend of the Rising Sun! we did not know you. We thought you were the *yatika-clucco* (the 'great speaker'—the commissioner). It is his blood we intended to spill. We expected to find him here; he has been here: where gone?"

I pointed in the direction of the fort.

"*Hulwak*!" exclaimed several in a breath, and in a tone that betokened disappointment; and then turning aside, they conversed with each other in a low voice.

"Fear not," said the first speaker, again standing before me, "friend of the Rising Sun! we will not do further harm to you; but you must go with us to the chiefs. They are not far off. Come!"

I was once more upon my feet, and perhaps by a desperate effort might have escaped. The attempt, however, might have cost me a second knock-down—perhaps my life. Moreover, the courtesy of my captors at once set my mind at ease. Go where they might, I felt that I had nothing to fear from them; and, without hesitation, I consented to accompany them.

My captors, throwing themselves into single file, and assigning me a position in their midst, at once started off through the woods. For some time we walked rapidly, the path taken by the leader of the party being easily followed, even in the darkness, by those behind. I observed that we were going in the direction whence had been heard the sounds of the conflict, that had long since ceased to vibrate upon the air. Of whatever nature had been the struggle, it was evidently brought to a close, and even the victors no longer uttered the *caha-queené*.

We had advanced about a mile when the moon arose; and the woods becoming more open, I could see my captors more distinctly. I recognised the features of one or two of them, from having seen them at the council. They were warriors of the Micosauc tribe, the followers of Osceola. From this I conjectured that he was one of the chiefs before whom I was being conducted.

My conjecture proved correct. We had not gone much further, when the path led into an opening in the woods, in the midst of which a large body of Indians, about a hundred in all, were grouped together. A little apart was a smaller group—the chiefs and head warriors. In their midst I observed Osceola.

The ground exhibited a singular and sanguinary spectacle. Dead bodies were lying about, gashed with wounds still fresh and bleeding. Some of the dead lay upon their backs, their unclosed eyes glaring ghastly upon the moon, all in the attitudes in which they had fallen. The scalping-knife had done its work, as the whitish patch upon the crowns, laced with seams of crimson red, shewed the skulls divested of their hirsute covering. Men were strolling about with the fresh scalps in their hands, or elevated upon the muzzles of their guns.

There was no mystery in what I saw; I knew its meaning well. The men who had fallen were of the traitor tribes—the followers of Lusta Hajo and Omatla.

According to the arrangement with the commissioner, the chiefs had left Fort Brooke, accompanied by a chosen band of their retainers. Their intention had become known to the patriots—their movements had been watched—they had been attacked on the way; and, after a short struggle, overpowered. Most of them had fallen in the melée—a few, with the chief Lusta Hajo, had contrived to escape; while still another few—among whom was Omatla himself—had been taken prisoners during the conflict, and were yet alive. They had been rescued from death only to suffer it in a more ceremonial shape.

I saw the captives where they stood, close at hand, and fast bound to some trees. Among them I recognised their leader, by the grace of Commissioner Thompson, "king of the Seminole nation."

By those around, his majesty was now regarded with but slight deference. Many a willing regicide stood near him, and would have taken his life without further ceremony. But these were restrained by the chiefs, who opposed the violent proceeding, and who had come to the determination to give Omatla a trial, according to the laws and customs of their nation.

As we arrived upon the ground, this trial was going on. The chiefs were in council.

One of my captors reported our arrival. I noticed a murmur of disappointment among the chiefs as he finished making his announcement. They were disappointed: I was not the captive they had been expecting.

No notice was taken of me; and I was left free to loiter about, and watch their proceedings, if I pleased.

The council soon performed its duty. The treason of Omatla was too well-known to require much canvassing; and, of course, he was found guilty, and condemned to expiate the crime with his life.

The sentence was pronounced in the hearing of all present. The traitor must die.

A question arose—who was to be his executioner?

There were many who would have volunteered for the office—for to take the life of a traitor, according to Indian philosophy, is esteemed an act of honour. There would be no difficulty in procuring an executioner.

Many actually did volunteer; but the services of these were declined by the council. This was a matter to be decided by vote.

The vote was immediately taken. All knew of the vow made by Osceola. His followers were desirous he should keep it; and on this account, he was unanimously elected to do the deed. He accepted the office.

Knife in hand, Osceola approached the captive, now cowering in his bonds. All gathered around to witness the fatal stab. Moved by an impulse I could not resist, I drew near with the rest.

We stood in breathless silence, expecting every moment to see the knife plunged into the heart of the criminal.

We saw the arm upraised, and the blow given, but there was no wound—no blood! The blow had descended upon the thongs that bound the captive, and Omatla stood forth free from his fastenings!

There was a murmur of disapprobation. What could Osceola mean? Did he design that Omatla should escape—the traitor condemned by the council—by all?

But it was soon perceived he had no such intention—far different was his design.

135

"Omatla!" said he, looking his adversary sternly in the face, "you were once esteemed a brave man, honoured by your tribe—by the whole Seminole nation. The white men have corrupted you—they have made you a renegade to your country and your cause; for all that, you shall not die the death of a dog. I will kill, but not *murder* you. My heart revolts to slay a man who is helpless and unarmed. It shall be a fair combat between us, and men shall see that the right triumphs. Give him back his weapons! Let him defend himself, if he can."

The unexpected proposal was received with some disapprobation. There were many who, indignant at Omatla's treason, and still wild with the excitement produced by the late conflict, would have butchered him in his bonds. But all saw that Osceola was determined to act as he had proposed; and no opposition was offered.

One of the warriors, stepping forward, handed his weapons to the condemned chief—only his tomahawk and knife, for so Osceola was himself armed.

This done, by a sort of tacit understanding, the crowd drew back, and the two combatants stood alone in the centre.

The struggle was brief as bloody. Almost at the first blow, Osceola struck the hatchet from his antagonist's hand, and with another stroke, rapidly following, felled Omatla to the earth.

For a moment the victor was seen bending over his fallen adversary, with his long knife unsheathed, and glittering in the moonlight.

When he rose erect, the steel had lost its sheen—it was dimmed with crimson blood.

Osceola had kept his oath. He had driven his blade through the heart of the traitor— Omatla had ceased to live.

White men afterwards pronounced this deed an assassination—a murder. It was not so, any more than the death of Charles, of Caligula, of Tarquin—of a hundred other tyrants, who have oppressed or betrayed their country.

Public opinion upon such matters is not honest; it takes its colour from the cant of the times, changing like the hues of the chameleon. Sheer hypocrisy, shameful inconsistency! He only is a murderer who kills from a murderer's motive. Osceola was not of this class.

My situation was altogether singular. As yet, the chiefs had taken no notice of my presence; and notwithstanding the courtesy which had been extended to me by those who conducted me thither, I was not without some apprehensions as to my safety. It might please the council, excited as they were with what had just transpired, and now actually at war with our people, to condemn me to a fate similar to that which had befallen Omatla. I stood waiting their pleasure therefore in anything but a comfortable frame of mind.

It was not long before I was relieved from *my* apprehensions. As soon as the affair with Omatla was ended, Osceola approached, and in a friendly manner stretched out his hand, which I was only too happy to receive in friendship.

He expressed regret that I had been wounded and made captive by his men— explained the mistake; and then calling one of his followers, ordered him to guide me back to the fort.

I had no desire to remain longer than I could help upon such tragic ground; and, bidding the chief adieu, I followed my conductor along the path.

Near the pond, the Indian left me; and, without encountering any further adventures, I re-entered the gates of the fort.

Chapter Sixty Four.

A Banquet with a Bad Ending.

As by duty bound, I delivered a report of the scene I had involuntarily been witness to. It produced a lively excitement within the fort, and an expedition was instantly ordered forth, with myself to act as guide.

A bit of sheer folly. The search proved bootless, as any one might have prophesied. Of course, we found the place, and the bodies of those who had fallen—upon which the wolves had already been ravening—but we discovered no living Indians—not even the path by which they had retreated!

The expedition consisted of several hundred men—in fact, the whole garrison of the fort. Had we gone out with a smaller force, in all probability, we should have seen something of the enemy.

The death of Omatla was the most serious incident that had yet occurred; at all events, the most important in its bearings. By the whites, Omatla had been constituted king; by killing, the Indians shewed their contempt for the authority that had crowned him, as well as their determination to resist all interference of the kind. Omatla had been directly under the protection of the white chiefs: this had been guaranteed to him by promise as by treaty; and therefore the taking his life was a blow struck against his patrons. The government would now be under the necessity of avenging his death.

But the incident had its most important bearings upon the Indians, especially upon Omatla's own people. Terrified by the example, and dreading lest similar retribution might be extended to themselves, many of Omatla's tribe—sub-chiefs and warriors—forsook their alliance, and enrolled themselves in the ranks of the patriots. Other clans that had hitherto remained undecided, acting under similar motives, now declared their allegiance to the national will, and took up arms without further hesitation.

The death of Omatla, besides being an act of stern justice, was a stroke of fine policy on the part of the hostile Indians. It proved the genius of him who had conceived and carried it into execution.

Omatla was the first victim of Osceola's vow of vengeance. Soon after appeared the second. It was not long before the tragedy of the traitor's death was eclipsed by another, far more thrilling and significant. One of the chief actors in this drama disappears from the stage.

On our arrival at the fort, it was found that the commissariat was rapidly running short. No provision had been made for so large a body of troops, and no supplies could possibly reach Fort King for a long period of time. We were to be the victims of the usual improvidence exhibited by governments not accustomed to warlike operations. Rations were stinted to the verge of starvation; and the prospect before us began to look very like starvation itself.

In this emergency, the commander-in-chief performed an act of great patriotism. Independent of his military command, General Clinch was a citizen of Florida—a proprietor and planter upon a large scale. His fine plantation lay at a short distance from Fort King. His crop of maize, covering nearly a hundred acres, was just ripening; and this, without more ado, was rationed out to the army.

Instead of bringing the commissariat to the troops, the reverse plan was adopted; and the troops were marched upon their food—which had yet to be gathered before being eaten.

Four-fifths of the little army were thus withdrawn from the fort, leaving rather a weak garrison; while a new stockade was extemporised on the general's plantation, under the title of "Fort Drane."

There were slanderous people who insinuated that in this curious matter the good old general was moved by other motives than those of mere patriotism. There was some talk about "Uncle Sam"—well-known as a solvent and liberal paymaster—being called upon to give a good price for the general's corn; besides, so long as an army bivouacked upon his plantation, no danger need be apprehended from the Indian incendiaries. Perhaps these insinuations were but the conceits of camp satire.

I was not among those transferred to the new station; I was not a favourite with the commander-in-chief, and no longer upon his staff. My duties kept me at Fort King, where the commissioner also remained.

The days passed tamely enough—whole weeks of them. An occasional visit to Camp Drane was a relief to the monotony of garrison-life, but this was a rare occurrence. The fort had been shorn of its strength, and was too weak for us to go much beyond its walls. It was well-known that the Indians were in arms. Traces of their presence had been observed near the post; and a hunting excursion, or even a romantic saunter in the neighbouring woods—the usual resources of a frontier station—could not have been made without some peril.

137

During this period I observed that the commissioner was very careful in his outgoings and incomings. He rarely passed outside the stockade, and never beyond the line of sentries. Whenever he looked in the direction of the woods, or over the distant savanna, a shadow of distrust appeared to overspread his features, as though he was troubled with an apprehension of danger. This was after the death of the traitor chief. He had heard of Osceola's vow to kill Omatla; perhaps he had also heard that the oath extended to himself; perhaps he was under the influence of a presentiment.

Christmas came round. At this season, wherever they may be found—whether amid the icy bergs of the north, or on the hot plains of the tropic—on board ship, within the walls of a fortress—ay, even in a prison—Christians incline to merry-making. The frontier post is no exception to the general rule; and Fort King was a continued scene of festivities. The soldiers were released from duty—alone the sentinels were kept to their posts; and, with such fare as could be procured, backed by liberal rations of "Monongahela," the week passed cheerily enough.

A "sutler" in the American army is generally a thriving adventurer—with the officers liberal both of cash and credit—and, on festive occasions, not unfrequently their associate and boon companion. Such was he, the sutler, at Fort King.

On one of the festal days, he had provided a sumptuous dinner—no one about the fort so capable—to which the officers were invited—the commissioner himself being the honoured guest.

The banquet was set out in the sutler's own house, which, as already mentioned, stood outside the stockade, several hundred yards off, and near to the edge of the woods.

The dinner was over, and most of the officers had returned within the fort, where—as it was now getting near night—it was intended the smoking and wine-drinking should be carried on.

The commissioner, with half a dozen others—officers and civilian visitors—still lingered to enjoy another glass under the hospitable roof where they had eaten their dinner.

I was among those who went back within the fort.

We had scarcely settled down in our seats, when we were startled by a volley of sharp cracks, which the ear well knew to be the reports of rifles. At the same instant was heard that wild intonation, easily distinguishable from the shouting of civilised men—the war-cry of the Indians!

We needed no messenger to inform us what the noises meant: the enemy was upon the ground, and had made an attack—we fancied upon the fort itself.

We rushed into the open air, each arming himself as best he could.

Once outside, we saw that the fort was not assailed; but upon looking over the stockade, we perceived that the house of the sutler was surrounded by a crowd of savages, plumed and painted in full fighting costume. They were in quick motion, rushing from point to point, brandishing their weapons, and yelling the *Yo-ho-ehee*.

Straggling shots were still heard as the fatal gun was pointed at some victim endeavouring to escape. The gates of the fort were standing wide open, and soldiers, who had been strolling outside, now rushed through, uttering shouts of terror as they passed in.

The sutler's house was at too great a distance for the range of musketry. Some shots were discharged by the sentries and others who chanced to be armed, but the bullets fell short.

The artillerists ran to their guns; but on reaching these, it was found that the stables—a row of heavy log-houses—stood directly in the range of the sutler's house—thus sheltering the enemy from the aim of the gunners.

All at once the shouting ceased, and the crowd of dusky warriors was observed moving off towards the woods.

In a few seconds they had disappeared among the trees—vanishing, as if by magic, from our sight.

He who commanded at the fort—an officer slow of resolve—now mustered the garrison, and ventured a sortie. It extended only to the house of the sutler, where a halt was made, while we contemplated the horrid scene.

The sutler himself, two young officers, several soldiers and civilians, lay upon the floor dead, each with many wounds.

Conspicuous above all was the corpse of the commissioner. He was lying upon his back, his face covered with gore, and his uniform torn and bloody. Sixteen bullets had been fired into his body; and a wound more terrible than all was observed over the left breast. It was the gash made by a knife, whose blade had passed through his heart.

I could have guessed who gave that wound, even without the living testimony that was offered on the spot. A negress—the cook—who had concealed herself behind a piece of furniture, now came forth from her hiding-place. She had been witness of all. She was acquainted with the person of Osceola. It was he who had conducted the tragedy; he had been the last to leave the scene; and before taking his departure, the negress had observed him give that final stab—no doubt in satisfaction of the deadly vow he had made.

After some consultation, a pursuit was determined upon, and carried out with considerable caution; but, as before, it proved fruitless: as before, even the track by which the enemy had retreated could not be discovered!

Chapter Sixty Five.

"Dade's Massacre."

This melancholy finale to the festivities of Christmas was, if possible, rendered more sad by a rumour that shortly after reached Fort King. It was the rumour of an event, which has since become popularly known as "Dade's massacre."

The report was brought by an Indian runner—belonging to one of the friendly clans—but the statements made were of so startling a character, that they were at first received with a cry of incredulity.

Other runners, however, continuously arriving, confirmed the account of the first messenger, until his story—tragically improbable as it appeared—was accepted as truth. It was true in all its romantic colouring; true in all its sanguinary details. The war had commenced in real earnest, inaugurated by a conflict of the most singular kind—singular both in character and result.

An account of this battle is perhaps of sufficient interest to be given.

In the early part of this narrative, it has been mentioned that an officer of the United States army gave out the vaunt that he "could march through all the Seminole reserve with only a corporal's guard at his back." That officer was Major Dade.

It was the destiny of Major Dade to find an opportunity for giving proof of his warlike prowess—though with something more than a corporal's guard at his back. The result was a sad contrast to the boast he had so thoughtlessly uttered.

To understand this ill-fated enterprise, it is necessary to say a word topographically of the country.

On the west coast of the peninsula of Florida is a bay called "Tampa"—by the Spaniards, "Espiritu Santo." At the head of this bay was erected "Fort Brooke"—a stockade similar to Fort King, and lying about ninety miles from the latter, in a southerly direction. It was another of those military posts established in connection with the Indian reserve—a dépôt for troops and stores—also an entrepôt for such as might arrive from the ports of the Mexican gulf.

About two hundred soldiers were stationed here at the breaking out of hostilities. They were chiefly artillery, with a small detachment of infantry.

Shortly after the fruitless council at Fort King, these troops—or as many of them as could be spared—were ordered by General Clinch to proceed to the latter place, and unite with the main body of the army.

In obedience to these orders, one hundred men with their quota of officers, were set in motion for Fort King. Major Dade commanded the detachment.

On the eve of Christmas, 1835, they had taken the route, marching out from Fort Brooke in high spirits, buoyant with the hope of encountering and winning laurels in a fight with the Indian foe. They flattered themselves that it would be the first conflict of the war,

139

and therefore, that in which the greatest reputation would be gained by the victors. They dreamt not of defeat.

With flags flying gaily, drums rolling merrily, bugles sounding the advance, cannon pealing their farewell salute, and comrades cheering them onwards, the detachment commenced its march—that fatal march from which it was destined never to return.

Just seven days after—on the 31st of December—a man made his appearance at the gates of Fort Brooke, crawling upon his hands and knees. In his tattered attire could scarcely be recognised the uniform of a soldier—a private of Dade's detachment—for such he was. His clothes were saturated with water from the creeks, and soiled with mud from the swamps. They were covered with dust, and stained with blood. His body was wounded in five places—severe wounds all—one in the right shoulder, one in the right thigh, one near the temple, one in the left arm, and another in the back. He was wan, wasted, emaciated to the condition of a skeleton, and presented the aspect of one. When, in a weak, trembling voice, he announced himself as "Private Clark of the 2nd Artillery," his old comrades had with difficulty identified him.

Shortly after, two others—privates Sprague and Thomas—made their appearance in a similar plight. Their report was similar to that already delivered by Clark: that Major Dade's command had been attacked by the Indians, cut to pieces, massacred to a man—that they themselves were the sole survivors of that band who had so lately gone forth from the fort in all the pride of confident strength, and the hopeful anticipation of glory.

And their story was true to the letter. Of all the detachment, these three miserable remnants of humanity alone escaped; the others—one hundred and six in all—had met death on the banks of the Amazura. Instead of the laurel, they had found the cypress.

The three who escaped had been struck down and left for dead upon the field. It was only by counterfeiting death, they had succeeded in afterwards crawling from the ground, and making their way back to the fort. Most of this journey Clark performed upon his hands and knees, proceeding at the rate of a mile to the hour, over a distance of more than sixty miles!

Chapter Sixty Six.

The Battle-Ground.

The affair of Dade's massacre is without a parallel in the history of Indian warfare. No conflict of a similar kind had ever occurred—at least, none so fatal to the whites engaged in it. In this case they suffered complete annihilation—for, of the three wounded men who had escaped, two of them shortly after died of their wounds.

Nor had the Indians any great advantage over their antagonists, beyond that of superior cunning and strategy.

It was near the banks of the Amazura ("Ouithlacoochee" of the Seminoles), and after crossing that stream, that Major Dade's party had been attacked. The assault was made in ground comparatively open—a tract of pine-woods, where the trees grew thin and straggling—so that the Indians had in reality no great advantage either from position or intrenchment. Neither has it been proved that they were greatly superior in numbers to the troops they destroyed—not more than two to one; and this proportion in most Indian wars has been considered by their white antagonists as only "fair odds."

Many of the Indians appeared upon the ground mounted; but these remained at a distance from the fire of the musketry; and only those on foot took part in the action. Indeed, their conquest was so soon completed, that the horsemen were not needed. The first fire was so deadly, that Dade's followers were driven into utter confusion. They were unable to retreat: the mounted Indians had already outflanked them, and cut off their chance of escape.

Dade himself, with most of his officers, fell at the first volley; and the survivors had no choice but fight it out on the ground. A breastwork was attempted—by felling trees, and throwing their trunks into a triangle—but the hot fire from the Indian rifles soon checked the progress of the work; and the parapet never rose even breast-high above the ground.

Into this insecure shelter the survivors of the first attack retreated, and there fell rapidly under the well-aimed missiles of their foes. In a short while the last man lay motionless; and the slaughter was at an end.

When the place was afterwards visited by our troops, this triangular inclosure was found, filled with dead bodies—piled upon one another, just as they had fallen—crosswise, lengthways, in every attitude of death!

It was afterwards noised abroad that the Indians had inhumanly tortured the wounded, and horribly mutilated the slain. This was not true. There were no wounded left to be tortured—except the three who escaped—and as for the mutilation, but one or two instances of this occurred—since known to have been the work of runaway negroes actuated by motives of personal revenge.

Some scalps were taken; but this is the well-known custom of Indian warfare; and white men ere now have practised the fashion, while under the frenzied excitement of battle.

I was one of those who afterwards visited the battle-ground on a tour of inspection, ordered by the commander-in-chief; and the official report of that tour is the best testimony as to the behaviour of the victors. It reads as follows:

"Major Dade and his party were destroyed on the morning of the 28th of December, about four miles from their camp of the preceding night. They were advancing in column of route when they were attacked by the enemy, who rose in a swarm out of the cover of long grass and palmettoes. The Indians suddenly appeared close to their files. Muskets were clubbed, knives and bayonets used, and parties clenched in deadly conflict. In the second attack, our own men's muskets, taken from the dead and wounded, were used against them; a cross-fire cut down a succession of artillerists, when the cannon were taken, the carriages broken and burned, and the guns rolled into a pond. Many negroes were in the field; but no scalps were taken by the Indians. On the other hand, the negroes, with hellish cruelty, pierced the throats of all whose cries or groans shewed that there was still life in them."

Another official report runs thus:

We approached the battle-field from the rear. Our advanced guard had passed the ground without halting when the commanding officer and his staff came upon one of the most appalling scenes that can be imagined. We first saw some broken and scattered boxes; then a cart, the two oxen of which were lying dead, as if they had fallen asleep, their yokes still on them: a little to the right, one or two horses were seen. We next came to a small inclosure, made by felling trees, in such a manner as to form a triangular breastwork. Within the triangle—along the north and west faces of it—were about thirty bodies, mostly mere skeletons, although much of the clothing was left upon them. They were lying in the positions they must have occupied during the fight. Some had fallen over their dead comrades, but most of them lay close to the logs, with their heads turned towards the breastwork, over which they had delivered their fire, and their bodies stretched with striking regularity parallel to each other. They had evidently been shot dead at their posts, and the Indians had not disturbed them, except by taking the scalps of some—which, it is said, was done by their negro allies. The officers were all easily recognised. Some still wore their rings and breastpins, and money was found in their pockets! The bodies of eight officers and ninety-eight men were interred.

"It may be proper to observe that the attack was not made from a hommock, but in a thinly-wooded country—the Indians being concealed by palmettoes and grass."

From this report, it appears that the Indians were fighting—not for plunder, not even from motives of diabolical revenge. Their motive was higher and purer—it was the defence of their country—of their hearths and homes.

The advantage they had over the troop of Major Dade was simply that of ambush and surprise. This officer, though a man of undoubted gallantry, was entirely wanting in those qualities necessary to a leader—especially one engaged against such a foe. He was a mere book-soldier—as most officers are—lacking the genius which enables the great military chieftain to adapt himself to the circumstances that surround him. He conducted the march of his detachment as if going upon parade; and by so doing he carried it into danger and subsequent destruction.

141

But if the commander of the whites in this fatal affair was lacking in military capacity, the leader of the Indians was not. It soon became known that he who planned the ambush and conducted it to such a sanguinary and successful issue, was the young chief of the Baton Rouge—Osceola.

He could not have stayed long upon the ground to enjoy his triumph. It was upon that same evening, at Fort King—forty miles distant from the scene of Dade's massacre—that the commissioner fell before his vow of vengeance!

Chapter Sixty Seven.

The Battle of "Ouithlacoochee."

The murder of the commissioner called for some act of prompt retribution. Immediately after its occurrence, several expresses had been dispatched by different routes to Camp Drane—some of whom fell into the hands of the enemy, while the rest arrived safely with the news.

By daybreak of the following morning the army, more than a thousand strong, was in motion; and marching towards the Amazura. The avowed object of this expedition was to strike a blow at the *families* of the hostile Indians—their fathers and mothers, their wives, sisters and children—whose lurking-place amidst the fastnesses of the great swamp—the "Cove"—had become known to the general. It was intended they should be *captured, if possible*, and held as hostages until the warriors could be induced to surrender.

With all others who could be spared from the fort, I was ordered to accompany the expedition, and accordingly joined it upon the march. From the talk I heard around me, I soon discovered the sentiment of the soldiery. They had but little thought of making captives. Exasperated by what had taken place at the fort—further exasperated by what they called "Dade's massacre," I felt satisfied that they would not stay to take prisoners—old men or young men, women or children, all would alike be slain—no quarter would be given.

I was sick even at the prospect of such a wholesale carnage as was anticipated. Anticipated, I say, for all confidently believed it would take place. The hiding-place of these unfortunate families had become known—there were guides conducting us thither who knew the very spot—how could we fail to reach it?

An easy surprise was expected. Information had been received that the warriors, or most of them, were absent upon another and more distant expedition, and in a quarter where we could not possibly encounter them. We were to make a descent upon the nest in the absence of the eagles; and with this intent the army was conducted by silent and secret marches.

But the day before, our expedition would have appeared easy enough—a mere exciting frolic, without peril of any kind; but the news of Dade's defeat had produced a magical effect upon the spirits of the soldiers, and whilst it exasperated, it had also cowed them. For the first time, they began to feel something like a respect for their foe, mingled perhaps with a little dread of him. The Indians, at least, knew how to kill.

This feeling increased as fresh messengers came in from the scene of Dade's conflict, bringing new details of that sanguinary affair. It was not without some apprehension, then, that the soldier marched onwards, advancing into the heart of the enemy's country; and even the reckless volunteer kept close in the ranks as he rode silently along.

About mid-day we reached the banks of the Amazura. The stream had to be crossed before the Cove could be reached, for the vast network of swamps and lagoons bearing this name extended from the opposite side.

A ford had been promised the general, but the guides were at fault—no crossing-place could be found. At the point where we reached it, the river ran past, broad, black, and deep—too deep to be waded even by our horses.

Were the guides playing traitor, and misleading us? It certainly began to assume that appearance; but no—it could not be. They were Indians, it is true, but well proved in their devotion to the whites. Besides, they were men compromised with the national party—doomed to death by their own people—our defeat would have been their ruin.

It was not treason, as shewn afterwards—they had simply been deceived by the trails, and had gone the wrong way.

It was fortunate for us they had done so! But for this mistake of the guides, the army of General Clinch might have been called upon to repeat on a larger scale the drama so lately enacted by Dade and his companions.

Had we reached the true crossing, some two miles further down, we should have entered an ambush of the enemy, skillfully arranged by that same leader who so well understood his forest tactics. The report of the warriors having gone on a distant expedition was a mere *ruse*, the prelude to a series of strategic manoeuvres devised by Osceola.

The Indians were at that moment where we should have been, but for the mistake of the guides. The ford was beset upon both sides by the foe—the warriors lying unseen like snakes among the grass, ready to spring forth the moment we should attempt the crossing. Fortunate it was for Clinch and his army that our guides possessed so little skill.

The general acted without this knowledge at the time—else, had he known the dangerous proximity, his behaviour might have been different. As it was, a halt was ordered; and, after some deliberation, it was determined we should cross the river at the point where the army had arrived.

Some old boats were found, "scows," with a number of Indian canoes. These would facilitate the transport of the infantry, while the mounted men could swim over upon their horses.

Rafts of logs were soon knocked together, and the passage of the stream commenced. The manoeuvre was executed with considerable adroitness, and in less than an hour one half of the command had crossed.

I was among those who got first over; but I scarcely congratulated myself on the success of the enterprise. I felt sad at the prospect of being soon called upon to aid in the slaughter of defenceless people—of women and children—for around me there was no other anticipation. It was with a feeling of positive relief, almost of joy, that I heard that wild war-cry breaking through the woods—the well-known Yo-ho-ehee of the Seminoles.

Along with it came the ringing detonations of rifles, the louder report of musketry; while bullets, whistling through the air, and breaking branches from the surrounding trees, told us that we were assailed in earnest, and by a large force of the enemy.

That portion of the army already over had observed the precaution to post itself in a strong position among heavy timber that grew near the river-bank; and on this account the first volley of the Indians produced a less deadly effect. For all that, several fell; and those who were exposed to view were still in danger.

The fire was returned by the troops, repeated by the Indians, and again answered by the soldiers—now rolling continuously, now in straggling volleys or single shots, and at intervals altogether ceasing.

For a long while but little damage was done on either side; but it was evident that the Indians, under cover of the underwood, were working themselves into a more advantageous position—in fact, *surrounding* us. The troops, on the other hand, dare not stir from the spot where they had landed, until a larger number should cross over. After that it was intended we should advance, and force the Indians from the covert at the point of the bayonet.

The troops from the other side continued to cross. Hitherto, they had been protected by the fire of those already over; but at this crisis a manoeuvre was effected by the Indians, that threatened to put an end to the passing of the river, unless under a destructive fire from their rifles.

Just below our position, a narrow strip of land jutted out into the stream, forming a miniature peninsula. It was a sand-bar caused by an eddy on the opposite side. It was lower than the main bank, and bare of timber—except at its extreme point, where a sort of island had been formed, higher than the peninsula itself.

On this island grew a thick grove of evergreen trees—palms, live-oaks, and magnolias—in short, a hommock.

It would have been prudent for us to have occupied this hommock at the moment of our first crossing over; but our general had not perceived the advantage. The Indians were not slow in noticing it; and before we could take any steps to hinder them, a body of warriors rushed across the isthmus, and took possession of the hommock.

The result of this skillful manoeuvre was soon made manifest. The boats, in crossing, were swept down by the current within range of the wooded islet—out of whose evergreen shades was now poured a continuous stream of blue fiery smoke, while the leaden missiles did their work of death. Men were seen dropping down upon the rafts, or tumbling over the sides of the canoes, with a heavy plunge upon the water, that told they had ceased to live; while the thick fire of musketry that was directed upon the hommock altogether failed to dislodge the daring band who occupied it.

There were but few of them—for we had seen them distinctly as they ran over the isthmus—but it was evident they were a chosen few, skilled marksmen every man. They were dealing destruction at every shot.

It was a moment of intense excitement. Elsewhere the conflict was carried on with more equality—since both parties fought under cover of the trees, and but little injury was sustained or inflicted by either. The band upon the islet were killing more of our men than all the rest of the enemy.

There was no other resource than to dislodge them from the hommock—to drive them forth at the bayonet's point—at least this was the design that now suggested itself to the commander-in-chief.

It seemed a forlorn hope. Whoever should approach from the land-side would receive the full fire of the concealed enemy—be compelled to advance under a fearful risk of life.

To my surprise, the duty was assigned to myself. Why, I know not—since it could not be from any superior courage or ardour I had hitherto evinced in the campaign. But the order came from the general, direct and prompt; and with no great spirit I prepared to execute it.

With a party of rifles—scarcely outnumbering the enemy we were to attack at such a serious disadvantage—I started forth for the peninsula.

I felt as if marching upon my death, and I believe that most of those who followed me were the victims of a similar presentiment. Even though it had been a certainty, we could not now turn back; the eyes of the whole army were upon us. We must go forwards—we must conquer or fall.

In a few seconds we were upon the island, and advancing by rapid strides towards the hommock. We had hopes that the Indians might not have perceived our approach, and that we should get behind them unawares.

They were vain hopes. Our enemies had been watchful; they had observed our manoeuvre from its beginning; had faced round, and were waiting with rifles loaded, ready to receive us.

But half conscious of our perilous position, we pressed forwards and had got within twenty yards of the grove, when the blue smoke and red flame suddenly jetted forth from the trees. I heard the bullets shower past my ears; I heard the cries and groans of my followers, as they fell thickly behind me. I looked around—I saw that every one of them was stretched upon the ground, dead or dying!

At the same instant a voice reached me from the grove:

"Go back, Randolph! go back! By that symbol upon your breast your life has been spared; but my braves are chafed, and their blood is hot with fighting. Tempt not their anger. Away! away!"

Chapter Sixty Eight.

A Victory Ending in a Retreat.

I saw not the speaker, who was completely hidden behind the thick trellis of leaves. It was not necessary I should see him, to know who addressed me; on hearing the voice I instantly recognised it. It was Osceola who spoke.

144

I cannot describe my sensations at that moment, nor tell exactly how I acted. My mind was in a chaos of confusion—surprise and fear mingling alike in my emotions.

I remember facing once more towards my followers. I saw that they were not all dead—some were still lying where they had fallen, doubled up, or stretched out in various attitudes of death—motionless—beyond doubt, lifeless. Some still moved, their cries for help showing that life was not extinct.

To my joy, I observed several who had regained their feet, and were running, or rather scrambling, rapidly away from the ground; and still another few who had risen into half-erect attitudes, and were crawling off upon their hands and knees.

These last were still being fired upon from the bushes; and as I stood wavering, I saw one or two of them levelled along the grass by the fatal bullets that rained thickly around me.

Among the wounded who lay at my feet, there was a young fellow whom I knew. He appeared to be shot through both limbs, and could not move his body from the spot. His appeal to me for help was the first thing that aroused me from my indecision; I remembered that this young man had once done me a service.

Almost mechanically, I bent down, grasped him around the waist, and raising his body, commenced dragging him away.

With my burden I hurried back across the isthmus—as fast as my strength would permit—nor did I stop till beyond the range of the Indian rifles. Here I was met by a party of soldiers, sent to cover our retreat. In their hands I left my disabled comrade, and hastened onward to deliver my melancholy report to the commander-in-chief.

My tale needed no telling. Our movement had been watched, and our discomfiture was already known throughout the whole army.

The general said not a word; and, without giving time for explanation, ordered me to another part of the field.

All blamed his imprudence in having ordered such a desperate charge—especially with so small a force. For myself, I had gained the credit of a bold leader; but how I chanced to be the only one, who came back unscathed out of that deadly fire, was a puzzle which at that moment I did not choose to explain.

For an hour or more the fight continued to be carried on, in the shape of a confused skirmish among swamps and trees, without either party gaining any material advantage. Each held the position it had taken up—though the Indians retained the freedom of the forest beyond. To have retired from ours, would have been the ruin of the whole army; since there was no other mode of retreat, but by recrossing the stream, and that could only have been effected under the fire of the enemy.

And yet to hold our position appeared equally ruinous. We could effect nothing by being thus brought to a stand-still, for we were actually besieged upon the bank of the river. We had vainly endeavoured to force the Indians from the bush. Having once failed, a second attempt to cut our way through them would be a still more perilous emprise; and yet to remain stationary had also its prospects of danger. With scanty provisions, the troops had marched out of their cantonments. Their rations were already exhausted—hunger stared the army in the face. Its pangs were already felt, and every hour would render them more severe.

We began to believe that we were *besieged*; and such was virtually the fact. Around us in a semi-circle swarmed the savages, each behind his protecting tree—thus forming a defensive line equal in strength to a fortified intrenchment. Such could not be forced, without the certainty of great slaughter among our men.

We perceived, too, that the number of our enemies was hourly increasing. A peculiar cry—which some of the old "Indian fighters" understood—heard at intervals, betokened the arrival of fresh parties of the foe. We felt the apprehension that we were being outnumbered, and might soon be overpowered. A gloomy feeling was fast spreading itself through the ranks.

During the skirmishes that had already occurred, we noticed that many of the Indians were armed with fusils and muskets. A few were observed in uniform, with military accoutrements! One—a conspicuous leader—was still more singularly attired. From his shoulders was suspended a large silken flag, after the fashion of a Spanish cloak of the times of the *conquistadores*. Its stripes of alternate red and white, with the blue starry field at the corner, were conspicuous. Every eye in the army looked upon it, and recognised in the fantastic draping, thus tauntingly displayed, the loved flag of our country.

These symbols were expressive. They did not puzzle us. Their presence among our enemies was easily explained. The flag, the muskets and fusils, the uniforms and equipments, were trophies from the battle-field where Dade had fallen.

Though the troops regarded these objects with bitter indignation, their anger was impotent: the hour for avenging the disastrous fate of their comrades had not yet arrived.

It is not improbable we might have shared their destiny, had we remained much longer upon the ground; but a plan of retreat offered, of which our general was not loath to take advantage. It was the happy idea of a volunteer officer—an old campaigner of the "Hickory" wars—versed in the tactics of Indian fighting.

By his advice, a feint was made by the troops who had not yet crossed—the volunteers. It was a pretended attempt to effect the passage of the river at a point higher up stream. It was good strategy. Had such a passage been possible, it would have brought the enemy between two fires, and thus put an end to the "surround;" but a crossing was not intended—only a ruse.

It had the effect designed; the Indians were deceived by it, and rushed in a body up the bank to prevent the attempt at crossing. Our beleaguered force took advantage of their temporary absence; and the "regulars," making an adroit use of the time, succeeded in getting back to the "safe side" of the river. The wily foe was too prudent to follow us; and thus ended the "battle of the Ouithlacoochee."

In the hurried council that was held, there was no two opinions as to what course of action we should pursue. The proposal to march back to Fort King was received with a wonderful unanimity; and, with little loss of time, we took the route, and arrived without farther molestation at the fort.

Chapter Sixty Nine.

Another "Swamp-Fight."

After this action, a complete change was observed in the spirit of the army. Boasting was heard no more; and the eagerness of the troops to be led against the enemy was no longer difficult to restrain. No one expressed desire for a second expedition across the Ouithlacoochee, and the "Cove" was to remain unexplored until the arrival of reinforcements. The volunteers were disheartened, wearied of the campaign, and not a little cowed by the resistance they had so unexpectedly encountered—bold and bloody as it was unlooked for. The enemy, hitherto despised, if it had aroused by its conduct a strong feeling of exasperation and vengeance, had also purchased the privilege of respect.

The battle of the Ouithlacoochee cost the United States army nearly a hundred men. The Seminole loss was believed to be much greater; though no one could give a better authority for this belief than that of a "guess." No one had *seen* the enemy's slain; but this was accounted for by the assertion, that during the fight they *had carried their dead and wounded from the field!*

How often has this absurd allegation appeared in the dispatches of generals both victorious and defeated! It is the usual explanation of a battle-field found too sparsely strewn by the bodies of the foe. The very possibility of such an operation argues either an easy conflict, or a strong attachment between comrade and comrade—too strong, indeed, for human nature. With some fighting experience, I can affirm that I never saw a *dead* body, either of comrade or foeman, moved from the ground where he had fallen, so long as there was a shot ringing upon the ear.

In the battle of the Ouithlacoochee, no doubt some of our enemies had "bit the dust;" but their loss was much less than that of our own troops. For myself—and I had ample opportunity for observation—I could not swear to a single "dead Indian;" nor have I met with a comrade who could.

Notwithstanding this, historians have chronicled the affair as a grand "victory," and the dispatch of the commander-in-chief is still extant—a curious specimen of warlike literature. In this document may be found the name of almost every officer engaged, each depicted as a peerless hero! A rare monument of vanity and boasting.

To speak the honest truth, we had been well "whipped" by the red skins; and the chagrin of the army was only equalled by its exasperation.

Clinch, although esteemed a kind general—the "soldier's friend," as historians term him—was no longer regarded as a great warrior. His glory had departed. If Osceola owed *him* any spite, he had reason to be satisfied with what he had accomplished, without molesting the "old veteran" further. Though still living, he was dead to fame.

A fresh commander-in-chief now made his appearance, and hopes of victory were again revived. The new general was Gaines, another of the "veterans" produced by seniority of rank. He had not been ordered by the Government upon this especial duty; but Florida being part of his military district, had volunteered to take the guidance of the war.

Like his predecessor, Gaines expected to reap a rich harvest of laurels, and, like the former, was he doomed to disappointment. Again, it was the cypress wreath.

Without delay, our army—reinforced by fresh troops from Louisiana and elsewhere—was put in motion, and once more marched upon the "Cove."

We reached the banks of the Amazura, but never crossed that fatal stream—equally fatal to our glory as our lives. This time, *the Indians crossed.*

Almost upon the ground of the former action—with the difference that it was now upon the nether bank of the stream—we were attacked by the red warriors; and, after some hours of sharp skirmishing, compelled to shelter our proud battalions within the protecting pickets of a stockade! Within this inclosure we were besieged for a period of nine days, scarcely daring to trust ourselves outside the wooden walls. Starvation no longer stared us in the face—it had actually come upon us; and but for the *horses* we had hitherto bestrode—with whose flesh we were fain to satisfy the cravings of our appetites—one half the army of "Camp Izard" would have perished of hunger.

We were saved from destruction by the timely arrival of a large force that had been dispatched to our rescue under Clinch, still commanding his brigade. Having marched direct from Fort King, our former general had the good fortune to approach the enemy from their rear, and, by surprising our besiegers, disentangled us from our perilous situation.

The day of our delivery was memorable by a singular incident—an armistice of a peculiar character.

Early in the morning, while it was yet dark, a voice was heard hailing us from a distance, in a loud "Ho there!—Halloa!"

It came from the direction of the enemy—since we were *surrounded*, it could not be otherwise—but the peculiar phraseology led to the hope that Clinch's brigade had arrived.

The hail was repeated, and answered; but the hope of a rescue vanished when the stentorian voice was recognised as that of Abram, the black chief, and quondam interpreter of the council.

"What do you want?" was the interrogatory ordered by the commander-in-chief.

"A talk," came the curt reply.

"For what purpose?"

"We want to stop fighting."

The proposal was agreeable as unexpected. What could it mean? Were the Indians starring, like ourselves, and tired of hostilities? It was probable enough: for what other reason should they desire to end the war so abruptly? They had not yet been defeated but, on the contrary, victorious in every action that had been fought.

But one other motive could be thought of. We were every hour expecting the arrival of Clinch's brigade. Runners had reached the camp to say that he was near, and, reinforced by it, we should be not only strong enough to raise the siege, but to attack the Indians with almost a certainty of defeating them. Perhaps they knew, as well as we, that Clinch was advancing, and were desirous of making terms before his arrival.

The proposal for a "talk" was thus accounted for by the commander-in-chief, who was now in hopes of being able to strike a decisive blow. His only apprehension was, that the enemy should retreat, before Clinch could get forward upon the field. An armistice would serve to delay the Indians upon the ground; and without hesitation, the distant speaker was informed that the talk would be welcome.

A meeting of *parlementaires* from each side was arranged; the hour, as soon as it should be light. There were to be three of the Indians, and three from the camp.

A small savanna extended from the stockade. At several hundred yards' distance it was bounded by the woods. As soon as the day broke, we saw three men emerge from the timber, and advance into the open ground. They were Indian chiefs in full costume; they were the commissioners. All three were recognised from the camp—Abram, Coa Hajo, and Osceola.

Outside musket-range, they halted, placing themselves side by side in erect attitudes, and facing the inclosure.

Three officers, two of whom could speak the native tongue, were sent forth to meet them. I was one of the deputation.

In a few seconds we stood face to face with the hostile chiefs.

Chapter Seventy.

The Talk.

Before a word was uttered, all six of us shook hands—so far as appearance went, in the most friendly manner. Osceola grasped mine warmly; as he did so, saying with a peculiar smile:

"Ah, Randolph! friends sometimes meet in war as well as in peace."

I knew to what he referred, but could only answer him with a significant look of gratitude.

An orderly, sent to us with a message from the general, was seen approaching from the camp. At the same instant, an Indian appeared coming out of the timber, and, keeping pace with the orderly, simultaneously with the latter arrived upon the ground. The deputation was determined we should not outnumber it.

As soon as the orderly had whispered his message, the "talk began."

Abram was the spokesman on the part of the Indians, and delivered himself in his broken English. The others merely signified their assent by a simple nod, or the affirmation "Ho;" while their negative was expressed by the exclamation "Cooree."

"Do you white folk want to make peace?" abruptly demanded the negro.

"Upon what terms?" asked the head of our party.

"Da tarms we gib you are dese: you lay down arm, an' stop de war; your sogas go back, an' stay in dar forts: *we Indyen* cross ober da Ouithlacoochee; an' from dis time forth, for ebber after, we make the grand ribber da line o' boundary atween de two. We promise lib in peace an' good tarms wi' all white neighbour. Dat's all got say."

"Brothers!" said our speaker in reply, "I fear these conditions will not be accepted by the white general, nor our great father, the president. I am commissioned to say, that the commander-in-chief can treat with you on no other conditions than those of your absolute submission, and under promise that you will now agree to the removal."

"*Cooree! cooree!* never!" haughtily exclaimed Coa Hajo and Osceola in one breath, and with a determined emphasis, that proved they had no intention of offering to surrender.

"An' what for we submit," asked the black, with some show of astonishment. "We not conquered! We conquer you ebbery fight—we whip you people, one, two, tree time—we whip you; dam! we kill you well too. What for we submit? We come here gib condition—not ask um."

"It matters little what has hitherto transpired," observed the officer in reply; "we are by far stronger than you—we must conquer you in the end."

Again the two chiefs simultaneously cried "*Cooree!*"

"May be, white men, you make big mistake 'bout our strength. We not so weak you tink for—dam! no. We show you our strength."

As the negro said this, he turned inquiringly towards his comrades, as if to seek their assent to some proposition.

Both seemed to grant it with a ready nod; and Osceola, who now assumed the leadership of the affair, faced towards the forest, at the same time giving utterance to a loud and peculiar intonation.

The echoes of his voice had not ceased to vibrate upon the air, when the evergreen grove was observed to be in motion along: its whole edge; and the next instant, a line of dusky warriors shewed itself in the open ground. They stepped forth a pace or two, then halted in perfect order of battle—so that their numbers could easily be told off from where we stood.

"Count the red warriors!" cried Osceola, in a triumphant tone—"count them, and be no longer ignorant of the strength of your enemy."

As the Indian uttered these words, a satirical smile played upon his lips; and he stood for some seconds confronting us in silence.

"Now," continued he, once more pointing to his followers, "do yonder braves—there are fifteen hundred of them—do they look starving and submissive? No! they are ready to continue the war till the blood of the last man sinks into the soil of his native land. If they must perish, it will be here—here in Florida—in the land of their birth, upon the graves of their fathers.

"We have taken up the rifle because you wronged us, and would drive us out. For the wrongs we have had revenge. We have killed many of your people, and we are satisfied with the vengeance we have taken. We want to kill no more. But about the removal, we have not changed our minds. We shall never change them.

"We have made you a fair proposition: accept it, and in this hour the war shall cease; reject it, and more blood shall be spilled—ay, by the spirit of Wykomé! rivers of blood shall flow. The red poles of our lodges shall be painted again and again with the blood of our pale-faced foes. Peace or war, then—you are welcome to your choice."

As Osceola ceased speaking, he waved his hand towards his dusky warriors by the wood, who at the sign disappeared among the trees, silently, rapidly, almost mysteriously.

A meet reply was being delivered to the passionate harangue of the young chief, when the speaker was interrupted by the report of musketry, heard in the direction of the Indians, but further off. The shots followed each other in rapid succession, and were accompanied by shouts, that, though feebly borne from the far distance, could be distinguished as the charging cheers of men advancing into a battle.

"Ha! foul play!" cried the chiefs in a breath; "pale-faced liars! you shall rue this treason;" and, without waiting to exchange another sentence, all three sprang off from the spot, and ran at full speed towards the covert of the woods.

We turned back within the lines of the camp, where the shots had also been heard, and interpreted as the advance of Clinch's brigade attacking the Indian outposts in the rear. We found the troops already mustered in battle-array, and preparing to issue forth from the stockade. In a few minutes, the order was given, and the army marched forth, extending itself rapidly both right and left along the bank of the river.

As soon as the formation was complete, the line advanced. The troops were burning for revenge. Cooped up as they had been for days, half-famished, and more than half disgraced, they had now an opportunity to retrieve their honour; and were fully bent upon the punishment of the savage foe. With an army in their rear, rapidly closing upon them by an extended line—for this had been pre-arranged between the commanders—another similarly advancing upon their front, how could the Indians escape? They must fight—they would be conquered at last.

This was the expectation of all—officers and soldiers. The commander-in-chief was himself in high spirits. His strategic plan had succeeded. The enemy was surrounded—entrapped; a great victory was before him—a "harvest of laurels."

We marched forward. We heard shots, but now only solitary or straggling. We could not hear the well-known war-cry of the Indians.

We continued to advance. The hommocks were carried by a charge, but in their shady coverts we found no enemy.

Surely they must still be before us—between our lines and those of the approaching reinforcement? Is it possible they can have retreated—escaped?

No! Yonder they are—on the other side of the meadow—just coming out from the trees. They are advancing to give us battle! Now for the charge—now—

Ha! those blue uniforms and white belts—those forage-caps and sabres—these are not Indians! It is not the enemy! They are our friends—the soldiers of Clinch's brigade!

Fortunate it was that at that moment there was a mutual recognition, else might we have annihilated one another.

Chapter Seventy One.

Mysterious Disappearance of an Army.

The two divisions of the army now came together, and after a rapid council had been held between the commanders, continued scouring the field in search of our enemy. Hours were spent in the search; but not an Indian foe could be found!

Osceola had performed a piece of strategy unheard of in the annals of war. He had carried an army of 1,600 men from between two others of nearly equal numbers, who had completely enfiladed him, without leaving a man upon the ground—ay, without leaving a trace of his retreat. That host of Indian warriors, so lately observed in full battle-array, had all at once broken up into a thousand fragments, and, as if by magic, had melted out of sight.

The enemy was gone, we knew not whither; and the disappointed generals once more marched their forces back to Fort King.

The "dispersion," as it was termed, of the Indian army, was of course chronicled as another "victory." It was a victory, however, that killed poor old Gaines—at least his military fame—and he was only too glad to retire from the command he had been so eager to obtain.

A third general now took the field as commander-in-chief—an officer of more notoriety than either of his predecessors—Scott. A lucky wound received in the old British wars, seniority of rank, a good deal of political buffoonery, but above all a free translation of the French "system of tactics," with the assumption of being their author, had kept General Scott conspicuously before the American public for a period of twenty years (Note 1). He who could contrive such a system of military manoeuvring could not be otherwise than a great soldier; so reasoned his countrymen.

Of course wonderful things were expected from the new commander-in-chief, and great deeds were promised. He would deal with the savages in a different way from that adopted by his predecessors; he would soon put an end to the contemptible war.

There was much rejoicing at the appointment; and preparations were made for a campaign on a far more extensive scale than had fallen to the lot of either of the chiefs who preceded him. The army was doubled—almost trebled—the commissariat amply provided for, before the great general would consent to set foot upon the field.

He arrived at length, and the army was put in motion.

I am not going to detail the incidents of this campaign; there were none of sufficient importance to be chronicled, much less of sufficient interest to be narrated. It consisted simply of a series of harassing marches, conducted with all the pomp and regularity of a parade review. The army was formed into three divisions, somewhat bombastically styled "right wing," "left wing," and "centre." Thus formed, they were to approach the "Cove of the Ouithlacoochee"—again that fatal Cove—from three different directions, Fort King, Fort Brooke, and the Saint John's. On arriving on the edge of the great swamp, each was to fire minute-guns as signals for the others, and then all three were to advance in converging lines towards the heart of the Seminole fastness.

The absurd manoeuvre was carried out, and ended as might have been expected, in complete failure. During the march, no man saw the face of a red Indian. A few of their camps were discovered, but nothing more. The cunning warriors had heard the signal guns, and well understood their significance. With such a hint of the position of their enemy, they had but little difficulty in making their retreat between the "wings."

Perhaps the most singular, if not the most important, incident occurring in Scott's campaign was one which came very near costing me my life. If not worthy of being given in detail, it merits mention as a curious case of "abandonment."

While marching for the "Cove" with his centre wing, the idea occurred to our great commander to leave behind him, upon the banks of the Amazura, what he termed a "post of observation." This consisted of a detachment of forty men—mostly our Suwanee volunteers, with their proportion of officers, myself among the number.

We were ordered to fortify ourselves on the spot, and *stay* there until we should be relieved from our duty, which was somewhat indefinitely understood even by him who was placed in command of us. After giving these orders, the general, at the head of his "central wing," marched off, leaving us to our fate.

Our little band was sensibly alive to the perilous position in which we were thus placed, and we at once set about making the best of it. We felled trees, built a blockhouse, dug a well, and surrounded both with a strong stockade.

Fortunately we were not *discovered* by the enemy for nearly a week after the departure of the army, else we should most certainly have been destroyed to a man. The Indians, in all probability, had followed the "centre wing," and thus for a time were carried out of our neighbourhood.

On the sixth day, however, they made their appearance, and summoned us to surrender.

We refused, and fought them—again, and again, at intervals, during a period of fifty days!

Several of our men were killed or wounded; and among the former, the gallant chief of our devoted band, Holloman, who fell from a shot fired through the interstices of the stockade.

Provisions had been left with us to serve us for *two weeks*; they were eked out to last for seven! For thirty days we subsisted upon raw corn and water, with a few handfuls of acorns, which we contrived to gather from the trees growing within the inclosure.

In this way we held out for a period of fifty days, and still no commander-in-chief—no army came to relieve us. During all that gloomy siege, we never heard word of either; no white face ever showed itself to our anxious eyes, that gazed constantly outward. We believed ourselves abandoned—forgotten.

And such in reality was the fact—General Scott, in his eagerness to get away from Florida, had quite forgotten to relieve the "post of observation;" and others believing that we had long since perished, made no effort to send a rescue.

Death from hunger stared us in the face, until at length the brave old hunter, Hickman, found his way through the lines of our besiegers, and communicated our situation to our "friends at home."

His tale produced a strong excitement, and a force was dispatched to our relief, that succeeded in dispersing our enemies, and setting us free from our blockhouse prison.

Thus terminated "Scott's campaign," and with it his command in Florida. The whole affair was a burlesque, and Scott was only saved from ridicule and the disgrace of a speedy recall, by a lucky accident, that fell in his favour. Orders had already reached him to take control of another, "Indian war"—the "Creek"—that was just breaking out in the States of the southwest; and this afforded the discomfited general a well-timed excuse for retiring from the "Flowery Land."

Florida was destined to prove to American generals a land of melancholy remembrances. No less than seven of them were successively beaten at the game of Indian warfare by the Seminoles and their wily chieftains. It is not my purpose to detail the history of their failures and mishaps. From the disappearance of General Scott, I was myself no longer with the main army. My destiny conducted me through the more romantic by-ways of the campaign—the paths of *la petite guerre*—and of these only am I enabled to write. Adieu, then, to the grand historic.

Note 1. Scott's whole career, political as well as military, had been a series of *faux pas*. His campaign in Mexico will not bear criticism. The numerous blunders he there committed would have led to most fatal results, had they not been neutralised by the judgment of his inferior officers, and the indomitable valour of the soldiery. The battle of Moline del Rey— the armistice with Santa Anna, were military errors unworthy of a cadet fresh from college. I make bold to affirm that every action was a mob-fight—the result depending upon mere chance; or rather on the desperate bravery of the troops upon one side, and the infamous cowardice of those on the other.

Chapter Seventy Two.

The Condition of Black Jake.

We had escaped from the blockhouse in boats, down the river to its mouth, and by sea to Saint Marks. Thence the volunteers scattered to their homes—their term of service having expired. They went as they listed; journeying alone, or in straggling squads of three and four together.

One of these groups consisted of old Hickman the hunter, a companion of like kidney, myself, and my ever faithful henchman.

Jake was no longer the "Black Jake" of yore. A sad change had come over his external aspect. His cheek-bones stood prominently out, while the cheeks themselves had fallen in; his eyeballs had retreated far within their sockets, and the neglected wool stood out over his temples in a thick frizzled shock. His skin had lost its fine ebon polish, and showed distinct traces of corrugation. Wherever "scratched" by his now elongated finger-nails, a whitish dandruffy surface was exhibited.

The poor fellow had fared badly in the blockhouse; and three weeks of positive famine had played sad havoc with his outward man.

Starvation, however, but little affected his spirits. Throughout all, he had preserved his jovial mood, and his light humour often roused me from my despondency. While gnawing the corn cob, and washing down the dry maize with a gourd of cold water, he would indulge in rapturous visions of "hominy and hog-meat," to be devoured whenever it should please fate to let him return to the "ole plantayshun." Such delightful prospects of future enjoyment enabled him the better to endure the pinching present—for anticipation has its joys. Now that we were free, and actually heading homewards; now that his visions were certain soon to become realities, Jake's joviality could no longer be kept within bounds; his tongue was constantly in motion; his mouth ever open with the double tier of "ivories" displayed in a continuous smile; while his skin seemed to be rapidly recovering its dark oily lustre.

Jake was the soul of our party, as we trudged wearily along; and his gay jokes affected even the staid old hunters, at intervals eliciting from both loud peals of laughter.—For myself I scarcely shared their mirth—only now and then, when the sallies of my follower proved irresistible. There was a gloom over my spirit, which I could not comprehend.

It should have been otherwise. I should have felt happy at the prospect of returning home—of once more beholding those who were dear—but it was not so.

It had been so on my first getting free from our blockhouse prison; but this was only the natural reaction, consequent upon escape from what appeared almost certain death. My joy had been short-lived: it was past and gone; and now that I was nearing my native home, dark shadows came over my soul; a presentiment was upon me that all was not well.

I could in no way account for this feeling, for I had heard no evil tidings. In truth, I had heard nothing of home or of friends for a period of nearly two months. During our long siege, no communication had ever reached us; and at Saint Marks we met but slight news from the settlements of the Suwanee. We were returning in ignorance of all that had transpired there during our absence—if aught *had* transpired worthy of being known.

This ignorance itself might have produced uncertainty, doubt, even apprehension; but it was not the sole cause of my presentiment. Its origin was different. Perhaps the recollection of my abrupt departure—the unsettled state in which I had left the affairs of our family—the parting scene, now vividly recalled—remembrances of Ringgold—reflections upon the wicked designs of this wily villain—all these may have contributed to form the apprehensions under which I was suffering. Two months was a long period; many events could happen within two months, even in the narrow circle of one's own family. Long since it had been reported that I had perished at the hands of the Indian foe; I was believed to be dead, at home, wherever I was known; and the belief might have led to ill results. Was my sister still true to her word, so emphatically pronounced in that hour of parting? Was I returning home to find her still my loved sister? Still single and free? or had she yielded to maternal solicitation, and become the wife of the vile caitiff after all?

With such conjectures occupying my thoughts, no wonder I was not in a mood for merriment. My companions noticed my dejection, and in their rude but kind way, rallied me as we rode along. They failed, however, to make me cheerful like themselves. I could not cast the load from my heart. Try as I would, the presentiment lay heavy upon me, that all was not well.

Alas, alas! the presentiment proved true—no, not true, but worse—worse than my worst apprehensions—worse even than that I had most feared.

The news that awaited me was not of marriage, but of death—the death of my mother—and worse than death—horrid doubt of my sister's fate. Before reaching home, a messenger met me—one who told an appalling tale.

The Indians had attacked the settlement, or rather my own plantation—for their foray had gone no further: my poor mother had fallen under their savage knives; my uncle too: and my sister? *She had been carried off!*

I stayed to hear no more; but, driving the spurs into my jaded horse, galloped forward like one suddenly smitten with madness.

Chapter Seventy Three.

A Bad Spectacle.

My rate of speed soon brought me within the boundaries of the plantation; and, without pausing to breathe my horse, I galloped on, taking the path that led most directly to the house. It was not the main road, but a wood-path here and there closed up with "bars." My horse was a spirited animal, and easily leaped over them.

I met a man coming from the direction of the house—a white man—a neighbour. He made motions as if to speak—no doubt, of the calamity. I did not stop to listen. I had heard enough. My eyes alone wanted satisfaction.

I knew every turn of the path. I knew the points where I should first come in sight of the house.

I reached it, and looked forwards. Father of mercy! there was no house to be seen!

Half-bewildered, I reined up my horse. I strained my eyes over the landscape—in vain—no house.

Had I taken the wrong road, or was I looking in the wrong direction? No—no. There stood the giant tulip-tree, that marked the embouchure of the path. There stretched the savanna; beyond it the home-fields of indigo and maize; beyond these the dark wood-knoll of the hommock; but beyond this last there was nothing—nothing I could recognise.

The whole landscape appeared to have undergone a change. The gay white walls—the green *jalousies*—the cheerful aspect of home, that from that same spot had so often greeted me, returning hungry and wearied from the hunt—were no longer to be seen. The sheds, the negro-cabins, the offices, even the palings had disappeared. From their steads I beheld thick volumes of smoke ascending to the sky, and rolling over the sun till his disc was red. The heavens were frowning upon me.

From what I had already learned, the spectacle was easy of comprehension. It caused no new emotion either of surprise or pain. I was not capable of suffering more.

Again putting my horse to his speed, I galloped across the fields towards the scene of desolation.

As I neared the spot, I could perceive the forms of men moving about through the smoke. There appeared to be fifty or a hundred of them. Their motions did not betoken excitement. Only a few were moving at all, and these with a leisurely gait, that told they were not in action. The rest stood in groups, in lounging attitudes, evidently mere spectators of the conflagration. They were making no attempt to extinguish the flames, which I now observed mingling with the smoke. A few were rushing to and fro—most of them on horseback—apparently in the endeavour to catch some horses and cattle, that, having escaped from the burnt inclosure, were galloping over the fields, neighing and lowing.

One might have fancied that the men around the fire were those who had caused it; and for a moment such an idea was in my mind. The messenger had said that the foray had just taken place—that very morning at daybreak. It was all I had heard, as I hurried away.

It was yet early—scarcely an hour after sunrise—for we had been travelling by night to avoid the hot hours. Were the savages still upon the ground? Were those men Indians? In the lurid light, amidst the smoke, chasing the cattle—as if with the intention of driving them off—the conjecture was probable enough.

But the report said they had gone away: how else could the details have been known?—the murder of my mother, the rape of my poor sister? With the savages still upon the ground, how had these facts been ascertained?

Perhaps they had gone, and returned again to collect the booty, and fire the buildings? For an instant such fancies were before my mind.

They had no influence in checking my speed. I never thought of tightening the rein—my bridle arm was not free; with both hands I was grasping the ready rifle.

Vengeance had made me mad. Even had I been certain that the dark forms before me were those of the murderers, I was determined to dash forwards into their midst, and perish upon the body of a savage.

I was not alone. The black was at my heels; and close behind, I could hear the clattering hoofs of the hunters' horses.

We galloped up to the selvidge of the smoke. The deception was at an end. They were not Indians or enemies, but friends who stood around, and who hailed our approach neither with words nor shouts, but with the ominous silence of sympathy.

I pulled up by the fire, and dismounted from my horse: men gathered around me with looks of deep meaning. They were speechless—no one uttered a word. All saw that it was a tale that needed no telling.

I was myself the first to speak. In a voice so husky as scarcely to be heard, I inquired: "Where?"

The interrogatory was understood—it was anticipated. One had already taken me by the hand, and was leading me gently around the fire. He said nothing, but pointed towards the hommock. Unresistingly I walked by his side.

As we neared the pond, I observed a larger group than any I had yet seen. They were standing in a ring, with their faces turned inwards, and their eyes bent upon the earth. *I knew she was there.*

At our approach, the men looked up, and suddenly the ring opened—both sides mechanically drawing back. He who had my hand conducted me silently onwards, till I stood in their midst. I looked upon the corpse of my mother.

Beside it was the dead body of my uncle, and beyond, the bodies of several black men—faithful slaves, who had fallen in defence of their master and mistress.

My poor mother!—shot—stabbed—*scalped.* Even in death had she been defeatured!

Though I had anticipated it, the spectacle shocked me.

My poor mother! Those glassy eyes would never smile upon me again—those pale lips would neither chide nor cheer me more.

I could control my emotions no longer. I burst into tears; and falling upon the earth, flung my arms around the corpse, and kissed the cold mute lips of her who had given me birth.

Chapter Seventy Four.

To the Trail.

My grief was profound—even to misery. The remembrance of occasional moments of coldness on the part of my mother—the remembrance more especially of the last parting scene—rendered my anguish acute. Had we but parted in affection—in the friendly confidence of former years—my loss would have been easier to endure. But no; her last words to me were spoken in reproach—almost in anger—and it was the memory of these that now so keenly embittered my thoughts. I would have given the world could she have heard but one word—to know how freely I forgave her.

My poor mother! all was forgiven. Her faults were few and venial. I remembered them not. Ambition was her only sin—among those of her station, almost universal—but I remembered it no more. I remembered only her many virtues—only that she was my *mother*. Never until that moment had I known how dearly I loved her.

It was no time to indulge in grief. Where was my sister?

I sprang to my feet, as I gave wild utterance to the interrogatory.

It was answered only by signs. Those around me pointed to the forest. I understood the signs—the savages had borne her away.

Up to this hour I had felt no hostility towards the red men; on the contrary, my sentiments had an opposite inclination. If not friendship for them, I had felt something akin to it. I was conscious of the many wrongs they had endured, and were now enduring at the hands of our people. I knew that in the end they would be conquered, and must submit. I had felt sympathy for their unfortunate condition.

It was gone. The sight of my murdered mother produced an instantaneous change in my feelings; and sympathy for the savage was supplanted by fierce hostility. Her blood called aloud for vengeance, and my heart was eager to obey the summons.

As I rose to my feet, I registered vows of revenge.

I stood not alone. Old Hickman and his fellow-hunter were at my back, and fifty others joined their voices in a promise to aid me in the pursuit.

Black Jake was among the loudest who clamoured for retribution. He too had sustained his loss. Viola was nowhere to be found—she had been carried off with the other domestics. Some may have gone voluntarily, but all were absent—all who were not dead. The plantation and its people had no longer an existence. I was homeless as well as motherless.

There was no time to be wasted in idle sorrowing; immediate action was required, and determined upon. The people had come to the ground armed and ready, and a few minutes sufficed to prepare for the pursuit.

A fresh horse was procured for myself; others for the companions of my late journey; and after snatching a breakfast hastily prepared, we mounted, and struck off upon the trail of the savages.

It was easily followed, for the murderers had been mounted, and their horses' tracks betrayed them.

They had gone some distance up the river before crossing, and then swam their horses over to the Indian side. Without hesitation, we did the same.

The place I remembered well. I had crossed there before—two months before—while tracking the steed of Osceola. It was the path that had been taken by the young chief. The coincidence produced upon me a certain impression; and not without pain did I observe it.

It led to reflection. There was time, as the trail was in places less conspicuous, and the finding it delayed our advance. It led to inquiry.

Had any one seen the savages?—or noted to what band they belonged? Who was their leader?

Yes. All these questions were answered in the affirmative. Two men, lying concealed by the road, had seen the Indians passing away—had seen their captives, too; my sister—Viola—with other girls of the plantation. These were on horseback, each clasped in the arms of a savage. The blacks travelled afoot. They were *not* bound. They appeared to go willingly. The Indians were "Redsticks"—*led by Osceola.*

Such was the belief of those around me, founded upon the report of the men who had lain in ambush.

It is difficult to describe the impression produced upon me. It was painful in the extreme. I endeavoured not to believe the report. I resolved not to give it credence, until I should have further confirmation of its truthfulness.

Osceola! O heavens! Surely he would not have done this deed? It could not have been he?

The men might have been mistaken. It was before daylight the savages had been seen. The darkness might have deceived them. Every feat performed by the Indians—every foray made—was put down to the credit of Osceola. Osceola was everywhere. Surely he had not been there?

Who were the two men—the witnesses? Not without surprise did I listen to the answer. They were *Spence and Williams*!

To my surprise, too, I now learned that they were among the party who followed me—volunteers to aid me in obtaining revenge for my wrongs!

Strange, I thought; but stranger still that Arens Ringgold was *not* there. He had been present at the scene of the conflagration; and, as I was told, among the loudest in his threats of vengeance. But he had returned home; at all events he was not one of the band of pursuers.

I called Spence and Williams, and questioned them closely. They adhered to their statement. They admitted that it was dark when they had seen the Indians returning from the massacre. They could not tell for certain whether they were the warriors of the "Redstick" tribe, or those of the "Long Swamp." They believed them to be the former. As to who was their leader, they had no doubt whatever. It was Osceola who led them. They knew him by the three ostrich feathers in his head-dress, which rendered him conspicuous among his followers.

These fellows spoke positively. What interest could they have in deceiving me? What could it matter to them, whether the chief of the murderous band was Osceola, Coa Hajo, or Onopa himself?

Their words produced conviction—combined with other circumstances, deep, painful conviction. The murderer of my mother—he who had fired my home, and borne my sister into a cruel captivity—could be no other than Osceola.

All memory of our past friendship died upon the instant. My heart burned with hostility and hate, for him it had once so ardently admired.

Chapter Seventy Five.

The Alarm.

There were other circumstances connected with the bloody affair, that upon reflection appeared peculiar and mysterious. By the sudden shock, my soul had been completely benighted; and these circumstances had escaped my notice. I merely believed that there had been an onslaught of the Indians, in which my mother had been massacred, and my sister borne away from her home—that the savages, not satisfied with blood, had added fire—that these outrages had been perpetrated in revenge for past wrongs, endured at the hands of their pale-faced enemies—that the like had occurred elsewhere, and was almost daily occurring—why not on the banks of the Suwanee, as in other districts of the country? In fact, it had been rather a matter of wonder, that the settlement had been permitted to remain so long unmolested. Others—far more remote from the Seminole strongholds—had already suffered a like terrible visitation; and why should ours escape? The immunity had been remarked, and the inhabitants had become lulled by it into a false security.

The explanation given was that the main body of the Indians had been occupied elsewhere, watching the movements of Scott's triple army; and, as our settlement was strong, no small band had dared to come against it.

But Scott was now gone—his troops had retired within the forts—their summer quarters—for winter is the season of campaigning in Florida; and the Indians, to whom all seasons are alike, were now free to extend their marauding expeditions against the trans-border plantations.

This appeared the true explanation why an attack upon the settlement of the Suwanee had been so long deferred.

During the first burst of my grief, on receiving news of the calamity, I accepted it as such: I and mine had merely been the victims of a general vengeance.

But the moments of bewilderment soon passed; and the peculiar circumstances, to which I have alluded, began to make themselves apparent to my mind.

First of all, why was our plantation the only one that had been attacked?—our house the only one given to the flames?—our family the only one murdered?

These questions startled me; and natural it was that they did so. There were other plantations along the river equally unprotected—other families far more noted for their hostility to the Seminole race—nay, what was yet a greater mystery, the Ringgold plantation lay in the very path of the marauders; as their trail testified, they had passed around it to reach our house; and both Arens Ringgold and his father had long been notorious for bitter enmity to the red men, and violent aggressions against their rights.

Why, then, had the Ringgold plantation been suffered to remain unmolested, while ours was singled out for destruction? Were we the victims of a *particular and special vengeance?*

It must have been so; beyond a doubt, it was so. After long reflection, I could arrive at no other conclusion. By this alone could the mystery be solved.

And Powell—oh! could it have been he?—my friend, a fiend guilty of such an atrocious deed? Was it probable? was it possible? No—neither.

Despite the testimony of the two men—vile wretches I knew them to be—despite what they had seen and said—my heart refused to believe it.

What motive could he have for such special murder?—ah! what motive?

True, my mother had been unkind to him—more than that, ungrateful; she had once treated him with scorn. I remembered it well—he, too, might remember it.

But surely he, the noble youth—to my mind the *beau idéal* of heroism—would scarcely have harboured such petty spite, and for so long?—would scarcely have repaid it by an act of such bloody retribution? No—no—no.

Besides, would Powell have left untouched the dwelling of the Ringgolds? of Arens Ringgold, one of his most hated foes—one of the four men he had sworn to kill? This of itself was the most improbable circumstance connected with the whole affair.

Ringgold had been at home—might have been entrapped in his sleep—his black retainers would scarcely have resisted; at all events, they could have been overcome as easily as ours.

Why was *he* permitted to live? Why was *his* house not given to the flames?

Upon the supposition that Osceola was the leader of the band, I could not comprehend why he should have left Arens Ringgold to live, while killing those who were scarcely his enemies.

New information imparted to me as we advanced along the route, produced new reflections. I was told that the Indians had made a hasty departure—that they had in fact retreated. The conflagration had attracted a large body of citizen soldiery—a patrol upon its rounds—and the appearance of these, unexpected by the savages, had caused the latter to scamper off to the woods. But for this, it was conjectured other plantations would have suffered the fate of ours—perhaps that of Ringgold himself.

The tale was probable enough. The band of marauders was not large—we knew by their tracks there were not more than fifty of them—and this would account for their retreat on the appearance even of a smaller force. The people alleged that it was a retreat.

This information gave a different complexion to the affair—I was again driven to conjectures—again forced to suspicions of Osceola.

Perhaps I but half understood his Indian nature; perhaps, after all, *he* was the monster who had struck the blow.

Once more I interrogated myself as to his motive—what motive?

Ha! my sister, Virginia—O God! could love—passion—fiendish desire to possess—
"The Indyens! Indyens! Indyens!"

Chapter Seventy Six.

A False Alarm.

The significant shout at once put a period to my reflections.

Believing the savages to be in sight, I spurred towards the front. The horsemen had drawn bridle and halted. A few, who had been straggling from the path, hurried up and ranged themselves close to the main body, as if for protection. A few others, who had been riding carelessly in the advance, were seen galloping back. It was from these last the cry of "Indyens" had come, and several of them still continued to repeat it.

"Indyuns?" cried Hickman, interrogatively, and with an air of incredulity. "Whar did ye see them?"

"Yonder," responded one of the retreating horsemen—"in yon clump o' live-oaks. It's full o' them."

"I'll be dog-goned if I believe it," rejoined the old hunter, with a contemptuous toss of the head. "I'll lay a plug o' Jeemes's River, it war stumps yez seed! Indyuns don't show 'emselves in timmer like this hyar—specially to sech verdunts as you. Ye'll *hear* 'em afore you see 'em, I kalklate."

"But we did hear them," replied one, "we heard them calling out to one another."

"Bah!" exclaimed the hunter; "y'all hear 'em different from that, I guess, when you gets near enough. It'll be the spang o' thar rifles y'ull hear fust thing. Dog-gone the Indyun's thar. Twar a coon or a cat-bird ye've heern a screamin'! I know'd ye'd make a scamper the fust thing as flittered afore ye."

"Stay whar yez are now," he added in a tone of authority, "jest stay whar yez are a bit."

So saying, he slipped down from his saddle, and commenced hitching his bridle to a branch.

"Come, Jim Weatherford," he said, addressing himself to his hunter comrade, "you come along—we'll see whether it be Indyuns or stumps thet's gin these fellows sech a dog-goned scare."

Weatherford, anticipating the request, had already dropped to the ground; and the two having secured their horses, rifle in hand, slunk silently off into the bushes.

The rest of the party, gathering still more closely together, remained in their saddles to await the result.

There was but slight trial upon their patience; for the two pioneers were scarce out of sight, when we heard their voices ringing together in loud peals of laughter.

This encouraged us to advance. Where there was so much merriment there could be but little danger; and, without waiting for the return of the scouts, we rode forwards, directing our course by their continued cachinnations.

An opening brought both of them into view; Weatherford was gazing downwards, as if examining some tracks; while Hickman, who saw us coming up, stood with extended arm, pointing toward the straggling woods that lay beyond.

We turned our eyes in the direction indicated. We observed a number of half-wild, horned cattle, that, startled by the trampling of our troops, were scampering off among the trees.

"Now," cried the hunter, triumphantly; "thar's yur Indyuns! Ain't they a savage consarn? Ha! ha! ha!"

Every one joined in the laugh except those who had given the false alarm.

"I know'd thar war no Indyuns," continued the alligator-hunter. "That ain't the way they'll make thar appearance. Yu'll hear 'em afore you sees 'em; an' jest one word o' advice to you greenhorns—as don't know a red Indyun from a red cow—let somebody as diz know, go in the devance, an' the rest o' ye keep well togither; or I'll stake high on't thet some o' yez 'll sleep the night 'ithout har on yur heads."

All acknowledged that Hickman's advice was sage and sound. The hint was taken, and leaving the two old hunters henceforth to lead the pursuit, the rest drew more closely together, and followed them along the trail.

The plan adopted in this instance, was that followed in all well-devised tracking parties when in pursuit of an enemy. It matters not of what elements the body is composed—be it naval, military or civilian—be there present, commodores, generals or governors—all yield the *pas* to some old hunter or scout, who follows the trail like a sleuth hound, and whose word is supreme law for the nonce.

It was evident the pursued party could not be far in advance of us. This we knew from the hour at which they had been seen retreating from the settlement. After my arrival on the plantation, no time had been lost—only ten minutes spent in preparation—and altogether there was scarce an hour's difference between the times of our starting. The fresh trail confirmed the fact—they could not be a league ahead of us, unless they had ridden faster than we. This was scarce probable, encumbered as they were with their black captives, whose larger tracks, here and there distinctly perceptible, showed that they were marching afoot. Of course, the savage horsemen would be detained in getting them forwards; and in this lay our main hope of overtaking them.

There were but few who feared for the result, should we only be able to come up with the enemy. The white men were full of wrath and revenge, and this precluded all thoughts of fear. Besides, we could tell by their trail that the Indians scarce outnumbered us. Not above fifty appeared to constitute the band. No doubt they were able warriors, and our equals man to man; but those who had volunteered to assist me were also the "true grit"— the best men of the settlement for such a purpose.

No one talked of going back. All declared their readiness to follow the murderers even to the heart of the Indian territory—even into the "Cove" itself.

The devotion of these men cheered me; and I rode forwards with lighter heart— lighter with the prospect of vengeance, which I believed to be near.

Chapter Seventy Seven.

"A Split Trail."

It proved not to be so near us as we had anticipated. Pressing forward, as fast as our guides could lift the trail, we followed it for ten miles. We had hoped to find revenge at half the distance.

The Indians either knew that we were after them; or, with their wonted wisdom were marching rapidly under the mere suspicion of a pursuit. After the committal of such horrid atrocities, it was natural for them to suppose they would be pursued.

Evidently they were progressing as fast as we—but not faster; though the sun was broiling hot, sap still oozed from the boughs they had accidentally broken—the mud turned up by their horses' hoofs, as the guides expressed it, had not yet "crusted over," and the crushed herbage was wet with its own juice and still procumbent.

To the denizen of the city, accustomed to travel from street to street by the assistance of sign boards at every corner and numbers on every door, it must appear almost incredible that the wild savage, or untutored hunter, can, without guide or compass, unerringly follow, day after day, the track of some equally cunning foe. To the pursuing party every leaf, every twig, every blade of grass is a "sign," and they read them as plainly as if the route were laid down upon a map. While the pursuing party is thus attentive to detect "sign," the escaping one is as vigilant to avoid leaving any—and many are the devices resorted to, to efface the trail.

"Jest helf a hour ahead," remarked old Hickman, as he rose erect after examining the tracks for the twentieth time—"jest helf a hour, dog-darn 'em! I never knowed red skins to travel so fast afore. Thar a streakin' it like a gang o' scared bucks, an' jest 'bout now thar breech clouts are in a purty considerable sweat, an' some o' thar duds is stannin at an angle o' forty-five, I reckon."

A peal of laughter was the reply to this sally of the guide.

"Not so loud, fellars! not so loud," said he, interrupting the laughter by an earnest wave of his hand. "By jeroozalim! tha'll hear ye; an if they do, tha'll be some o' us 'ithout scalps afore sundown. For yer lives, boys, keep still as mice—not a word, or we'll be heern—tha'r as sharp eared as thar own dogs, and, darn me, if I believe thar more'n helf a mile ahead o' us."

The guide once more bent himself over the trail, and after a short reconnoissance of the tracks, repeated his last words with more emphasis.

"No, by —! not more'n half a mile—Hush, boys, keep as quiet as possums, an' I promise ye we'll tree the varmints in less'n a hour. Hush!"

Obedient to the injunctions, we rode forwards, as silently as it was possible for us to proceed on horseback.

We strove to guide our horses along the softer borders of the path to prevent the thumping of their hoofs. No one spoke above a whisper; and even then there was but little conversation, as each was earnestly gazing forwards, expecting every moment to see the bronzed savages moving before us.

In this way we proceeded for another half mile, without seeing aught of the enemy except their tracks.

A new object, however, now came in view—the clear sky shining through the trunks of the trees. We were all woodsmen enough to know that this indicated an "opening" in the forest.

Most of my companions expressed pleasure at the sight. We had now been riding a long way through the sombre woods—our path often obstructed by slimy and fallen logs, so that a slow pace had been unavoidable. They believed that in the open ground we should move faster; and have a better chance of sighting the pursued.

Some of the older heads, and especially the two guides, were affected differently by the new appearance. Hickman at once gave expression to his chagrin.

"Cuss the clarin," he exclaimed; "it are a savanner, an' a big 'un, too—dog-gone the thing—it'll spoil all."

"How?" I inquired.

"Ye see, Geordy, if thar a'ready across it, they'll leave some on t'other side to watch—they'll be sarten to do that, whether they know we're arter 'em or not. Wall, what follers? We kin no more cross 'ithout bein' seen, than a carryvan o' kaymils. An' what follers that? Once they've sighted us, in coorse they'll know how to git out o' our way; judjin' from the time we've been a travellin'—hey! it's darned near sundown!—I reckon we must be clost to thar big swamp. If they spy us a-comin' arter, they'll make strait custrut for thar, and then I know what they'll do."

"What?"

"They'll scatter thar; and ef they do, we might as well go sarchin' for bird's-nests in snow time."

"What should we do?"

"It are best for the hul o' ye to stop here a bit. Me and Jim Weatherford'll steal forbad to the edge of the timmer, an' see if they're got acrosst the savanner. Ef they are, then we must make roun' it the best way we kin, an' take up thar trail on the tother aide. Thar's no other chance. If we're seen crossin' the open ground, we may jest as well turn tail to 'em, and take the back-track home agin."

To the counsel of the alligator-hunter there was no dissenting voice. All acknowledged its wisdom, and he was left to carry out the design without opposition.

He and his companion once more dismounted from their horses, and, leaving us standing among the trees, advanced stealthily towards the edge of the opening.

It was a considerable time before they came back; and the other men were growing impatient. Many believed we were only losing time by this tardy reconnoissance, and the Indians would be getting further away. Sonde advised that the pursuit should be continued at once, and that, seen or not, we ought to ride directly onwards.

However consonant with my own feelings—burning as I was for a conflict with the murderers—I knew it would not be a prudent course. The guides were in the right.

These returned at length, and delivered their report. There *was* a savanna, and the Indians had crossed it. They had got into the timber on its opposite side, and neither man nor horse was to be seen. They could scarcely have been out of sight, before Hickman and Weatherford arrived upon its nearer edge, and the former averred that he had seen the tail of one of their horses, disappearing among the bushes.

During their absence, the cunning trackers had learned more. From the sign they had gathered another important fact—that there was no longer *a trail for us to follow!*

On entering the Savanna the Indians had *scattered*—the paths they had taken across the grassy meadow, were as numerous as their horses. As the hunter expressed it, the trail "war split up into fifty pieces." The latter had ascertained this by crawling out among the long grass, and noting the tracks.

One in particular had occupied their attention. It was not made by the hoof-prints of horses, though some of these ran alongside, but by the feet of men. They were naked feet; and a superficial observer might have fancied that but one pair of them had passed over the ground. The skilled trackers, however, knew this to be a *ruse*. The prints were large, and misshapen, and too deeply indented in the soil to have been produced by a single individual. The long heel, and scarcely convex instep—the huge balls, and broad prints of the toes, were all signs that the hunters easily understood. They knew that it was the trail of the negro captives who had proceeded thus by the direction of their captors.

This unexpected ruse on the part of the retreating savages created chagrin, as well as astonishment. For the moment all felt outwitted—we believed that the enemy was lost—we should be cheated of our revenge. Some even talked of the idleness of carrying the pursuit further. A few counselled us to go back; and it became necessary to appeal to their hatred of the savage foe—with most of them a hereditary passion—and once more to invoke their vengeance.

At this crisis, old Hickman cheered the men with fresh hope. I was glad to hear him speak.

"We can't get at 'em to-night, boys," said he, after much talk had been spent; "we dasent cross over this hyar clearin' by daylight, an' it's too big to git roun' it. It 'ud take a twenty mile ride to circumvent the durned thing. Ne'er a mind! Let us halt hyar till the dark comes on. Then we kin steal across; an' if me an' Jim Weatherford don't scare up the trail on the tother side, then this child never ate allygator. I know they'll come thegither agin, an' we'll be like enough to find the durned varments camped somewhar in a clump. Not seein' us arter 'em any more, they'll be feelin' as safe as a bear in a bee tree—an' that's jest the time to take 'em."

The plan was adopted; and, dismounting from our jaded horses, we awaited the setting of the sun.

There are few situations more trying to the boiling blood and pent-up fury of the pursuer—especially if he have bitter cause for vengeance—than a "check" in the chase; the loss of the trail of course often involves the escape of the foe, and though it may be after a while recovered, yet the delay affords such advantage to the enemy, that every moment serves only to increase the anxiety and whet the fury of the pursuer. This then was my case on the present occasion. While yielding to the advice of the hunter, because I knew it to be the best plan under the circumstances, I nevertheless could scarce control my impatience, or submit to the delay—but felt impelled to hurry forward, and alone and single-handed, if need be, inflict upon the savage miscreants the punishment due to their murderous deeds.

Chapter Seventy Eight.

Crossing the Savanna.

We now suffered the very acme of misery. While riding in hot haste along the trail, there was an excitement, almost continuous, that precluded the possibility of intense reflection, and kept my mind from dwelling too minutely upon the calamity that had befallen me. The prospect of retribution, ever appearing nearer at hand—at every step nearer—all but cancelled my emotions of grief; and motion itself—knowing it to be forward, and towards the object of hatred—had a certain effect in soothing my troubled soul.

Now that the pursuit was suspended, and I was free to reflect on the events of the morning, my soul was plunged into the deepest misery. My fancy distressed me with dire images. Before me appeared the corpse of my murdered mother—her arms outstretched, waving me on to vengeance. My sister, too, wan, tearful, dishevelled! dishonoured!

No wonder that with painful impatience I awaited the going down of the sun. I thought I had never seen that grand orb sink so slowly. The delay tortured me almost to distraction.

The sun's disc was blood red, from a thick haze that hung over the woods. The heavens appeared lowering, and angry—they had the hue of my own spirit.

At length, twilight came on. Short it was—as is usual in Southern latitudes—though it appeared long and tardy in passing away. Darkness followed, and once more springing to my saddle, I found relief in motion.

Emerging from the timber, we rode out upon the open savanna. The two hunters, acting as guides, conducted us across. There was no attempt made to follow any of the numerous trails. In the darkness, it would have been impossible, but even had there been light enough left them, the guides would have pursued a different course.

Hickman's conjecture was, that on reaching the opposite side, the marauding party would come together at some rendezvous previously agreed upon. The trail of any one, therefore, would be sufficient for our purpose, and in all probability would conduct us to their camp. Our only aim, then, was to get across the savanna unobserved; and this the darkness might enable us to accomplish.

Silently as spectres we marched over the open meadow. We rode with extreme slowness, lest the hoof-strokes should be heard. Our tired steeds needed no taming down. The ground was favourable—a surface of soft, grassy turf, over which our animals glided with noiseless tread. Our only fears were, that they should scent the horses of the Indians, and betray us by their neighing.

Happily our fears proved groundless; and, after half an hour's silent marching, we reached the other side of the savanna, and drew up under the shadowy trees.

It was scarce possible we could have been observed. If the Indians had left spies behind them, the darkness would have concealed us from their view, and we had made no noise by which our approach could have been discovered, unless their sentinels had been placed at the very point where we re-entered the woods. We saw no signs of any, and we believed that none of the band had lingered behind, and we had not been seen.

We congratulated one another in whispers; and in like manner deliberated on our future plans of proceeding. We were still in our saddles—with the intention to proceed further. We should have dismounted upon the spot, and waited for the light of morning to enable us to take up the trail, but circumstances forbade this. Our horses were suffering from thirst, and their riders were no better off. We had met with no water since before noon, and a few hours under the burning skies of Florida are sufficient to render thirst intolerable. Whole days in a colder climate would scarce have an equal effect.

Both horses and men suffered acutely—we could neither sleep nor rest, without relief—water must be sought for, before a halt could be made.

We felt hunger as well, for scarce any provision had been made for the long march—but the pangs of this appetite were easier to be endured. Water of itself would satisfy us for the night, and we resolved to ride forward in search of it.

In this dilemma, the experience of our two guides promised relief. They had once made a hunting excursion to the savanna we had crossed. It was in the times when the tribes were friendly, and white men were permitted to pass freely through the "reserve." They remembered a pond, at which, upon that occasion, they had made their temporary encampment. They believed it was not far distant from the spot where we had arrived. It might be difficult to find in the darkness, but to suffer on or search for it were our only alternatives.

The latter was of course adopted; and once more allowing Hickman and Weatherford to pioneer the way, the rest of us rode silently after.

We moved in single file, each horse guided by the one that immediately preceded him; in the darkness no other mode of march could be adopted. Our party was thus strung out into a long line, here and there curving according to the sinuosities of the path, and gliding like some monstrous serpent among the trees.

Chapter Seventy Nine.

Groping among the Timber.

At intervals the guides were at fault; and then the whole line was forced to halt and remain motionless. Several times both Hickman and Weatherford were puzzled as to the direction they should take. They had lost the points of the compass, and were bewildered.

Had there been light, they could have recovered this knowledge by observing the bark upon the trees—a craft well-known to the backwoods hunter—but it was too dark to make such an observation. Even amidst the darkness, Hickman alleged he could tell north from south by the "feel" of the bark: and for this purpose I now saw him groping against the trunks. I noticed that he passed from one to another, trying several of them, the better to confirm his observations.

After carrying on these singular manoeuvres for a period of several minutes, he turned to his comrade with an exclamation that betokened surprise:—

"Dog-gone my cats, Jim," said he, speaking in an undertone, "these woods are altered since you and I war hyar—what the ole scratch kin be the matter wi' 'em? The bark's all peeled off and thar as dry as punk."

"I was thinkin' they had a kewrious look," replied the other, "but I s'posed it was the darkness o' the night."

"Neer a bit of it—the trees is altered someways, since we war hyar afore! They are broom pines—that I recollect well enough—let's git a bunch o' the leaves, and see how they looks."

Saying this, he reached his hand upwards, and plucked one of the long fascicles that drooped overhead.

"Ugh!" continued he, crushing the needles between his fingers, "I see how it are now. The darnationed moths has been at 'em—the trees are dead."

"D'yer think thar all dead?" he inquired after a pause, and then advancing a little, he proceeded to examine some others.

"Dead as durnation!—every tree o' 'em—wal! we must go by guess-work—thar's no help for it, boys. Ole Hick kin guide you no furrer. I'm dead beat, and know no more 'bout the direkshun o' that ere pond, than the greenest greenhorn among ye."

This acknowledgment produced no very pleasant effect. Thirst was torturing all those who heard it. Hitherto, trusting that the skill of the hunters would enable them to find water, they had sustained it with a degree of patience. It was now felt more acutely than ever.

"Stay," said Hickman, after a few moments had elapsed. "All's not lost that's in danger. If I arn't able to guide ye to the pond, I reckon I've got a critter as kin. Kin you, ole hoss?" he continued, addressing himself to the animal he bestrode—a wiry old jade that Hickman had long been master of—"kin you find the water? Gee up, ole beeswax! and let's see if you kin."

Giving his "critter" a kick in the ribs, and at the same time full freedom of the bridle, he once more started forwards among the trees.

We all followed as before, building fresh hopes upon the instinct of the animal.

Surely the pride of man ought to be somewhat abased, when he reflects, that he, "the lord of the creation," is oftentimes foiled in attempts which, by the mere instincts of the lower animals, are of easy accomplishment. What a lesson of humility this ought to teach to the wanton and cruel oppressor of those noble animals, whose strength, and instinct, and endurance, are all made subservient to his comfort. It is in the hour of danger and peril alone, that man realises his dependence upon agencies other than his own lordly will.

163

We had not proceeded far, when it became known that Hickman's horse had got scent of the water. His owner alleged that he "smelt" it, and the latter knew this, as well as if it had been one of his hounds taking up the trail of a deer.

The horse actually exhibited signs of such an intelligence. His muzzle was protruded forwards, and now and then he was heard to sniff the air; while, at the same time, he walked forward in a direct line—as if making for some object. Surely he was heading for water. Such was the belief.

It produced a cheering effect, and the men were now advancing in better spirits, when, to their surprise, Hickman suddenly drew up, and halted the line I rode forward to him to inquire the cause. I found him silent and apparently reflective.

"Why have you stopped?" I inquired.

"You must all o' ye wait here a bit."

"Why must we?" demanded several, who had pressed along side.

"'Taint safe for us to go forrad this way; I've got a idea that them red skins is by the pond—they've camped there for sartin—it's the only water that is about hyar; and its devilitch like that thar they've rendevoozed an' camped. If that be the case, an' we ride forrad in this fashion, they'll hear us a-comin' an' be off agin into the bushes, whar we'll see no more o' them. Ain't that like enough, fellers?"

This interrogatory was answered in the affirmative.

"Wal then," continued the guide; "better for yous all to stay hyar, while me and Jim Weatherford goes forrad to see if the Indyuns is thar. We kin find the pond now. I know whar it lies by the direkshun the hoss war taken. It aint fur off. If the red skins aint thar, we'll soon be back, an' then ye kin all come on as fast as ye like."

This prudent course was willingly agreed to, and the two hunters, once more dismounting, stole forwards afoot. They made no objection to my going along with them. My misfortunes gave me a claim to be their leader; and, leaving my bridle in the hands of one of my companions, I accompanied the guides upon their errand.

We walked with noiseless tread. The ground was thickly covered with the long needles of the pine, forming a soft bed, upon which the footstep made no sound. There was little or no underwood, and this enabled us to advance with rapidity, and in a few minutes we were a long way from the party we had left behind.

Our only care was about keeping the right direction, and this we had almost lost—or believed so—when, to our astonishment we beheld a light shining through the trees. It was the gleam of a fire that appeared to be blazing freely. Hickman at once pronounced it the camp fire of the Indians.

At first we thought of returning, and bringing on our comrades to the attack; but upon reflection, we determined to approach nearer the fire, and make certain whether it was the enemy's camp.

We advanced no longer in erect attitudes; but crawling upon our hands and knees. Wherever the glare penetrated the woods, we avoided it, and kept under the shadow of the tree-trunks. The fire burned in the midst of an opening. The hunters remembered that the pond was so placed; and now observing the sheen of water, we knew it must be the same.

We drew nearer and nearer, until it was no longer safe to advance. We were close to the edge of the timber that concealed us. We could see the whole surface of the open ground. There were horses picketed over it, and dark forms recumbent under the fire light. They were murderers asleep.

Close to the fire, one was seated upon a saddle. He appeared to be awake, though his head was drooped to the level of his knees. The blaze was shining upon this man's face; and both his features and complexion might have been seen, but for the interposition of paint and plumes.

The face appeared of a crimson red, and three black ostrich feathers, bending over the brow, hung straggling down his cheeks. These plumed symbols produced painful recognition. I knew that it was the head-dress of Osceola.

I looked further. Several groups were beyond—in fact, the whole open space was crowded with prostrate human forms.

There was one group, however, that fixed my attention. It consisted of three or four individuals, seated or reclining along the grass. They were in shade, and from our position, their features could not be recognised; but their white dresses, and the outlines of their forms, soft even in the obscurity of the shadow, told that they were females.

Two of them were side by side, a little apart from the others; one appeared to be supporting the other, whose head rested in her lap.

With emotions fearfully vivid, I gazed on these two forms. I had no doubt they were Viola and my sister.

Chapter Eighty.

Signal Shots.

I shall not attempt to depict my emotions at that moment. My pen is unequal to the task. Think of my situation, and fancy them if you can.

Behind me, a mother murdered and basely mutilated—a near relative slain in like fashion—my home—my whole property given to the flames. Before me, a sister torn from the maternal embrace—borne ruthlessly along by savage captors—perhaps defiled by their fiendish leader. And he, too, before my eyes—the false, perfidious friend, the ravisher—the murderer! Had I not cue for indulging in the wildest emotions?

And wild they were—each moment growing wilder, as I gazed upon the object of my vengeance. They were fast rising beyond my control. My muscles seemed to swell with renewed rage—the blood coursed through my veins like streams of liquid fire.

I almost forgot the situation in which we were. But one thought was in my mind—vengeance. Its object was before me—unconscious of my presence as if he had been asleep—almost within reach of my hand; perfectly within range of my rifle.

I raised the piece to the level of those drooping plumes. I sighted their tips—I knew that the eyes were underneath them—my finger rested against the trigger.

In another instant, that form—in my eyes, hitherto heroic—would have been lifeless upon the grass; but my comrades forbade the act.

With a quick instinct, Hickman grasped the lock of my gun. Covering the nipple with his broad palm; while Weatherford clutched at and held the barrel. I was no longer master of the piece.

I was angry at the interruption, but only for an instant. A moment's reflection convinced me they had acted right. The old hunter, putting his lips close to my ear, addressed me in an earnest whisper:

"Not yit, Geordie, not yit; for your life, don't make a fuss! 'Twould be no use to kill *him*. The rest o' the varmints ud be sartin to git off, and sartin to toat the weemen along wi' 'em. We three aint enough to stop 'em—we'd only get scalped ourselves. We must slide back for the others; an' then we'll be able to surround 'em—that's the idea, aint it, Jim?"

Weatherford, fearing to trust his voice, nodded an affirmative.

"Come, then," added Hickman, in the same low whisper, "we musn't lose a minute; let's get back as rapidly as possible. Keep your backs low down—genteely, genteely;" and as he continued giving these injunctions, he faced towards the ground, extended his body to its full length, and, crawling off like an alligator, was soon lost behind the trunks of the trees.

Weatherford and I followed in similar fashion, until safe beyond the circle of the fire light, when all three of us came to a stop, and arose erect to our feet.

We stood for a moment listening *backwards*. We were not without anxiety lest our retreat might have disturbed the camp; but no sounds reached us save those to which we had been listening—the snore of some sleeping savage, the "crop-crop" of the browsing horses, or the stamp of a hoof upon the firm turf.

Satisfied that we had passed away unobserved, we started upon the back-track, which the hunters could now follow like a path well-known to them.

We advanced, dark as it was, almost in a run; and were progressing rapidly, when our speed was suddenly checked by the report of a gun.

Each halted as if shot. Surprise it was that stopped us; for the report came not from the Indian camp, but the opposite direction—that in which our party had been left.

But it could not be one of them who had fired. They were at too great a distance for their guns to have been heard so distinctly. Had they advanced nearer, tired of waiting for our return? Were they still advancing? If so, the shot was most imprudent; it would be certain to put the camp on the *qui vive*. What had they fired at? It might have been an accidental discharge—it must have been.

These conjectures were rapid as thought itself. We did not communicate them to one another; each fancied them for himself.

We had scarce time even to speak, when a second shot rang in our ears. It came from the same direction as the former, appearing almost a repetition; and had there been time to reload, we should so have judged it; but there had not been time, even for the most accomplished rifleman. Two guns, therefore, had been fired.

My companions were puzzled as well as myself. The firing was inexplicable under any other hypothesis than that some Indians had strayed from their camp and were making signals of distress.

We had no time to reflect. We could now hear behind us the camp in full alarm, and we knew it was the shots that had caused it. We heard the shouts of men, the neighing and hurried trampling of horses.

Without pausing longer, we again hurried onwards in the direction of our friends.

Further on we perceived some men on horseback. Two there appeared to be; but in the darkness we were not certain, as their forms were scarce distinguishable.

They appeared to retreat as we approached, gliding off, like ghosts, among the trees.

No doubt these were they who had fired the shots. They were just in the direction whence the reports had come, and at the proper distance.

Were they Indians or whites? Hoping they were our friends, risking the chances of their being our foes, Old Hickman hailed them.

We paused to listen. There was no reply, not even an exclamation from either. We could hear, by the hoof-strokes of their horses, that they were hurrying off in a direction altogether different from either our party or the camp.

There was something mysterious in the behaviour of these horsemen. For what purpose had they fired their guns? If to signal the camp, why had they retreated from us, as we came from it? Why, moreover, had they gone off in a direction that did not lead to it? for its position was now known to them by the noise of the alarm they had themselves occasioned. To me their behaviour was inexplicable. Hickman appeared to have found some clue to it, and the knowledge seemed to have a angular effect upon him. He exhibited signs of surprise, mingled with strong feelings of indignation.

"Devil swamp 'em! the wuthless skunks, if't are them, an' I'm good as sure it are. I can't a be mistaken in the crack o' them two guns. What say ye, Jim Weatherford? D'ye recognise 'em?"

"I war thinkin' I'd heern them afore somewhars, but I can't 'zactly tell whar—stay; one on 'em's precious like the ring o' Ned Spence's rifle."

"Preecious like—it are the same; and t'other's Bill Williams's. What on airth kin the two be arter? We left 'em long wi' the rest, and hyar they are now—I'm sartint it's them, gallivantin' about through the woods, an' firin' off their guns to spoil everything we've done. They've sot the Indyuns off to a sartinty. Devil swamp 'em both!—what*kin* they be arter?—some hellnifferous game, I 'spect! By the tarnal catawampus, I'll make both on 'em pay for this when we git thegither! Come along, quick, fellers! Let's git the party up, or we'll be too late. Them Indyuns'll make track, and slope afore we git near 'em. Darn the shots! they've spoilt the hull bizness. Quick! come along hyar!"

Obedient to the old hunter's directions, we hurried on after him.

Chapter Eighty One.

An Empty Camp.

We had not gone far before we came within ear-shot of voices, mingled with the hollow thumping of horses' hoofs.

We recognised the voices as those of our comrades, and hailed them as they came nearer, for we perceived that they were advancing towards us.

They had heard the reports; and, believing them to proceed from our rifles, had fancied we were engaged with the Indians, and were now riding forwards to our aid.

"Hollow, boys!" shouted Hickman, as they drew nearer. "Is Bill Williams and Ned Spence among ye? Speak out, if ye be!"

There was no reply to this interrogatory. It was succeeded by a dead silence of some seconds' duration. Evidently the two men were not there, else they would have answered for themselves.

"Where are they?" "Where have they gone to?" were the inquiries that passed through the crowd.

"Ay, whar are they?" repeated Hickman. "Thar not hyar, that's plain. By the 'tarnal allygator, thar's some ugly game afoot atween them two fellers! But, come, boys, we must forrad. The Indyuns is jest afore ye: it's no use creepin' any more. Thar a gwine to slope; and if we don't git up to 'em in three shakes o' a squirrel's tail, thar won't be a cussed varmint o' 'em on the groun'. Hooraw for redskins' scalps! Look to your guns. Let's forrad, and gie 'em partickler hell!"

And with this emphatic utterance, the old hunter dashed into the front, and led the way towards the camp of the savages.

The men followed, helter-skelter, the horses crowding upon each other's heels. No strategic method was observed. Time was the important consideration, and the aim was to get up to the camp before the Indians could retreat from it. A bold charge into their midst, a volley from our guns, and then with knives and pistols to close the conflict. This was the programme that had been hastily agreed upon.

We had arrived near the camp—within three hundred yards of it. There was no uncertainty as to the direction. The voices of the savages, that continued to be heard ever since the first alarm, served to guide us on the way.

All at once these voices became hushed. No longer reached us, either the shouting of the men, or the hurried trampling of their horses. In the direction of the camp all was still as death.

But we no longer needed the guidance of sounds. We were within sight of the camp fires—or at least of their light, that glittered afar among the trees. With this as our beacon, we continued to advance.

We rode forwards, but now less recklessly. The change from confused noise to perfect silence had been so sudden and abrupt as to have the effect of making us more cautious. The very stillness appeared ominous—we read in it a warning—it rendered us suspicious of an ambuscade—the more so as all had heard of the great talent of the "Redstick Chief" for this very mode of attack.

When within a hundred yards of the fires, our party halted. Several dismounted, and advanced on foot. They glided from trunk to trunk till they had reached the edge of the opening, and then came back to report.

The camp was no longer in existence—its occupants were gone. Indians, horses, captives, plunder, had all disappeared from the ground!

The fires alone remained. They showed evidence of being disturbed in the confusion of the hasty decampment. The red embers were strewed over the grass—their last flames faintly flickering away.

The scouts continued to advance among the trees, till they had made the full circuit of the little opening. For a hundred yards around it the woods were searched with caution and ease; but no enemy was encountered—no ambuscade. We had arrived too late, and the savage foes had escaped us—had carried off their captives from under our very eyes.

It was impossible to follow them in the darkness; and, with mortified spirits, we advanced into the opening, and took possession of the deserted camp. It was our determination to remain there for the rest of the night, and renew the pursuit in the morning.

Our first care was to quench our thirst by the pond—then that of our animals. The fires were next extinguished, and a ring of sentries—consisting of nearly half the number of our party—was placed among the tree-trunks, that stood thickly around the opening. The horses were staked over the ground, and the men stretched themselves along the sward so lately occupied by the bodies of their savage foes. In this wise we awaited the dawning of day.

To none of our party—not even to myself—was this escape of the enemy, or "circumvention," as he termed it, so mortifying as to old Hickman, who, though priding himself upon his superior cunning and woodcraft, was obliged to confess himself outwitted by a rascally Redstick.

Chapter Eighty Two.

A Dead Forest.

My comrades, wearied with the long ride, were soon in deep slumber—the sentries only keeping awake. For me, was neither rest nor sleep—my misery forbade repose.

Most of the night I spent in passing to and fro around the little pond, that lay faintly gleaming in the centre of the open ground.

I fancied I found relief in thus roving about; it seemed to still the agitation of my spirit, and prevented my reflections from becoming too intense.

A new regret occupied my thoughts—I regretted that I had not carried out my intention to fire at the chief of the murderers—I regretted I had not killed him on the spot—the monster had escaped, and my sister was still in his power—perhaps beyond the hope of rescue. As I thought thus, I blamed the hunters for having hindered me.

Had they foreseen the result, they might have acted otherwise; but it was beyond human foresight to have anticipated the alarm.

The two men who had caused it were again with us. Their conduct, so singular and mysterious, had given rise to strong suspicion of their loyalty, and their re-appearance—they had joined us while advancing towards the camp—had been hailed with an outburst of angry menace. Some even talked of shooting them out of their saddles, and this threat would most probably have been carried into effect, had the fellows not offered a ready explanation.

They alleged that they had got separated from the troop before it made its last halt, how they did not say; that they knew nothing of the advance of the scouts, or that the Indians were near; that they had got lost in the woods, and had fired their guns as signals in hopes that we should answer them. They acknowledged having met three men afoot, but they believed them to be Indians, and kept out of their way; that afterwards seeing the party near, they had recognised and ridden up to it.

Most of the men were contented with this explanation. What motive, reasoned they, could the two have in giving an alarm to the enemy? Who could suspect them of rank treason?

Not all, however, were satisfied; I heard old Hickman whisper some strange words to his comrade, as he glanced significantly towards the estrays.

"Keep yur eye skinned, Jim, and watch the skunks well; thares somethin' not hulsome about 'em."

As there was no one who could openly accuse them, they were once more admitted into the ranks, and were now among those who were stretched out and sleeping.

They lay close to the edge of the water. In my rounds, I passed them repeatedly; and in the sombre darkness, I could just distinguish their prostrate forms. I regarded them with strange emotions, for I shared the suspicions of Hickman and Weatherford. I could scarce doubt that these fellows had strayed off on purpose—that, actuated by some foul motive, they had fired their guns to warn the Indians of the approach of our party.

After midnight there was a moon. There were no clouds to intercept her beams, and on rising above the tree-tops, she poured down a flood of brilliant light.

The sleepers were awakened by the sudden change; some rose to their feet, believing it to be day. It was only upon glancing up to the heavens they became aware of their mistake.

The noise had put every one on the alert, and some talked of continuing the pursuit by the light of the moon.

Such a course would have coincided with my own wishes; but the hunter-guides opposed it. Their reasons were just. In open ground they could have lifted the trail, but under the timber the moon's light would not have availed them.

They could have tracked by torch-light, but this would only be to expose us to an ambuscade of the enemy. Even to advance by moonlight would be to subject ourselves to a like danger. Circumstances had changed. The savages now knew we were after them. In a night-march the pursued have the advantage of the pursuers—even though their numbers be inferior. The darkness gives them every facility of effecting a surprise.

Thus reasoned the guides. No one made opposition to their views, and it was agreed that we should keep our ground till daylight.

It was time to change the sentinels. Those who had slept now took post, and the relieved guard came in and flung themselves down, to snatch a few hours of rest.

Williams and Spence took their turn with the rest. They were posted on one side the glade, and next to one another Hickman and Weatherford had fulfilled their guard tour.

As they stretched themselves along the grass, I noticed that they had chosen a spot near to where the suspected men were placed. By the moonlight, they must have had a view of the latter.

Notwithstanding their recumbent attitudes, the hunters did not appear to go to sleep. I observed them at intervals. Their heads were close together, and slightly raised above the ground, as if they were whispering to one another.

As before, I walked round and round—the moonlight enabling me to move more rapidly. Ofttimes did I make the circuit of the little pond—how oft, it would be difficult to determine.

My steps were mechanical—my thoughts had no connection with the physical exertions I was making, and I took no note of how I progressed.

After a time there came a lull over my spirits. For a short interval both my griefs and vengeful passions seemed to have departed.

I knew the cause. It was a mere psychological phenomenon—one of common occurrence. The nerves that were organs of the peculiar emotions under which I had been suffering, had grown wearied and refused to act. I knew it was but a temporary calm—the lull between two billows of the storm.

During its continuance, I was sensible to impressions from external objects. I could not help noticing the singularity of the scene around me. The bright moonlight enabled me to note its features somewhat minutely.

We were encamped upon what, by backwoodsmen, is technically termed a *glade*—oftener, in their idiom, a "gleed"—a small opening in the woods, without timber or trees of any sort. This one was circular—about fifty yards in diameter—with the peculiarity of having a pond in its midst. The pond, which was only a few yards in circumference, was also a circle, perfectly concentric with the glade itself. It was one of those singular natural basins found throughout the peninsula, and appearing as if scooped out by mechanic art. It was deeply sunk in the earth, and filled with water till within three feet of its rim. The liquid was cool and clear, and under the moonbeams shone with a silvery effulgence.

Of the glade itself nothing more—except that it was covered with sweet-smelling flowers, that now, crushed under the hoofs of horses and the heels of man, gave forth a redoubled fragrance.

The picture was pretty.

Under happier circumstances, I should have contemplated it with pleasure. But it was not the picture that so much occupied my attention at that moment. Rather was it the framing.

Around the glade stood a ring of tall trees, as regular as if they had been planted; and beyond these, as far as the eye could penetrate the depths of the forest, were others of like size and aspect. The trunks of all were nearly of one thickness—few of them reaching a diameter of two feet, but all rising to the height of many yards, without leaf or branch. They stood somewhat densely over the ground, but in daylight the eye might have ranged to a considerable distance through the intervals, for there was no underwood—save the low dwarf palmetto—to interrupt the view. They were straight, and almost cylindrical as palms; and they might have been mistaken for trees of this order, had it not been for their large heads of leaves terminating in cone-shaped summits.

They were not palms—they were pines—"broom" pines (*Pinus Australis*), a species of trees with which I was perfectly familiar, having ridden many hundreds of miles shaded by the pendant fascicles of their acicular foliage.

The sight of these trees, therefore, would have created no curiosity, had I not noticed in their appearance something peculiar. Instead of the deep green which should have been exhibited by their long, drooping leaves, they appeared of a brownish yellow.

Was it fancy? or was it the deceptive light of the moon that caused this apparent change from their natural hue?

One or the other, soliloquised I, on first noticing them; but as I continued to gaze, I perceived that I was in error. Neither my own fancy nor the moon's rays were at fault; the foliage was really of the colour it appeared to be. Drawing nearer to them, I observed that the leaves were withered, though still adhering to the twigs. I noticed, moreover, that the trunks were dry and dead-like—the bark scaled or scaling off—that the trees, in short, were dead and decaying.

I remembered what Hickman had stated while groping for the direction. That was at some distance off; but, as far as I could see, the woods presented the same dim colour.

I came to the conclusion that the *whole forest was dead.*

The inference was correct, and the explanation easy. The sphinx (Note 1) had been at work. The whole forest was dead.

Note 1. *Sphinae coniferarum.* Immense swarms of insects, and especially the larva of the above species, insinuate themselves under the bark of the "long-leafed" (broom) pine, attack the trunk, and cause the tree to perish in the course of a year. Extensive tracts are met with in Florida covered solely with dead pines that have been thus destroyed.

Chapter Eighty Three.

A Circular Conflict.

Strange as it may seem, even in that hour these observations had interested me; but while making them I observed something that gratified me still more. It was the blue dawn that, mingling with the yellower light of the moon, affected the hue of the foliage upon which I had been gazing. Morning was about to break.

Others had noticed it at the same instant, and already the sleepers were rising from their dewy couch, and looking to the girths of their saddles.

We were a hungry band; but there was no hope of breakfast, and we prepared to start without it.

The dawn was of only a few minutes' duration, and, as the sky continued to brighten, preparations were made for the start. The sentries were called in—all except four, who were prudently left to the last minute, to watch in four different directions. The horses were unpicketed and bridled—they had worn their saddles all night—and the guns of the party were carefully re-primed or capped.

Many of my comrades were old campaigners, and every precaution was taken that might influence our success in a conflict.

It was expected that before noon we should come up with the savages, or track them home to their lair. In either case, we should have a fight, and all declared their determination to go forwards.

Some minutes were spent in arranging the order of our march. It was deemed prudent that a few of the more skilled of the men should go forwards as scouts on foot, and thoroughly explore the woods before the advance of the main body. This would secure us from any sudden attack, in case the enemy had formed an ambuscade. The old hunters were once more to act as trackers, and lead the van.

These arrangements were completed, and we were on the point of starting—the men had mounted their horses, the scouts were already entering the edge of the timber, when, all on a sudden, several shots were heard, and at the same time, the alarm-cries of the sentries who had fired them. The four had discharged their pieces almost simultaneously.

The woods appeared to ring with a hundred echoes. But they were not echoes—they were real reports of rifles and musketry; and the shrill war-cry that accompanied them was easily distinguished above the shouting of our own sentries. The Indians were upon us.

Upon us, or, to speak less figuratively, *around* us. The sentries had fired all at once, therefore, each must have seen Indians in his own direction. But it needed not this to guide us to the conclusion that we were surrounded. From all sides came the fierce yells of the foe—as if echoing one another—and their bullets whistled past us in different directions. Beyond doubt, the glade was encompassed within their lines.

In the first volley two or three men were hit, and as many horses. But the balls were spent and did but little damage.

From where they had fired, the glade was beyond the "carry" of their guns. Had they crept a little nearer, before delivering their fire, the execution would have been fearful—clumped together as we were at the moment.

Fortunately, our sentries had perceived their approach, and in good time given the alarm.

It had saved us.

There was a momentary confusion, with noise—the shouting of men—the neighing and prancing of horses; but above the din was heard the guiding voice of old Hickman.

"Off o' yer horses, fellers! an' take to the trees—down wi' ye, quick! To the trees, an' keep 'em back! or by the tarnal arthquake, every mother's son o' us'll git sculped! To the trees! to the trees!"

The same idea had already suggested itself to others; and before the hunter had ceased calling out, the men were out of their saddles and making for the edge of the timber.

Some ran to one side, some to another—each choosing the edge that was nearest him, and in a few seconds our whole party had ensconced itself—the body of each individual sheltered behind the trunk of a tree. In this position we formed a perfect circle, our backs turned upon each other, and our faces to the foe.

Our horses, thus hurriedly abandoned, and wild with the excitement of the attack, galloped madly over the ground, with trailing bridles, and stirrups striking against their flanks. Most of them dashed past us; and, scampering off, were either caught by the savages, or breaking through their lines, escaped into the woods beyond.

We made no attempt to "head" them. The bullets were hurtling past our ears. It would have been certain death to have stepped aside from the trunks that sheltered us.

The advantage of the position we had gained was apparent at a single glance. Fortunate it was, that our sentries had been so tardily relieved. Had these been called in a moment sooner, the surprise would have been complete. The Indians would have advanced to the very edge of the glade, before uttering their war-cry or firing a shot, and we should have been at their mercy. They would have been under cover of the timber, and perfectly protected from our guns, while we in the open ground must have fallen before their fire.

But for the well-timed alarm, they might have massacred us at will.

Disposed as we now were, our antagonists had not much advantage. The trunks of the trees entrenched us both. Only the concave side of our line was exposed, and the enemy might fire at it across the opening. But as the glade was fifty yards in diameter, and at no point had we permitted the Indians to get up to its edge, we knew that their bullets could not carry across; and were under no apprehension on this score.

The manoeuvre, improvised though it was, had proved our salvation. We now saw it was the only thing we could have done to save ourselves from immediate destruction. Fortunate it was that the voice of Hickman had hurried us so quickly to our posts.

Our men were not slow in returning the enemy's fire. Already their pieces were at play; and every now and then was heard the sharp whip-like "spang" of the rifles around the circle of the glade. At intervals, too, came a triumphant cheer, as some savage, who had too rashly exposed his red body, was known to have fallen to the shot.

Again the voice of the old hunter rang over the glade. Cool, calm, and clear, it was heard by every one.

"Mind yer hind sights, boys! an' shoot sure. Don't waste neer a grain o' yer powder. Ye'll need the hul on't, afore we've done wi' the cussed niggers. Don't a one o' ye pull trigger till ye've drawed a bead on a red skin."

These injunctions were full of significance. Hitherto the younger "hands" had been firing somewhat recklessly—discharging their pieces as soon as loaded, and only wounding the trunks of the trees. It was to stay this proceeding that Hickman had spoken.

His words produced the desired effect. The reports became less frequent, but the triumphant cheer that betokened a "hit," was heard as often as ever. In a few minutes after the first burst of the battle, the conflict had assumed altogether a new aspect. The wild yells uttered by the Indians in their first onslaught—intended to frighten us into confusion—were no longer heard; and the shouts of the white men had also ceased. Only now and then were heard the deep "hurrah" of triumph, or a word spoken by some of our party to give encouragement to his comrades. At long intervals only rang out the "yo-ho-ehee," uttered by some warrior chief to stimulate his braves to the attack.

The shots were no longer in volleys, but single, or two or three at a time. Every shot was fired with an aim; and it was only when that aim proved true, or he who fired it believed it so, that voices broke out on either side. Each individual was too much occupied in looking for an object for his aim, to waste time in idle words or shouts. Perhaps in the whole history of war, there is no account of a conflict so quietly carried on—no battle so silently fought. In the interludes between the shots there were moments when the stillness was intense— moments of perfect but ominous silence.

Neither was battle ever fought, in which both sides were so oddly arrayed against each other. We were disposed in two concentric circles—the outer one formed by the enemy, the inner, by the men of our party, deployed almost regularly around the glade. These circles were scarce forty paces apart—at some points perhaps a little less, where a few of the more daring warriors, sheltered by the trees, had worked themselves closer to our line. Never was battle fought where the contending parties were so near each other without closing in hand-to-hand conflict. We could have conversed with our antagonists, without raising our voices above the ordinary tone; and were enabled to aim, literally, at the "whites of their eyes."

Under such circumstances was the contest carried on.

Chapter Eighty Four.

A Dead Shot by Jake.

For fall two hours this singular conflict was continued, without any material change in the disposition of the combatants. Now and then an odd man might be seen darting from tree to tree, with a velocity as if projected from a howitzer—his object either to find a trunk that would afford better cover to his own body, or a point that would uncover the body—or a portion of it—of some marked antagonist.

The trunks were barely thick enough to screen us; some kept on their feet, taking the precaution to make themselves as "small" as possible, by standing rigidly erect, and keeping their bodies carefully aligned. Others, perceiving that the pines "bulged" a little at the roots, had thrown themselves flat upon their faces, and in this attitude continued to load and fire.

The sun was long since ascending the heavens—for it had been near sunrise when the conflict began. There was no obscurity to hide either party from the view of the other, though in this the Indians had a slight advantage on account of the opening in our rear. But even in the depth of the forest there was light enough for our purpose. Many of the dead fascicles had fallen—the ground was deeply bedded with them—and those that still drooped overhead formed but a gauzy screen against the brilliant beams of the sun. There was light sufficient to enable our marksmen to "sight" any object as large as a dollar piece, that chanced to be within range of their rifles. A hand—a portion of an arm—a leg badly aligned—a jaw bone projecting outside the bark—a pair of shoulders too brawny for the trunk that should have concealed them—even the outstanding skirt of a dress, was sure to draw a shot—perhaps two—from one side or the other. A man to have exposed his full face for ten seconds would have been almost certain of receiving a bullet through his skull, for on both sides there were sharpshooters.

Thus two hours had passed, and without any great injury received or inflicted by either party. There were some "casualties," however, and every now and then a fresh incident added to the number, and kept up the hostile excitement. We had several wounded—one or two severely—and one man killed. The latter was a favourite with our men, and his death strengthened their desire for vengeance.

The Indian loss must have been greater. We had seen several fall to our shots. In our party were some of the best marksmen in Florida. Hickman was heard to declare he "had drawed a bead upon three, and wherever he drawed his bead he was dog-goned sartin to put his bullet." Weatherford had shot his man, killing him on the spot. This was beyond conjecture, for the dead body of the savage could be seen lying between two trees where it had fallen. His comrades feared that in dragging it away, they might expose themselves to that terrible rifle.

The Indians had not yet learned that refinement of civilised warriors, who seek from their opponents a temporary truce in which to pay an empty compliment to the dead, while with cunning eye and wary step they seize the opportunity to scrutinise where to make the most effectual onslaught upon the living.

After a time, the Indians began to practise a chapter of tactics, which proved that in this mode of warfare they were our superiors. Instead of one, two of them would place themselves behind a tree, or two trees that stood close together, and as soon as one fired, the other was ready to take aim. Of course, the man at whom the first shot had been discharged, fancying his *vis-à-vis* now carried an empty gun, would be less careful about his person, and likely enough to expose it.

This proved to be the case, for before the bit of craft was discovered, several of our men received wounds, and one man of our number was shot dead by his tree. This ruse freshly exasperated our men—the more so that they could not reciprocate the strategy, since our numbers were not sufficient to have taken post by "twos." It would have thinned our line so that we could not have defended the position.

We were compelled, therefore, to remain as we were—more careful not to expose ourselves to the cunning "fence" of our enemies.

There was one case, however, in which the savages were paid back in their own coin. Black Jake and I were partners in this *revanche*.

We occupied two trees almost close together; and had for antagonists no less than three savages, who had been all the morning most active in firing at us. I had received one of their bullets through the sleeve of my coat, and Jake had the dandruff driven out of his wool, but neither of us had been wounded.

During the contest I had got "sight" upon one, and fancied I had spilled his blood. I could not be certain, however, as the three were well sheltered behind a clump of trees, and covered, also, by a thicket of dwarf palmettoes.

One of these Indians, Jake wished particularly to kill. He was a huge savage—much larger than either of the others. He wore a head-dress of king vulture plumes, and was otherwise distinguished by his costume. In all probability, a chief. What was most peculiar in this man's appearance was his face, for we could see it at intervals, though only for an instant at a time. It was covered all over with a scarlet pigment—vermilion it was—and shone through the trees like a counterpart of the sun.

It was not this, however, that had rendered the Indian an object of Jake's vengeance. The cause was different. The savage had noticed Jake's peculiar colour, and had taunted him with it several times during the fray. He spoke in his native tongue, but Jake comprehended it well enough. He was spited—exasperated—and vowed vengeance against the scarlet chief.

I contrived at length to give him an opportunity. Cunningly adjusting my cap, so that it appeared to contain my head, I caused it to protrude a little around the trunk of the tree. It was an old and well-known ruse, but for all that, in Jake's phraseology, it "fooled" the Indian.

173

The red countenance appeared above the palmettoes. A puff of smoke rose from below it. The cap was jerked out of my hand as I heard the report of the shot that had done it.

A little after, I heard another crack, louder and nearer—the report of the negro's piece. I peeped around the tree to witness the effect. A spot of darker red dappled the bright disk of the Indian's face—the vermilion seemed suddenly encrimsoned. It was but a glance I had, for in the next instant the painted savage doubled back among the bushes.

During all the time we had been engaged, the Indians did not appear desirous of advancing upon us—although, certainly, they were superior to us in point of numbers. The party we had been pursuing must have been joined by another one as numerous as itself. Not less than a hundred were now upon the ground, and had been so from the beginning of the fight. But for this accession they would hardly have dared to attack us, and but for it we should have charged them at once, and tried the chances of a hand-to-hand conflict. We had seen, however, that they far outnumbered us, and were content to hold our position.

They appeared satisfied with theirs, though by closing rapidly inwards they might have overpowered us. After all, their ranks would have been smartly thinned before reaching our line, and some of their best men would have fallen. No men calculate such chances more carefully than Indians; and perhaps none are inferior to them in charging a foe that is entrenched. The weakest fort—even the most flimsy stockade—can be easily defended against the red warriors of the West.

Their intention having been foiled by the failure of their first charge, they appeared not to contemplate another—contented to hold us in siege—for to that situation were we, in reality, reduced. After a time, their firing became less frequent, until it nearly ceased altogether, but we knew that this did not indicate any intention to retreat; on the contrary, we saw some of them kindling fires afar off in the woods, no doubt with the design of cooking their breakfasts.

There was not a man among us who did not envy them their occupation.

Chapter Eighty Five.

A Meagre Meal.

To us the partial armistice was of no advantage. We dared not stir from the trees. Men were athirst, and water within sight—the pond glittering in the centre of the glade. Better there had been none, since they dared not approach it. It only served to tantalise them. The Indians were seen to eat, without leaving their lines. A few waited on the rest, and brought them food from the fires. Women were observed passing backwards and forwards, almost within range of our guns.

We were, all of us, hungry as famished wolves. We had been twenty-four hours without tasting food—even longer than that—and the sight of our enemies, feasting before our very faces, gave a keen edge to our appetites, at the same time rekindling our indignation. They even taunted us on our starving condition.

Old Hickman had grown furious. He was heard to declare that he "war hungry enough to eat a Indyen raw, if he could git his teeth upon one," and he looked as if he would have carried but the threat.

"The sight o' cussed red skins," continued he, "swallerin' hul collops o' meat, while Christyian whites haint neery a bone to pick, are enough to rile one to the last jeint in the eends o' the toes—by the tarnal allygator, it ar!"

It is a bare place, indeed, where such men as Hickman and Weatherford will not find resources; and the energies of both were now bent upon discovery. They were seen scratching among the dead needles of the pines, that, as already stated, formed a thick layer over the surface of the ground.

Of what were they in search? worms?—grubs?—larvae or lizards? One might have fancied so; but no—it had not come to that. Hungry as they were, they were not yet ready to feed upon the *reptilia*. A better resource had suggested itself to them; and shortly after, an exclamation of joy announced that they had discovered the object of their search.

Hickman was seen holding up a brownish coloured mass, of conical form, somewhat resembling a large pineapple. It was a cone of the broom pine, easily recognisable by its size and shape.

"Now, fellers!" shouted he, in a voice loud enough to be heard by all around the glade, "jest gather a wheen o' these hyar tree-eggs, and break 'em open; ye'll find kurnels inside o' 'em that aint bad chawin'—they aint equal to hog an' hominy; but we hant got hog an' hominy, and these hyar'll sarve in a pinch, I reck'n. Ef ye'll only root among the rubbage aroun' ye, ye'll scare up a wheen—jest try it."

The suggestion was eagerly adopted, and in an instant "all hands" were seen scratching up the dead leaves in search of pine cones.

Some of these were found lying upon the surface, near at hand, and were easily procured, while others, were jerked within reach by ramrods or the barrels of rifles. Less or more, every one was enabled to obtain a supply.

The cones were quickly cut open, and the kernels greedily devoured. It was by no means an inferior food; for the seeds of the broom pine are both nutritive and pleasant to the palate. Their quality gave universal satisfaction—it was only in quantity they were deficient, for there was not enough of them within reach to stay the cravings of fifty stomachs hungry as ours were.

There was some joking over this dry breakfast, and the more reckless of the party laughed while they ate, as though it had been a nutting frolic. But the laughter was short-lived—our situation was too serious to admit of much levity.

It was an interval while the firing of the enemy had slackened, almost ceased; and we had ample time to consider the perils of our position. Up to this time, it had not occurred to us that, in reality, we were *besieged*. The hurried excitement of the conflict had left us no time for reflection. We only looked upon the affair as a skirmish that must soon come to an end, by one side or the other proving victorious.

The contest no longer wore that look; it had assumed the aspect of a regular siege. We were encompassed on every side—shut up as if in a fortress, but not half so secure. Our only stockade was the circle of standing trees, and we had no blockhouse to retire to—no shelter in the event of being wounded. Each man was a sentry, with a *tour* of guard duty that must be continual!

Our situation was indeed perilous in the extreme. There was no prospect of escape. Our horses had all galloped off long since; one only remained, lying dead by the side of the pond. It had been killed by a bullet, but it was not from the enemy. Hickman had fired the shot; I saw him, and wondered at the time what could be his object. The hunter had his reasons, but it was only afterwards I learned them.

We could hold our ground against five times our number—almost any odds—but how about food? Thirst we did not fear. At night we should have relief. Under the cover of night we could approach the pond, one after another.

We had no apprehension from want of water; but how about food? The cones we had gathered were but a bite; there were no more within reach; we must yield to hunger—to famine.

We conversed with one another freely, as if face to face. We canvassed our prospects; they were gloomy enough.

How was the affair to end? How were we to be delivered from our perilous situation? These were the questions that occupied the thoughts of all.

We could think of only one plan that offered a plausible chance of escape; and that was to hold our position until nightfall, make a sally in the darkness, and fight our way through the lines of our foes. It would be running the gauntlet; a few of us would certainly fall—perhaps many—but some would escape. To stay where we were would be to expose our whole party to certain sacrifice. There was no likelihood of our being rescued by others; no one entertained such a hope. As soon as hunger overcame us, we should be massacred to a man.

Rather than patiently abide such a fate, we resolved, while yet strong, to risk all chances, and fight our way through the enemy's line. Darkness would favour the attempt; and thus resolved, we awaited the going down of the sun.

175

Chapter Eighty Six.

A Bullet from Behind.

If we thought the time long, it was not from want of occupation. During the day, the Indians at intervals renewed their attack; and notwithstanding all our vigilance, we had another man killed, and several slightly wounded.

In these skirmishes, the savages showed a determination to get nearer our line, by making their advances from tree to tree.

We perfectly understood their object in this. It was not that they had any design of closing with us, though their numbers might have justified them in doing so. They were now far more numerous than at the beginning of the fight. Another fresh band had arrived upon the ground—for we had heard the shouts of welcome that hailed their coming.

But even with this accession of strength, they did not design to come to the encounter of sharp weapons. Their purpose in advancing was different. They had perceived that by getting close to our convex line, they would be near enough to fire upon those on the opposite side of the glade, who, of course, were then exposed to their aim.

To prevent this, therefore, became our chief object and anxiety, and it was necessary to redouble our vigilance.

We did so, regarding with scrutinous glances the trunks behind which we knew the savages were skulking, and eyeing them as keenly as the ferret hunter watches the burrows of the warren.

They had but slight success in their endeavours to advance. It cost them several of their boldest men; for the moment one of them essayed to rush forwards, the cracks of three or four rifles could be heard; and one of these was sure to deliver its messenger of death. The Indians soon became tired of attempting this dangerous manoeuvre; and as evening approached, appeared to give up their design, and content themselves by holding us in siege.

We were glad when the sun set and the twilight came on; it would soon pass, and we should be able to reach the water. The men were maddened with thirst, for they had been suffering from it throughout the whole day. During the daylight many would have gone to the pond, had they not been restrained by the precepts of the more prudent, and perhaps more effectually by an example of which they had all been witnesses. One, more reckless than the rest, had risked the attempt; he succeeded in reaching the water, drank to satisfaction, and was hastening back to his post, when a shot from the savages stretched him dead upon the sward. He was the man last killed; and his lifeless body now lay in the open ground, before the eyes of his comrades.

It proved a warning to all; for, despite the torture of thirst, no one cared to repeat the rash experiment.

At length the welcome darkness descended—only a glimmer of grey light lingered in the leaden sky. Men in twos and threes were now seen approaching the pond. Like spectres they moved, silently gliding over the open ground, but in stooping attitudes, and heads bent eagerly forwards in the direction of the water.

We did not all go at once—though all were alike eager to quench their thirst—but the admonitions of the old hunter had their effect: and the more continent agreed to bear their pangs a little longer, and wait till the others should get back to their posts.

It was prudent we so acted; for, at this crisis, the Indians—no doubt suspecting what was going forward—renewed their fire with fresh energy.

Whole volleys were discharged inwards and without aim, the darkness must have hindered an aim, but for all that, the bullets buzzed past our ears as thickly as hornets upon their flight. There was a cry raised that the enemy was closing upon us; and those who had gone to the water rushed rapidly back—some even without staying to take the much desired drink.

During all this time I had remained behind my tree. My black follower had also stuck to his post like a faithful sentinel as he was. We talked of relieving one another by turns. Jake insisted that I should "drink first."

I had partially consented to this arrangement, when the fire of the enemy suddenly reopened. Like others, we were apprehensive that the savages were about to advance; and we knew the necessity of keeping them back. We agreed to keep our ground for a little longer.

I had "one eye round the trunk of the tree, with my rifle raised" to the level—and was watching for a flash from the gun of some savage, to guide me in my aim—when, all on a sudden, I felt my arm jerked upwards, and my gun shaken out of my grasp.

There was no mystery about it. A bullet had passed through my arm, piercing the muscles that upheld it. I had shown too much of my shoulder, and was wounded—nothing more.

My first thought was to look to my wound. I felt it distinctly enough, and that enabled me to discover the place. I saw that the ball had passed through the upper part of my right arm, just below the shoulder, and in its further progress had creased the breast of my uniform coat, where its trace was visible in the torn cloth.

There was still light sufficient to enable me to make these observations; and furthermore, that a thick stream of blood was gushing from the wound.

I commenced unbuttoning my coat, the better to get at the wound. The black was ready by my side, rending his shirt into ribbons.

All at once I heard him uttering an exclamation of surprise followed by the words, "Gorramighty! Mass George—dat shot come from ahind!"

"From behind?" I shouted, echoing his words, and once more looking to the wound.

"Yes, mass, yes—sartin he come from ahind."

Some suspicion of this had already been in my thoughts: I fancied that I had "*felt*" the shot from that quarter.

It had been no fancy. On a more minute examination of the wound, and the torn traces upon the breast of my coat, the direction of the bullet was plainly perceived. Undoubtedly it had struck me from behind.

"Good God, Jake!" I exclaimed, "it is so. The Indians have advanced to the other side of the glade—we are lost!"

Under this belief, we both faced towards the opening, when at that moment, as if to confirm us, another bullet whistled past our ears, and struck with a heavy "thud" into the tree by which we were kneeling. This one had certainly been fired from the other side of the glade—we saw the flash and heard the report of the gun that had sent it.

What had become of our comrades on that side? Had they abandoned their posts, and permitted the Indians to advance? Were they all by the pond, and thus neglecting their duty?

These were the first conjectures both of my companion and myself. It was too dark for us to see our men under the shadows of the pines, but neither did they appear in the open ground. We were puzzled, and shouted aloud for an explanation.

If there were replies, we heard them not—for at that moment a wild yell from our savage enemies drowned all other cries, and a sight burst upon our eyes that caused the blood to curdle within our veins.

Directly in point of the position that Jake and I held, and close to the Indian line, a red flame was seen suddenly springing up from the earth. It rose in successive puffs, each leaping higher and higher, until it had ascended among the tops of the trees. It resembled the flashes of large, masses of gunpowder ignited upon the ground, and such in reality it was. We read the intention at a glance. The Indians were attempting to fire the forest!

Their success was almost instantaneous. As soon as the sulphureous blaze came in contact with the withered fascicles of foliage, the latter caught as though they had been tinder; and with the velocity of projected rockets, the flames shot out in different directions, and danced far above the tops of the tree. We looked around; on all sides we beheld a similar spectacle. That wild yell had been the signal for a circle of fires. The glade was encompassed by a wall of flame—red, roaring, and gigantic. The whole forest was on fire. From all points the flame appeared closing inwards, sweeping the trees as if they had been withered grass, and leaping in long spurts high into the heavens.

The smoke now came thick and heavy around us—each moment growing denser as the fire approached—while the heated atmosphere was no longer endurable. Already it stifled our breathing.

Destruction stared us in the face, and men shouted in despair. But the roar of the burning pines drowned their voices, and one could not hear even his comrade who was nearest. Their looks were significant—for before the smoke fell, the glade was lit up with intense brilliance, and we could see one another with unnatural distinctness. In the faces of all appeared the anxiety of awe.

Not long continued I to share it. Too much blood had escaped from my neglected wound; I tried to make into the open ground, as I saw others doing; but, before I got two steps from the tree, my limbs tottered beneath me, and I fell fainting to the earth.

Chapter Eighty Seven.

A Jury Amid the Fire.

I had a last thought, as I fell. It was that my life had reached its termination—that in a few seconds my body would be embraced by the flames, and I should horribly perish. The thought drew from me a feeble scream; and with that scream my consciousness forsook me. I was as senseless as if dead—indeed, so far as sensibility went, I *was* dead; and, had the flames at that moment swept over me, I should not have felt them. In all probability, I might have been burned to a cinder without further pain.

During the interval of my unconsciousness, I had neither dream nor apparition. By this, I knew that my soul must have forsaken its earthly tenement. It may have been hovering above or around, but it was no longer within me. It had separated from my senses, that were all dead.

Dead, but capable of being restored to life, and haply a restorative was at hand, with one capable to administer it.

When my soul returned, the first perception I had was that I was up to my neck in water. I was in the pond, and in a recumbent position—my limbs and body under the water, with only my head above the surface, resting against the bank. A man was kneeling over me, himself half immersed.

My returning senses soon enabled me to tell who the man was—my faithful Jake. He had my pulse in his hand, and was gazing into my features with silent earnestness. As my open eyes replied to his gaze, he uttered an exclamation of joy, and the words: "Golly, Massa George! you lib—thank be to Gorramighty, you lib. Keep up ya heart, young massa—you's a gwine to git ober it—sartin, your a gwine to git ober it."

"I hope so, Jake," was my reply, in a weak voice; but, feeble though it was, it roused the faithful fellow into a transport of delight, and he continued to utter his cheering ejaculations.

I was able to raise my head and look around. It was a dread spectacle that on all sides greeted my eyes, and there was plenty of light wherewith to view it. The forest was still on fire, burning with a continued roar, as of thunder or a mighty wind—varied with hissing noises, and loud crackling that resembled the platoon firing of musketry. One might have fancied it a fusilade from the Indians, but that was impossible. They must have long since retreated before the spreading circle of that all-consuming conflagration. There was less flame than when I had last looked upon it; and less smoke in the atmosphere. The dry foliage had been suddenly reduced to a cinder, and the twiggy fragments had fallen to the earth, where they lay in a dense bed of glowing embers.

Out of this rose the tall trunks, half stripped of their branches, and all on fire. The crisp scaling bark had caught freely, and the resinous sapwood was readily yielding to the flames. Many had burned far inwards, and looked like huge columns of iron heated to redness. The spectacle presented an aspect of the infernal world.

The sense of feeling, too, might have suggested fancies of the same region. The heat was intense to an extreme degree. The atmosphere quivered with the drifting caloric. The hair had crisped upon our heads—our skins had the feel of blistering, and the air we inhaled resembled steam from the 'scape pipe of an engine.

Instinctively I looked for my companions. A group of a dozen or more were upon the open ground near the edge of the pond, but these were not all. There should have been nearer fifty. Where were the others? Had they perished in the flames? Where were they?

Mechanically, I put the question to Jake.

"Thar, massa," he replied, pointing downwards, "Tha dey be safe yet—ebbery one ob un, I blieve."

I looked across the surface of the pond. Three dozen roundish objects met my glance. They were the heads of my companions. Like myself, their bodies were submerged, most of them to the neck. They had thus placed themselves to shun the smoke, as well as the broiling heat.

But the others—they on the bank—why had they not also availed themselves of this cunning precaution? Why were they still standing exposed to the fierce heat, and amid the drifting clouds of smoke?

The latter had grown thin and gauze-like. The forms of the men were seen distinctly through it, magnified as in a mist. Like giants they were striding over the ground, and the guns in their hands appeared of colossal proportions. Their gestures were abrupt, and their whole bearing showed they were in a state of half frenzied excitement.

It was natural enough amidst the circumstances that surrounded them. I saw they were the principal men of our party. I saw Hickman and Weatherford both gesticulating freely among them. No doubt they were counselling how we should act.

This was the conjecture I derived from my first glance; but a further survey of the group convinced me I was in error. It was no deliberation about our future plans. In the lull between the volleys of the crackling pines, I could hear their voices. They were those of men engaged in angry dispute. The voices of Hickman and Weatherford especially reached my ear, and I perceived they were talking in a tone that betokened a high state of indignation.

At this moment, the smoke drifting aside, discovered a group still further from the edge of the pond. There were six men standing in threes, and I perceived that the middle man of each three was tightly grasped by the two others. Two of them were prisoners! Were they Indians? two of our enemies, who, amid the confusion of the fire, had strayed into the glade, and been captured?

It was my first thought; but at that instant, a jet of flame, shooting upwards, filled the glade with a flood of brilliant light. The little group thus illuminated could be seen as distinctly as by the light of day.

I was no longer in doubt about the captives. Their faces were before me, white and ghastly as if with fear. Even the red light failed to tinge them with its colour; but wan as they were, I had no difficulty in recognising them. They were Spence and Williams.

Chapter Eighty Eight.

Quick Executioners.

I turned to the black for an explanation, but before he could make reply to my interrogatory, I more than half comprehended the situation.

My own plight admonished me. I remembered my wound—I remembered that I had received it from *behind*. I remembered that the bullet that struck the tree, came from the same quarter. I thought we had been indebted to the savages for the shots; but no, worse savages—Spence and Williams were the men who had fired them!

The reflection was awful—the motive mysterious.

And now returned to my thoughts the occurrences of the preceding night—the conduct of these two fellows in the forest—the suspicious hints thrown out by old Hickman and his comrades, and far beyond the preceding night, other circumstances, well marked upon my memory, rose freshly before me.

Here again was the hand of Arens Ringgold. O God, to think that this arch-monster—

"Dar only a tryin' them two daam raskell," said Jake, in reply to the interrogatory I had put, "daat's what they am about, Mass'r George, dat's all."

"Who?" I asked mechanically, for I already knew who were meant by the "two daam raskell."

"Lor, Massr George? doant you see um ober yonder—Spence an' William—golly! tha'r boaf as white as peeled pumpkins! It war them that shot you, an' no Indians, arter all. I knowd dat from tha fust, an' I tol' Mass' Hickman de same; but Mass' Hickman 'clare he see um for hisself—an' so too Mass' Weatherford—boaf seed 'um fire tha two shots. Thar a tryin' 'on 'em for tha lives, dat's what tha men am doin'."

With strange interest I once more turned my eyes outward, and gazed, first at one group, then the other. The fire was now making less noise—the sapwood having nearly burnt out—and the detonations caused by the escape of the pent gases from the cellular cavities of the wood had grown less frequent. Voices could be heard over the glade, those of the improvised jury.

I listened attentively. I perceived that a dispute was still raging between them. They were not agreed upon their verdict—some advocating the immediate death of the prisoners; while others, adverse to such prompt punishment, would have kept them for further inquiry. There were some who could not credit their guilt—the deed was too atrocious, and hence improbable; under what motive could they have committed it? At such a time, too, with their own lives in direst jeopardy?

"Ne'er a bit o' jeppurdy," exclaimed Hickman in reply to the interrogatory, "ne'er a bit o' jeppurdy. Thar haint been a shot fired at eyther on 'em this hul day. I tell ye, fellers, thar's a un'erstannin' 'atween them an' the Indyens. Thar no better'n spies, an' thar last night's work proves it; an' but for the breakin' out of the fire, which they didn't expect, they'd been off arter firin' the shots. 'Twar all bamfoozle about thar gettin' lost—them fellers git lost, adeed! Both on 'em knows these hyar wuds as well as the anymals thet lives in 'em. Thum both been hyar many's the time, an' a wheen too often, I reckin. Lost! wagh! Did yez iver hear o' a coon gittin' lost?" Some one made reply, I did not hear what was said, but the voice of the hunter again sounded distinct and clear.

"Ye palaver about thar motive—I s'pose you mean thar reezuns for sech bloody bizness! Them, I acknullidge, aint clar, but I hev my sespicions too. I aint a gwine to say who or what. Thar's some things as mout be, an' thar's some as moutn't; but I've seed queer doin's in these last five yeern, an' I've heern o' others; an if what I've heern be's true—what I've seed I know to be—then I tell ye, fellers, thar's a bigger than eyther o' thesen at the bottom o' the hul bizness—that's what thar be."

"But do you really say you saw them take aim in that direction; are you sure of that?"

This inquiry was put by a tall man who stood in the midst of the disputing party—a man of advanced age, and of somewhat severe aspect. I knew him as one of our neighbours in the settlement—an extensive planter—who had some intercourse with my uncle, and out of friendship for our family had joined the pursuit.

"Sure," echoed the old hunter with emphasis, and not without some show of indignation; "didn't me an' Jim Weatherford see 'em wi' our own two eyes? an' thar good enough, I reckin, to mark sich varmints as them. We'd been a watchin' 'em all day, for we knowd thar war somethin' ugly afoot. We seed 'em both fire acrost the gleed—an' sight plum-centre at young Randolph; besides, the black himself sez that the two shots comed that away. What more proof kin you want?"

At this moment I heard a voice by my side. It was that of Jake, calling out to the crowd.

"Mass' Hickman," cried he, "if dey want more proof, I b'lieve dis nigger can gib it. One ob de bullets miss young mass'r, an' stuck in da tree; yonner's the verry tree itself, that we wa behind, it ain't burn yet, it no take fire; maybe, gen'lem'n, you mout find tha bullet tha still? maybe you tell what gun he 'longs to?"

The suggestion was instantly adopted. Several men ran towards the tree behind which Jake and I had held post; and which, with a few others—near it, for some reason or other—had escaped the flames, and still stood with trunks unscathed in the foreground of the conflagration.

180

Jake ran with the rest and pointed out the spot.

The bark was scrutinised, the hole found, and the leaden witness carefully picked out. It was still in its globe shape, slightly torn by the grooves of the barrel. It was a rifle ballet, and one of the very largest size.

It was known that Spence carried a piece of large calibre. But the guns of all the party were paraded, and their measure taken. The bullet would enter the barrel of no other rifle save that of Spence.

The conclusion was evident—the verdict was no longer delayed. It was unanimous, that the prisoners should die.

"An' let 'em die like dogs as they are," cried Hickman, indignantly raising his voice, and at the same time bringing his piece to the level, "Now, Jim Weatherford! look to yer sights! Let 'em go thar, fellers! an' git yerselves out o' the way. We'll gie 'em a chance for thar cussed lives. They may take to yonner trees if they like, an' git 'customed to it—for they'll be in a hotter place than that afore long. Let 'em go I let 'em go! I say, or by the tarnal I'll fire into the middle o' ye!"

The men who had hold of the prisoners, perceiving the menacing attitude of the hunter, and fearing that he might make good his words, suddenly dropped their charge, and ran back towards the group of jurors.

The two wretches appeared bewildered. Terror seemed to hold them speechless, and fast glued to the spot. Neither made any effort to leave the ground. Perhaps the complete impossibility of escape was apparent to them, and prostrated all power to make the attempt. Of course, they could not have got away from the glade. Their taking to the trees was only mockery on the part of the indignant hunter. In ten seconds, they would have been roasted among the blazing branches.

It was a moment of breathless suspense. Only one voice was heard—that of Hickman:

"Now Jim, you sight Spence—gie tother to me." This was said in a hurried undertone, and the words had scarcely passed, when the two rifles cracked simultaneously.

The execution was over. The renegades had ceased to live.

This speedy punishment of convicted rascals is a severe commentary upon the more refined proceedings of our judicial trials, in which every effort is made, and every argument strained to enable the culprit—known to be guilty—to escape the punishment due to his crimes, a result which is generally effected, either by some legal technicality or political machinery.

Chapter Eighty Nine.

An Enemy Unlooked For.

As, upon the stage of a theatre, the farce follows the grand melodrama, this tragic scene was succeeded by an incident ludicrous to an extreme degree. It elicited roars of laughter from the men, that, under the circumstances, sounded like the laughter of madmen; maniacs indeed might these men have been deemed—thus giving way to mirth, with a prospect before them so grim and gloomy—the prospect of almost certain death, either at the hands of our savage assailants, or from starvation.

Of the former we had no present fear. The flames that had driven us out of the timber, had equally forced them from their position; and we knew they were now far from us. They could not be near.

Now that the burnt branches had fallen from the pines, and the foliage was entirely consumed, the eye was enabled to penetrate the forest to a great distance. On every side we commanded a *vista* of at least a thousand yards, through the intervals between the red glowing trunks; and beyond this we could hear by the "swiz" of the flames, and the continual crackling of the boughs, that fresh trees were being embraced within the circle of conflagration, that was each moment extending its circumference.

The sounds grew fainter apace, until they bore a close resemblance to the mutterings of distant thunder. We had fancied that the fire was dying out; but the luminous ring around the horizon proved that the flames were still ascending. It was only that the noise came from a greater distance, that we heard it less distinctly.

Our human foes must have been still further away, they must have retired before the widening rim of the conflagration. But they had calculated upon doing so before applying the torch. In all likelihood, they had retreated to the savanna, to await the result.

Their object in firing the forest was not so easily understood. Perhaps they expected that the vast volume of flame would close over and consume us, or, more like, that we should be smothered under the dense clouds of smoke. This might in reality have been our fate, but for the proximity of the pond. My companions told me, that their sufferings from the smoke had been dreadful in the extreme—that they should have been stifled by it, had they not thrown themselves into the pond, and kept their faces close to the surface of the water, which was several feet below the level of the ground. It had been to me an hour of unconsciousness. My faithful black had carried me lifeless, as he supposed, to the water, and placed me among the rest.

It was afterwards—when the smoke had partially cleared away—that the spies were brought to account. Hickman and Weatherford, deeply indignant at the conduct of these monsters, would not hear of delay. They insisted upon immediate punishment; and the wretches were seized upon, dragged out of the pond, and put upon their trial. It was at this crisis that my senses returned to me.

As soon as the dread sentence had been carried into execution, the *ci-devant* jurors came rushing back to the pond, and plunged their bodies into the water. The heat was still intense, and painful of endurance.

There were two only who appeared to disregard it, and still remained upon the bank. These were the two hunters.

Knives in hand, I saw them stooping over a dark object that lay near. It was the horse that Hickman had shot in the morning; and I now perceived the old hunter's motive, that had hitherto mystified me. It was an act of that cunning foresight that characterised this man, apparently instinctive.

They proceeded to skin the horse, and, in a few seconds, had pealed off a portion of the hide—sufficient for their purpose. They then cut out several large pieces of the flesh, and laid them aside. This done, Weatherford stepped off to the edge of the burning timber, and presently returned with an armful of half consumed fagots. These were erected into a fire, near the edge of the pond; and the two, squatting down by its side, commenced broiling the pieces of horse-flesh upon sapling spits, and conversing as coolly and cheerily as if seated in the chimney corner of their own cabins.

There were others as hungry as they, who took the hint, and proceeded to imitate their example. The pangs of hunger were harder to bear than the hot atmosphere, and in a few minutes' time, a dozen men might have been observed, grouped like vultures around the dead horse hacking and hewing at the carcass.

At this crisis occurred the incident which I have characterised as ludicrous.

With the exception of the few engaged in their coarse *cuisine*, the rest of us remained in the water. We were lying around the circular rim of the basin—our bodies parallel to one another, and our heads upon the bank. We were not dreaming of being disturbed by an intruder of any kind—at least for a time. We were no longer in fear of the fire, and our savage foemen were far off.

All at once, however, an enemy was discovered in an unexpected quarter—right in the midst of us.

Just in the centre of the pond, where the water was deepest, a monstrous form rose suddenly to the surface; at the same time that our ears were greeted with a loud bellowing, as if half a score of bulls were let loose into the glade.

In an instant, the water was agitated and lashed into foam, and the spray fell in showers around our heads.

Weird-like and sudden, as was the apparition, there was nothing mysterious about it. The hideous form, and deep barytone were well-known to all. It was simply an alligator.

But for its enormous size the presence of the reptile would scarce have been regarded; but it was one of the largest of its kind—its long body almost equalling the diameter of the pond, with huge gaunt jaws that seemed capable of swallowing a man at a single "gulp." Its roar, too, was enough to inspire even the boldest with terror.

It produced this effect; and the wild frightened looks of those in the water—their confused plunging and splashing, as they scrambled to their feet and hastened to get out of it—their simultaneous rushing up the bank, and scattering off into the open ground—all contributed to form a spectacle ludicrous in the extreme.

In less than ten seconds' time the great saurian had the pond to himself; where he continued to bellow, and lash the water in his rage.

He was not permitted to exult long in his triumph. The hunters, with several others, seized their rifles, and ran forwards to the edge of the pond, when a volley from a dozen guns terminated the monster's existence.

Those who had been "ashore," were already convulsed with laughter at the scared fugitives; but the latter, having recovered from their momentary affright, now joined in the laugh, till the woods rang with a chorus of wild cachinnations.

Could the Indians have heard us at that moment, they must have fancied as mad, or more likely dead, and that our voices were those of their own fiends, headed by Wykomé himself—rejoicing over the holocaust of their pale-faced foes.

Chapter Ninety.

A Conflict in Darkness.

The forest continued to burn throughout the night, the following day, and the night after. Even on the second day, most of the trees were still on fire.

They no longer blazed, for the air was perfectly still, and there was no wind to fan the fire into flame. It was seen in red patches against the trunks, smouldering and gradually becoming less, as its strength spontaneously died out.

From many of the trees it had disappeared altogether, and these no longer bore any resemblance to trees, but looked like huge, sharp-pointed stakes, charred and black, as though profusely coated with coal-tar.

Though there were portions of the forest that might now have been traversed, there were other places where the fire still burned fiercely enough to oppose our progress. We were still besieged by the igneous element—as completely confined within the circumscribed boundaries of the glade, as if encompassed by a hostile army of twenty times our number—indeed, more so. No rescue could possibly reach us. Even our enemies, so far as *our* safety was concerned, could not have "raised the siege."

So far the old hunter's providence had stood us in good stead. But for the horse some of us must have succumbed to hunger; or, at all events, suffered its extreme. We had been now four days without food—except what the handful of pine cones and the horse-flesh afforded us; and still the fiery forest hemmed us in. There was no alternative but to stay where we were until, as Hickman phrased it, "the woods should git *cool.*"

We were cheered with the hope that another day would effect this purpose, and we might travel with safety.

The prospect before us was gloomy as that around us. As our dread of the fire declined, that of our human foes increased in an inverse proportion. We had but little hope of getting off without an encounter. They could traverse the woods as soon as we, and were certain to be on the look-out. With them the account was still to be settled. The gauntlet was yet to be run.

But we had grown fierce and less fearful. The greatest coward of our party had become brave, and no one voted for either skulking or hanging back. Stand or fall, we had resolved upon keeping together, and cutting our way through the hostile lines, or dying in the attempt. It was but the old programme, with a slight change in the *mise-en-scène.*

We waited only for another night to carry our plans into execution. The woods would scarce be as "cool" as we might have desired, but hunger was again hurrying us. The horse—a small one—had disappeared. Fifty starved stomachs are hard to satisfy. The bones lay around clean picked—those that contained marrow, broken into fragments and emptied of their contents; even the hideous saurian was a skeleton!

A more disgusting spectacle was presented by the bodies of the two criminals. The heat had swollen them to enormous proportions, and decomposition had already commenced. The air was loaded with that horrid effluvia peculiar to the dead body of a human being.

Our comrades who fell in the fight had been buried, and there was some talk of performing the like office for the others. No one objected; but none volunteered to take the trouble. In such cases men are overpowered by an extreme apathy; and this was chiefly the reason why the bodies of these wretches were suffered to remain without interment.

With eyes bent anxiously towards the west, we awaited the going down of the sun. So long as his bright orb was above the horizon, we could only guess at the condition of the fire. The darkness would enable us to distinguish that part of the forest that was still burning, and point out the direction we should take. The fire itself would guide us to the shunning of it.

Twilight found us on the tiptoe of expectation, and not without hope. There was but little redness among the scathed pines—the smoke appeared slighter than we had yet observed it. Some believed that the fires were nearly out—all thought the time had arrived when we could pass through them.

An unexpected circumstance put this point beyond conjecture. While we stood waiting, the rain began to fall—at first in big solitary drops, but in a few moments it came pouring down as if all heaven's fountains had been opened together.

We hailed the phenomenon with joy. It appeared an omen in our favour. We could hardly restrain ourselves from setting forth at once; but the more cautious counselled the rest to patience, and we stood awaiting the deeper darkness.

The rain continued to pour—its clouds hastening the night. As it darkened, scarce a spark appeared among the trees.

"It is dark enough," urged the impatient. The others yielded, and we started forth into the bosom of the ruined forest. We moved silently along amid the black, calcined trunks. Each grasped his gun tight and ready for use. Mine was held only in one hand—the other rested in a sling.

In this plight I was not alone. Half a dozen of my comrades had been also "winged;" and together we kept in the rear. The better men marched in front, Hickman and Weatherford acting as guides.

The rain beat down upon us. There was no longer a foliage to intercept it. As we walked under the burnt branches, the black char was driven against our faces, and as quickly washed off again. Most of the men were bareheaded—their caps were over the locks of their guns to keep them dry—some sheltered their priming with the skirts of their coats.

In this manner we had advanced nearly half a mile, we knew not in what direction; no guide could have found path in such a forest. We only endeavoured to keep straight forward, with the view of getting *beyond* our enemies. So long unmolested, we had begun to hope that we might.

Alas! it was a momentary gleam. We were underrating the cunning of our red foes. They had watched us all the time—had dogged our steps, and at some distance off, were marching on both sides of us, in two parallel lines. While dreaming of safety we were actually in their midst!

The flashes of a hundred guns through the misty rain—the whistling of as many bullets—were the first intimation we had of their presence.

Several fell under the volley. Some returned the fire—a few thought only of making their escape.

Uttering their shrill cries, the savages closed in upon us. In the darkness they appeared to outnumber the trees.

Save the occasional report of a pistol, no other shot was heard—no one thought of reloading. The foe was upon us before there was time to draw a ramrod. The knife and hatchet were to be the arbiters of the fight.

184

The struggle was sanguinary as it was short. Many of our brave fellows met their death; but each killed his foeman—some two or three of them—before he fell.

We were soon vanquished. The enemy was five to one—how could it be otherwise? They were fresh and strong; we weak with hunger—almost emaciated—many of us wounded—how could it be otherwise?

I saw but little of the conflict—perhaps no one saw more; it was a straggle amidst opaque darkness.

With my one hand—and that the left—I was almost helpless. I fired my rifle at random, and had contrived to draw a pistol; but the blow of a tomahawk hindered me from using it, at the same time felling me senseless to the earth.

I was only stunned, and when my senses returned to me, I saw that the conflict was over. Dark as it was, I could perceive a number of black objects lying near me upon the ground. They were the bodies of the slain.

Some were those of my late comrades—others their foes—in many instances locked in each other's embrace!

The savages were stooping over, as if separating them. On the former they were executing their last hideous rite of vengeance—they were scalping them.

A group was nearer; the individuals composing it were standing erect. One in their midst appeared to issue commands. Even in the grey light I could distinguish three waving plumes. Again Osceola!

I was not free, or at that moment I should have rushed forwards and grappled him, vain though the vengeful effort might have been. But I was not free.

Two savages knelt over me, as if guarding me against such an attempt. I perceived my black follower near at hand—still alive, and similarly cared for. Why had they not killed us?

At this moment a man was seen approaching. It was not he with the ostrich-plumes, though the latter appeared to have sent him.

As he drew near, I perceived that he carried a pistol. My hour was come. The man stooped over me, and placed the weapon close to my ear. To my astonishment he fired it into the air!

I thought he had missed me, and would try again. But this was not his purpose. He only wanted a light.

While the powder was ablaze, I caught a glance of the countenance. It was an Indian's, but I thought I had seen it before; and from some expression the man made use of, he appeared to know me.

He passed quickly from me, and proceeded to the spot where Jake was held captive. The pistol must have had two barrels, for I saw him fire it again, stooping in the same manner over the prostrate form of the black. He then rose and called out:

"It is they—still alive."

This information appeared meant for him of the black plumes, for the moment it was given he uttered some exclamation I did not comprehend, and then walked away.

His voice produced a singular impression upon me. I fancied it did not sound like Osceola's!

We were kept upon the ground only for a few minutes longer, and then a number of horses were brought up. Upon two of these Jake and I were mounted, and fast tied to the saddles. A signal was then given, and, with an Indian riding on each side of us, we were carried off through the woods.

Chapter Ninety One.

The Black Plumes.

We journeyed throughout the whole night. The burnt woods were left behind, and having crossed a savanna, we rode for several hours through a forest of giant oaks, palms, and magnolias. I knew this by the fragrance of the magnolia blossoms, that, after the fetid atmosphere that we had been breathing, smelt sweet and refreshing. Just as day was breaking, we arrived at an opening in the woods, where our captors halted.

185

The opening was of small extent—a few acres only—bounded on all sides by a thick forest of palms, magnolias, and live-oaks. Their foliage drooped to the ground, so that the glade appeared encompassed by a vast wall of green, through which no outlet was discernible.

Through the grey light, I perceived the outlines of an encampment. There were two or three tents with horses picketed around them, and human forms, some of them upright and moving about, others recumbent upon the grass, singly, or in clusters, as if sleeping together for mutual warmth. A large fire was burning in the midst, and around it were men and women, seated and standing.

Within the limits of this camp we had been carried, but no time was left us for observation. The moment we halted, we were dragged roughly from our horses, and flung prostrate upon the grass. We were next turned upon our backs. Thongs were tied around our waists and ancles, our arms and limbs drawn out to their full extent, and we were staked firmly to the ground, like hides spread out for drying. Of course, in this attitude, we could see no more of the camp—nor the trees—nor the earth itself—only the blue heavens above us.

Under any circumstances, the position would have been painful, but my wounded arm rendered it excruciating.

Our arrival had set the camp in motion. Men came out to meet us, and women stooped over us, as we lay on our backs. There were Indian squaws among them, but, to my surprise, I noticed that most of them were of African race—mulattoes, samboes, and negresses!

For some time they stood over, jeering and taunting us. They even proceeded to inflict torture—they spit on us, pulled out handfuls of our hair by the roots, and stuck sharp thorns into our skin, all the while yelling with a fiendish delight, and jabbering an unintelligible patois, that appeared a mixture of Spanish and Yamassee.

My fellow-captive fared as badly as myself. The homogenous colour of his skin elicited no sympathy from these female fiends. Black and white were alike the victims of their hellish spite.

Part of their jargon I was able to comprehend, aided by a slight acquaintance with the Spanish tongue, I made out what was intended to be done with us—we were to be *tortured*.

We had been brought to the camp to be *tortured*. We were to be the victims of a grand spectacle, and these infernal hags were exulting in the prospect of the sport our sufferings should afford them. For this only had, we been *captured*, instead of being *killed*.

Into whose hound hands had we fallen? Were they human beings? Were they Indians? Could they be Seminoles, whose behaviour to their captives hitherto, had repelled every insinuation of torture?

A shout arose as if in answer to my questions. The voices of all around were mingled in the cry, but the words were the same:

"*Mulato-mico! mulato-mico! viva, mulato-mico!*"

The trampling of many hoofs announced the arrival of a band. They were the warriors who had been engaged in the fight—who had conquered and made us captive. Only half a dozen guards had been with us on the night-march, and had reached the camp at daybreak. The new comers were the main body, who had stayed upon the field to complete the despoliation of their fallen foes. I could not see them, though they were near, for I heard their horses trampling around.

I lay listening to that significant shout:

"*Mulato-mico! viva, mulato-mico!*"

To me the words were full of terrible import. The phrase "Mulato-mico" was not new to me, and I heard it with a feeling of dread. But it was scarce possible to increase apprehensions already excited to the full. A hard fate was before me. The presence of the fiend himself could not make it more certain.

My fellow-victim shared my thoughts. We were near, and could converse. On comparing our conjectures, we found that they coincided.

But the point was soon settled beyond conjecture. A harsh voice sounded in our ears, issuing an abrupt order, that scattered the women away; a heavy footstep was heard behind—the speaker was approaching.

In another instant his shadow fell upon my face; and the man himself stood within the limited circle of my vision.

Despite the pigment that disguised his natural complexion—despite the beaded shirt, the sash, the embroidered leggins—despite the *three black plumes*, that waved over his brow, I easily identified the man. He was no Indian, but a mulatto—"yellow Jake" himself.

Chapter Ninety Two.

Buried Alive.

I had expected the man. The cry "Mulato-mico," and afterwards his voice—still well remembered—had warned me of his coming. I expected to gaze upon him with dread; strange it may seem, but such was not the case. On the contrary, I beheld him, with a feeling akin to joy. Joy at the sight of *those three blade plumes* that nodded above his scowling temples.

For a moment I marked not his angry frowns, nor the wicked triumph that sparkled in his eye. The ostrich feathers were alone the objects of my regard—the cynosure of my thoughts. Their presence upon the crest of the "mulatto king" elucidated a world of mystery—foul suspicion was plucked from out my bosom—the preserver of my life—the hero of my heart's admiration was still true—Osceola was true!

In the momentary exultation of this thought, I almost forgot the gloom of my situation; but soon the voice of the mulatto once more roused me to a consciousness of its peril.

"*Carajo!*" cried he, in a tone of malignant triumph. "*Al fin venganza!* (At last vengeance!)—Both, too, white and black—master and slave—my young tyrant and my rival! ha! ha! ha!

"Me tie to tree," continued he, after a burst of hoarse laughter. "Me burn, eh? burn 'live? Your turn come now—trees plenty here; but no, me teach you better plan. *Corrambo, sí!* far better plan. Tie to tree, captive sometime 'scape, ha! ha! ha! Before burn, me show you sight. Ho, there!" he shouted, motioning to some of the bystanders to come near. "Untie hands—raise 'em up—both faces turn to camp—*basta! basta!* that do. Now white rascal—Black rascal look!—what see yonder?"

As he issued these orders, several of his creatures pulled up the stakes that had picketed down our arms, and raised us into a sitting posture, our bodies slewed round, till our faces bore full upon the camp. It was broad daylight—the sun shining brightly in the heavens. Under such a light every object in the camp was distinctly visible—the tents—the horses—the motley crowd of human occupants. We regarded not these. On two forms alone our eyes rested—they were my sister and Viola.

They were close together, as I had seen them once before—Viola seated with her head drooping, while that of Virginia rested in her lap. The hair of both was hanging in dishevelled masses—the black tresses of the maid mingling with the golden locks of her mistress. They were surrounded by guards, and appeared unconscious of our presence. But one was dispatched to warn them.

As the messenger reached them, we saw them both start, and look inquiringly abroad. In another instant their eyes were upon us. A thrilling scream announced that we were recognised. They cried out together. I heard my sister's voice pronouncing my name. I called to her in return. I saw her spring to her feet, toss her arms wildly above her head, and attempt to rush towards me. I saw the guards taking hold of her, and rudely dragging her back. Oh, it was a painful sight! death itself could not have been so hard to endure. But we were allowed to look upon them no longer. Suddenly jerked upon our backs, our wrists were once more staked down, and we lay in our former recumbent attitudes.

Painful as were our reflections, we were not allowed to indulge in them alone. The monster continued to stand over us, taunting us with spiteful words, and, worse than all, gross allusions to my sister and Viola. Oh, it was horrible to bear! Molten lead poured into our ears could scarce have tortured us more.

It was almost a relief when he desisted from speech, and we saw him commence making preparations for our torture. We knew that the hour was nigh; for he had himself said so, as he issued the orders to his fellows. Some horrible mode of death had been promised, but what it was we were yet in ignorance.

Not long did we remain so. Several men were seen approaching the spot, with spades and pickaxes in their hands. They were negroes—old field-hands—and knew how to use such implements.

They stopped near us, and commenced digging the ground. O God! were we to be buried alive?

This was the conjecture that first suggested itself. If true, it was terrible enough; but it was not true. We were designed to undergo a still more horrible fate!

Silently, and with the solemn air of grave-diggers, the men worked on. The mulatto stood over directing them. He was in high glee, occasionally calling to us in mockery, and boasting how skillfully he should perform the office of executioner.

The women and savage warriors clustered around, laughing at his sallies, or contributing their quota of grotesque wit, at which they uttered yells of demoniac laughter. We might easily have fancied ourselves in the infernal regions, in the middle of a crowd of jibbering fiends, who stood grinning down upon us, as if they drew delight from our anguish.

We noticed that few of the men were Seminoles. Indians there were; but these were of dark complexion, nearly black. They were of the tribe of Yamassees—a race conquered by the Seminoles, and partially engrafted into their nation. But most of those we saw were black negroes, samboes, and mulattoes, descendants of Spanish maroons, or "runaways" from the American plantations. There were many of the latter; for I could hear English spoken among them. No doubt there were some of my own slaves mixing with the motley crew, though none of them came near, and I could only note the faces of those who stood over me.

In about half an hour the diggers had finished their work. Our stakes were drawn, and we were dragged forwards to the spot where they had been engaged.

As soon as I was raised up, I bent my eyes upon the camp; but my sister was no longer there. Viola, too, was gone. They had been taken either inside the tents or back among the bushes.

I was glad they were not there: they would be spared this pang of a horrid spectacle; though it was not likely that from any such motive the monster had removed them.

Two dark holes yawned before us, deeply dug into the earth. They were not graves; or if so, it was not intended our bodies should be placed vertically in them.

If their shape was peculiar, so too was the purpose for which they were made. We were soon to become acquainted with it.

We were conduced to the edge of the cavities, seized by the shoulders, and each of us plunged into the one that was nearest. They proved just deep enough to bring our throats on a level with the surface, while standing erect. The loose earth was then shovelled in, and kneaded firmly around us. More was added, until our shoulders were covered up, and only our heads appeared above ground.

The position was ludicrous enough; and we might have laughed ourselves, but that we were standing in our graves. From the fiendish spectators it drew yells of laughter. What next? Was this to be the end of their proceedings? Were we to be thus left to perish, miserably, and by inches? Hunger and thirst would in time terminate our existence; but, oh, the long hours of anguish that must be endured! Whole days of misery we must suffer before the spark of life should forsake us—whole days of horror and—Ha! they had not yet done with us!

No: a death like that we had been fancying appeared too easy to the monster who directed them. The resources of his hatred were far from being exhausted: he had still other, and far keener, torture in store for us.

"Carajo! good!" cried he, as he stood admiring his contrivance; "better than tie to tree—good fix, eh! No fear 'scape—*Carrai*, no. *Bring fire!*"

188

Bring fire! It was to be fire, then, the extreme instrument of torture. We heard the word—that word of fearful sound. We were to die by fire!

Our terror had arrived at its height. It rose no higher when we saw fagots carried up to the spot, and built in a ring around our heads. It rose no higher when we saw the torch applied, and the dry wood catching the flame. It rose no higher as the blaze grew red, and redder, and we felt its angry glow upon our skulls, soon to be calcined like the sticks themselves.

No; we could suffer no more. Our agony had reached the acme of endurance, and we longed for death to relieve us. If another pang had been possible, there was cause for it in those screams now proceeding from the opposite edge of the camp. Even in that dread hour, we could recognise the voices of my sister and Viola. The unmerciful monster had brought them out again to witness the execution. We saw them not; but their wild plaints proved that they were spectators of the horrid scene.

Hotter and hotter grew the fire, and nearer licked the flames. I heard my hair crisping and singing at the fiery contact.

Objects swam dizzily before my eyes. The trees tottered and reeled, the earth whirled round. My skull ached as if it would soon split; my brain was drying up; my senses were fast forsaking me.

Chapter Ninety Three.

Devils or Angels.

Was I enduring the tortures of the future world? Were these its fiends that grinned and jibbered around me? See! they scatter and fall back! Some one approaches who can command them. Pluto himself? No; it is a woman—a woman here?—is it Proserpine? If a woman, surely *she* will have mercy upon me! Vain hope! There is no mercy in hell. Oh, my brain! Horror! horror!

There *are* women—these are women—they look not fiends! No, they are angels! Would they were angels of mercy!

But they are. See! one interferes with the fire. With her foot she dashes it back, scattering the fagots in furious haste. Who is she? If I were alive, I would call her Haj-Ewa; but dead, it must be her spirit below.

But there is another. Ha! another, younger and fairer. If they be angels, this must be the loveliest in heaven. It is the spirit of Maümee!

How comes she in this horrid place among fiends? It is not the abode for her. She was guilty of do crime that should send her here.

Where am I? Have I been dreaming? I was on fire just now—only my brain it was that was burning; my body was cold enough—where am I?

Who are you, that stand over me, pouring coolness upon my head? Are you not Haj-Ewa, the mad queen?

Whose soft fingers are those I feel playing upon my temples? Oh—the exquisite pleasure imparted by their touch! Bend down, that I may look upon your face, and thank you—"Maümee! Maümee!"

Then I am not dead. I live. I am saved!

It was Haj-Ewa, and not her spirit. It was Maümee herself—whose beautiful, brilliant eyes were looking into mine. No wonder I had believed it to be an angel.

"Carajo!" sounded a voice, that appeared hoarse with rage. "Remove those women!—pile back the fires. Away, mad queen!—go back to your tribe! these my captives—your chief no claim—*Carrambo!*—you not interfere; pile back the fires!"

"Yamassees!" cried Haj-Ewa, advancing towards the Indians; "Obey him not! or dread the wrath of Wykomé! His spirit will be angry, and follow you in vengeance. Wherever you go the *chitta mico* will be on your path, and its rattle in your ears. *Hulwak*! It will bite your heel as you wander in the woods. Speak I not truth, thou king of the Serpents?"

As she uttered the interrogatory, she raised the rattlesnake in her hands, holding it so that it might be distinctly seen by those whom she addressed. The reptile hissed, accompanying the sibilation with a sharp "skirr" of its tail. Who could doubt that it was an answer in the affirmative?

Not the Yamassees, who stood awe-bound and trembling in the presence of the mighty sorceress.

"And you, black runaways and renegades," she continued to the negro allies—"you who have no god, and fear not Wykomé—dare to rebuild the fires—dare to lift one fagot—and you shall take the place of your captives. A greater than yon yellow monster, your chief, will soon be on the ground. *Hinklas*! Ho! yonder the Rising Sun! he comes—he comes!"

As she ceased speaking, the hoof-strokes of a horse echoed through the glade, and a hundred voices simultaneously raised the shout: "Osceola! Osceola!" That cry was grateful to my ears. Though already rescued, I had begun to fear it might prove only a short relief. Our delivery from death was still far from certain—our advocates were but weak women. The mulatto king, in the midst of his fierce satellites, would scarce have yielded to their demands. Alike disregarded would have been their entreaties. The fire would have been re-kindled, and the execution carried out to its end.

In all probability this would have been the event, had not Osceola in good time arrived upon the ground.

His appearance, and the sound of his voice, at once reassured me. Under his protection we had nothing more to fear, and a soft voice whispered in my ear that he came as our *deliverer*.

His errand was soon made manifest. Drawing bridle, he halted near the middle of the camp, directly in front of us. I saw him dismount from his fine black horse—like himself, splendidly caparisoned—and handing the reins to a bystander, he came walking towards us. His port was superb—his costume brilliantly picturesque; and once more, I beheld those three ostrich-plumes—the real ones; that had played such a part in my suspicious fancy.

When near the spot, he stopped, and gazed inquiringly towards us. He might have smiled at our absurd situation, but his countenance betrayed no signs of levity. On the contrary, it was serious and sympathetic. I fancied it was sad.

For some moments he stood in a fixed attitude, without saying a word. His eyes wandered from one to the other—my fellow-victim and myself; as if endeavouring to distinguish us. No easy task. Smoke, sweat and ashes, must have rendered us extremely alike, and both difficult of identification.

At this moment, Maümee glided up to him, whispered a word in his ear, and returning again, knelt over me, and chafed my temples with her soft hands.

With the exception of the young chief himself, no one heard what his sister had said; but upon *him* her words appeared to produce an instantaneous effect. A change passed over his countenance. The look of sadness gave place to one of furious wrath; and turning suddenly to the yellow king, he hissed out the word "Fiend!"

For some seconds he spoke no more, but stood gazing upon the mulatto, as though he would annihilate him by his look. The latter quailed under the conquering glance, and trembled like a leaf, but made no answer.

"Fiend and villain!" continued Osceola, without changing either tone or attitude. "Is this the way you have carried out my orders? Are these the captives I commanded you to take? Vile runaway of a slave! who authorised you to inflict the fiery torture? Who taught you? Not the Seminoles, whose name you have adopted and disgraced. By the spirit of Wykomé! but that I have sworn never to torture a foe, I should place you where these now stand, and burn your body to ashes! From my sight—begone! No—stay where you are. On second thoughts, I may need you." And with this odd ending to his speech, the young chief turned upon his heel, and came walking towards us.

The mulatto did not vouchsafe a reply, though his looks were full of vengeance. Once, during the flagellation, I thought I noticed him turn his eyes towards his ferocious followers, as if to invoke their interference.

But these knew that Osceola was not alone. As he came up, the trampling of a large troop had been heard, and it was evident that his warriors were in the woods not far distant. A single *yo-ho-ehee*, in the well-known voice of their chief, would bring them upon the ground before its echoes had died.

190

The yellow king seemed himself to be aware of their proximity. Hence it was that he replied not. A word at that minute might have proved his last; and with a sulky frown upon his face, he remained silent.

"Release them!" said Osceola, addressing the *ci-devant* diggers; "and be careful how you handle your spades."

"Randolph!" he continued, bending over me; "I fear I have scarce been in time. I was for off when I heard of this, and have ridden hard. You have been wounded—are you ill hurt?"

I attempted to express my gratitude, and assure him I was not much injured; but my voice was so freak and hoarse as to be hardly intelligible. It grew stronger, however, as those fair fingers administered the refreshing draught, and we were soon conversing freely.

Both of us were quickly "unearthed," and with free limbs stood once more upon the open ground. My first thoughts were to rush towards my sister, when, to my surprise, I was restrained by the chief.

"Patience," said he; "not yet, not yet—Maümee will go and assure her of your safety. See! she knows it already! Go, Maümee! Tell Miss Randolph, her brother is safe! and will come presently. But she must remain where she is, only for a little while. Go, sister, and cheer her."

Turning to me, he added in a whisper; "She has been placed there for a purpose—you shall see. Come with me—I shall show you a spectacle that may astonish you—there is not a moment to be lost; I hear the signal from my spies. A minute more, and we are too late—come! come!"

Without opposing a word, I hastened after the chief, who walked rapidly towards the nearest edge of the woods.

He entered the timber, but went no farther. When fairly under cover of the thick foliage, he stopped, turned round, and stood facing towards the camp.

Obedient to a sign, I imitated his example.

Chapter Ninety Four.

The End of Arens Ringgold.

I had not the slightest idea of the chief's intention, or what was the nature of the spectacle I had been promised. Somewhat impatient, I questioned him.

"A new way of winning a mistress," said he, with a smile.

"But who is the lover?—who to be the mistress?" I inquired.

"Patience, Randolph, and you shall see. Oh! it is a rare experiment—a most cunning plot, and would be laughable were it not for the tragedy mixed up with it. You shall see. But for a faithful friend, I should not have known of it, and would not have been here to witness it. For my presence and your life, as it now appears—more still, perhaps, the safety of your sister—you are indebted to Haj-Ewa."

"Noble woman!"

"Hist! they are near—I hear the tread of hoofs. One—two—three. It must be they—yes—yonder. See!"

I looked in the direction pointed out, a small party of horsemen—half a dozen in all—was seen emerging from the timber, and riding with a brush into the open ground. As soon as they were fairly uncovered, they spurred their horses to a gallop, and with loud yells dashed rapidly into the midst of the camp. On reaching this point they fired their pieces—apparently into the air—and then continuing their shouts, rode on.

I saw that they were *white* men, and this surprised me, but what astonished me still more, was that I *knew* them. At least I knew their faces, and recognised the men as some of the most worthless scamps of our own settlement.

A third surprise awaited me, on looking more narrowly at their leader. Him I knew well. Again it was Arens Ringgold.

I had not time to recover from the third surprise, when still a fourth was before me. The men of the camp—both negroes and Yamassees—appeared terrified at this puny attack, and scattering off, hid themselves in the bushes. They yelled loudly enough, and some fired their guns as they retreated; but, like the attacking party, their shots appeared directed into the air! Mystery of mysteries! what could it mean?

I was about to inquire once more, when I observed that my companion was occupied with his own affairs, and did not desire to be disturbed. I saw that he was looking to his rifle, as if examining the sights.

Glancing back into the glade, I saw that Ringgold had advanced close to where my sister was seated, and was just halting in front of the group. I heard him address her by name, and pronounce some phrase of congratulation. He appeared about to dismount with the design of approaching her on foot, while his men, still upon horseback, were galloping through the camp, huzzaing fiercely and firing pistols through the air.

"His hour is come," muttered Osceola, as he glided past me; "a fate deserved and long delayed—it is come at last," and with these words, he stepped forth into the open ground.

I saw him raise his piece to the level, its muzzle pointed towards Ringgold, and the instant after, the report rang over the camp.

The shrill *"Car-ha-queene"* pealed from his lips, as the planter's horse sprang forwards with an empty saddle, and the rider himself was seen struggling upon the grass.

The others uttered a terrific cry, and with fear and astonishment depicted in their looks, galloped back into the bushes—without waiting to exchange a word with their wounded leader, or a shot with the man who had wounded him.

"My aim has not been true," said Osceola, with singular coolness; "he still lives. I have received much wrong from him and his—ay, very much wrong—or I might spare his wretched life. But no—my vow must be kept—he must die!"

As he said this, he rushed after Ringgold, who had regained his feet, and was making towards the bushes, as with a hope of escape.

A wild scream came from the terrified wretch, as he saw the avenger at his heels. It was the last time his voice was heard.

In a few bounds Osceola was by his side—the long blade glittered for an instant in the air—and the downward blow was given, so rapidly, that the stroke could scarce be perceived.

The blow was instantaneously fatal. The knees of the wounded man suddenly bent beneath him, and he sank lifeless on the spot where he had been struck—his body after death remaining doubled up as it had fallen.

"The fourth and last of my enemies," said Osceola, as he returned to where I stood; "the last of those who deserved my vengeance, and against whom I had vowed it."

"Scott?" I inquired.

"He was the third—he was killed yesterday, and by this hand. Hitherto I have fought for revenge—I have had it—I have slain many of your people—I have had full satisfaction, and henceforth—"

The speaker made a long pause.

"Henceforth?" I mechanically inquired.

"I care but little how soon they kill me."

As Osceola uttered these strange words, he sank down upon a prostrate trunk, covering his face with his hands. I saw that he did not expect a reply.

There was a sadness in his tone, as though some deep sorrow lay upon his heart, that could neither be controlled nor comforted. I had noticed it before; and thinking he would rather be left to himself, I walked silently away.

A few moments after I held my dear sister in my arms, while Jake was comforting Viola in his black embraces.

His old rival was no longer near. During the sham attack he had imitated his followers, and disappeared from the field; but though most of the latter soon returned, the yellow king, when sought for, was not to be found in the camp. His absence roused the suspicions of Osceola, who was now once more in action. By a signal his warriors were summoned; and came galloping up. Several were instantly dispatched in search of the missing chief, but after a while these came back without having found any traces of him.

One only seemed to have discovered a clue to his disappearance. The followers of Ringgold consisted of only five men.

The Indian had gone for some distance on the path by which they had retreated. Instead of five, there were six sets of horse tracks upon the trail.

The report appeared to produce an unpleasant impression upon the mind of Osceola. Fresh scouts were sent forth, with orders to bring back the mulatto, *living* or *dead*.

The stern command proved that there were strong doubts about the fealty of the Yellow Chief, and the warriors of Osceola appeared to share the suspicions of their leader.

The patriot party had suffered from defections of late. Some of the smaller clans, wearied of fighting, and wasted by a long season of famine, had followed the example of the tribe Omatla, and delivered themselves up at the forts. Though in the battles hitherto fought, the Indians had generally been successful, they knew that their white foemen far outnumbered them, and that in the end the latter must triumph. The spirit of revenge, for wrongs long endured, had stimulated them at the first; but they had obtained full measure of vengeance, and were content. Love of country—attachment to their old homes—mere patriotism was now balanced against the dread of almost complete annihilation. The latter weighed heaviest in the scale.

The war spirit was no longer in the ascendant. Perhaps at this time had overtures of peace been made, the Indians would have laid down their arms, and consented to the removal. Even Osceola could scarce have prevented their acceptance of the conditions, and it was doubted whether he would have made the attempt.

Gifted with genius, with full knowledge of the strength and character of his enemies, he must have foreseen the disasters that were yet to befall his followers and his nation. It could not be otherwise.

Was it a gloomy forecast of the future that imparted to him that melancholy air, now observable both in his words and acts? Was it this, or was there a still deeper sorrow—the anguish of a hopeless passion—the drear heart-longing for a love he might never obtain?

To me it was a moment of strong emotions, as the young chief approached the spot where my sister was seated. Even then was I the victim of unhappy suspicions, and with eager scrutiny I scanned the countenances of both.

Surely I was wrong. On neither could I detect a trace of aught that should give me uneasiness. The bearing of the chief was simply gallant and respectful. The looks of my sister were but the expressions of a fervent gratitude. Osceola spoke first.

"I have to ask your forgiveness, Miss Randolph, for the scene you have been forced to witness; but I could not permit this man to escape. Lady, he was your greatest enemy, as he has been ours. Through the cooperation of the mulatto, he had planned this ingenious deception, with the design of inducing you to become his wife; but failing in this, the mask would have been thrown off, and you—I need not give words to his fool intent. It is fortunate I arrived in time."

"Brave chief!" exclaimed Virginia—"twice have you preserved the lives of my brother and myself—more than our lives. We have neither words nor power to thank you. I can offer only this poor token to prove my gratitude."

As she said this, she advanced towards the chief, and handed him a folded parchment, which she had drawn from her bosom.

Osceola at once recognised the document. It was the title deeds of his patrimonial estate.

"Thanks, thanks!" he replied, while a sad smile played over his features. "It is, indeed, an act of disinterested friendship. Alas! it has come too late. She who so much desired to possess this precious paper, who so much longed to return to that once loved home, is no more. My mother is dead. On yesternight her spirit passed away."

It was news even to Maümee, who, bursting into a wild paroxysm of grief, fell upon the neck of my sister. Their arms became entwined, and both wept—their tears mingling as they fell.

There was silence, broken only by the sobbing of the two girls and at intervals the voice of Virginia murmuring words of consolation. Osceola himself appeared too much affected to speak.

After a while, the chief aroused himself from his sorrowing attitude.

"Come, Randolph!" said he—"we must not dwell on the past, while such a doubtful future is before us. You must go back to your home and rebuild it. You have lost only a house. Your rich lands still remain, and your negroes will be restored to you. I have given orders; they are already on the way. This is no place for her," and he nodded towards Virginia. "You need not stay your departure another moment. Horses are ready for you; I myself will conduct you to the borders, and beyond that *you have no longer an enemy to fear.*"

As he pronounced the last words, he looked significantly towards the body of the planter, still lying near the edge of the woods. I understood his meaning, but made no reply.

"And she," I said—"the forest is a rude home, especially in such times—may *she go* with us?"

My words had reference to Maümee. The chief grasped my hand and held it with earnest pressure. With joy I beheld gratitude sparkling in his eye.

"Thanks!" he exclaimed, "thanks for that friendly offer. It was the very favour I would have asked. You speak true; the trees must shelter her no more. Randolph, I can trust you with her life—with her honour. Take her to your home!"

Chapter Ninety Five.

The Death Warning.

The sun was going down as we took our departure from the Indian camp. For myself, I had not the slightest idea of the direction in which we were to travel, but with such a guide there was no danger of losing the way.

We were far from the settlements of the Suwanee—a long day's journey—and we did not expect to reach home before another sun should set. That night there would be moonlight, if the clouds did not hinder it; and it was our intention to travel throughout the early part of the night, and then encamp. By this means the journey of to-morrow would be shortened.

To our guide the country was well-known, and every road that led through it.

For a long distance the route conducted through open woods, and we could all ride abreast; but the path grew narrower, and we were compelled to go by twos or in single file.

Habitually the young chief and I kept in the advance—our sisters riding close behind us. Behind them came Jake and Viola, and in the rear half a dozen Indian horsemen—the guard of Osceola. I wondered he had not brought with him more of his followers, and even expressed my surprise.

He made light of the danger.

The soldiers, he said, knew better than to be out after night, and for that part of the country through which we would travel by daylight, no troops ever strayed into it. Besides, there had been no scouting of late—the weather was too hot for the work. If we met any party they would be of his own people. From them, of course, we had nothing to fear. Since the war began he had often travelled most of the same route alone. He appeared satisfied there was no danger.

For my part, I was not satisfied. I knew that the path we were following would pass within a few miles of Fort King. I remembered the escape of Ringgold's crew. They were likely enough to have ridden straight to the fort, and communicated an account of the planter's death, garnished by a tale of their own brave attack upon the Indian camp. Among the authorities, Ringgold was no common man; a party might be organised to proceed to the camp. We were on the very road to meet them.

Another circumstance I thought of—the mysterious disappearance of the mulatto, as was supposed, in company with these men. It was enough to create suspicion. I mentioned my suspicion to the chief:

"No fear," said he, in reply, "my trackers will be after them—they will bring me word in time—but no," he added, hesitatingly, and for a moment appearing thoughtful; "they may not get up with them before the night falls, and then—you speak true, Randolph—I have acted imprudently. I should not care for these foolish fellows—but the mulatto—that is different—he knows all the paths, and if it should be that he is turning traitor—if it— Well! we are astart now, and we must go on. *You* have nothing to fear—and as for me—Osceola never yet turned his back upon danger, and will not now. Nay, will you believe me, Randolph, I rather seek it than otherwise?"

"Seek danger?"

"Ay—death—death!"

"Speak low—do not let *them* hear you talk thus."

"Ah! yes," he added, lowering his tone, and speaking in a half soliloquy, "in truth, I long for its coming."

The words were spoken with a serious emphasis that left no room to doubt of their earnestness.

Some deep melancholy had settled upon his spirit and preyed upon it continually. What could be its cause?

I could remain silent no longer. Friendship, not curiosity, incited me. I put the inquiry.

"*You* have observed it, then? But not since we set out—not since you made that friendly offer? Ah! Randolph, you have rendered me happy. It was she alone that made the prospect of death so gloomy."

"Why speak you of death?"

"Because it is near."

"Not to you?"

"Yes—to me. The presentiment is upon me that I have not long to live."

"Nonsense, Powell."

"Friend, it is true—I have had my death warning."

"Come, Osceola! This is unlike—unworthy of you. Surely you are above such vulgar fancies. I will not believe you can entertain them."

"Think you I speak of supernatural signs? Of the screech of the war-bird, or the hooting of the midnight owl? Of omens in the air, the earth, or the water? No—no. I *am* above such shallow superstitions. For all that, I know I must soon die. It was wrong of me to call my death warning a presentiment—it is a physical fact that announces my approaching end—it is *here*."

As he said this, he raised his hand, pointing with his fingers as if to indicate the chest.

I understood his melancholy meaning.

"I would rather," he continued, after a pause, "rather it had been my fate to fall upon the field of battle. True, death is not alluring in any shape, but that appears to me most preferable. I would choose it rather than linger on. Nay, I have chosen it. Ten times have I thus challenged death—gone half-way to meet it; but like a coward, or a coy bride, it refuses to meet *me*."

There was something almost unearthly in the laugh that accompanied these last words—a strange simile—a strange man!

I could scarce make an effort to cheer him. In fact, he needed no cheering: he seemed happier than before. Had it not been so, my poor speech, assuring him of his robust looks, would have been words thrown away. He knew they were but the false utterances of friendship.

I even suspected it myself. I had already noticed the pallid skin—the attenuated fingers—the glazed and sunken eye. This, then, was the canker that was prostrating that noble spirit—the cause of his deep melancholy. I had assigned to it one far different.

The future of his sister had been the heaviest load upon his heart. He told me so as we moved onward.

I need not repeat the promises I then made to him. It was not necessary they should be vows: my own happiness would hinder me from breaking them.

Chapter Ninety Six.

Osceola's Fate—Conclusion.

We were seated near the edge of the little opening where we had encamped, a pretty parterre, fragrant with the perfume of a thousand flowers. The moon was shedding down a flood of silvery light, and objects around appeared almost as distinct as by day. The leaves of the tall palms—the waxen flowers of the magnolias—the yellow blossoms of the zanthoxylon trees could all be distinguished in the clear moonbeams.

The four of us were seated together, brothers and sisters, conversing freely, as in the olden times, and the scene vividly recalled those times to all of us. But the memory now produced only sad reflections, as it suggested thoughts of the future. Perhaps we four should never thus meet again. Gazing upon the doomed form before me, I had no heart for reminiscences of joy.

We had passed Fort King in safety—had encountered no white face—strange I should fear to meet men of my own race—and no longer had we any apprehension of danger, either from ambush or open attack.

The Indian guards, with black Jake in their midst, were near the centre of the glade, grouped by a fire, and cooking their suppers. So secure did the chieftain feel that he had not even placed a sentinel on the path. He appeared indifferent to danger.

The night was waning late, and we were about retiring to the tents, which the men had pitched for us, when a singular noise reach us from the woods. To my ears it sounded like the surging of water—as of heavy rain, or the sough of distant rapids.

Osceola interpreted it otherwise. It was the continuous "whistling" of leaves, caused by numerous bodies passing through the bushes, either of men, or animals.

We instantly rose to our feet, and stood listening.

The noise continued, but now we could hear the snapping of dead branches, and the metallic clink of weapons.

It was too late to retreat. The noise came from every ride. A circle of armed men were closing around the glade.

I looked towards Osceola. I expected to see him rush to his rifle that lay near. To my surprise he did not stir.

His few followers were already on the alert, and had hastened to his side to receive his orders. Their words and gestures declared their determination to die in his defence.

In reply to their hurried speeches, the chieftain made a sign that appeared to astonish them. The butts of their guns suddenly dropped to the ground, and the warriors stood in listless attitudes, as if they had given up the intention of using them.

"It is too late," said Osceola in a calm voice, "too late! we are completely surrounded. Innocent blood might be spilled, and mine is the only life they are in search of. Let them come on—they are welcome to it now. Farewell, sister! Randolph, farewell!—farewell, Virg—."

The plaintive screams of Maümee—of Virginia—my own bursting, and no longer silent grief, drowned the voice that was uttering those wild adieus.

Clustered around the chief, we knew not what was passing, until the shouts of men, and the loud words of command proceeding from their officers, warned us that we were in the midst of a battalion of soldiers. On looking up we saw that we were hemmed in by a circle of men in blue uniform, whose glancing barrels and bayonets formed a *chevaux de frise* around us.

As no resistance was offered, not a shot had been fired; and save the shouting of men, and the ringing of steel, no other sounds were heard. Shots were fired afterwards, but not to kill. It was a *feu-de-joie* to celebrate the success of this important capture.

The capture was soon complete—Osceola, held by two men, stood in the midst of his pale-faced foes a prisoner. His followers were also secured, and the soldiers fell back into more extended line—the prisoners still remaining in their midst.

At this moment a mail appeared in front of the ranks, and near to where the captives were standing. He was in conversation with the officer who commanded. His dress bespoke him an Indian; but his yellow face contradicted the supposition. His head was turbaned, and three black plumes drooped over his brow. There was no mistaking the man. The sight was maddening. It restored all his fierce energy to the captive chief; and flinging aside the soldiers, as if they had been tools, he sprang forth from their grasp, and bounded towards the yellow man. Fortunate for the latter, Osceola was unarmed. He had no weapon left him—neither pistol nor knife—and while wringing a bayonet from the gun of a soldier, the traitor found time to escape.

The chief uttered a groan as he saw the mulatto pass through the serried line, and stand secure beyond the reach of his vengeance.

It was but a fancied security on the part of the mulatto. The death of the renegade was decreed, though it reached him from an unexpected quarter.

As he stood outside, bantering the captives, a dark form was seen gliding up behind him. The form was that of a woman—a majestic woman—whose grand beauty was apparent even in the moonlight. But few saw either her or her beauty. The prisoners alone were facing towards her, and witnessed her approach.

It was a scene of only a few seconds' duration. The woman stole close up to the mulatto, and for a moment her arms appeared entwined around his neck. There was the sheen of some object that in the moonlight gleamed like metal. It was a living weapon—it was the dread *crotalus*!

Its rattle could be heard distinctly, and close following came a wild cry of terror, as its victim felt the cold contact of the reptile around his neck, and its sharp fangs entering his flesh.

The woman was seen suddenly to withdraw the serpent, and holding its glistening body over her head, she cried out:

"Grieve not, Osceola! thou art avenged!—the chitta mico has avenged you!"

Saying this, she glided rapidly away, and before the astonished listeners could intercept her retreat, she had entered among the bushes and disappeared.

The horror-struck wretch tottered over the ground, pale and terrified, his eyes almost starting from their sockets.

Men gathered around and endeavoured to administer remedies. Gunpowder and tobacco were tried, but no one knew the simples that would cure him.

It proved his death-stroke; and before another sun went down, he had ceased to live.

With Osceola's capture the war did not cease—though I bore no further part in it. Neither did it end with his death, which followed a few weeks after—not by court-martial execution, for he was no rebel, and could claim the privilege of a prisoner of war, but of that disease which he knew had long doomed him. Captivity may have hastened the event. His proud spirit sank under confinement, and with it the noble frame that contained it.

Friends and enemies stood around him in his last hour, and listened to his dying words. Both alike wept. In that chamber there was not a tearless cheek—and many a soldier's eye was moist as he listened to the muffled dram that made music over the grave of the *noble Osceola.*

After all, it proved to be the jovial captain who had won the heart of my capricious sister. It was long before I discovered their secret—which let light in upon a maze of mysteries—and I was so spited about their having concealed it from me, that I almost refused to share the plantation with them.

When I did so at length, under threat of Virginia—not her solicitor—I kept what I considered the better half for myself and Maümee. The old homestead remained ours, and a new house soon appeared upon it—a fitting casket for the jewel it was destined to contain.

I had still an out-plantation to spare—the fine old Spanish clearing on the Tupelo Greek. I wanted a man to manage it—or rather a "man and wife of good character without incumbrances."

And for the purpose, who could have been better than black Jake and Viola, since they completely answered the above conditions?

I had another freehold at my disposal—a very small one. It was situated by the edge of the swamp, and consisted of a log cabin, with the most circumscribed of all "clearings" around it. But this was already in possession of a tenant whom, although he paid no rent, I would not have ejected for the world. He was an old alligator-hunter of the name of Hickman.

Another of like "kidney"—Weatherford by name—lived near on an adjoining plantation; but the two were oftener together than apart. Both had suffered a good deal of rough handling in their time, from the claws of "bars," the jaws and tails of alligators, and the tomahawk of Indians. When together or among friends, they were delighted to narrate their hair-breadth escapes, and both were often heard to declare that the "toughest scrape they ever come clar out o', wor when they wor on a jury-trial, surrounded by a burnin' forest o' dog-goned broom pines, an' about ten thousand red Indyuns."

They did come clear out of it, however, and lived long after to tell the tale with many a fanciful exaggeration.

The End.

Made in the USA
Las Vegas, NV
24 November 2020